MW00886327

THE TREASURE OF THE INCAS

A Story Of Adventure In Peru

By

G. A. Henty

About G. A. Henty

George Alfred Hent was born in Trumpington, near Cambridge but spent some of his childhood in Canterbury. He was a sickly child who had to spend long periods in bed. During his frequent illnesses he became an avid reader and developed a wide range of interests which he carried into adulthood. He attended Westminster School, London, as a half-boarder when he was fourteen, :2and later Gonville and Caius College, Cambridge, where he was a keen sportsman.

He left the university early without completing his degree to volunteer for the (Army) Hospital Commissariat of the Purveyors Department when the Crimean War began. He was sent to the Crimea and while there he witnessed the appalling conditions under which the British soldier had to fight. His letters home were filled with vivid descriptions of what he saw. His father was impressed by his letters and sent them to the Morning Advertiser newspaper which printed them. This initial writing success was a factor in Henty's later decision to accept the offer to become a special correspondent, the early name for journalists now better known as war correspondents.

Shortly before resigning from the army as a captain in 1859 he married Elizabeth Finucane. The couple had four children. Elizabeth died in 1865 after a long illness and shortly after her death Henty began writing articles for the Standard newspaper. In 1866 the newspaper sent him as their special correspondent to report on the Austro-Italian War where he met Giuseppe Garibaldi. He went on to cover the 1868 British punitive expedition to Abyssinia, the Franco-Prussian War, the Ashanti War, the Carlist Rebellion in Spain and the Turco-Serbian War. He also witnessed the opening of the Suez Canal and travelled to Palestine, Russia and India.

Henty was a strong supporter of the British Empire all his life; according to literary critic Kathryn Castle: "Henty ... exemplified the ethos of the [British Empire], and glorified in its successes". Henty's ideas about politics were influenced by writers such as Sir Charles Dilke and Thomas Carlyle.

Henty once related in an interview how his storytelling skills grew out of tales told after dinner to his children. He wrote his first children's book, Out on the Pampas in 1868, naming the book's main characters after his children. The book was published by Griffith and Farran in November 1870 with a title page date of 1871. While most of the 122 books he wrote were for children and published by Blackie and Son of London, he also wrote adult novels, non-fiction such as The March to Magdala and Those Other Animals, short stories for the likes of The Boy's Own Paper and edited the Union Jack, a weekly boy's magazine.

Henty was "the most popular Boy's author of his day." Blackie, who published his children's fiction in the UK, and W. G. Blackie estimated in February 1952 that they were producing about 150,000 Henty books a year at the height of his popularity, and stated that their records showed they had produced over three and a half million Henty books. He further estimated that considering the US and other overseas authorised and pirated editions, a total of 25 million was not impossible. Arnold notes this estimate and that there have been further editions since that estimate was made.

His children's novels typically revolved around a boy or young man living in troubled times. These ranged from the Punic War to more recent conflicts such as the Napoleonic Wars or the American Civil War. Henty's heroes – which occasionally included young ladies – are uniformly intelligent, courageous, honest and resourceful with plenty of 'pluck' yet are also modest. These themes have made Henty's novels popular today among many conservative Christians and homeschoolers.

Henty usually researched his novels by ordering several books on the subject he was writing on from libraries, and consulting them before beginning writing. Some of his books were written about events (such as the Crimean War) that he witnessed himself; hence, these books are written with greater detail as Henty drew upon his first-hand experiences of people, places, and events.

On 16 November 1902, Henty died aboard his yacht in Weymouth Harbour, Dorset, leaving unfinished his last novel, By Conduct and Courage, which was completed by his son Captain C.G. Henty.

Henty is buried in Brompton Cemetery, London.

Henty wrote 122 works of historical fiction and all first editions had the date printed at the foot of the title page.[15] Several short stories published in book form are included in this total, with the stories taken from previously published full-length novels. The dates given below are those printed at the foot of the title page of the very first editions in the United Kingdom. It is a common misconception that American Henty titles were published before those of the UK. All Henty titles bar one were published in the UK before those of America.

The simple explanation for this error of judgement is that Charles Scribner's Sons of New York dated their Henty first editions for the current year. The first UK editions published by Blackie were always dated for the coming year, to have them looking fresh for Christmas. The only Henty title published in book form in America before the UK book was In the Hands of the Cave-Dwellers dated 1900 and published by Harper of New York. This title was published in book form in the UK in 1903, although the story itself had already been published in England prior to the first American edition, in The Boy's Own Annual.

LITERARY CRITIQUES

George Alfred Henty (1832–1902) was a British novelist and writer known for his historical adventure stories for children and young adults. His works often combined fictional characters with real historical events, aiming to educate young readers about history while also providing entertaining narratives. Henty's writing style and themes have been the subject of various literary critiques over the years. Here are some common points made by critics:

Formulaic Structure: One common critique of Henty's works is that they tend to follow a formulaic structure. Many of his novels share similar plotlines, where a young British protagonist overcomes challenges, exhibits moral values, and plays a significant role in historical events. Critics argue that this predictable structure might make his stories less engaging for older or more experienced readers.

Simplistic Characterization: Some critics have noted that Henty's characters can be rather one-dimensional, often falling into stereotypical roles. The heroes are typically brave, resourceful, and morally upright, while the villains are often portrayed as scheming and unscrupulous. This lack of complexity in character development can limit the emotional depth of the stories.

Colonial and Imperialist Views: Henty's works are reflective of the time period in which he lived, which saw the height of the British Empire's power and influence. Some critics argue that his novels promote colonial and imperialist viewpoints, as they often depict British characters as heroic figures bringing civilization to "uncivilized" regions. This portrayal can be seen as ethnocentric and insensitive to the experiences and perspectives of other cultures.

Educational Value: Henty's novels have been praised for their educational value, as they introduce readers to historical events and periods that might not be covered in traditional history textbooks. However, critics have pointed out that his narratives sometimes prioritize historical accuracy at the expense of engaging storytelling, resulting in passages that read more like history lessons than compelling fiction.

Language and Style: Henty's writing style can be considered somewhat dated by modern standards. His prose tends to be formal and descriptive, which might not resonate with contemporary readers, especially younger ones. Some critics argue that the language could create a barrier for readers seeking fast-paced and accessible narratives.

Relevance to Modern Readers: Another point of critique is the relevance of Henty's works to modern readers. While his stories offer insights into historical contexts, some critics question whether his themes and values align with contemporary sensibilities and whether young readers today would find his narratives engaging.

Limited Diversity: Henty's works often lack diverse representation, both in terms of characters and perspectives. Critics have noted that his novels predominantly focus on white, male British protagonists, which can limit the inclusivity and relatability of his stories for a broader readership.

In summary, while George Alfred Henty's historical adventure novels have been cherished by many readers over the years for their educational content and engaging narratives, they have also faced criticism for their formulaic structure, simplistic characterization, colonial viewpoints, and limited relevance to modern audiences. It's important to approach his works with an understanding of the historical context in which they were written and to consider these critiques alongside their literary merits.

CONTENTS

IT DID NOT TAKE LONG TO TRANSFER THE SACKS INTO THE BOAT

PREFACE TO THE ORIGINAL EDITION

The mysterious loss of a large portion of the treasure of the Incas has never been completely cleared up. By torturing the natives to whom the secret had been entrusted, the Spaniards made two or three discoveries, but there can be little doubt that these finds were only a small proportion of the total amount of the missing hoards, although for years after their occupation of the country the Spaniards spared no pains and hesitated at no cruelty to bring to light the hidden wealth. The story of the boat which put to sea laden with treasure is historical, and it was generally supposed that she was lost in a storm that took place soon after she sailed. It was also morally certain that the Peruvians who left the country when the Spaniards became masters carried off with them a very large amount of treasure into that part of South America lying east of Peru. Legends are current that they founded a great city there, and that their descendants occupy it at the present time. But the forests are so thick, and the Indian tribes so hostile, that the country has never yet been explored, and it may be reserved for some future traveller, possessing the determination of my two heroes, to clear up the mystery of this city as they penetrated that of the lost treasure-ship. It need hardly be said that the state of confusion, misrule, and incessant civil wars which I have described as prevailing in Peru presents a true picture of the country at the period in which this story is laid.

G. A. HENTY.

CHAPTER I — HOW IT CAME ABOUT

Two men were sitting in the smoking-room of a London club. The room was almost empty, and as they occupied arm-chairs in one corner of it, they were able to talk freely without fear of being overheard. One of them was a man of sixty, the other some five or six and twenty.

"I must do something," the younger man said, "for I have been kicking my heels about London since my ship was paid off two years ago. At first, of course, it didn't matter, for I have enough to live upon; but recently I have been fool enough to fall in love with a girl whose parents would never dream of allowing her to marry a half-pay lieutenant of the navy with no chance in the world of getting employed again, for I have no interest whatever."

"It is an awkward case certainly, Prendergast," the other said; "and upon my word, though I sympathize with you, I cannot blame Fortescue. He is not what you might call a genial man, but there is no doubt that he was a splendid lawyer and a wonderful worker. For ten years he earned more than any man at the bar. I know that he was twice offered the solicitor-generalship, but as he was making two or three times the official salary, he would not take it. I believe he would have gone on working till now had he not suddenly come in for a very fine estate, owing to the death, in the course of two or three years, of four men who stood between him and it. Besides, I fancy he got hints that in the general opinion of the bar he had had a wonderfully good innings, and it was about time that younger men had a share in it. What his savings were I do not know, but they must be very large. His three sons are all at the bar, and are rising men, so there was no occasion for him to go on piling up money for them. But, as I say, he has always had the reputation of being a hard man, and it is practically certain that he would never allow his daughter to marry a man whom he would regard as next door to a pauper. Now, what are you thinking of doing?"

"Well, sir, Miss Fortescue has agreed to wait for me for two years, and of course I am eager to do something, but the question is what? I can sail a ship, but even could I get the command of a merchantman, it would not improve my position in the eyes of the parents of the lady in question. Now, you have been knocking about all over the world, I do wish you would give me your advice. Where is there money to be got? I am equally ready to go to the North Pole or the Equator, to enter the service of an Indian prince, or to start in search of a treasure hidden by the old bucaneers."

"You talk Spanish, don't you?"

"Yes; all my service has been in the Mediterranean. We were two years off the coast of Spain, and in and out of its ports, and as time hung heavily on our hands, I got up the language partly to amuse myself and partly to be able to talk fluently with my partners at a ball."

The elder man did not speak for a minute or two.

"You have not thought of South America?" he said at last.

"No, Mr. Barnett; I don't know that I have ever thought of one place more than another."

The other was again silent.

"I don't think you could do better anywhere," he said slowly. "It is a land with great possibilities; at any rate it is a land where you could be understood, and of course it would be folly to go anywhere without a knowledge of the language. I was, as you know, five years out there, and came home when the war broke out between Chili and the Spaniards. I have been more in Peru than in Chili, and as Peru was still in the hands of the Spanish, it would have been impossible for me to go there again as long as the war lasted. Knocking about as I did, I heard a great deal from the natives (I mean the Indians). I gathered from them a number of their traditions, and I am convinced that they know of any number of gold mines that were formerly worked, but were blocked up when the Spaniards invaded the country, and have been kept secret ever since.

"The natives have never spoken on the subject at all to the Spaniards. If they had, they would have been flogged until they revealed all they knew—that is to say, they would have been flogged to death, for no tortures will wring from an Indian anything he knows about gold. They look upon that metal as the source of all the misfortunes that have fallen upon their race. With an Englishman whom they knew and trusted, and who, as they also knew, had no wish whatever to discover gold mines, they were a little less reticent. I never asked them any questions on a subject in which I had not a shadow of interest, but I certainly had some curiosity, not of a pecuniary kind, because the matter had always been a riddle as to the hiding-place of the Incas' treasures. And from what I learned I should say it is absolutely certain that a great portion of these escaped the search of their Spanish tyrants.

"Whether the men who were employed in the work all died without revealing the secret, or whether it had been trusted to a chosen few, I know not; but the natives believe that there are still a few among them to whom the secret has been passed down from father to son. Anyhow, all had heard vague traditions. Some said that part of the treasure was carried hundreds of miles inland and given over to a tribe of fierce savages, in a country into which no European can enter. Another tradition is that a portion of it was carried off by sea in a great canoe, which was never heard of again and was believed to have been lost. I am not for a moment supposing, Prendergast, that if you went out there you would have the most remote chance of discovering what the Spaniards, ever since they landed there, have been in vain trying to find, and I certainly should not think of recommending a mad-brained adventure, but undoubtedly there are many rich gold mines yet to be found. There are openings for trade, too; and I can give you introductions to merchants both in Chili and Peru. It is not a thing I should recommend to everyone, far from it; but if you want to combine adventure with a chance, however small, of making money, I don't know that you can do better than go to South America. You are fitted for no calling here; your income, counting your half-pay, would suffice to keep you out there, and a couple of years of such a life would do you no harm."

"It is just what I should like," the young man said enthusiastically; "though I don't know how I should set to work if I did find a mine."

"You would have to bring home specimens, with particulars of the width of the lode. Of course you would crush pieces up and wash them yourself, or get your Indian to wash them; that would give you an approximate idea of the percentage of gold. If it were rich, I could introduce you to men who would advance money for working it, giving you a share of the profits. They would send out a mining expert with you. He would verify your report, and then you would take up the concession. I don't know whether there have been any changes in the regulations, but there is no difficulty in learning how to proceed from one or other of the men to whom I will give you introductions. The thing would not be worth thinking of were it not that the man who always went with me as guide and muleteer is an Indian, and has, I am convinced, a knowledge of some of these places. He was with me all the time I was out there. I saved his life when a puma sprang upon him, and he more than once hinted that he could make me a rich man, but I had no inclination that way, my income being sufficient for all my wants. Still, on the chance that he is alive—and he was about thirty when he was with me fifteen years ago, so it is probable that he is still to the fore—I will give you a letter to him telling him that you are a dear friend of mine, and that I trust to him to do any service he can for you just as he would have done for myself. Had it not been for that I should never have mentioned the matter to you. These old mines are the dream of every

Peruvian. They have been searching for them ever since the conquest of the country, and as they have failed, it is absurd to think that an Englishman would have the slightest chance of lighting upon a mine, still less of finding any of the Incas' treasures. But with the Indian's aid it is just possible that you may find something, though I should advise you most strongly not to build in any way upon the chance. I consider that you cannot possibly win Miss Fortescue; that being so, two years of knocking about will not make your position worse, and by the time you come back, you may have ceased to struggle against fate. It will afford you a remote—but distinctly remote—opportunity of bettering your position, will give you something else to think about besides that young lady's charms, and you may even come to recognize that life is, after all, possible without her. You may shake your head, lad; but you know children cry for the moon sometimes, yet afterwards come to understand that it would not be a desirable plaything."

"Well, at any rate, Mr. Barnett, I am extremely obliged for your suggestion and for your offer of introductions. It is just the life that I should enjoy thoroughly. As you say, the chance that anything will come of it is extremely small, but at least there is a possibility, and I take it as a drowning man catches at a straw."

"By the way, you mustn't think only of gold; silver is, after all, the chief source of the riches of Peru, and there are numbers of extraordinarily rich mines. It is calculated that three hundred millions have been produced since the first occupation by the Spaniards. Quicksilver is also very abundant; copper and lead are found too, but there is not much to be done with them at present, owing to the cost of carriage. There is good shooting in the mountains on the eastern side of the Andes, and you will find plenty of sport there."

They talked over the matter for some time before they separated, and Harry Prendergast became quite excited over it. On his return to his rooms he was astonished to find the candles alight and a strong smell of tobacco pervading the place. A lad of about sixteen leapt from the easy-chair in which he had been sitting, with his feet on another.

"Hullo, Harry, I didn't expect you back so soon! The maid said you were dining out, and I suppose that generally means one o'clock before you are back."

"Well, what brings you here, Bert? I thought I had got you off my hands for a year at least."

"I thought so, myself," the lad said coolly; "but circumstances have been too strong for me. We were running down the Channel the night before last, when a craft that was beating up ran smack into us. I don't know that it was his fault more than ours; the night was dark, and it was very thick, and we did not see each other until she was within a length of us. Luck was against us; if she had been a few seconds quicker we should have caught her broadside, but as it was she rammed us, knocking a hole in our side as big as a house, and we had just time to jump on board her. Our old craft went down two minutes after the skipper, who was of course the last man, left her. The other fellow had stove his bow in. Luckily we were only about a couple of miles off Dungeness, and though she leaked like a sieve, we were able to run her into the bay, where she settled down in two and a half fathoms of water. As soon as it was light we landed and tramped to Dover. A hoy was starting for the river that evening, and most of us came up in her, arriving at the Pool about three hours ago. It is a bad job, Harry, and I am horribly put out about it. Of course nothing could be saved, and there is all the new kit you bought for me down at the bottom. I sha'n't bother you again; I have quite made up my mind that I shall ship before the mast this time, and a five-pound note will buy me a good enough outfit for that."

"We need not talk about that now, Bertie. You are certainly an unlucky beggar; this is the second time you have been wrecked."

"It is a frightful nuisance," the boy said. "It is the kit I am thinking of, otherwise I should not mind. I didn't care for the skipper. He seemed all right and decent enough before we started, but I soon heard from fellows who had sailed with him before that he was a tartar; and what was worse, they said he was in the habit of being drunk two nights out of three. However, that has nothing to do with it. I am really awfully sorry, Harry. You have been a thundering good elder brother. I hated to think that you had to shell out last time, and I have quite made up my mind that you sha'n't do it again."

"Well, it cannot be helped; it is no fault of yours; still, of course, it is a nuisance. Thank God that no harm has come to you, that is the principal thing. Now, sit down and go on with your pipe, you young monkey. I did not think you had taken to smoking."

"One has to," the lad said, "everyone else does it; and there is no doubt that, when you have got the middle watch on cold nights with foul winds, it is a comfort."

"Well, go on smoking," his brother said. "I will light up too. Now shut your mouth altogether. I want to think."

They were silent for fully ten minutes, then Harry said;

"I told you about that business of mine with Miss Fortescue."

Bertie grinned all over his face, which, as he sat, was not visible to his brother. Then with preternatural gravity he turned towards him.

"Yes, you told me about it; an uncomfortable business wasn't it?—surly old father, lovely daughter, and so on."

"I will pull your ear for you, you young scamp," Harry said wrathfully, "if you make fun of it; and I have a good mind not to say what I was going to."

"Say it, Harry, don't mind my feelings," the lad said. "You can't say I did not stand it well when I was here last week, and gave you no end of sympathy. Go ahead, old fellow; I dare say I shall be taken bad some day, and then I shall be able to make allowances for you."

"I'll have nothing more to say to you, you young imp."

"Don't say that, Harry," the lad said in a tone of alarm. "You know how sympathizing I am, and I know what a comfort it is for you to unburden yourself; but I do think that it won't be necessary to go into personal descriptions, you know, or to tell me what you said to her or she said to you, because you told me all that ten days ago, also what her tyrannical old father said. But really seriously I am awfully sorry about it all, and if there is anything that I can possibly do for you I shall be only too pleased. I don't see that it would be any advantage for me to go and give the old gentleman my opinion of him; but if you think it would, and can coach me in some of his sore points, we might see how we could work upon them."

"I always thought you were a young ass, Bertie," Harry said sternly, "but I have not realized before how utterly assified you are."

"All right, Harry!" the lad said cheerfully; "hit me as hard as you like, under the circumstances I feel that I cannot kick."

Harry said nothing for another five minutes.

"This is a serious matter," he said at last, "and I don't want any tomfoolery."

"All right, Harry! I will be as serious as a judge."

"I am thinking of going away for two years."

The lad turned half round in his chair and had a good look at his brother.

"Where are you going to?" seeing by Harry's rather gloomy face that he was quite in earnest.

"I believe I am going to Peru."

"What are you going there for, Harry?" the lad said quietly.

"I told you," the other went on, "that Mr. Fortescue said that he had no personal objection to me, but that if I was in a position to give his daughter a home equal to that which I wanted her to leave, he would be content."

Bertie nodded.

"This seemed to me hopeless," Harry went on. "I told you that she was willing to wait for two years, but that she couldn't promise much longer than that, for her father had set his mind on her making a good match; he has certainly put a tremendous pressure upon her. When I was talking at the club this evening to Mr. Barnett—you know that he is our oldest friend and is one of our trustees—I told him about it, and said that though I was ready to do anything and go anywhere I could not see my way at all to making a big fortune straight away. He agreed with me. After talking it over he said he knew of but one way by which such a thing would be at all possible, but the betting would be twenty thousand to one against it. Of course I said that if there was even a possibility I would try it. Well, you know he was in Peru for some years. He says that the natives have all sorts of legends about rich mines that were hidden when the Spaniards came first, and that it is certain that, tremendous as was the amount of loot they got, a great part of the Incas' treasure was hidden away. Once or twice there had been great finds-in one case two million and a half dollars. It is believed that the secret is still known to certain Indians. When he went out there he had a muleteer, whose life he saved when he was attacked by some beast or other, and this man as much as hinted that he knew of a place where treasure might be concealed; but as Barnett was interested in beasts and plants and that sort of thing, and had a comfortable fortune, he never troubled himself about it one way or another. Well, he offered to give me a letter to this man, and he regarded it as just possible that the fellow, who seems to be a descendant of some of the people who were members of the Incas' court at the time the Spaniards came, may have some knowledge of the rich mines that were then closed down, and that he may be able to show them to me, from his feeling of gratitude to Barnett. It is but one chance in a million, and as I can see no other possibility of making a fortune in two years, I am going to try it."

"Of course you will," the lad said excitedly, "and I should think that you would take me with you."

"I certainly had not dreamt of doing so, Bertie. But if I have to keep on getting fresh outfits for you, the idea has come into my mind during the last half-hour that I could not do better."

"Harry, you are sure to be disappointed lots of times before you hit on a treasure, and then if you were all by yourself you would get down in the mouth. Now, I should be able to keep you going, pat you on the back when you felt sick, help you to fight Indians and wild beasts, and be useful in all sorts of ways."

"That is like your impudence, Bertie," the other laughed. "Seriously, I know I shall be a fool to take you, and if I really thought I had any chance to speak of I should not do so; but though I am going to try, I don't expect for a moment that I shall succeed. I feel that really it would be a comfort to have someone with me upon whom I could rely in such a life as I should have to lead. It certainly would be lonely work for one man. The only doubt in my mind is whether it will be fair to you—you have got your profession."

"But I can go back to it if nothing good turns up, Harry. I can visit the firm and tell them that I am going to travel with you for a bit, and hope that on my return they will take me back again and let me finish my apprenticeship. I should think they would be rather glad, for they always build and never buy ships, and it will take them six months to replace the *Stella*. Besides, it will do me a lot of good. I shall pick up Spanish—at least, I suppose that is the language they speak out there—and shall learn no end of things. As you know, we trade with the west coast of America, so I should be a lot more useful to the firm when I come back than I am now."

"Well, I will think it over, and let you know in the morning. I must certainly consult Mr. Barnett, for he is your trustee as well as mine. If we go I shall work my way out. It will be a big expense, anyhow, and I don't mean, if possible, to draw upon my capital beyond three or four hundred pounds. I believe living is cheap out there, and if I buy three or four mules I shall then have to pay only the wages for the muleteers, and the expenses of living. Of course I shall arrange for my income and half-pay to be sent out to some firm at Lima. Now, you had better go off to bed, and don't buoy yourself up with the belief that you are going, for I have by no means decided upon taking you yet."

"You will decide to take me, Harry," the lad said confidently, and then added with a laugh: "the fact that you should have adopted a plan like this is quite sufficient to show that you want somebody to look after you."

Harry Prendergast did not get much sleep that night. He blamed himself for having mentioned the matter at all to Bertie, and yet the more he thought over it the more he felt that it would be very pleasant to have his brother with him. The lad was full of fun and mischief, but he knew that he had plenty of sound sense, and would be a capital companion, and the fact that he had been three years at sea, and was accustomed to turn his hand to anything, was all in his favour. If nothing came of it he would only have lost a couple of years, and, as the boy himself had said, the time would not have been altogether wasted. Bertie was down before him in the morning. He looked anxiously at his brother as he came in.

"Well, Harry?"

"Well, I have thought it over in every light. But in the first place, Bertie, if you go with me you will have to remember that I am your commanding officer. I am ten years older than you, and besides I am a lieutenant in the King's Navy, while you are only a midshipman in the merchant service. Now, I shall expect as ready obedience from you as if I were captain of my own ship and you one of my men; that is absolutely essential."

"Of course, Harry, it could not be otherwise."

"Very well, then; in the next place I shall abide by what Mr. Barnett says. He is your guardian as well as trustee, and has a perfect right to put a veto upon any wild expedition of this sort. Lastly, I should hope, although I don't say that this is absolutely necessary, that you may get your employer's promise to take you back again in order that you may complete your time."

"Thank you very much, Harry!" the lad said gratefully. "The first condition you may rely upon being performed, and I think the third will be all right, for I know that I have always been favourably reported upon. Old Prosser told me so himself when he said that I should have a rise in my pay this voyage. As to Mr. Barnett, of course I can't say, but I should think, as it was he who put you up to this, he must see that it would be good for you to have someone to take care of you."

"I think he is much more likely to say that I shall have quite enough to do to take care of myself, without having the bother of looking after you. However, I will go and see him this morning. You had better call upon your employers."

"Don't you think I had better go to Mr. Barnett with you, Harry?"

"Not as you are now anyhow, Bertie. Your appearance is positively disgraceful. You evidently had on your worst suit of clothes when you were wrecked, and I can see that they have not been improved by the experience. Why, there is a split right down one sleeve, and a big rent in your trousers!"

"I got them climbing on board, for I had no time to pick and choose, with the *Stella* sinking under my feet."

"Well, you may as well go as you are, but you had better borrow a needle and thread from the landlady and mend up the holes. You really cannot walk through the city in that state. I will see about getting you some more clothes when we get back, for I cannot have you coming here in these in broad daylight. Here are three guineas; get yourself a suit of pilot cloth at some outfitter's at the East End. It will be useful to you anyhow, whether you go with me or ship again here."

"There is a good deal in what you say, Harry," Mr. Barnett said when Prendergast asked his opinion as to his taking his brother with him. "Two years would not make any material difference in his career as a sailor; it simply means that he will be so much older when he passes as mate. There is no harm in that. Two or three and twenty is quite young enough for a young fellow to become an officer, and I don't think that many captains care about having lads who have just got their certificate. They have not the same sense of responsibility or the same power of managing. Then, too, Bertie will certainly have a good deal of knocking about if he spends a couple of years in South America, and the knowledge he will gain of Spanish will add to his value with any firm trading on that coast. As far as you are concerned, I think it would be a great advantage to have him with you. In a long expedition, such as you propose, it is a gain to have a companion with you. It makes the work more pleasant, and two men can laugh over hardships and disagreeables that one alone would grumble at; but apart from this, it is very important in case of illness.

"A lonely man laid up with fever, or accidental injury, fares badly indeed if he is at a distance from any town where he can obtain medical attendance, and surrounded only by ignorant natives. I was myself at one time down with fever for six weeks in a native hut, and during that time I would have given pretty nearly all that I was worth for the sight of a white face and the sound of an English voice. As to the fact that it is possible that the lad might catch fever, or be killed in an affray with natives, that must, of course, be faced; but as a sailor he runs the risk of shipwreck, or of being washed overboard, or killed by a falling spar. Everything considered, I think the idea of his going with you is a good one. I don't suppose that many guardians would be of the same opinion, but I have been so many years knocking about in one part of the world or another, that I don't look at things in the same light as men who have never been out of England."

"I am glad you see it in that way, sir. I own that it would be a great satisfaction to have him with me. He certainly would be a cheery companion, and I should say that he is as hard as nails, and can stand as much fatigue and hardship as myself. Besides, there is no doubt that in case of any trouble two men are better than one."

"I cannot advance any money out of the thousand pounds that will come to him when he is of age. By your father's will it was ordered that, in the event of his own death before that time, the interest was to accumulate. Your father foresaw that, like you, probably Bertie would take to the sea, and as the amount would be fully two thousand pounds by the time he comes of age, it would enable him to buy a share in any ship that he might, when he passed his last examination, command; but I will myself draw a cheque for a hundred pounds, which will help towards meeting expenses. I feel myself to some extent responsible for this expedition. I somewhat regret now having ever spoken to you on the subject, for I cannot conceal from myself that the chance of your making a discovery, where the Spaniards, with all their power of putting pressure on the natives for the past two or three hundred years, have failed, is so slight as to be scarcely worth consideration.

"I tell you frankly that I broached the subject chiefly because I thought it was much better for you to be doing something than kicking your heels about London, and mooning over this affair with Miss Fortescue. There is nothing worse for a young man than living in London with just enough to keep him comfortably without the necessity of working. Therefore I thought you would be far better travelling and hunting for treasure in Peru, than staying here. Even if you fail, as I feel is almost certain, in the object for which you go out, you will have plenty to occupy your thoughts, and not be dwelling continually upon an attachment which in all probability will not turn out satisfactorily. I do not suppose that you are likely to forget Miss Fortescue, but by the time you return you will have accustomed yourself to the thought that it is useless to cry for the moon, and that, after all, life may be very endurable even if she does not share it. Therefore I propounded this Peruvian adventure, feeling sure that, whatever came of it, it would be a benefit to you."

"No doubt it will, sir. I see myself the chance of success is small indeed, but there is none at all in any other way. It is just the sort of thing I should like, and I quite feel myself that it would be good for me to have plenty to think about; and now that you have consented to Bertie's going with me, I feel more eager than before to undertake the expedition. The place is in rather a disturbed state, isn't it?"

"If you are going to wait until Peru ceases to be in a disturbed state, Harry, you may wait another hundred years. The Spanish rule was bad, but Peru was then a pleasant place to live in compared with what it is now. It is a sort of cock-pit, where a succession of ambitious rascals struggle for the spoils, and the moment one gets the better of his rivals fresh intrigues are set on foot, and fresh rebellions break out. There are good Peruvians—men who have estates and live upon them, and who are good masters. But as to the politicians, there is no principle whatever at stake. It is simply a question of who shall have the handling of the national revenue, and divide it and the innumerable posts among his adherents. But these struggles will not affect you largely. In one respect they will even be an advantage. Bent upon their own factious aims, the combatants have no time to concern themselves with the doings of an English traveller, whose object out there is ostensibly to botanize and shoot. Were one of them to obtain the undisputed control of affairs he might meddle in all sorts of ways; but, as it is, after you have once got pretty well beyond the area of their operations, you can regard their doings with indifference, knowing that the longer they go on fighting the fewer scoundrels there will be in the land.

"But even were they to think that it was mining, and not science or sport that took you out there, they would scarcely interfere with you. It is admitted by all the factions that Peru needs capital for her development, and at present that can best be got from this country. The discovery of a fresh mine means employment to a large number of people, and the increase of the revenues by a royalty or taxation. English explorers who have gone out have never had any reason to complain of interference on the part of the authorities. You will find the average better class of Peruvians a charming people, and extremely hospitable. The ladies are pretty enough to turn the head of anyone whose affections are not already engaged. The men are kindly and courteous in the extreme. However, you would have little to do with these.

"In the mountains you would largely depend upon your rifle for food, and on what you could get in the scattered native villages. The Indians have no love for the Peruvians. They find their condition no better off under them than it was under the Spaniards. Once they find out that you are English they will do all in their power for you. It is to Cochrane and the English officers with him that they owe the overthrow and expulsion of their Spanish tyrants, and they are vastly more grateful than either the Chilians or Peruvians have shown themselves to be."

On returning to their lodgings Harry met his brother, who had been into the city.

"Old Prosser was very civil," said Bertie. "He said that as their ships were chiefly in the South American trade it would be a great advantage for me to learn to speak Spanish well. They had not yet thought anything about whether they should order another ship to replace the *Stella*; at any rate, at present they had no vacancy, and would gladly give me permission to travel in South America, and would find me a berth to finish my apprenticeship when I returned. More than that, they said that as I had always been so favourably reported upon they would put me on as a supernumerary in the *Para*, which will sail in a fortnight for Callao. I should not draw pay, but I should be in their service, and the time would count, which would be a great pull, and I should get my passage for nothing."

"That is capital. Of course I will take a passage in her too."

"And what does Mr. Barnett say?"

"Rather to my surprise, Bertie, he did not disapprove of the plan at all. He thought it would be a good thing for me to have you with me in case of illness or anything of that sort. Then no doubt he thought to some extent it would keep you out of mischief."

"I don't believe he thought anything of the sort. Did he say so?"

"Well, no, he didn't; but I have no doubt he felt it in some way a sort of relief."

"That is all very fine. I know, when I have been down to his place in the country between voyages, I have always been as well behaved as if I had been a model mid."

"Well, I have heard some tales of your doings, Bertie, that didn't seem quite in accord with the character you give yourself."

"Oh, of course I had a few larks! You cannot expect a fellow who has been away from England for a year to walk about as soberly as if he were a Methodist parson!"

"No, I should not expect that, Bertie. But, on the other hand, I should hardly have expected that he would, for example, risk breaking his neck by climbing up to the top of the steeple and fastening a straw-hat on the head of the weathercock."

"It gave it a very ornamental appearance; and that weathercock was never before watched so regularly by the people of the village as it was from that time till the hat was blown away in a gale."

"That I can quite believe. Still, Mr. Barnett told me that the rector lodged a complaint about it."

"He might complain as much as he liked; there is no law in the land, as far as I know, that makes the fixing of a straw-hat upon a weathercock a penal offence. It did no end of good in the village, gave them something to talk about, and woke them up wonderfully."

"And there were other things too, I think," his brother went on.

"Oh, well, you need not go into them now! they are an old story. Besides, I fancy I have heard of various tricks played by Mr. Midshipman Harry Prendergast, and, as I heard them from your lips, I cannot doubt but that they were strictly veracious. Well, this is jolly now. When are we going to begin to get our outfit?"

"We will lose no time about that. But really there is not much to get—a couple of good rifles and two brace of pistols, with a good store of ammunition, those clothes you have just bought, and two or three suits of duck for the voyage. I shan't get any special kit until we arrive there, and can take the advice of people at Lima whether we had better travel in European clothes or in those worn by the Peruvians. Of course saddles and bridles and all that sort of thing we can buy there, and we shall want a small tent to use when we get into out-of-the-way places. I shall take three hundred pounds in gold. I have no doubt we can exchange it into silver profitably; besides, it is much more handy for carrying about. I shall go down this afternoon and see Prosser and secure a berth."

"I think you will have to arrange that with the captain. Very few of our ships have accommodation for passengers, but the captains are allowed to take one or two if they like."

"All right! At any rate I must go to the office first. They can refer me to the skipper if they like; that would be better than my going to him direct."

CHAPTER II — THE START

Harry Prendergast went down to Leadenhall Street and saw the managing owner of the *Para.* As Bertie had anticipated, Mr. Prosser, after hearing Harry's statement that he wished to take a passage to Callao in the vessel advertised to start in a week's time, and that he was much obliged to them for giving Bertie a berth as supernumerary midshipman, said:

"We shall certainly have pleasure in putting your brother's name on the ship's books. He has already explained to me his desire to go out with you; we have had every reason to be satisfied with him since he entered our service, and he had better draw pay as usual, as his service during the voyage will then count towards his time. As for yourself, we do not book passengers, it is more bother than it is worth; but we have no objection to our masters taking one or two. The addition of a mouth or so practically makes very little difference in the amount of ships' stores consumed. The masters pay us a small sum a head and make their own terms with the passengers they take. In that way we are saved all complaints as to food and other matters. Of course a passenger would put on board for himself a stock of such wines, spirits, and little luxuries as he may choose.

"You will find Captain Peters down at the docks. The last cargo has been discharged, and they are giving an overhaul to the rigging and making a few repairs; he is not a man to leave his ship if he can help it while work is going on there."

Harry at once went down.

"Well, sir," the captain said, when he had told him that he wished to take a passage to Callao, and that the owners had referred him to him, "I had fully made up my mind that I would not take passengers again. On my last voyage they were always grumbling at the food, expecting to be treated as if they were in a first-class hotel."

"I am not likely to grumble, Captain; I have been knocking about the King's service since I was fourteen."

"Oh, you are a royal navy man, are you, sir?"

"I am; I am a lieutenant."

"That makes a difference; and I have no doubt we can arrange the matter to our satisfaction."

"I may tell you," Harry said, "that I have a younger brother coming out with me. He is an apprentice nearly out of his time, and was on board the *Stella* when she was sunk in the Channel. Your owners have kindly arranged that he shall go out with you as a supernumerary; that is one reason why I wish to go in your ship."

The Master thought for a minute or two. "Well, Mr. Prendergast," he said, "I like having one of you naval gentlemen on board; if anything goes wrong it is a comfort to have your advice. If we have bad weather round the Horn, could I rely upon you to give me a helping hand should I need it? I don't mean that you should keep watch or anything of that sort, but that you should, as it were, stand by me. I have a new first mate, and there is no saying how he may turn out. No doubt the firm would make every enquiry. Still, such enquiries don't mean much; a master doesn't like to damn a man by refusing to give him a good character. I dare say he is all right. Still, I should certainly feel very much more comfortable if I had a naval officer with me. Now, sir, I pay the firm twelve pounds for each passenger I take as his share of the cabin stores; you pay me that, and I will ask for nothing for your passage. I cannot say fairer than that."

"You cannot indeed, Captain, and I feel very much obliged to you for the offer—very much obliged. It will suit me admirably, and in case of any emergency you may rely upon my aid; and if you have a spell of bad weather I shall be quite willing to take a watch, for I know that in the long heavy gales you meet with going round the Horn the officers get terribly overtaxed."

"And how about your brother?" the captain said; "as he is to be a supernumerary, I suppose that only means that the firm are willing that he shall put in his time for his rating. I have never had a supernumerary on board, but I suppose he is to be regarded as a passenger rather than one of the ship's complement."

"No, Captain, he is to be on the pay-sheet; and I think he had much better be put into a watch. He would find the time hang very heavy on his hands if he had nothing to do, and I know he is anxious to learn his profession thoroughly. As he is to be paid, there is no reason why he should not work."

"Very well; if you think so we will say nothing more about it. I thought perhaps you would like to have him aft with you."

"I am much obliged to you, but I think the other way will be best; and I am sure he would feel more comfortable with the other apprentices than as a passenger."

"Are you going out for long, may I ask you, Mr. Prendergast?"

"For a couple of years or so. I am going to wander about and do some shooting and exploring and that sort of thing, and I am taking him with me as companion. I speak Spanish fairly well myself, and shall teach him on the voyage, if you will allow me to do so. A knowledge of that language will be an advantage to him when he comes back into Prosser & Co.'s service."

"A great advantage," the captain agreed. "Most of us speak a little Spanish, but I have often thought that it would pay the company to send a man who could talk the lingo well in each ship. They could call him supercargo, and I am sure he would pay his wages three or four times over by being able to bargain and arrange with the Chilians and Peruvians. In ports like Callao, where there is a British consul, things are all right, but in the little ports we are fleeced right and left. Boatmen and shopkeepers charge us two or three times as much as they do their own countrymen, and I am sure that we could get better bargains in hides and other produce if we had someone who could knock down their prices."

"When do you sail, Captain?"

"This day week. It will be high tide about eight, and we shall start to warp out of dock a good half-hour earlier, so you can either come on board the night before or about seven in the morning."

"Very well, sir; we shall be here in good time. I shall bring my things on board with me; it is of no use sending them on before, as they will not be bulky and can be stored away in my cabin."

"This will be your state-room," the captain said, opening a door. "I have the one aft, and the first mate has the one opposite to you. The others are empty, so you can stow any baggage that you have in one of them; the second and third officers and the apprentices are in the deck-house cabins."

"In that case, Captain, I will send the wine and spirits on board the day before. Of course I shall get them out of bond; I might have difficulty in doing that so early in the morning. You will perhaps be good enough to order them to be stowed in one of the empty cabins."

"That will be the best plan," the captain said.

"When do the apprentices come on board?"

"The morning before we sail. There is always plenty to be done in getting the last stores on board."

"All right! my brother will be here. Good-morning, Captain, and thank you!"

The following morning at eleven Harry Prendergast was standing in front of the entrance to the British Museum. A young lady came up. "It is very imprudent of you, Harry," she said, after the first greeting, "to ask me to meet you."

"I could not help it, dear; it was absolutely necessary that I should see you."

"But it is of no use, Harry."

"I consider that it is of particular use, Hilda."

"But you know, Harry, when you had that very unpleasant talk with my father, I was called in, and said that I had promised to wait two years for you. When he found that I would not give way, he promised that he would not press me, on the understanding that we were not to meet again except in public, and I all but promised."

"Quite so, dear; but it appears to me that this is surely a public place."

"No, no, Harry; what he meant was that I was not to meet you except at parties."

"Well, I should have asked you to meet me to-day even if I had had to storm your father's house to see you. I am going away, dear, and he could scarcely say much if he came along and found us talking here. You see, it was not likely that I should stumble across a fortune in the streets of London. I have talked the matter over with Barnett—you know our trustee, you have met him once or twice—and we came to the conclusion that the only possible chance of my being able to satisfy your father as to my means, was for me to go to Peru and try to discover a gold mine there or hidden treasure. Such discoveries have been made, and may be made again; and he has supplied me with a letter to an Indian, who may possibly be able to help me."

"To Peru, Harry! Why, they are always fighting there."

"Yes, they do a good deal of squabbling, but the people in general have little to do with it; and certainly I am not going out to take any part in their revolutions. There is not a shadow of doubt that a number of gold mines worked by the old people were never discovered by the Spaniards, and it is also certain that a great portion of the treasures of the Incas is still lying hid. Barnett saved the life of a muleteer out there, and from what he said he believed that the man did know something about one of these lost mines, and might possibly let me into the secret. It is just an off chance, but it is the only chance I can see. You promised your father that you would never marry without his consent, and he would never give it unless I were a rich man. If nothing comes of this adventure I shall be no worse off than I am at present. If I am fortunate enough to discover a rich mine or a hidden treasure, I shall be in a position to satisfy his demand. I am going to take Bertie with me; he will be a cheerful companion, and even now he is a powerful young fellow. At any rate, if I get sick or anything of that sort, it would be an immense advantage to have him with me."

"I don't like the idea of your going, Harry," she said tearfully. "No, dear; and if I had the chance of seeing you sometimes, and of some day obtaining your father's consent to the marriage, all the gold mines in Peru would offer no temptation to me. As it is, I can see nothing else for it. In some respects it is better; if I were to stay here I should only be meeting you frequently at dances and dinners, never able to talk to you privately, and feeling always that you could never be mine. It would be a constant torture. Here is a possibility—a very remote one, I admit, but still a possibility—and even if it fails I shall have the satisfaction of knowing that I have done all that a man could do to win you."

"I think it is best that you should go somewhere, Harry, but Peru seems to be a horrible place."

"Barnett speaks of it in high terms. You know he was four or five years out there. He describes the people as being delightful, and he has nothing to say against the climate."

"I will not try to dissuade you," she said bravely after a pause. "At present I am hopeless, but I shall have something to hope and pray for while you are away. We will say good-bye now, dear. I have come to meet you this once, but I will not do so again, another meeting would but give us fresh pain. I am very glad to know that your brother is going with you. I shall not have to imagine that you are ill in some out-of-the-way place without a friend near you; and in spite of the dangers you may have to run, I would rather think of you as bravely doing your best than eating your heart out here in London. I shall not tell my father that we have met here; you had better write to him and say that you are leaving London at once, and that you hope in two years to return and claim me in accordance with his promise. I am sure he will be glad to know that you have gone, and that we shall not be constantly meeting. He will be kinder to me than he has been of late, for as he will think it quite impossible that you can make a fortune in two years he will be inclined to dismiss you altogether from his mind."

For another half-hour they talked together, and then they parted with renewed protestations on her part that nothing should induce her to break her promise to wait for him for two years. He had given her the address of one of the merchants to whom Mr. Barnett had promised him a letter of introduction, so that she might from time to time write, for the voyage would take at least four months and as much more would be required for his first letter to come back. He walked moodily home after parting with her.

"Hullo, Harry! nothing wrong with you, I hope? why, you look as grave as an owl."

"I feel grave, Bertie. I have just said good-bye to Hilda; and though I kept up my spirits and made the best of this expedition of ours, I cannot but feel how improbable it is that we shall meet again—that is to say, in our present relations; for if I fail I certainly shall not return home for some years; it would be only fair to her that I should not do so. I know that she would keep on as long as there was any hope, but I should not care to think that she was wasting her life. I was an ass to believe it could ever be otherwise, and I feel that the best thing for us both would have been for me to go away as soon as I found that I was getting fond of her."

"Well, of course I cannot understand it, Harry, and it seems to me that one girl is very like another; she may be a bit prettier than the average, but I suppose that comes to all the same thing in another twenty years. I can understand a man getting awfully fond of his ship, especially when she is a clipper. However, some day I may feel different; besides, how could you tell that her father would turn out such a crusty old beggar?"

"I suppose I did not think about it one way or the other, Bertie," Harry said quietly. "However, the mischief is done, and even if there was no chance whatever of making money I should go now for my own sake as well as hers. Well, it is of no use talking more about it; we will go out now and buy the rifles. I shan't get them new, one can pick up guns just as good at half the price, and as I know something about rifles I am not likely to be taken in. Of course I have got my pistols and only have a brace to buy for you. You will have time on the voyage to practise with them; if you did not do that you would be as likely to shoot me as a hostile Indian."

"Oh, that is bosh!" the boy said; "still, I certainly should like to be a good shot."

After getting the rifles and pistols, Harry went into the city and ordered six dozen of wine and three dozen of brandy to be sent on board out of bond; he also ordered a bag of twenty pounds of raw coffee, a chest of tea, and a couple of dozen bottles of pickles and sauces, to be sent down to the docks on the day before the *Para* sailed. Another suit of seafaring clothes and a stock of underclothing was ordered for Bertie. Harry spent the intervening time before the vessel sailed in looking up his friends and saying good-bye to them, and drove down to the docks at the appointed time, his brother having joined the ship on the previous day.

The *Para* was a barque-rigged ship of some eight hundred tons. At present she did not show to advantage, her deck being littered with stores of all kinds that had come on board late. The deck planks where they could be seen were almost black, the sails had been partly loosed from the gaskets, and to an eye accustomed to the neatness and order of a man-of-war her appearance was by no means favourable; but her sides shone with fresh paint, and, looking at her lines from the wharf, Harry thought she would be both fast and a good sea-boat. She was not heavily laden, and stood boldly up in the water. Nodding to Bertie, who was working hard among the men, he went up on to the poop, from which Captain Peters was shouting orders.

"Glad to see you, sir," the captain said; "she looks rather in a litter at present, doesn't she? We shall get her all ataunto before we get down to the Nore. These confounded people won't send their stores on board till the last moment. If I were an owner I should tell all shippers that no goods would be received within five or six hours of the ship's time for sailing; that would give us a fair chance, instead of starting all in a muddle, just at the time, too, when more than any other one wants to have the decks free for making short tacks down these narrow reaches. I believe half the wrecks on the sands at the mouth of the river are due to the confusion in which the ships start. How can a crew be lively in getting the yards over when they have to go about decks lumbered up like this, and half of them are only just recovering from their bout of drink the day before?"

Up to the last moment everyone on board was hard at work, and when the order was given to throw off the hawsers the deck was already comparatively clear. Half an hour later the vessel passed out through the dock gates, with two boats towing ahead so as to take her well out into the river; the rest of the crew were employed in letting the sails drop. As soon as she gathered way the men in the boats were called in, the boats themselves being towed behind in case they might again be required.

The passage from the Pool to the mouth of the river was in those days the most dangerous portion of the voyage. There were no tugs to seize the ships and carry them down to the open water, while the channels below the Nore were badly buoyed and lighted, and it was no uncommon thing for twenty vessels to get upon the sands in the course of a single tide.

The wind was light, and being northerly helped them well on their way, and it was only in one or two reaches that the *Para* was unable to lay her course. She overtook many craft that had been far ahead of her, and answered the helm quickly.

"She is both fast and handy, I see," Harry Prendergast, who had been watching her movements with interest, remarked.

"Yes; there are not many craft out of London can show her their heels when the wind is free. She does not look quite so well into the wind as I should wish; still, I think she is as good as most of them."

"I suppose you will get down to Gravesend before the tide turns?"

"Yes, we shall anchor there. The wind is not strong enough for us to stem the tide, which runs like a sluice there. Once past the Nore one can do better, but there is no fighting the tide here unless one has a steady breeze aft. I never feel really comfortable till we are fairly round the South Foreland; after that it is plain sailing enough. Though there are a few shoals in the Channel, one can give them a wide berth; fogs are the things we have to fear there."

"Yes. I have never been down the river, having always joined my ships either at Portsmouth or Plymouth, so I know very little about it; but I know from men who have been on board vessels commissioned at Chatham or Sheerness that they are thankful indeed when they once get round the Goodwins and head west."

"Well, Mr. Prendergast, I am against these new-fangled steamboats—I suppose every true sailor is; but when the *Marjory* began to run between London and Gravesend eighteen years ago—in '15 I think it was—folks did say that it would not be long before sailing craft would be driven off the sea. I did not believe that then, and I don't believe it now; but I do say that I hope before long there will be a lot of small steamers on the Thames, to tow vessels down till they are off the North Foreland. It would be a blessing and a comfort to us master mariners. Once there we have the choice of going outside the Goodwins, or taking a short cut inside if the wind is aft. Why, sir, it would add years to our lives and shorten voyages by weeks. There we are, now, sometimes lying off the Nore, five hundred sail, waiting for the wind to shift out of the east, and when we do get under weigh we have always to keep the lead going. One never knows when one may bump upon the sands. Some masters will grope their way along in the dark, but for my part I always anchor. There are few enough buoys and beacons in daytime, but I consider that it is tempting Providence to try and go down in a dark night. The owners are sensible men and they know that it is not worth while running risks just to save a day or two when you have got a four months' voyage before you. Once past Dover I am ready to hold on with anyone, but between the Nore and the North Foreland I pick my way as carefully as a woman going across a muddy street."

"You are quite right, Captain; I thoroughly agree with you. More ships get ashore going down to the mouth of the Thames than in any other part of the world; and, as you say, if all sailing ships might be taken down by a steamer, it would be the making of the port of London."

"Your brother is a smart young chap, Mr. Prendergast. I was watching him yesterday, and he is working away now as if he liked work. He has the makings of a first-rate sailor. I hold that a man will never become a first-class seaman unless he likes work for its own sake. There are three sorts of hands. There is the fellow who shirks his work whenever he has a chance; there is the man who does his work, but who does it because he has to do it, and always looks glad when a job is over; and there is the lad who jumps to his work, chucks himself right into it, and puts his last ounce of strength on a rope. That is the fellow who will make a good officer, and who, if needs be, can set an example to the men when they have to go aloft to reef a sail in a stiff gale. So, as I understand, Mr. Prendergast, he is going to leave the sea for a bit. It seems a pity too."

"He will be none the worse for it, Captain. A year or so knocking about among the mountains of Peru will do more good to him than an equal time on board ship. It will sharpen him up, and give him habits of reliance and confidence. He will be all the better for it afterwards, even putting aside the advantage it will be to him to pick up Spanish."

"Yes, it may do him good," the captain agreed, "if it does not take away his liking for the sea."

"I don't think it will do that. If the first voyage or two don't sicken a lad, I think it is pretty certain he is cut out for the sea. Of course it is a very hard life at first, especially if the officers are a rough lot, but when a boy gets to know his duty things go more easily with him; he is accustomed to the surroundings, and takes to the food, which you know is not always of the best, with a good appetite. Bertie has had three years of it now, and when he has come home I have never heard a grumble from him; and he is not likely to meet with such luxuries while we are knocking about as to make him turn up his nose at salt junk."

The tide was already turning when they reached Gravesend. As soon as the anchor was down the steward came up to say that dinner was ready.

"I am not at all sorry," Harry said as he went below with the captain. "I ate a good breakfast before I started at half-past six, and I went below and had a biscuit and bottle of beer at eleven, but I feel as hungry as a hunter now. There is nothing like a sea appetite. I have been nearly two years on shore, and I never enjoyed a meal as I do at sea."

The crew had been busy ever since they left the dock, and the deck had now been scrubbed and made tidy, and presented a very different appearance from that which met Harry's eye as he came on board.

Johnson, the first mate, also dined with the skipper. He was a tall, powerfully-built man. He was singularly taciturn, and took no share in the conversation unless directly asked. He seemed, however, to be able to appreciate a joke, but never laughed audibly, contenting himself with drawing his lips apart and showing his teeth.

The wind was light and baffling, so that they did not round the South Foreland until the seventh day after leaving dock. After that it was favourable and steady, and they ran without any change until they approached the line; then there was a fortnight of calm. At last they got the wind again, and made a rapid run until within five hundred miles of Cape Horn. The captain was in high glee.

"We have done capitally so far, Mr. Prendergast. I don't think I ever made so rapid a run. If she goes on like this we shall reach Callao within three months of starting."

"I don't think the weather will continue like this," the mate said.

This was the first original observation he had made since he had sailed, and Harry and the captain looked at him in surprise.

"You think there is going to be a change, Mr. Johnson?" the captain said, after a short pause to recover from his astonishment.

The mate nodded.

"Glass falling, sky hazy."

"Is the glass falling? I am ashamed to say I have not looked at it for the past twenty-four hours. It has stuck so long at the same point that I have quite ceased to look at it two or three times a day as I usually do."

"It has not fallen much, but it is sinking."

The captain got up from the table, and went to look at the glass.

"You are right, it has fallen a good eighth; but that may mean a change of wind. Did you notice any change, Mr. Prendergast?"

"No, I can't say that I did. I looked up, as a sailor always does, when I was on deck this morning, but it was clear enough then, and I have not noticed it particularly since."

But when they went up on deck half an hour later both agreed that the mate was right. The change overhead was slight, but away to the west a dull reddish mist seemed to obscure the horizon.

"We will get the upper sails off at once, Mr. Johnson. These storms come so suddenly off the coast that it is as well to lose no time in shortening sail when one sees any indication of such a change."

The mate at once gave the necessary orders. The sailors started up with looks of surprise.

"Look sharp, men!" the mate said. "We shall have wind, and plenty of it. It will be here before long."

The men, who were by no means sorry for a spell of work after going so long without shifting sail or tack, worked hard, and the white sheets of canvas were soon snugly furled. By this time all the sailors who had been to sea for any time recognized the utility of their work. The low bank had risen and extended the whole width of the western horizon.

"What do you think, Mr. Prendergast? Have we got enough off her?"

"I don't know about your storms here, Captain; but if it were in the Levant I should get every stitch of canvas off her excepting closely-reefed topsails, a storm jib, and fore stay-sail. The first burst over, one can always shake out more canvas. However, you know these seas, and I do not."

"I think you are right. These pamperos, as we call them, are not to be trifled with."

"In that case there is no time to be lost, Captain, and with your permission I will lend a hand."

"All hands take in sail!" the captain shouted.

The mate led the way up the starboard shrouds, while Harry, throwing off his coat, mounted those to port, closely followed by Bertie. Five minutes' hard work, and the *Para* was stripped for the struggle.

"That is a good job done," the skipper said to Harry as he reached the deck.

"A very good job, sir. The wind may come, but we are prepared for it; there is nothing like being ready in time."

"She is in good trim for it," said the captain, "not above two-thirds laden, and as the wind is off the land, there is nothing to worry us except the Falklands. I shall go outside them. Of course that will lengthen the voyage, but with this westerly wind I should not care about being between them and the mainland. You think the same, Mr. Prendergast?"

"I do, sir; they are a scattered group, and it would not be pleasant to have them under lee."

It had grown sensibly darker, but the line of mist had not risen higher. Harry remarked upon this.

"I almost doubt whether it is coming after all," he said.

The captain shook his head.

"It does not spread over the sky," he said, "because it is largely dust blown off the land. After the first burst you will see that we shall have a bright blue sky and a roaring wind, just as one gets it sometimes in an easterly gale in the Channel. We shall have it in another five minutes, I fancy. I don't think it will be very strong, or we should have had it here before this."

It was not long before a dull, moaning sound was heard, the brown-red fog changed its appearance, swirls of vapour seemed to dash out in front of it, and the whole swelled and heaved as if it were being pushed forward by some tremendous pressure in its rear.

The ship's head was pointing nearly east, the canvas hung down motionless, and there was not a breath of wind.

"Hold on all!" the captain shouted. Half a minute later the billowly clouds swept across the vessel, and a sudden darkness overspread them. Then there was a glow of white light, a line of foam approached as fleet as a race-horse, and with a shriek the gale was upon them. The vessel shook from stem to stern as if she had struck against a rock, and her bow was pressed down lower and lower until she seemed as if she were going to dive head-foremost. But as she gathered way, her bow rose, and in a minute she was flying along at some eighteen knots an hour.

"She is all right now, Mr. Prendergast," the captain said. "It is well we stripped her so thoroughly, and that she is not heavily laden."

Four men had been placed at the wheel, and it needed all their strength to keep her from yawing. In half an hour the sea began to get up, and the captain laid her course south-east, which put the wind on her quarter.

"It is well we were not a degree or so farther south, Captain."

"Yes; it would have been as much as we could do to weather the Falklands; for with this small amount of sail we should have made a terrible amount of leeway. As it is, all is fair sailing."

The darkness gradually passed away, and in an hour after the gale had struck her the *Para* was sailing under a bright blue sky. Although but few points off the wind, she was lying down till her lee scuppers were under water. The spray was flying over her sparkling in the sun; the sailors were crouched under the weather bulwark, lashed to belaying-pins and stanchions to prevent themselves from shifting down to leewards. Six hours later it was evident that there was some slight diminution in the force of the wind.

"She is going about fourteen knots now," the captain said; "we can head her more to the south. We must be nearly abreast of the islands, and according to my reckoning forty or fifty miles to the east of them."

It was now dark, and the watch was sent below.

"To-morrow morning we shall be able to get some more sail on her," the master said, "and I hope by the next morning the squall will be over, for we shall then have made our southing, and the wind will be right in our teeth when we turn her head west. There is no saying which way it will come when the squall dies out. What do you think, Johnson?"

"We are pretty sure to get it hot from one quarter or another," the man said. "I should say most likely from the south."

"Except for the cold that would be better than west," Harry remarked.

"Yes, if it is not too strong; but it is likely to be strong. After such a gale as we have had, it seldom settles down for some time. As like as not there will be bad weather for the next month."

The next morning when Harry went on deck he saw that the reefs had been shaken out of the topsails and the spanker hoisted. There was still a fresh wind, but it had backed round more to the south, and there was so sharp a nip in it that he went below and put on a pea-jacket. Then he beckoned to Bertie, who was off duty, to join him on the poop.

"That has been a smart blow, Bertie."

"Yes, but I had it worse than that the last time I came round the Horn. I think we shall be shortening sail again before long. The clouds are banking up to the south-west. She is a good sea-boat, isn't she?"

"She has behaved uncommonly well. We shall want all our clothes before night, Bertie. It was May when we started, and it is nearly mid-winter down here."

"There is one thing, we shan't have so much risk of coming across drifting icebergs, most of them will be frozen up hard and fast down in the south. They don't matter much when the weather is clear, but if it is thick one has an awful time of it. On my first voyage it was like that, and I tell you I didn't think I was going to see England again. We had some desperately close shaves."

The wind speedily freshened, and by evening the ship was under close-reefed canvas again. The clouds were flying fast overhead and the air was thick. Before the evening watch was set the ship was brought round on the other tack, and was running to the east of south.

"We will lie on this course till morning, Mr. Prendergast," said the captain, "and then if the wind holds, I think we shall be able to make a long leg and weather the Horn."

For six days the storm raged with unabated violence. The cold was intense, the spray breaking over the bows froze as it fell, and the crew were engaged for hours at a time in breaking up the masses of ice thus formed. Harry had volunteered to take a watch in turn with the first and second mates. The captain was almost continuously on deck. Twice they encountered icebergs, and once in a driving snow-storm nearly ran foul of one. Fortunately it was daylight, and the whole crew being on deck, they were able to put the vessel about just in time. During this time the vessel had only gained a few miles' westing. All on board were utterly exhausted with the struggle against the bitter wind; their hands were sore and bleeding through pulling upon frozen ropes, their faces inflamed, and their eyelids so swollen and sore that they could scarcely see. Then the wind began to abate, and more sail being got on the *Para*, she was able to lie her course.

CHAPTER III — AT LIMA

Three days later the sky cleared, and the captain, getting an observation, found that they had rounded the southernmost point of the Cape. Another day and the *Para's* head was turned north, and a week later they were running smoothly along before a gentle breeze, with the coast of Chili twenty miles away. The heavy wraps had all been laid aside, and although the air was still frosty, the crew felt it warm after what they had endured. The upper spars and yards had all been sent up, and she was now carrying a crowd of canvas. The mate had thawed out under the more congenial surroundings. He had worked like a horse during the storm, setting an example, whether in going aloft or in the work of clearing off the ice from the bows, and even when his watch was relieved he seldom went below.

"Well, I hope, Mr. Johnson, we shall sail together until you get your next step," the captain said. "I could not wish for a better first officer."

"I want nothing better, sir. She is a fine ship, well manned and well commanded. I begin to feel at home in her now; at first I didn't. I hate changes; and though the last captain I sailed with was a surly fellow, we got on very well together. I would rather sail with a man like that than with a skipper who is always talking. I am a silent man myself, and am quite content to eat my meal and enjoy it, without having to stop every time I am putting my fork into my mouth to answer some question or other. I was once six months up in the north without ever speaking to a soul. I was whaling then, and a snow-storm came on when we were fast on to a fish. It was twenty-four hours before it cleared off, and when it did there was no ship to be seen. We were in an inlet at the time in Baffin's Bay. We thought that the ship would come back, and we landed and hauled up the boat. The ship didn't come back, and, as I learned long afterwards, was never heard of again. I suppose she got nipped between two icebergs.

"Winter was coming on fast, and the men all agreed that they would rather try and make their way south overland than stay there. I told them that they were fools, but I admit that the prospect of a winter there was enough to frighten any man. I did not like it myself, but I thought it was wiser to remain there than to move. Some of the men went along the shore, or out in the boat, and managed to kill several sea-cows. They made a sledge, piled the meat on it, and started.

"Meanwhile I had been busy building a sort of hut. I piled great stones against the foot of the cliffs, and turned the boat upside down to form a roof. The men helped me to do that job the last thing before they started. Then I blocked up the entrance, leaving only just room for me to crawl in and out. The snow began to fall steadily three days after the others had gone, and very soon covered my hut two feet deep. I melted the blubber of the whale in the boat's baler, for we had towed the fish ashore. The first potful or two I boiled over a few bits of drift-wood. After that it was easy enough, as I unravelled some of the boat's rope, dipped it in the hot blubber, and made a store of big candles. There was a lot of meat left on the sea-cows, so I cut that up, froze it, and stowed as much as I could in the hut. I was bothered about the rest, as I knew the bears were likely to come down; but I found a ledge on the face of the perpendicular rock, and by putting the boat's mast against it I was able to get up to it. Here I piled, I should say, a ton of meat and blubber. Then I set to work and collected some dried grass, and soon I had enough to serve as bed and covers. It took me a month to do all this, and by that time winter was down on me in earnest. I had spent my evenings in making myself, out of the skins of the three cows, breeches, high boots, and a coat with a hood over the head, and in order to make these soft I rubbed them with hot oil. They were rough things, but I hoped that I might get a bear later on. Fortunately the boat had two balers, for I required one in which to melt the snow over the lamp.

"Well, sir, I lived there during that winter. I did not find it altogether dull, for I had several bits of excitement. For a month or so bears and wolves came down and fought over the carcass of the whale. When that was eaten up they turned their attention to me, and over and over again they tried to break in. They had better have left me alone, for though they were strong enough to have pulled away the rocks that blocked the entrance, they could not stand fire. As I had any amount of rope, I used to soak it in rock-oil, set it on fire, and shove it out of the entrance. Twice small bears managed to wriggle up the passage, but I had sharpened the boat-hook and managed to kill them both. One skin made me a whole suit, and the other a first-rate blanket. Not that it was ever unpleasantly cold, for a couple of my big candles, and the thick coating of snow over it, kept the place as warm as I cared for. Occasionally, when the bears had cleared off, I went out, climbed the mast, and got fresh supplies down. They had made desperate efforts to get at the meat, but the face of the rock was luckily too smooth for them to get any hold. When spring came and the ice broke up, I planted the mast on the top of the cliff with the sail fastened as a flag, and a month after the sea was clear a whaler came in and took me off. That was how I pretty well lost the use of my tongue, and though I am better than I was, I don't use it much now except on duty."

S. Antonio
Marañon R.
Ucayali R.
AMAZON R.
Yacarana R.
SCALE OF MILES
0 50 100 150 200
Moyobamba
EASTERN CORDILLERA
CENTRAL CORDILLERA
WESTERN CORDILLERA
Shapaja
R. Jurua
B R A Z I L
Pisana
Calleria
Tarauaca R.
Truxillo
Sta. Rosa
Purus R.
Pozuzu
Paucartambo
Junin
P E R U
Paucartambo R.
Oraya
Callao
LIMA
Huancayelica
Ayacucho
Pachacamac
Paucartambo
Cuzco
Abancay
Pisco Bay
Huacas Pt.
ANDES
Sicuani
Crucero
C. Nasca
C. Lomas
Puno
Atico Pt.
Arequipa
PACIFIC
OCEAN
Coles Pt.
Tacna
CHILE
BOLIVIA

"That certainly accounts for it," Harry said; "you must have had an awful time."

"I don't think I minded it very much, sir. Except when I was bothered by the bears I slept a good lot. I think at first I used to talk out loud a good deal. But I soon dropped that, though I used to whistle sometimes when I was cooking the food. I don't think I should have held on so long if I had only had the sea-cow flesh, but the bears made a nice change, and I only wished that one or two more had managed to crawl in."

"I wonder you were able to kill them with a boat-hook."

"I didn't, sir. You know every whaler carries an axe to cut the line if necessary, and I was able to split their skulls as they crawled in before they could get fairly on to their feet and use their paws. I was getting very weak with scurvy towards the end; but as soon as the snow melted plants began to shoot, and I was able to collect green stuff, so that I was nearly well by the time I was picked up."

The weather continued fine all the time they were coasting up the Chilian coast. They were a week at Valparaiso getting out the cargo they had brought for that town, and did some trading at smaller ports; but at last, just four months after leaving England, they dropped anchor off Callao. "Well, it has been a jolly voyage, Harry," his brother said as they were rowed ashore, after a hearty farewell from the captain and the first officer.

"I am glad you enjoyed it, Bertie. I was sorry all the time I hadn't taken a passage for you aft."

"I am better pleased to have been at work; it would have been awfully slow otherwise. The mates were both good fellows, and I got on well with the other apprentices. I tried at first not to turn out on night watch, as I was not obliged to do so, but I soon gave it up; it seemed disgusting to be lying there when the others had to turn out. It has been a jolly voyage, but I am glad that we are here at last, and are going to set to work in search of treasures."

"I had begun to think that we should not get on shore to-day," Harry said as they neared the landing-place. "What with three hours' waiting for the medical officer, and another three for that bumptious official whom they call the port officer, and without whose permission no one is allowed to land, I think everyone on board was so disgusted that we should have liked nothing better than to pitch the fellow overboard. It was rather amusing to watch all those boatmen crowding round shouting the praises of their own craft and running down the others. But a little of it goes a long way. It is the same pretty nearly at every port I have entered. Boatmen are harpies of the worst kind. It is lucky that we had so little baggage; a tip of a couple of dollars was enough to render the custom-house officer not only civil but servile."

As they mounted the steps they were assailed by a motley crowd, half of whom struggled to get near them to hold out their hands for alms, while the other half struggled and fought for the right of carrying their baggage. Accustomed to such scenes, Harry at once seized upon two of them, gave them the portmanteaux, and, keeping behind them, pushed them through the crowd, telling them to lead the way to the hotel that the captain had recommended as being the least filthy in the place. They crossed a square covered with goods of all kinds. There were long rows of great jars filled with native spirit, bales of cinchona bark, piles of wheat from Chili, white and rose-coloured blocks of salt, pyramids of unrefined sugar, and a block of great bars of silver; among these again were bales and boxes landed from foreign countries, logs of timber, and old anchors and chains. Numbers of people who appeared to have nothing to do sauntered about or sat on logs. In odd corners were native women engaged in making the picanties upon which the poor largely exist; these were composed of fresh and salt meat, potatoes, crabs, the juice of bitter oranges, lard, salt, and an abundance of pepper pods.

"That is the sort of thing we shall have to eat, Bertie."

"Well, I should not mind if I had not got to look on at the making; they smell uncommonly good."

The hotel was larger and even more dirty than the captain's description had led them to expect. However, the dinner that was served to them was better than they had looked for, and being very hungry after their long wait, they did full justice to it.

"It might have been a good deal worse, Bertie."

"I should think so; after four months of salt junk it is splendid!"

A cup of really good coffee, followed by a little glass of native spirits, added to their satisfaction. They had hesitated before whether to push on at once to Lima or wait there till next morning. Their meal decided them—they would start at daybreak, so as to get to Lima before the sun became really hot. Harry asked the landlord to bargain for two riding mules and one for baggage to be ready at that hour, and they then strolled out to view the place, although Bertie assured his brother that there was nothing whatever to see in it.

"That may be, Bertie; but we are not going to begin by being lazy. There is always something to see in foreign lands by those who keep their eyes open."

After an hour's walk Harry was inclined to think that his brother was right. The houses were generally constructed of canes, plastered with mud, and painted yellow. As the result of earthquakes, scarce a house stood upright—some leaned sideways, and looked as if they were going to topple over into the road; while others leaned back, as if, were you to push against them, they would collapse and crush the inmates.

Their night was not a pleasant one. The beds were simple, consisting only of hides stretched across wooden frames, but, as they very speedily found, there were numerous other inhabitants. They therefore slept but little, and were heartily glad when the first gleam of dawn appeared.

Slipping on their clothes, they ran down to the shore and had a bath. By the time they returned breakfast was ready—coffee, fish, and eggs. The mules did not appear for another hour, by which time their patience was all but exhausted. The portmanteaux were speedily strapped on to the back of the baggage mule, and they mounted the two others. The muleteer had brought one for himself, and, fastening the baggage animal behind it, they started.

It was six miles to Lima, but as the city is five hundred and twelve feet above the sea, the ascent was steady and somewhat steep. The road was desperately bad, and the country uninteresting, being for the most part dried up. Occasionally they saw great mounds of adobe bricks, the remains of the ancient habitations. As they neared the town vegetation became general, small canals irrigating the country. Here were fruit and vegetable gardens, with oranges, plantains, vines, and flowers.

Passing through a gate in the walls they entered the town, which afforded a pleasant contrast to the squalid misery of Callao. The city, however, could not be called imposing; the houses were low and irregular, fantastically painted in squares or stripes, and almost all had great balconies shut in with trellis-work.

Few of the houses had any windows towards the street, the larger ones being constructed with a central courtyard, into which the rooms all opened. The streets were all built at right angles, the principal ones leading from the grand square, in which stood the cathedral and the palace of the Spanish viceroys, the other sides consisting of private houses, with shops and arcades below them. The hotel to which they had been recommended was a large building with a courtyard, with dining and other rooms opening from it, and above them the bedrooms. In comparison with the inn at Callao it was magnificent, but in point of cleanliness it left a great deal to be desired. After settling themselves in their room they went out. The change in temperature since they had left Callao had been very great.

"The first thing to do, Bertie, is to buy ourselves a couple of good ponchos. You see all the natives are wearing them."

"We certainly want something of the sort, Harry. I thought it was heat that we were going to suffer from, but it seems just the other way. To judge from the temperature we might be in Scotland, and this damp mist chills one to the bone."

"I am not much surprised, for of course I got the subject up as much as I could before starting; and Barnett told me that Lima was altogether an exceptional place, and that while it was bright and warm during the winter months, from May till November on the plains only a few miles away, even in the summer months there was almost always a clammy mist at Lima, and that inside the house as well as outside everything streamed with moisture. He said that this had never been satisfactorily accounted for. Some say that it is due to the coldness of the river here—the Rimac—which comes down from the snowy mountains. Others think that the cold wind that always blows down the valley of the river meets the winds from the sea here, and the moisture contained in them is thus precipitated. I believe that a few miles higher up we shall get out of this atmosphere altogether. Still, the ponchos will be very useful, for it will be really cold up in the mountains. They serve for cloaks in the daytime and blankets at night. The best are made of the wool of the guanacos, a sort of llama. Their wool is very fine, and before we start we will get two of coarser wool to use as blankets to sleep on, while we have the finer ones to cover us."

There was no difficulty in finding a shop with the goods they wanted, and the prices, even of the best, were very moderate. They next bought two soft felt hats with broad brims.

"That is ever so much more comfortable. We will wait until to-morrow before we begin what we may call business, Bertie. Of course I shall deliver the other letters of introduction that Mr. Barnett gave me; but the principal one—that to his former muleteer—is more important than all put together. If anything has happened to him, there is an end of any chance whatever of finding treasure. Of course he may have moved away, or be absent on a journey with his mules, in which case we shall have either to follow him or wait for his return."

"That would be a frightful nuisance."

"Yes; still, it is one of the things that we foresaw might happen."

"I vote we go at once, Harry, and see if he is here."

"I don't think we shall find him here; for Barnett said that he lived in the village of Miraflores, five miles away on the north, and that if he is not there, Señor Pasquez, to whom I have a letter, will be likely to tell me where he is to be found, for he is often employed by him. However, I am as anxious as you to see him. As it is only eleven o'clock yet, there is no reason why we should not go to Miraflores. They will get mules for us at the hotel, and tell us which road to take."

It was not necessary, however, to go into the hotel, for when they returned, two or three men with mules were waiting to be hired. They engaged two animals, and as the man of whom they hired them had a third, and he was ready to accompany them for a small fee, they agreed to take him with them.

Before they were a mile out of the town the mist cleared off and the sun shone brightly. The heat, however, was by no means too great to be pleasant. Miraflores was a charming village, or rather small town, nestling among gardens and orchards.

"I want to find a muleteer named Dias Otero," Harry said to their guide as they rode into the place.

"I know him well," he said. "Everyone about here knows Dias. His wife was a cousin of my mother's."

"Do you know whether he is at home now?"

"Yes, señor; I saw him in Lima three days ago. He had just come down from the mountains. He had been away two months, and certainly will not have started again so soon. Shall I lead you to his house at once?"

"Do so; it is to see him that I have come to this town. He worked for a long time with a friend of mine some years ago, and I have brought a message from him. I may be some time talking with him, so when I go in you can tie up your mules for a while."

"That is his house," the man said presently.

It lay in the outskirts of the town, and was neater than the generality of houses, and the garden was a mass of flowers. They dismounted, handed over the mules to their owner, and walked to the door. An Indian of some fivc-and-forty years came out as they did so.

"Are you Dias Otero?" Harry asked.

"The same, señor."

"I have just arrived from England, and bring a letter to you from Señor Barnett, with whom you travelled for two or three years some time ago."

The man's face lit up with pleasure. "Will you enter, señor. Friends of Señor Barnett may command my services in any way. It is a delight to hear from him. He writes to me sometimes, but in these troubles letters do not always come. I love the señor; there never was a kinder master. He once saved my life at the risk of his own. Is there any hope of his coming out again?"

"I do not think so, Dias. He is strong and well, but I do not think he is likely to start again on a journey of exploration. He is my greatest friend. My brother and I were left under his charge when we were young, and he has been almost a father to us. It is he who has sent us out to you. Here is his letter."

"Will you read it to me, señor. I cannot read; I am always obliged to get somebody to read my letters, and write answers for me."

The letter was of course in Spanish, and Harry read:

"Dear friend Dias,

"I am sending out to you a gentleman, Mr. Prendergast, an officer of the British Navy, in whom I am deeply interested. His brother accompanies him. I beg that you will treat them as you would me, and every service you can render him consider as rendered to myself. From a reason which he will no doubt explain to you in time, it is of the deepest importance to him that he should grow rich in the course of the next two years. He asked my advice, and I said to him, 'There is no one I know of who could possibly put you in the way of so doing better than my friend Dias Otero. I believe it is in his power to do so if he is willing.' I also believe that for my sake you will aid him. He will place himself wholly in your hands. He does not care what danger he runs, or what hardships he has to go through in order to attain his purpose. I know that I need not say more to you. He has two years before him; long before that I am sure you will be as interested in him as you were in me. He has sufficient means to pay all expenses of travel for the time he will be out there. I know that you are descended from nobles of high rank at the court of the Incas when the Spaniards arrived, and that secrets known to but few were passed down from father to son in your family. If you can use any of those secrets to the advantage of my friend, I pray you most earnestly to do so. I trust that this letter will find you and your good wife in health. Had I been ten years younger I would have come out with my friends to aid them in their adventure, but I know that in putting them into your hands I shall be doing them a vastly greater service than I could do were I able to come in person."

HARRY AND BERTIE INTRODUCE THEMSELVES TO DIAS

When Harry ceased, the Indian sat for some time without speaking, then he said:

"It is a matter that I must think over, señor. It is a very grave one, and had any other man than Señor Barnett asked this service of me no money could have tempted me to assent to it. It is not only that my life would be in danger, but that my name would be held up to execration by all my people were I to divulge the secret that even the tortures of the Spaniards could not wring from us. I must think it over before I answer. I suppose you are staying at the Hotel Morin; I will call and see you when I have thought the matter over. It is a grave question, and it may be three or four days before I can decide."

"I thank you, Dias; but there is no occasion for you to give a final decision now. Whether or no, we shall travel for a while, and I trust that you will go with us with your mules and be our guide, as you did to Mr. Barnett. It will be time enough when you know us better to give us a final answer; it is not to be expected that even for Señor Barnett's sake you would do this immense service for strangers, therefore I pray you to leave the matter open. Make arrangements for your mules and yourself for a three months' journey in the mountains, show us what there is to see of the gold and silver placers, and the quicksilver mines at Huanuco. At the end of that time you will know us and can say whether you are ready to aid us in our search."

The native bowed his head gravely.

"I will think it over," he said; "and now, señors, let us put that aside. My wife has been busy since you entered in preparing a simple meal, and I ask you to honour me by partaking of it."

"With pleasure, Dias."

It consisted of *puchero*, a stew consisting of a piece of beef, cabbage, sweet-potatoes, salt pork, sausage-meat, pigs' feet, yuccas, bananas, quinces, peas, rice, salt, and an abundance of Chili peppers. This had been cooked for six hours and was now warmed up. Two bottles of excellent native wine, a flask of spirits, and some water were also put on the table. The Indian declined to sit down with them, saying that he had taken a meal an hour before.

While they ate he chatted with them, asking questions of their voyage and telling them of the state of things in the country.

"It is always the same, señors, there is a revolution and two or three battles; then either the president or the one who wants to be president escapes from the country or is taken and shot, and in a day or two there is a fresh pronunciamiento. We thought that when the Spaniards had been driven out we should have had peace, but it is not so; we have had San Martin, and Bolivar, and Aguero, and Santa Cruz, and Sucre. Bolivar again finally defeated the Spaniards at Ayacucho. Rodil held possession of Callao castle, and defended it until January of this year. We in the villages have not suffered—those who liked fighting went out with one or other of the generals; some have returned, others have been killed—but Lima has suffered greatly. Sometimes the people have taken one side, sometimes the other, and though the general they supported was sometimes victorious for a short time, in the end they suffered. Most of the old Spanish families perished; numbers died in the castle of Callao, where many thousands of the best blood of Lima took refuge, and of these well-nigh half died of hunger and misery before Rodil surrendered."

"But does not this make travelling very unsafe?"

The Indian shrugged his shoulders.

"Peru is a large country, señor, and those who want to keep out of the way of the armies and lighting can do so; I myself have continued my occupation and have never fallen in with the armies. That is because the fighting is principally in the plains, or round Cuzco; for the men do not go into the mountains except as fugitives, as they could not find food there for an army. It is these fugitives who render the road somewhat unsafe; starving men must take what they can get. They do not interfere with the great silver convoys from Potosi or other mines—a loaf of bread is worth more than a bar of silver in the mountains—but they will plunder persons coming down with goods to the town or going up with their purchases. Once or twice I have had to give up the food I carried with me, but I have had little to grumble at, and I do not think you need trouble yourself about them; we will take care to avoid them as far as possible."

After chatting for an hour they left the cottage, and, mounting their mules, returned to Lima.

"I think he will help us, Harry," Bertie said as soon as they set out.

"I think so too, but we must not press him to begin with. Of course there is a question too as to how far he can help us. He may know vaguely where the rich mines once existed; but you must remember that they have been lost for three hundred years, and it may be impossible for even a man who has received the traditions as to their positions to hit upon the precise spot. The mountains, you see, are tremendous; there must be innumerable ravines and gorges among them. It is certain that nothing approaching an accurate map can ever have been made of the mountains, and I should say that in most cases the indications that may have been given are very vague.

They would no doubt have been sufficient for those who lived soon after the money was hidden, and were natives of that part of the country and thoroughly acquainted with all the surroundings, but when the information came to be handed down from mouth to mouth during many generations, the local knowledge would be lost, and what were at first detailed instructions would become little better than vague legends. You know how three hundred years will alter the face of a country—rocks roll down the hills, torrents wash away the soil, forests grow or are cleared away. I believe with you that the Indian will do his best, but I have grave doubts whether he will be able to locate any big thing."

"Well, you don't take a very cheerful view of things, Harry; you certainly seemed more hopeful when we first started."

"Yes. I don't say I am not hopeful still, but it is one thing to plan out an enterprise at a distance and quite another when you are face to face with its execution. As we have come down the coast, and seen that great range of mountains stretching along for hundreds of miles, and we know that there is another quite as big lying behind it, I have begun to realize the difficulties of the adventures that we are undertaking. However, we shall hear, when Dias comes over to see us, what he thinks of the matter. I fancy he will say that he is willing to go with us and help us as far as he can, but that although he will do his best he cannot promise that he will be able to point out, with anything like certainty, the position of any of the old mines."

Next day they called on Señor Pasquez, who received them very cordially.

"So you are going to follow the example of Señor Barnett and spend some time in exploring the country and doing some shooting. Have you found Dias?"

"Yes, señor, and I think he will go with us, though he has not given a positive answer."

"You will be fortunate if you get him; he is one of the best-known muleteers in the country, and if anyone comes here and wants a guide Dias is sure to be the first to be recommended. If he goes with you he can give you much useful advice; he knows exactly what you will have to take with you, the best districts to visit for your purpose, and the best way of getting there. For the rest, I shall be very happy to take charge of any money you may wish to leave behind, and to act as your banker and cash any orders you may draw upon me. I will also receive and place to your account any sums that may be sent you from England."

"That, sir, is a matter which Mr. Barnett advised me to place in your hands. After making what few purchases we require, and taking fifty pounds in silver, I shall have two hundred and fifty pounds to place in your hands. Mr. Barnett will manage my affairs in my absence, and will send to you fifty pounds quarterly."

"You will find difficulty in spending it all in two years," the merchant said with a smile. "If you are content to live on what can be bought in the country, it costs very little; and as for the mules, they can generally pick up enough at their halting-places to serve them, with a small allowance of grain. You can hire them cheaply, or you can buy them. The latter is cheaper in the end, but you cannot be sure of getting mules accustomed to mountains, and you would therefore run the risk of their losing their foothold, and not only being dashed to pieces but destroying their saddles and loads. However, if you secure the services of Dias Otero, you will get mules that know every path in the mountains. He is famous for his animals, and he himself is considered the most trusty muleteer here; men think themselves lucky in obtaining his services. I would send him with loads of uncounted gold and should be sure that there would not be a piece missing."

Next day Dias came to the hotel.

"I have thought it over, señor," he said. "I need not say that were it only ordinary service, instead of exploring the mountains, I should be glad indeed to do my best for a friend of Señor Barnett; but as to the real purpose of your journey I wish, before making any arrangement, that the matter should be thoroughly understood. I have no certain knowledge whatever as to any of the lost mines, still less of any hidden treasures; but I know all the traditions that have passed down concerning them. I doubt whether any Indians now possess a certain knowledge of these things. For generations, no doubt, the secrets were handed down from father to son, and it is possible that some few may still know of these places; but I doubt it. Think of the hundreds and thousands of our people who have been killed in battle, or died as slaves in the mines, and you will see that numbers of those to whom the secrets were entrusted must have taken their knowledge to the grave with them.

"In each generation the number of those who knew the particulars of these hiding-places must have diminished. Few now can know more than I do, yet I am sure of nothing. I know generally where the mines were situated and where some treasures were concealed, and what knowledge I have I will place at your service; but so great a care was used in the concealment of the entrances to the mines, so carefully were the hiding-places of the treasures chosen, and so cunningly concealed, that, without the surest indications and the most minute instructions, we might search for years, as men indeed have done ever since the Spanish came here, without finding them. I am glad that I can lay my hand upon my heart and say, that whatever may have been possessed by ancestors of mine, no actual details have ever come down to me; for, had it been so, I could not have revealed them to you. We know that all who were instructed in these were bound by the most terrible oaths not to reveal them. Numbers have died under the torture rather than break those oaths; and even now, were one of us to betray the secrets that had come down to him, he would be regarded as accursed. No one would break bread with him, every door would be closed against him, and if he died his body would rot where it fell. But my knowledge is merely general, gathered not only from the traditions known to all our people, but from confidences made by one member of our family to another. Full knowledge was undoubtedly given to some of them; but all these must have died without initiating others into the full particulars. Such knowledge as I have is at your disposal. I can take you to the localities, I can say to you, 'Near this place was a great mine,' but unless chance favours you you may search in vain."

"That is quite as much as I had hoped for, Dias, and I am grateful for your willingness to do what you can for us, just as you did for Señor Barnett."

CHAPTER IV — A STREET FRAY

"Now, señor," Dias said, "as we have settled the main point, let us talk over the arrangements. What is the weight of your baggage?"

"Not more than a mule could carry. Of course we shall sling our rifles over our shoulders. We have a good stock of ammunition for them and for our pistols. We shall each take two suits of clothes besides those we wear, and a case of spirits in the event of accident or illness. We shall each have three flannel shirts, stockings, and so on, but certainly everything belonging to us personally would not mount up to more than a hundred and fifty pounds. We should, of course, require a few cooking utensils, tin plates, mugs, and cups. What should we need besides these?"

"A tent and bedding, señor. We should only have, at the start, to carry such provisions as we could not buy. When we are beyond the range of villages in the forests we might often be weeks without being able to buy anything; still, we should probably be able to shoot game for food. We should find fruits, but flour we shall have to take with us from the last town we pass through before we strike into the mountains, and dried meat for an emergency; and it would be well to have a bag of grain, so that we could give a handful or so to each of the mules. I am glad you have brought some good spirits—we shall need it in the swamps by the rivers. Your tea and coffee will save your having to buy them here, but you will want some sugar. We must take two picks and a shovel, a hammer for breaking up ore, a small furnace, twenty crucibles and bellows, and a few other things for aiding to melt the ore. You would want for the journey five baggage mules, and, of course, three riding mules. I could hardly manage them, even with aid from you, in very bad places, and I would rather not take any strange man with me on such business as we have in hand. But some assistance I must have, and I will take with me my nephew José. He has lost his father, and I have taken him as my assistant, and shall train him to be a guide such as I am. He is but fifteen, but he already knows something of his business, and such an expedition will teach him more than he would learn in ten years on the roads."

"That would certainly be far better than having a muleteer whom you could not trust, Dias. My brother and myself will be ready to lend you a hand whenever you want help of any kind. We have not had any experience with mules, but sailors can generally turn their hands to anything. Now, how about the eight mules?"

"I have five of my own, as good mules as are to be found in the province; we shall have to buy the three others for riding. Of course I have saddles and ropes."

"But you will want four for riding."

"No, señor; yours and the one I ride will be enough. José at times will take my place, and can when he likes perch on one of the most lightly laden animals."

"How much will the riding mules cost?"

"I can get fair ones for about fifty dollars apiece; trade is slack at present owing to the troubles, and there are many who would be glad to get rid of one or two of their train."

"And now, Dias, we come to the very important question, what are we to pay you for yourself, your nephew, and the five mules—say by the month?"

"I have been thinking the matter over, señor—I have talked it over with my wife"—he paused for a moment, and then said: "She wishes to go with me, señor."

Harry opened his eyes in surprise. "But surely, Dias, you could not think of taking her on such an expedition, where, as you say yourself, you may meet with many grave dangers and difficulties?"

"A woman can support them as well as a man," Dias said quietly. "My wife has more than once accompanied me on journeys when I have been working on contract. We have been married for fifteen years, and she has no children to keep her at home. She is accustomed to my being away for weeks. This would be for months, perhaps for two years. I made no secret to her that we might meet with many dangers. She says they will be no greater for her than for me. At first she tried to dissuade me from going for so long a time; but when I told her that you were sent me by the gentleman who saved my life a year after I married her, and that he had recommended you to me as standing to him almost in the relation of a son, and I therefore felt bound to carry his wishes into effect, and so to pay the debt of gratitude that I owed him, she agreed at once that it was my duty to go and do all in my power for you, and she prayed me to take her with me. I said that I would put it before you, señor, and that I must abide by your decision."

"By all means bring her with you, Dias. If you and she are both willing to share the dangers we should meet with, surely we cannot object in any way."

"Thank you, señor; you will find her useful. You have already seen that she can cook well; and if we have José to look after the animals when we are searching among the hills, you will find it not unpleasant, when we return of an evening, to find a hot supper ready for us."

"That is quite true, and I am sure we shall find your wife a great acquisition to our party. The only difference will be, that instead of one large tent we must have two small ones—it does not matter how small, so long as we can crawl into them and they are long enough for us to lie down. And now about payment?"

"I shall not overcharge you," Dias said with a smile. "If my wife had remained behind I must have asked for money to maintain her while we were away. It would not have been much, for she has her garden and her house, and there is a bag hid away with my savings, so that if she had been widowed she could still live in the house until she chose someone else to share it with her; she is but thirty-two, and is as comely as when I first married her. However, as she is going with us, there will be no need to trouble about her. If misfortune comes upon us and I am killed, it is likely she will be killed also. We shall have no expenses on the journey, as you will pay for food for ourselves and the animals. You will remember, señor, that I make this journey not as a business matter—no money would buy from me any information that I may have as to hidden mines or treasures,—I do it to repay a debt of gratitude to my preserver, Don Henry Barnett, and partly because I am sure that I shall like you and your brother as I did him. I shall aid you as far as lies in my power in the object for which you are undertaking this journey. Therefore until it is finished there shall be no talk about payment. You may have many expenses beyond what you calculate upon. If we meet with no success, and return to Lima empty-handed, I shall have lost nothing. I shall have had no expenses at home, my wife and I will have fed at your expense, and José will have learned so much that he would be as good a guide as any in the country. You could then give me the three mules you will buy, to take the place of any of mine that may have perished on the journey, and should you have them to spare, I will take a hundred dollars as a *bueno mano*. If we succeed, and you discover a rich mine or a hidden treasure, you shall then pay me what it pleases you. Is it a bargain?"

"The bargain you propose is ridiculously one-sided, Dias, and I don't see how I could possibly accept the offer you make to me."

"Those are my terms, señor," Dias said simply, "to take or to leave."

"Then I cannot but accept them, and I thank you most heartily;" and he held out his hand to Dias, and the Indian grasped it warmly.

"When do you propose we shall start?"

"Will this day week suit you, señor? There are the mules to buy, and the tents to be made—they should be of vicuña skin with the wool still on, which, with the leather kept well oiled, will keep out water. We shall want them in the hills, but we shall sometimes find villages where we can sleep in shelter."

"Not for us, Dias. Mr. Barnett has told me that the houses are for the most part alive with fleas, and I should prefer to sleep in a tent, however small, rather than lie in a bed on the floor of any one of them. We don't want thick beds, you know—a couple of thicknesses of well-quilted cotton, say an inch thick each, and two feet wide. You can get these made for us, no doubt."

The Indian nodded.

"That would be the best for travel; the beds the Peruvian caballeros use are very thick and bulky."

"You will want two for yourself and your wife, and two for José. By the by, we shall want a tent for him."

Dias smiled. "It will not be necessary, señor; muleteers are accustomed to sleep in the open air, and with two thick blankets, and a leathern coverlet in case of rain, he will be more than comfortable. I shall have five leather bags made to hold the beds and blankets. But the making of the beds and tents will take some time—people do not hurry in Lima,—and there will be the riding saddles and bridles to get, and the provisions. I do not think we can be ready before another week. It will be well, then, that you should, before starting away, visit the ruins of Pachacamac. All travellers go there, and it will seem only natural that you should do so, for there you will see the style of the buildings, and also the explorations that were everywhere made by the Spaniards in search of treasure."

"Very well, Dias; then this day week we shall be ready to start. However, I suppose I shall see you every day, and learn how you are getting on with your preparations."

Bertie had been sitting at the window looking down into the street while this conversation was going on. "Well, what is it all about?" he asked, turning round as the Indian left the room. "Is it satisfactory?"

"More than satisfactory," his brother answered. "In the first place his nephew, a lad of fifteen, who is training as a mule-driver, is going with us, which is much better than getting an outsider; in the next place his wife is going with us."

"Good gracious!" Bertie exclaimed, "what in the world shall we do with a woman?"

"Well, I think we shall do very well with her, Bertie; but well or ill she has to go. She will not let her husband go without her, which is natural enough, considering how long we shall be away, and that the journey will be a dangerous one. But really I think she will be an acquisition to the party. She is bright and pretty, as you no doubt noticed, and what is of more importance, she is a capital cook."

"She certainly gave us a good meal yesterday," Bertie said, "and though I could rough it on anything, it is decidedly pleasanter to have a well-cooked meal."

"Well, you see, that is all right."

"And how many mules are we to take?"

"Five for baggage, and three for riding. I have no doubt Dias's wife will ride behind him, and the boy, when he wants to ride, will perch himself on one of the baggage mules. Dias has five mules, and we shall only have to buy the three for riding."

"What is it all going to cost, Harry?" Bertie said when his brother had told him all the arrangements that had been made. "That is the most important point after all."

"Well, you will be astonished when I tell you, Bertie, that if we don't succeed in finding a treasure of any kind I shall only have to pay for the three riding mules, and the expenses of food and so on, and a hundred dollars."

"Twenty pounds!" Bertie said incredulously; "you are joking!"

"No, it is really so; the man said that he considered that in going with me he is only fulfilling the obligation he is under to Mr. Barnett. Of course I protested against the terms, and would have insisted upon paying the ordinary prices, whatever they might be, for his services and the use of his mules; but he simply said that those were the conditions on which he was willing to go with me, and that I could take them or leave them, so I had to accept. I can only hope that we may find some treasure, in which case only he consented to accept proper payment for his services."

"Well, it is awfully good of him," Bertie said; "though really it doesn't seem fair that we should be having the services of himself, his wife, his boy, and his mules for nothing. There is one thing, it will be an extra inducement to him to try and put us in the way of finding one of those mines."

"I don't think so, Bertie; he said that not for any sum of money whatever would he do what he is going to do, but simply from gratitude to Barnett. It is curious how the traditions, or superstitions, or whatever you like to call them, of the time of the Incas have continued to impress the Indians, and how they have preserved the secrets confided to their ancestors. No doubt fear that the Spaniards would force them to work in the mines till they died has had a great effect in inducing them to conceal the existence of these places from them. Now that the Spaniards have been cleared out there is no longer any ground for apprehension of that kind, but they may still feel that the Peruvians would get the giant's share in any mine or treasure that might be found, and that the Indians would, under one pretence or another, be defrauded out of any share of it. It is not wonderful that it should be so considering how these poor people have been treated by the whites, and it would really seem that the way in which Spain has gone to the dogs is a punishment for her cruelties in South America and the Islands. It may be said that from the very moment when the gold began to flow the descent of Spain commenced; in spite of the enormous wealth she acquired she fell gradually from her position as the greatest power in Europe.

"In 1525, after the battle of Pavia, Spain stood at the height of her power. Mexico was conquered by Cortez seven years before, Peru in 1531, and the wealth of those countries began to flow into Spain in enormous quantities, and yet her decline followed speedily. She was bearded by our bucaneers among the Islands and on the western coast; the Netherlands revolted, and after fierce fighting threw off her yoke; the battle of Ivry and the accession of Henry of Navarre all but destroyed her influence in France; the defeat of the Armada and the capture of Cadiz struck a fatal blow both to her power on the sea and to her commerce, and within a century of the conquest of Peru, Spain was already an enfeebled and decaying power. It would almost seem that the discoveries of Columbus, from which such great things were hoped, proved in the long run the greatest misfortune that ever befell Spain."

"It does look like it, Harry; however, we must hope that whatever effect the discovery of America had upon Portugal or Spain, it will make your fortune."

Harry laughed.

"I hope so, Bertie, but it is as well not to be too hopeful. Still, I have great faith in Dias, at any rate I feel confident that he will do all he can; but he acknowledges that he knows nothing for certain. I am sure, however, that he will be a faithful guide, and that though we may have a rough time, it will not be an unpleasant one. Now, you must begin to turn to account what Spanish you have learned during the voyage; I know you have worked regularly at it while you have not been on duty."

"I have learned a good lot," Bertie said; "and I dare say I could ask for anything, but I should not understand the answers. I can make out a lot of that Spanish *Don Quixote* you got for me, but when Dias was talking to you I did not catch a word of what he was saying. I suppose it will all come in time."

"But you must begin at once. I warn you that when I am fairly off I shall always talk to you in Spanish, for it would look very unsociable if we were always talking together in English. If you ride or walk by the side of the boy you will soon get on; and there will be Donna Maria for you to chat away with, and from what we saw of her I should say she is sociably inclined. In three months I have no doubt you will talk Spanish as well as I do."

"It will be a horrid nuisance," Bertie grumbled; "but I suppose it has got to be done."

Three days later Dias said he thought they might as well start the next day to Pachacamac.

"We shall only want the three riding mules and one for baggage. Of course we shall not take José or my wife. By the time we return everything will be ready for us."

"I shall be very glad to be off, Dias. We know no one here except Señor Pasquez; and although he has been very civil and has begged us to consider his house as our own, he is of course busy during the day, and one can't do above a certain amount of walking about the streets. So by all means let us start to-morrow morning. We may as well go this time in the clothes we wear, it will be time enough to put on the things we have bought when we start in earnest."

Starting at sunrise, they rode for some distance through a fertile valley, and then crossed a sandy plain until they reached the little valley of Lurin, in which stand the ruins of Pachacamac. This was the sacred city of the natives of the coast before their conquest by the Incas. During their forty-mile ride Dias had told them something of the place they were about to visit. Pachacamac, meaning "the creator of the world," was the chief divinity of these early people, and here was the great temple dedicated to him. The Incas after their conquest erected a vast Temple of the Sun, but they did not attempt to suppress the worship of Pachacamac, and the two flourished side by side until the arrival of the Spaniards. The wealth of the temple was great; the Spaniards carried away among their spoils one thousand six hundred and eighty-seven pounds of gold and one thousand six hundred ounces of silver; but with all their efforts they failed to discover the main treasure, said to have been no less than twenty-four thousand eight hundred pounds of gold, which had been carried away and buried before their arrival.

"If the Spaniards could not succeed in getting at the hiding-place, although, no doubt, they tortured everyone connected with the temple to make them divulge the secret, it is evident there is no chance for us," Harry said.

"Yes, señor, they made every effort; thousands of natives were employed in driving passages through the terraces on which the temple stood. I believe that they did find much treasure, but certainly not the great one they were searching for. There is no tradition among our people as to the hiding-place, for so many of the natives perished that all to whom the secret was known must have died without revealing it to anybody. Had it not been so, the Spaniards would sooner or later have learned it, for although hundreds have died under torture rather than reveal any of the hiding-places, surely one more faint-hearted than the rest would have disclosed them. Certain it is that at Cuzco and other places they succeeded in obtaining almost all the treasures buried there, though they failed in discovering the still greater treasures that had been carried away to be hidden in different spots. But Pachacamac was a small one in comparison with Cuzco, and it was believed that the treasures had not been carried far. Tradition has it that they were buried somewhere between this town and Lima. Doubtless all concerned in the matter fled before the Spaniards arrived, at any rate with all their cruelty the invaders never discovered its position. The report that it was buried near may have been set about to prevent their hunting for it elsewhere, and the gold may be lying now somewhere in the heart of the mountains."

Harry Prendergast and his brother looked in astonishment at the massive walls that rose around the eminence on which the temple had stood. The latter had disappeared, but its situation could be traced on the plateau buttressed by the walls. These were of immense thickness, and formed of huge adobe bricks almost as hard as stone; even the long efforts of the Spaniards had caused but little damage to them. The plateau rose some five hundred feet above the sea, which almost washed one face of it. Half-way up the hill four series of these massive walls, whose tops formed terraces, stood in giant steps some fifty feet high. Here and there spots of red paint could be seen, showing that the whole surface was originally painted. The ascent was made by winding passages through the walls. On the side of the upper area facing the sea could be seen the remains of a sort of walk or esplanade, with traces of edifices of various kinds. On a hill a mile and a half away were the remains of the Incas' temple and nunnery, the style differing materially from that of the older building; it was still more damaged than the temple on the hill by the searchers for treasure.

Pachacamac was the most sacred spot in South America, vast numbers of pilgrims came here from all points. The city itself had entirely disappeared, covered deeply in sand, but for a long distance round, it had, like the neighbourhood of Jerusalem and Mecca, been a vast cemetery, and a small amount of excavation showed the tombs of the faithful, occupied in most cases by mummies.

"We will ride across to the Incas' temple. There is not much to see there, but it is as well that you should look at the vaults in which the treasures were hid. There are similar places at Cuzco and several of the other ruins."

"It may certainly be useful to see them," Harry agreed, and they rode across the plain. Leaving their mules outside they entered the ruins. The Indian led them into some underground chambers. He had brought a torch with him, and this he now lit.

"You have to be careful or you might otherwise tumble into one of these holes and break a limb; and in that case, if you were here by yourselves, you would certainly never get out again."

They came upon several of these places. The openings were sometimes square and sometimes circular, and had doubtless been covered with square stones. They were dug out of the solid ground. For about six feet the sides of the pit were perpendicular; in some it swelled out like a great vase with a broad shoulder, in others it became a square chamber of some size.

"Some of these places were no doubt meant to store grain and other provisions," the Indian said, "some were undoubtedly treasuries."

"Awkward places to find," Harry said; "one might spend a lifetime in searching for them in only one of these temples."

"They were the last places we should think of searching," Dias said. "For years the Spaniards kept thousands of men at work. I do not say that there may not be some few places that have escaped the searchers, but what they could not with their host of workers find certainly could not be found by four or five men. It is not in the temples that the Incas' wealth has been hidden, but in caves, in deep mountain gorges, and possibly in ruins on the other side of the mountains where even the Spaniards never penetrated.

There are such places. I know of one to which I will take you if our search fails elsewhere. It is near the sea, and yet there are not half a dozen living men who have ever seen it, so strangely is it hidden. Tradition says that it was not the work of the Incas, but of the people before them. I have never seen it close. It is guarded, they say, by demons, and no native would go within miles of it. The traditions are that the Incas, when they conquered the land, found the place and searched it, after starving out the native chief who had fled there with his followers and family. Some say that they found great treasure there, others that they discovered nothing; all agree that a pestilence carried off nearly all those who had captured it. Others went, and they too died, and the place was abandoned as accursed, and in time its very existence became forgotten; though some say that members of the tribe have always kept watch there, and that those who carelessly or curiously approached it have always met with their death in strange ways. Although I am a Christian, and have been taught to disbelieve the superstitions of my countrymen, I would not enter it on any condition."

"If we happen to be near it I shall certainly take a close look at it," Harry said with a laugh. "I don't fancy we should see anything that our rifles and pistols would find invulnerable."

It was getting dark by the time they had finished their inspection of the rooms, so, riding two or three miles away, they encamped in a grove up the valley. Next morning they returned to Lima. Dias had given out that the two white señors intended to visit all the ruined temples of the Incas, and as other travellers had done the same their intention excited neither surprise nor comment.

On the following evening after dark Harry and his brother were returning from the house of Señor Pasquez.

"It is a pleasant house," Harry said; "the girls are pretty and nice, they play and sing well, and are really charming. But what a contrast it was the other morning when we went in there and accidentally ran against them when we were going upstairs with their father, utterly untidy, and, in fact, regular sluts—a maid of all work would look a picture of neatness beside them."

Bertie was about to answer, when there was an outburst of shouts from a wine-shop they were passing, and in a moment the door burst open and half a dozen men engaged in a fierce conflict rushed out. Knives were flashing, and it was evident that one man was being attacked by the rest. By the light that streamed out of the open door they saw that the man attacked was Dias. It flashed across Harry's mind that if this man was killed there was an end to all hope of success in their expedition.

"Dash in to his rescue, Bertie," he cried; "but whatever you do, mind their knives."

With a shout he sprang forward and struck to the ground a man who was dodging behind Dias with uplifted knife, while Bertie leapt on to the back of another, the shock throwing the man down face forward. Bertie was on his feet in a moment, and brought the stick he carried with all his force down on the man's head as he tried to rise. Then, springing forward again, he struck another man a heavy blow on the wrist. The knife dropped from the man's hand, and as he dashed with a fierce oath upon Bertie the stick descended again, this time on his head, and felled him to the ground. In the meantime one of the assailants had turned fiercely on Harry and aimed a blow at him with his knife; but with the ease of a practised boxer Harry stepped back, and before the man could again raise the knife he leaped in and struck him a tremendous blow on the point of his chin. The fifth man took to his heels immediately. The other four lay where they had fallen, evidently fearing they would be stabbed should they try to get on to their feet.

"Are you hurt, Dias?" Harry exclaimed.

"I have several cuts, señor, but none of them, I think, serious. You have saved my life."

"Never mind that now, Dias. What shall we do with these fellows—hand them over to the watch?"

"No, señor, that would be the last thing to do; we might be detained here for months. I will take all their knives and let them go."

"Here are two of them," Bertie said, picking up those of the men he had struck.

Dias stood over the man Harry had first knocked down, and with a fierce whisper ordered him to give up his knife, which he did at once. The other was still stupid from the effect of the blow and his fall, and Dias had only to take his knife from his relaxed fingers.

"Now, señor, let us be going before anyone comes along."

"What was it all about, Dias?" Harry asked as he walked away.

"Many of the muleteers are jealous, señor, because I always get what they consider the best jobs. I had gone into the wine-shop for a glass of pulque before going round to see that the mules were all right. As I was drinking, these men whispered together, and then one came up to me and began to abuse me, and directly I answered him the whole of them drew their knives and rushed at me. I was ready too, and wounded two of them as I fought my way to the door. As I opened it one of them stabbed me in the shoulder, but it was a slanting blow. Once out they all attacked me at once, and in another minute you would have had to look for another muleteer. 'Tis strange, señors, that you should have saved my life as Mr. Barnett did. It was a great deed to risk your lives with no weapons but your sticks against five ruffians with their knives."

"I did not use my stick," Harry said. "I am more accustomed to use my fists than a stick, and can hit as hard with them, as you saw. But my brother's stick turned out the most useful. He can box too, but cannot give as heavy a blow as I can. Still, it was very lucky that I followed your advice, and bought a couple of heavy sticks to carry with us if we should go out after dark. Now you had better come to the hotel, and I will send for a surgeon to dress your wound."

"It is not necessary, señor; my wife is waiting for me in my room, she arrived this afternoon. Knife cuts are not uncommon affairs here, and she knows quite enough to be able to bandage them."

"At any rate we shall have to put off our start for a few days."

"Not at all, señor; a bandage tonight and a few strips of plaster in the morning will do the business. I shall be stiff for a few days, but that will not interfere with my riding, and José will be able to load and unload the mules, if you will give him a little assistance. Adios! and a thousand thanks."

"That was a piece of luck, Bertie," Harry said when they had reached their room in the hotel. "In the first place, because neither of us got a scratch, and in the second, because it will bind Dias more closely to us. Before, he was willing to assist us for Barnett's sake, now it will be for our own also, and we may be quite sure that he will do his best for us."

"It is my first scrimmage," Bertie said, "and I must say that I thought, as we ran in, that it was going to be a pretty serious one. We have certainly come very well out of it."

"It was short and sharp," Harry laughed. "I have always held that the man who could box well was more than a match for one with a knife who knew nothing of boxing. One straight hit from the shoulder is sure to knock him out of time."

Next morning Dias and his wife came up early. The former had one arm in a sling. As they entered, the woman ran forward, and, throwing her arms round Bertie, she kissed him on both cheeks. The lad was too much surprised at this unexpected salute to return it, as his brother did when she did the same to him. Then, drawing back, she poured out her thanks volubly, the tears running down her cheeks.

"Maria asked me if she might kiss you," Dias said gravely when she stopped. "I said that it was right that she should do so, for do we not both owe you my life?"

"You must not make too much of the affair, Dias; four blows were struck, and there was an end to it."

"A small matter to you, señor, but a great one to us. A Peruvian would not interfere if he saw four armed men attacking one. He would be more likely to turn down the next street, so that he might not be called as a witness. It is only your countrymen who would do such things."

"And you still think that you will be ready to start the day after to-morrow?"

"Quite sure, señor. My shoulder will be stiff and my arm in a sling for a week, but muleteers think nothing of such trifles,—a kick from a mule would be a much more serious affair."

"You don't think those rascals are likely to waylay us on the road, and take their revenge?"

"Not they, señor. If you could do such things unarmed, what could you not do when you had rifles and pistols? The matter is settled. They have not been seriously hurt. If one of them had been killed I should be obliged to be careful the next time I came here; as it is, no more will be said about it. Except the two hurt in the wine-shop they will not even have a scar to remind them of it. In two years they will have other things to think about, if it is true that Colombia means to go to war with Chili."

"What is the quarrel about, Dias?"

"The Colombians helped us to get rid of the Spaniards, but ever since they have presumed a right to manage affairs here."

"Perhaps nothing will come of it."

"Well, it is quite certain that there is no very good feeling between Chili, Bolivia, Colombia, and Peru."

"I suppose they will be fighting all round some day?"

"Yes, and it will interfere with my business. Certainly we are better off than when the Spaniards were here; but the taxes are heavy, and things don't go as people expected they would when we got rid of the Spaniards. All the governments seem jealous of each other. I don't take any interest in these matters except so far as they interfere with trade. If every man would attend to his own affairs it would be better for us all."

"I suppose so, Dias; but one can hardly expect a country that has been so many years governed by a foreign power to get accustomed all at once to governing itself."

"Now, señor, I shall be glad if you will go with me and look at the stores that are already collected. I think you will find that everything is ready."

CHAPTER V — AMONG THE MOUNTAIN

Two days later the mules were brought round to the door at sunrise, and Harry and his brother sallied out from the hotel, dressed for the first time in the Peruvian costume. They were both warmly clothed. On their heads were felt hats with broad brims, which could be pulled down and tied over the ears, both for warmth and to prevent their being blown away by the fierce winds that sweep down the gorges. A thick poncho of llama wool fell from their shoulders to their knees, and loosely tied round their necks were thick and brightly-coloured scarves. They wore high boots, and carried large knives stuck in a strap below the knee. The rifles were fastened at the bow of their saddles, and their wallets, with provisions for the day, were strapped behind. By the advice of Dias each had in his pocket a large pair of green goggles, to protect their eyes from the glare of sun and snow. They tied these on before coming downstairs, and both agreed that had they met unexpectedly in the street they would have passed each other without the slightest recognition.

"It is a pity, Harry," Bertie said seriously, "that you did not have your portrait taken to send home to a certain young lady. You see, she would then have been able to hang it up in her room and worship it privately, without anyone having the slightest idea that it was her absent lover."

"You young scamp," Harry said, "I will pull your ears for you."

"If you attempt anything of the sort, I shall tie the brim of my hat tightly over them. I really think it is very ungrateful of you not to take my advice in the spirit in which I gave it."

"If you intend to go on like this, Bert, I shall leave you behind."

"You can't do it."

"Oh, yes, I can! I might give you in charge for some crime or other; and in lack of evidence, the expenditure of a few dollars would, I have no doubt, be sufficient to induce the judge, magistrate, or whatever they call him, to give you six months' imprisonment."

"Then you are an unnatural brother, and I will make no more suggestions for your good."

So they had come downstairs laughing, though feeling a little shy at their appearance as they issued out of the courtyard. Speedily, however, they gained courage as they saw that passers-by paid no attention to them.

They had spent the previous afternoon in packing the bundles, in which every item was put away so that it could be got at readily, and in making sure that nothing had been omitted. The five baggage mules were fastened one behind another, and José stood at the head of the leading one. As they came out Dias swung his wife on to a cushion strapped behind his saddle, and mounted himself before her. Harry and his brother climbed into theirs. They had both refused to put on the heavy and cruel spurs worn by the Peruvians, but had, at the earnest request of the Indian, put them in their saddle-bags.

"You will want them," he said. "You need not use them cruelly, but you must give your mules an occasional prick to let them know that you have spurs."

On leaving the town the road ran up the valley of the Rimac, a small river, but of vital importance to the country through which it passes, as small canals branching from it irrigate the land.

"The Spaniards have done some good here at least," Harry said to Dias, who was riding beside him.

"Some of these canals were constructed in their time, but the rest existed long before they came here, and, indeed, long before the Incas came. The Incas' work lies chiefly beyond the mountains; on this side almost all the great ruins are of cities and fortresses built by the old people. Cuzco was the Incas' capital, and almost all the towns between the two ranges of the Andes were their work. It is true that they conquered the people down to the sea, but they do not seem to have cared to live here. The treasures of Pachacamac and the other places on the plains were those of the old people and the old religion. The inhabitants of the plains are for the most part descendants of those people. The Incas were strong and powerful, but they were not numerous. That was why the Spaniards conquered them so easily. The old people, who regarded them as their masters, did not care to fight for them, just as the Peruvians did not care to fight for the Spaniards."

"I expect it was a good deal like the Normans in England," Bertie put in. "They conquered the Saxons because they were better armed and better disciplined, but they were few in number in comparison with the number they governed, and in their quarrels with each other the bulk of the people stood aloof; and it was only when the Normans began their wars in France and Scotland, and were obliged to enlist Saxon archers and soldiers, that the two began to unite and to become one people."

"I have no doubt that was so, Bertie; but you are breaking our agreement that you should speak in Spanish only."

"Oh, bother! you know very well that I cannot talk in it yet, and you surely do not expect that I am going to ride along without opening my lips."

"I know you too well to expect that," Harry laughed, "and will allow an occasional outbreak. Still, do try to talk Spanish, however bad it may be. You have got cheek enough in other things, and cheek goes a long way in learning to talk a foreign language. You have been four months at your Spanish books, and should certainly begin to put simple sentences together."

"But that is just what one does not learn from books," the lad said. "At any rate, not from such books as I have been working at. I could do a high-flown sentence, and offer to kiss your hand and to declare that all I have is at your disposal. But if I wanted to say, 'When are we going to halt for dinner? I am feeling very peckish,' I should be stumped altogether."

"Well, you must get as near as you can, Bertie. I dare say you cannot turn slang into Spanish; but you can find other words to express your meaning, and when you cannot hit on a word you must use an English one. Your best plan is to move along on the other side of Dias, and chat to his wife."

"What have I got to say to her?"

"Anything you like. You can begin by asking her if she has ever gone a long journey with her husband before, how far we shall go to-day—things of that sort."

"Well, I will try anyhow. I suppose I must. But you go on talking to Dias, else I shall think that you are both laughing at me."

Five miles from Lima they passed through the little village of Quiraz. Beyond this they came upon many cotton plantations, and in the ravines by the side of the valley or among the ruins of Indian towns were several large fortresses. They also passed the remains of an old Spanish town and several haciendas, where many cattle and horses were grazing. They were ascending steadily, and after passing Santa Clara, eleven miles from Lima, the valley narrowed and became little more than a ravine. On either side were rents made in the hills by earthquakes, and immense boulders and stones were scattered about at the bottom of the narrow gorge. Four hours' travelling brought them to Chosica, where the valley widened again near the foot of the hills.

Here they halted for the day. There was an inn here which Dias assured them was clean and comfortable, and they therefore took a couple of rooms for the night in preference to unpacking their tents.

"It is just as well not to begin that till we get farther away," Harry said. "We have met any number of laden mules coming down, and if we were to camp here we should cause general curiosity."

He accordingly ordered dinner for himself and his brother, Dias preferring to take his meal in a large room used by passing muleteers. The fare was as good as they had had at the hotel at Lima.

"I am not sorry that we halted here," Bertie said; "I feel as stiff as a poker."

"I think you got on very well, Bertie, with Mrs. Dias. I did not hear what you were saying, but you seemed to be doing stunningly."

"She did most of the talking. I asked her to speak slowly, as I did not manage to catch the sense of what she said. She seems full of fun, and a jolly little woman altogether. She generally understood what I meant, and though she could not help laughing sometimes, she did it so good-temperedly that one did not feel put out. Each time I spoke she corrected me, told me what I ought to have said, and made me say it after her. I think I shall get on fairly well at the end of a few weeks."

"I am sure you will, Bertie; the trouble is only at the beginning, and now that you have once broken the ice, you will progress like a house on fire."

There were still four hours of daylight after they had finished their meal, so they went out with Dias to explore one of the numerous burying-grounds round the village. It consisted of sunken chambers. In these were bones, with remains of the mats in which the bodies had been clothed. These wrappings resembled small sacks, and they remarked that the people must have been of very small size, or they could never have been packed away in them. With them had been buried many of the implements of their trade. One or two had apparently not been opened. Here were knitting utensils, toilet articles, implements for weaving, spools of thread, needles of bone and bronze. With the body of a girl had been placed a kind of work-box, containing the articles that she had used, and the mummy of a parrot, some beads, and fragments of an ornament of silver. Dias told them that all these tombs were made long before the coming of the Incas. He said that round the heads of the men and boys were wound the slings they had used in life, while a piece of cotton flock was wrapped round the heads of the women. Many of the graves communicated with each other by very narrow passages; the purpose of these was not clear, but probably they were made to enable the spirits of the dead to meet and hold communion with each other.

"I don't want to see any more of them," Bertie said after they had spent three hours in their investigations; "this sort of thing is enough to give one a fit of the blues."

Beyond Chosica civilization almost ceased. The road became little more than a mule track, and was in many places almost impassable by vehicles of any kind. Nothing could be wilder than the scenery they passed. At times rivers ran through perpendicular gorges, and the track wound up and down steep ravines. Sometimes they would all dismount, though Dias assured them it was not necessary; still, it made a change from the monotonous pace of little over two miles an hour at which the mules breasted the steep incline.

José rode on the first of the baggage mules, which was very lightly loaded; he generally sang the whole time. When on foot, Donna Maria stepped gaily along and Bertie had hard work to keep pace with her. He was making rapid progress with the language, though occasionally a peal of laughter from his companion told of some egregious error.

There were villages every few miles, but now when they halted they did so as a rule a mile before they got to one of these. Dinner was cooked over a fire of dead sticks, and after the meal Harry's tent was erected and the bed spread in it. The Indians went on to the village for the night, while Harry and his brother sat and smoked for a time by the fire and then turned in. At daybreak Dias rode back leading their riding mules and a baggage animal; the tent, beds, and the cooking utensils were packed up, and they rode in to the village and passed on at a trot until they overtook Maria and José, who had started with the other four mules when Dias rode away. At last they reached the head of the pass, and two days' journey took them to Oroya, standing on an elevated plateau some ten thousand feet above the sea, and five thousand below the highest point of the road.

The scenery had now completely changed. Villages were scattered thickly over the plain, cultivation was general. The hillsides were lined by artificial terraces, on which were perched chalets and small hamlets—they had seen similar terraces on the way up. These were as the Spaniards found them, and must at one time have been inhabited by a thriving population. Even now gardens and orchards flourished upon them up to the highest points on the hills. Oroya was a large place, and, avoiding the busy part of the town, they hired rooms, as it was necessary to give the mules two days' rest. On the first evening after their arrival they gathered round a fire, for the nights were cold, and even in the daytime they did not find their numerous wraps too hot for them.

"Now, Dias," Harry said, "we must talk over our plans. You said that we would not decide upon anything till we got here."

"In the first place, señor, I think it would be well to go to the north to see the Cerro de Pasco silver mine, they say it is the richest in the world. It is well that you should see the formation of the rocks and the nature of the ore; we may in our journeyings come across similar rock."

"It is gold rather than silver that one wants to find, Dias. I do not say that a silver mine would not be worth a very large sum of money, but it would be necessary to open it and go to a large expense to prove it. Then one would have to go to England and get up a company to work it, which would be a long and difficult matter. Still, I am quite ready to go and see the place."

Dias nodded.

"What you say is true, señor. I could take you to a dozen places where there is silver. They may be good or may not, but even if they were as rich as Potosi the silver would have to be carried to Lima, so great a distance on mules' backs that it would swallow up the profits. And it would be almost impossible to convey the necessary machinery there, indeed to do so would involve the making of roads for a great distance."

"At the same time, Dias, should you know of any silver lodes that might turn out well, I would certainly take some samples, and send two or three mule-loads of the stuff home. They might be of no good for the purpose for which I have come out here, but in time I might do something with them; the law here is that anyone who finds a mine can obtain a concession for it."

"That is so, señor, but he must proceed to work it."

"I suppose it would be sufficient to put two or three men on for that purpose."

"But if you were away for a year difficulties might arise. It would be better for you only to determine the course of the lode, its thickness and value, to trace it as far as possible, and then hide all signs of the work, and not to make your claim until you return here."

"Very well, I will take your advice, Dias. And now about the real object of our journey."

"I have been thinking it over deeply," Dias said. "First as to mines; at present almost all the gold that is obtained is acquired by washing the sands of rivers. Here and there gold has been found in rocks, but not in sufficient quantities to make mining pay. The rivers whose sands are richest in gold are in the mountains that lie behind Lake Titicaca, which lies to the south of Cuzco and on the border of Bolivia. No one doubts that in the time of the Incas there existed gold mines, and very rich ones; for if it had not been so it is impossible to account for the enormous amount of gold obtained by the Spanish conquerors, and no one doubts that they got but a small portion of the gold in existence when they arrived. It is of no use whatever for us to search the old ruins of the Incas in Cuzco, or their other great towns; all that can be found there has already been carried away.

"Now you see, señor, Huanuco, Jauja, Cuzco, and Puno all lie near the eastern range of the Andes, and when the alarm caused by the arrogant conduct of the Spaniards began, it was natural that the treasures should be sent away into the heart of those mountains. The towns on the western sides of this plateau, Challhuanca, Tanibobamba, Huancavelica, would as naturally send theirs for safety into the gorges of the western Andes, but all traditions point to the fact that this was not done by the Incas. As soon as the Spaniards arrived and struck the first blow, the great chiefs would naturally call together a band of their followers on whose fidelity they could rely, load the treasures on llamas, of which they possessed great numbers, and hurry them off to the mountains.

"It is among the mountains, therefore, that our search must be made. All our traditions point to the fact that it was along the eastern range of the Cordilleras, and the country beyond, that by far the greater portion of the treasures were taken for concealment. At any rate, as we have but eighteen months for the search it is on that side that we must try, and ten times that length of time would be insufficient for us to do it thoroughly. As to the gold mines, it is certain that they lie in that portion of the range between Cuzco and Lake Titicaca. It was near Puno, a short distance from the lake, that the Spaniards, owing to the folly of an Indian, found great treasures in a cave. They would probably have found much more had not a stream suddenly burst out which flooded the whole valley and converted it into a lake. Which do you think we had better look for first, gold mines or hidden treasures?"

"Of course that must depend on you, Dias, and how much you know about these matters. I need not say that a hidden treasure would be of vastly more use to me than the richest gold mine in the world. To obtain the gold from a mine an abundance of labour is required, besides machinery for crushing quartz and separating the gold from it. In the bed of a river, if it is rich and abounding in nuggets, three or four men, with rough machinery, could wash out a large quantity of gold in a short time, and a place of that sort would be far better than a rich mine, which could not be worked without a large amount of capital."

"I have heard tales of such places on the other side of the mountains to the south. From time to time gold-seekers have returned with as much as they could carry, but not one in a hundred of those that go ever come back; some doubtless die from hunger and hardship, but more are killed by the Indians. Most of the tribes there are extremely savage, and are constantly at war with each other, and they slay every white man who ventures into their country."

"Then is it not probable, Dias, that the gold could have come from their country?"

"Not from the plains, but from the streams running down into them; and although the Incas never attempted to subdue the tribes beyond the mountains, they may have had bodies of troops to protect the workers from incursions by these savages."

"Are there many wild beasts there?"

"In some parts of the mountains pumas and jaguars abound."

"That is not altogether satisfactory, though I should not mind if we fell in with one occasionally. But how about game, Dias?"

"The chief game are the wild vicuñas, which are very numerous in some parts; but they are very shy and difficult to hunt. Deer are plentiful, and there are foxes, bears, and hogs; but the great article of food is fish. On the plains the manatee, which is very like the seal, is caught; turtles are found in great numbers, and the people make oil from their eggs; and the buffo, a sort of porpoise, also abounds. The natives do not eat these, except when very pressed for food; they catch them for the sake of their oil. There are many kinds of fish: the sunaro, which I heard an English traveller say are like the fish the English call the pike; these grow to the length of seven or eight feet. And many smaller kinds of fish are caught by throwing the juice of the root of the barbasto into small streams. This makes the fish stupid, and they float on the surface so that they may easily be caught by hand. There are also many sorts of fruit."

"Well, then, we ought to do fairly well, Dias."

"Yes, señor; but many of these creatures are only found in the forests and in the rivers of the plains, and they are so much hunted by the savages there that they are very shy. But there are some creatures with which we certainly do not wish to meet, and unfortunately these are not uncommon. I mean the alligators and the great serpents. The natives fear the alligators much, for their weapons are of no avail against them, and they would never venture to attack a great snake."

"And besides these, what other disagreeables are there, Dias?" Bertie asked cheerfully.

"There is one other disagreeable," Dias replied, "and it is a serious one. There are in the mountains many desperate men. Some have slain an enemy who had friends influential enough to set the law in motion against them, or have escaped from prison; some have resisted the tax-collectors; many have been suspected of plotting against the government; and others are too lazy to work."

"And how do they live?" Harry asked.

"They live partly on game and partly on plunder. They steal from cultivators; they are paid a small sum by all muleteers passing through the mountains; they rob travellers who are worth robbing; and sometimes they carry off a proprietor of land, and get a ransom for him. Occasionally they will wash the sand, and get gold enough to send one of their number into a town to buy articles they require."

"And do they go in large bands?"

"No, señor; as a rule some ten or twelve keep together under the one they have chosen as their chief. Sometimes, if people make complaints and troops are sent against them, they will join to resist them; but this is not often. The authorities know well enough that they have no chance of catching these men among the mountains they are so well acquainted with, and content themselves with stationing a few troops in the villages."

"And is it through the robbers or the savages that so few of the gold explorers ever return?"

"It is chiefly, I think, from hardship," Dias said; "but undoubtedly many who venture down near the Indians' country are killed by them. Some who have done well, and are returning with the gold they have accumulated, fall victims to these robbers. You must not, of course, suppose that there are great numbers of them, señor. There may be some hundreds, but from Huancabamba—the northern frontier of the western Cordilleras, where the Maranon crosses the eastern range—down to Lake Titicaca on the one side, and Tacna on the other, is nigh a thousand miles, and the two ranges cover more square leagues than can be reckoned, and even a thousand men scattered over these would be but so many grains of sand on a stretch of the sea-shore."

"It certainly sounds like it, Dias; but perhaps those worthy people congregate chiefly in the neighbourhood of the passes."

"That is so, señor; but even through these a traveller might pass many times without being troubled by them."

"Have you fallen in with them often, Dias?"

"Yes; but, as you see, they have done me no harm. Sometimes, when I get to the end of my journey, the mules are not so heavily laden as when I started; but generally the people for whom I work say to me, 'Here are so many dollars, Dias; they are for toll.' There are places in the villages at the foot of the most-frequented passes where it is understood that a payment of so many dollars per mule will enable you to pass without molestation. In return for your money, you receive a ribbon, or a rosette, or a feather, and this you place in your hat as a passport. You may meet a few men with guns as you pass along, but when they see the sign they salute you civilly, ask for a drink of wine if you are carrying it, then wish you good-day. It is only in little-frequented passes that you have to take your chance. I may say that though these men may plunder, they never kill a muleteer. They know that if they did, all traffic on that road would cease, and the soldiers would find guides who knew every path and hiding-place in the mountains."

"Anyhow, I think it is well, Dias, that I took your advice, and handed over my gold to Señor Pasquez, for if we do fall into the hands of any of these gentry, we can lose practically nothing."

"No money, señor, but we might lose everything else, except perhaps the mules, which they could not use in the mountains. But if they were to take our blankets, and tents, and provisions, and your firearms, we should be in a bad way if we happened to be a couple of hundred miles in the heart of the mountains."

"Well, I don't think they will take them," Harry said grimly, "without paying pretty dearly for them. With your gun and our rifles, and that old fowling-piece which you got for José, which will throw a fairly heavy charge of buck-shot, I think we can make a very good fight against any band of eight men, or even one or two more."

"I think so," Dias said gravely. "It is seldom I miss my mark. Still, I hope we shall not be troubled with them, or with the Indians. You see, it is not so much an attack by day that we have to fear, as a surprise at night. Of course, when we are once on the hills, José and I will keep watch by turns.

He is as sharp as a needle. I should have no fear of any of these robbers creeping up to us without his hearing them. But I can't say so much for him in the case of the Indians, who can move so noiselessly that even a vicuña would not hear them until they were within a spear's-throw."

"The spear is their weapon then, Dias?"

"Some tribes carry bows and arrows, others only spears, and sometimes they poison the points of both these weapons."

"That is unpleasant. Are there remedies for the poisons?"

"None that I know of, nor do I think the savages themselves know of any. The only chance is to pour ammonia at once into the hole that is made by an arrow, and to cut out all the flesh round a spear-wound, and then to pour in ammonia or sear it with a hot iron."

"That accounts for your buying that large bottle of ammonia at Lima. I wondered what you wanted it for. When we get into the country these unpleasant people inhabit, I will fill my spirit-flask with it, so that it will always be handy if required. Now we understand things generally, Dias. It only remains for you to decide where we had best leave the plain and take to the mountains."

Dias was silent for a minute. "I should say, señor, that first we had better journey down to Cuzco and then down to Sicuani, where the western Cordilleras, after making a bend, join the eastern branch, and there cross the Tinta volcano. On the other side are many gorges. In one of these I know there is some very rich gold sand. Explorers have sought for this spot in vain, but the secret has been well kept by the few who know it. It has been handed down in my father's family from father to son ever since the Spaniards came. He told it to me, and I swore to reveal it to none but my son. I have no son, and the secret therefore will die with me. Whether it has been passed down in any other family I cannot say. It may be, or it may not be; but as I owe you my life, and also the debt of gratitude to Señor Barnett, I feel that you are more to me than a son. Moreover, the secret was to be kept lest it should come to the knowledge of the Spaniards. The Spaniards have gone, and with them the reason for concealment, so I feel now that I am justified in taking you there."

"I am glad of that, Dias. Assuredly the gold can be of service to no man as long as it lies there, and it would be better to utilize it than allow it to waste. I need not say how grateful I shall feel if you can put me in the way of obtaining it."

"That I cannot absolutely promise," he said. "I have the indications, but they will be difficult to find. Three hundred years bring great changes—rocks on which there are marks may be carried away by torrents, figures cut in the cliffs may be overgrown by mosses or creepers. However, if but a few remain, I hope to be able to find my way. If I fail we must try elsewhere; but this is the only one of which I have been told all the marks. I know generally several places where great treasure was hidden, but not the marks by which they could be discovered, and as we may be sure that every measure was taken to hide the entrances to the caves, the chances would be all against our lighting upon them. I may say, señor, that, great as was the treasure of the Incas, that of the Chimoos or Chincas, a powerful people who inhabited part of this country, was fully as large; and traditions say that most of the treasures hidden were not those of the Incas, but of the Chimoos, who buried them when their country was invaded by the Incas.

"This is certainly the case with most of the treasures hidden to the west of the mountains. It was so at Pachacamac; it was so at Truxillo, where the Spaniards found three million and a half dollars of gold; and it is known that this was but a small hoard, and that the great one, many times larger, has never been discovered. Probably the secret has long been lost; for if there are but few who know where the Incas buried their gold, it may well be believed that the exact locality of the Chimoo treasures, which were buried more than eight hundred years ago, is now unknown, and that nothing but vague traditions have been handed down."

"That one can quite understand," Harry agreed, "when we consider how many of the Chimoos must have fallen in the struggle with the Incas, and how more than half the population were swept away by the Spaniards, to say nothing of those who have died in the wars of the last thirty years. It seems strange, however, that the treasures in the temple of Pachacamac were left untouched by the Incas and allowed to accumulate afterwards."

"It was so generally regarded as the sacred city," Dias said, "that, powerful as they were, the Incas did not attempt to interfere with it, as to do so would certainly have stirred up a formidable insurrection of the natives throughout the whole of their territory; and instead, therefore, of taking possession of the temple and dedicating it to their own god, they allowed it to remain untouched and the worship of the old gods to be carried on there, contenting themselves with building a temple of their own to the Sun-god close at hand."

"Whether any treasure we find belonged to the Incas or to the Chimoos is of no consequence whatever. I certainly think that before entering upon what would seem to be almost a hopeless search for such stores, we should try this place that you know of. In that case it seems to me, Dias, that if we had gone down the coast to Islay, and up through Arequipa to Cuzco, our journey would have been considerably shorter."

"That is true, señor, but we should have found it difficult to take a passage for our mules; the steamers are but small craft, with poor accommodation even for passengers. And besides, until we had made all our arrangements for the journey from Lima, I could hardly say that I had made up my mind to bring you to this place. Only when you and your brother saved my life did I feel that I was bound to aid you, even to the point of divulging the secret. It is different now from what it was when it was first handed down. At that time the Spaniards were mercilessly slaying all known to be in the possession of any secret connected with gold, and every discovery of gold entailed the forced labour of thousands more of the natives. Well, señor, all that is changed; we are our own masters, and those who find mines are allowed to work them on payment of certain royalties. There is, therefore, no good in keeping a secret that has been useless for hundreds of years."

"Certainly, Dias, you will have the satisfaction of knowing that you are injuring no one by the act, and are besides doing a very good action to my brother and myself.

"Well, Bertie," Harry said when Dias had left the room, "I think we may congratulate ourselves. For the first time I really think there is a chance of the expedition turning out a success."

"It certainly looks like it," Bertie agreed. "For your sake I hope it will be so. As for me, I am quite content; what with Indians and brigands, wild beasts, alligators, and snakes, the journey is likely to be an exciting one."

CHAPTER VI — A TROPICAL FOREST

It took them over three weeks to reach Cuzco. They did not hurry, for they wished to keep the mules in good condition for the serious work before them. They were travelling across a plateau thickly dotted with villages and small towns, and everywhere richly cultivated. Near the summit of the mountains large flocks of alpacas were grazing, and lower down herds of cattle and sheep, while near the plain were patches of wheat, barley, and potatoes, which in turn were succeeded by fields of maize, apple and peach trees, and prickly-pears. At the foot were fields of sugar-cane, oranges, citron, pine-apples, cacao, and many other tropical fruits; while in the deeper ravines cotton was grown in abundance for the wants of the population. Here, in fact, were all varieties of climate, from the perpetual snow on the summits of the lofty mountains to a tropical heat in the valleys.

"If the Incas had been contented with this glorious plateau, which for centuries constituted their kingdom, and had passed a law against the gathering of gold and the mining for silver, they might still have been lords here," Harry said one day. "There would have been nothing to tempt the avarice of the Spaniards, for owing to the distance of the mines from the coast, the cost of carriage would have been immense, and the long sea journey would have rendered the exportation of the natural products of the country impossible. Some of the more sober-minded of the Dons might have settled down here and taken wives from among the daughters of the nobles, and, bringing with them the civilization of Spain, become valuable colonists. The Incas, before they extended their conquest over the whole of the west of South America, must have been a comparatively simple people, and would have had none of the habits of luxury and magnificence that tempted the Spaniards. The gold of South America was the ruin of the Incas, as it was afterwards the chief cause of the ruin of Spain."

"Well, Harry, then I should very strongly advise you to give up treasure-hunting and to remain poor, for the curse of the gold may not have worked itself out yet."

"I must risk that, Bertie. I have no desire for luxury or magnificence; it is for a laudable purpose that I seek the gold. However, if you have any scruples on the subject there is no occasion for you to have any share in what I may discover."

"No, I think I will agree with you and risk it; though certainly at present I don't see what advantage any amount of money would be to me."

The houses of the peasants were for the most part comfortable, although small, for since the expulsion of the Spaniards, the people had had no reason to make a pretence of poverty. During the Spanish rule no one dared, by the size of his house or by his mode of living, to show signs of wealth above his fellows, for to do so would be to expose himself to the cruel exactions of the tax-collectors and local officials; and even now they had hardly recognized the change that had taken place, and remained wedded to the habits that had become rooted in them by centuries of oppression.

The travellers had no difficulty whatever in purchasing food and forage on the way. They always slept in their tents now, and preferred Donna Maria's cooking to that which they could obtain in the small and generally dirty inns in the towns.

By the time they reached Cuzco, Bertie was able to converse in Spanish with some fluency. On the way he rode either beside Dias and his wife, or with José; in either case an animated conversation was kept up, sometimes on the stirring events of the war of independence and the subsequent struggles, sometimes about life in England, its ways and customs, concerning which neither Maria nor José had any knowledge whatever. Bertie also endeavoured to gain some information concerning the history of Peru prior to the rising against Spain; but neither the woman nor boy knew anything of the subject beyond the fact that the Incas were great people, and that the natives still mourned for them.

"You see that black apron most of the women wear over one hip, as a sign of mourning; it is still worn for the Incas. They must have been good people, and not cruel like the Spanish, or they would not be so much regretted," Maria said. "I don't wear the apron, because both Dias and I are of mixed blood, descendants on one side of natives, and on the other of Creoles, that is of Spaniards whose families were settled here, and who hated their countrymen just as much as we do. Well, there is Cuzco in sight. I have never seen it, and am glad that we shall stay there for a few days."

The old capital of the Incas lay at the end of a valley about two miles in length, and about a mile in width. To the north of the city rose an abrupt hill, crowned by the great citadel with its three lines of walls, the hill being divided from those forming the side of the valley by two deep ravines, in which flowed little streams that ran through the city. The appearance of the town was striking. There were numerous churches, its streets ran at right angles to each other, and the massive stone houses dated from the early Spanish days, though they were surmounted for the most part by modern brickwork additions. Where the great Temple of the Sun once stood, the church of Santo Domingo had been built, a portion of the splendid building of the old faith being incorporated in it.

"What is the use of staying here?" Bertie asked his brother impatiently, two days after they had arrived at Cuzco. "I dare say these old ruins and fortresses, and so on, are very interesting to people who understand all about the Incas; but as I know nothing about them, I don't see how you can expect me to get up any interest in an old wall because you tell me that it is one of the remains of a palace belonging to some old chap I never heard of. I shall be very glad when Dias says that the mules have had enough rest and that we can set out on our business."

"I am afraid you are a Goth, Bert," Harry said, looking at him with an expression of pity. "Here you are in one of the most interesting cities of the world, a place that thousands and thousands of people would travel any distance to investigate, and in forty-eight hours you are tired of it. You have no romance in your nature, no respect for the past; you are a Goth and a Philistine."

"I am afraid you are mixing up localities, Harry. I may be a Goth or a Philistine, but perhaps you are not aware that these peoples or tribes had no connection with each other. Your education in matters unconnected with the Royal Navy seems to have been even more deplorably neglected than my own."

"Shut up, youngster!"

"No, Lieutenant Prendergast, you are not on the quarter-deck of one of Her Majesty's ships at present. You are not even the leader of a small caravan on the march. We are in this locanda on terms of perfect equality, save and except in any small advantage that you may possess in the matter of years."

Harry laughed.

"Well, Bertie, I do not altogether disagree with what you say. If I had come here to get up the history of the Incas, and investigate the ruins of their palaces, I should be content to stay here for some weeks; but as it is, I am really just as anxious as you are to be on the move. I was speaking to Dias half an hour ago, and he says that in two more days we shall be able to start again. We have been discussing how much flour and other things it is absolutely necessary to take. Of course the better provided we are the more comfortable we shall be; but on the other hand, as Dias says, it is of great importance that the mules should carry as little weight as possible.

"In crossing the passes we shall have the benefit of the old roads of the Incas, but once we leave these the difficulties will be enormous. Dias said that it might be better to dispose of our mules altogether and get trained llamas in their place, as these can climb over rocks where no mule could obtain a foothold. But then it would be necessary to take with us one or two natives accustomed to their ways, and this would not suit us at all. However, I do think that it would be worth while to take two or three of these animals with us. They can carry a hundred pounds apiece; but as we may be going over extraordinarily rough country, fifty pounds would be sufficient. The advantage would be that we could establish a sort of central camp at the farthest spot to which the mules could go, and then make exploring expeditions with the llamas to carry provisions and tools. The llamas are not bad eating, so that if we found no other use for them they would assist our commissariat."

"How far can they go in a day, Harry?"

"Ten or twelve miles, and you may be sure that that is as much as we can do when we are among the mountains."

"Then I should think they would be very useful. I suppose there will be no difficulty in buying them?"

"None at all. A good many are brought in for sale to the market every day. Of course it would be necessary to get strong animals accustomed to burdens."

Before starting there was another long consultation between Harry and Dias as to which course it would be better to adopt. The most-frequented pass through the mountains was that to Paucartambo, forty miles north-east from Cuzco, at the mouth of the pass that leads down into the plains. Between this town and the Carabaya range, a hundred and fifty miles to the south, was to be found the rich gold deposit to which Dias had referred. So far, however, as the traditions he had received informed him, it was situated near the slopes of the Tinta volcano, and between that and Ayapata. The direct road to this spot was extremely difficult, and he was of opinion that the journey could be more easily performed by going to Paucartambo and then skirting the foot of the mountains.

"You will find no difficulty in obtaining food as you go along," he said; "wild turkeys, pheasants, and other birds are to be met with in that district. Moreover, there are many plantations which have been deserted owing to the depredations of the Chincas, a tribe who live on the tributaries of the

Pueros, or as it used to be called, Rio Madre de Dios. Here you will find fields of maize still growing, sugar-cane, cacao, and rice. One after another the estates have been abandoned; at some of them the whole of the people on the farms were massacred, and in all the danger was so great that the proprietors found it impossible to work them. The one drawback to that road is that we may fall in with the Chincas, in which case they will certainly attack us. However, they are widely scattered through the forests, and we may not fall in with them. On the other hand, the track by the Tinta mountain from Sicuani is extremely difficult and dangerous, We might lose several of our animals in traversing it, and should have to depend entirely on what we carried for food."

"Then by all means let us go the other way, Dias. Were we to lose some of our mules it would be impossible to replace them, and it would be useless to find gold if we could not carry it away."

Two days later they started, four llamas having been added to the caravan. Dias explained that it would not be necessary to take any natives to attend to these animals, as, once started, they would follow the mules without difficulty, especially if they were fed with them before starting. Three days' travelling brought them to the little town, which lay very high up in the hills. The cold here was bitter, and the party needed all their wraps, and were glad to get in motion as soon as it was light. Passing over a range of mountains above Paucartambo, where a thin layer of snow crunched under their feet, they began the tremendous descent into the plain. In a short time the morning mist cleared away. The road led through a tropical forest. It took them over three hours to reach the river Chirimayu, a descent of eleven thousand feet in the course of eight miles.

Here they halted by the side of a splendid waterfall. The hills rose up perpendicularly on every side except where the little river made its way through the gorge; they were covered with brushwood, ferns, and creepers, thick with flowers of many colours, while lofty palms and forest trees grew wherever their roots could find a hold. Splendid butterflies of immense size flitted about; birds of many kinds and beautiful plumage flew hither and thither among the trees; humming-birds sucked the honey from the bright flowers; parrots chattered and screamed in the upper branches of the trees, and the foam and spray of the torrent sparkled in the sun. Harry and his brother stood struck with admiration at the loveliness of the scene, even Donna Maria and José ceased their chatter as they looked at a scene such as they had never before witnessed.

THEY HALTED BY THE SIDE OF A SPLENDID WATERFALL

"It is worth coming all the way from England to see this, Bertie."

"It is, indeed. If it is all like this I sha'n't mind how long Dias takes to find the place he is in search of."

At a word from Dias they all set to work to take the burdens off the animals. A place was cleared for the tents. When these had been erected José collected dried sticks. A fire was soon lighted, and Maria began to prepare breakfast.

"Is it unhealthy here, Dias?"

"Not here, señors; we are still many hundred feet above the plain. In the forest there it is unhealthy for whites, the trees grow so thickly that it is difficult to penetrate them, swamps and morasses lie in many places, and the air is thick and heavy. We shall not go down there until we need. When we must descend we shall find an abundance of maize, and fruits of all sorts. The savages kill the people they find on the estates, but do not destroy the crops or devastate the fields. They are wise enough to know that these are useful to them, and though they are too lazy to work themselves they appreciate the good things that others have planted."

"It is rather early to make a halt, Dias."

"We have work to do, señor. In the first place we must find a spot where large trees stand on the bank of the torrent. Two or three of these must be felled so that they fall across it; then we shall have to chop off the branches, lay them flat side by side, and make a bridge over which to take animals. After breakfast we must set about this work, and it will be too late before we finish to think of going farther to-day."

"It is well that we bought four good axes and plenty of rope at Cuzco," Harry said.

"We shall want them very often, señor. Three large torrents come down between this and the Tinta volcano, besides many smaller ones. Some rise from the hills to the north of us. These fall into others, which eventually combine to make the Madre de Dios. So far as is known boats can descend the river to the Amazon without meeting with any obstacle, from a point only a few miles from the head of the Pueros, which we shall presently cross. The fact that there are no cataracts during the whole course from the hills to the junction of the rivers, shows how perfectly flat the great plain is."

"And did either the Incas or the Spaniards ever conquer the Chincas and cultivate these splendid plains?"

"The Incas drove them back some distance, señor, and forced them to pay a tribute, but they never conquered them. Doubtless they cultivated the land for some leagues from the foot of the mountains, as did the Spaniards, and it was considered the most fertile part of the Montaña, as their possessions this side of the Cordilleras were called. The Spaniards tried to push farther, but met with such stout opposition by the savages that they were forced to desist."

All were ready when Maria announced breakfast. After the meal they sat smoking for half an hour, reluctant to commence the heavy work before them.

"We had better be moving, señor," Dias said as he rose to his feet, "or we shall not get the bridge made before dark."

A hundred yards from the camp they found three large trees growing close to each other near the edge of the stream. Bertie looked at them with an air of disgust.

"This will be worse for the hands than rowing for twelve hours in a heavy boat."

"I dare say it will," Harry agreed; "but it has got to be done, and the sooner we set about it the better."

"I shall take off my flannel shirt," Bertie said.

"You had better not, señor," Dias said, as he saw what the lad was about to do. "There are many insects here that will sting you, and the bites of some of them swell up and turn into sores. Now, señor, I will take this tree. The next is not quite so large, will you take that? I will help you when I am finished with my own. Your brother and José can work by turns at the other."

It was hard work, for the trees were over two feet across near the foot. Dias had felled his before the others had cut half-way through, and he then lent his aid to Harry, who was streaming with perspiration.

"You are not accustomed to it, señor. You will manage better when you have had two or three months' practice at the work."

"I did not bargain for this, Harry," Bertie said as he rested for the twentieth time from his work. "Jaguars and alligators, Indians and bandits, and hard climbing I was prepared for, but I certainly never expected that we should have to turn ourselves into wood-cutters."

"It is hard work, Bertie, but it is useless to grumble, and, as Dias says, we shall become accustomed to it in two or three months."

"Two or three months!" Bertie repeated with a groan; "my hands are regularly blistered already, and my arms and back ache dreadfully."

"Well, fire away! Why, José has done twice as much as you have, and he has hardly turned a hair. I don't suppose that he has had much more practice than you have had, and he is nothing like so strong."

"Oh, I dare say! if he has never cut, his ancestors have, and I suppose it is hereditary. Anyhow, I have been doing my best. Well, here goes!"

Harry laughed at his brother's theory for explaining why José had done more work than he had. He was himself by no means sorry that Dias had come to his assistance, and that his tree was nearly ready to fall. José climbed it with the end of a long rope, which he secured to an upper bough. Dias then took the other end of the rope, crossed the torrent by the tree he had felled, and when José had come down and Harry had given a few more cuts with the axe, he was able to guide the tree in its fall almost directly across the stream. Then he took Bertie's tree in hand. In ten minutes this was lying beside the others. It took three hours' more work to cut off the branches and to lay the trees side by side, which was done with the aid of one of the mules. The smaller logs were packed in between them to make a level road, and when this was done the workers went back to the little camp. The sun was already setting, and Donna Maria had the cooking-pots simmering over the fire.

"That has been a hard day's work," Harry said, when he and his brother threw themselves down on the grass near the fire.

"Hard is no name for it, Harry. I have never been sentenced to work on a tread-mill, but I would cheerfully chance it for a month rather than do another day's work like this. The palms of my hands feel as if they had been handling a red-hot iron, my arms and shoulders ache as if I had been on a rack. I seem to be in pain from the tips of my toes to the top of my head."

Harry laughed.

"It is only what every settler who builds himself a hut in the backwoods must feel, Bert. It is the work of every wood-cutter and charcoal-burner; it is a good deal like the work of every miner. You have been brought up too soft, my boy."

"Soft be hanged!" the lad said indignantly; "it is the first time I have heard that the life of an apprentice on board a ship was a soft one. I have no doubt you feel just as bad as I do."

"But you don't hear me grumbling, Bert; that is all the difference. I expect that, of the two, I am rather the worse, for my bones and muscles are more set than yours, and it is some years now since I pulled at either a rope or an oar."

Bertie was silent for a minute or two, and then said rather apologetically:

"Well, Harry, perhaps I need not have grumbled so much, but you see it is a pretty rough beginning when one is not accustomed to it. We ought to have had a short job to begin with, and got into it gradually, instead of having six hours on end; and I expect that the backwoods settler you were talking about does not work for very long when he first begins. If he did he would be a fool, for he certainly would not be fit for work for a week if he kept on till he had nearly broken his back and taken the whole skin off his hands by working all day the first time he tried it."

"There is something in that, Bertie; and as we are in no extraordinary hurry I do think we might have been satisfied with felling the trees to-day, and cutting off the branches and getting them into place to-morrow. Still, as Dias seemed to make nothing of it, I did not like to knock off at the very start."

"The meal is ready, señor," Maria said, "and I think we had better eat it at once, for the sky looks as if we were going to have rain."

"And thunder too," Dias said. "You had better begin; José and I will picket the mules and hobble the llamas. If they were to make off, we should have a lot of trouble in the morning."

The aspect of the sky had indeed changed. Masses of cloud hung on the tops of the hills, and scud was flying overhead.

Maria placed one of the cooking-pots and two tin plates, knives, and forks beside Harry and his brother, with two flat cakes of ground maize.

"Sit down and have your food at once," Harry said to her. "The rain will be down in bucketfuls before many minutes."

They were soon joined by Dias and José, the latter bringing up a large can of water from the stream. They had just finished when large drops of rain began to patter on the ground.

"Never mind the things," Harry said as he leapt to his feet. "Crawl under shelter at once; it is no use getting a wetting."

All at once made for the tents; and they were but just in time, for the rain began to fall in torrents, and a peal of thunder crashed out overhead as they got under the canvas.

"This is our first experience of this sort of thing," Harry said, as he and his brother lit their pipes half-sitting and half-reclining on their beds. "I rather wondered why Dias put the tents on this little bit of rising ground, which did not look so soft or tempting as the level; but I see now that he acted very wisely, for we should have been flooded in no time if we had been lower down. As it is, I am by no means sure that we shan't have the water in. Another time we will take the precaution to make trenches round the tents when we pitch them. However, we have got a waterproof sheet underneath the beds, so I expect it will be all right."

"I hope so. Anyhow, we had better see that the edges are turned up all round, so that the water cannot run over them. By Jove! it does come down. We can hardly hear each other speak."

Suddenly the entrance to the tent was thrust aside.

"Here is a candle, señors."

It was thrown in, and Dias ran back into his own tent, which was but a few yards away, before Harry could remonstrate at his coming out.

"The candle will be useful, anyhow," Bertie said. "It is almost pitch-dark now. What with the sun going down and the clouds overhead, it has turned from day into night in the past five minutes."

Striking a match he lit the candle, and stuck it in between his shoes, which he took off for the purpose.

"That is more cheerful, Harry."

"Hullo! what is that?"

A deep sound, which was certainly not thunder, rose from the woods. It was answered again and again from different directions.

"They must be either pumas or jaguars, which are always called here lions and tigers, and I have no doubt Dias will know by the roar which it is. I should not mind if it were daylight, for it is not pleasant to know that there are at least half a dozen of these beasts in the neighbourhood. We may as well drop the cartridges into our rifles and pistols. I believe neither of these beasts often attacks men, but they might certainly attack our mules."

The storm continued, and each clap of thunder was succeeded by roars, snarls, and hissing, and with strange cries and shrieks. During a momentary lull Harry shouted:

"Is there any fear of these beasts attacking us or the mules, Dias?"

"No, señor, they are too frightened by the thunder and lightning to think of doing so."

"What are all those cries we hear?"

"Those are monkeys, señor. They are frightened both by the storm and by the roaring of the lions and tigers."

"Which is the bigger, Harry, the puma or the jaguar?"

"I believe the jaguar is the bigger, but the puma is the more formidable and fiercer. The latter belongs to the same family as the lion, and the former to that of the leopards. The jaguar is more heavily built than the leopard, and stronger, with shorter legs, but it is spotted just as the leopard is. The puma is in build like the lion, but has no mane. Both prey on animals of all kinds. The natives say they catch turtles, turn them over on their backs as a man would do, and tear the shells apart. They will also eat fish; but they are both scourges to the Indians and white planters, as they will kill sheep, horses, and cattle. Of course, if they are attacked by men and wounded, they will fight desperately, as most wild creatures will; but if man does not molest them, they are quite content to leave him alone, unless he chances to pass under a tree among the branches of which they are lying in wait for prey. Both of them can climb trees."

"Well, I thought I should have slept like a log, Harry, after the work that I have done, but what with the thunder and the patter of the rain, and all those noises of beasts, I don't think I am likely to close my eyes."

"We shall get accustomed to the noises after a time, Bert; but at present I feel as if I were in the middle of a travelling menagerie which had been caught in a thunderstorm. It is curious that all animals should be frightened at lightning, for they cannot know that it is really dangerous."

"Yes, I know. We had two dogs on the last ship I was in. A clap of thunder would send them flying down the companion into the cabin, and they would crouch in some dark corner in a state of absolute terror. They would do just the same if cannon were fired in salute, or anything of that sort. I suppose they thought that was thunder."

In spite, however, of the noises, Harry and his brother both dropped off to sleep before long, being thoroughly worn out by the day's work. They were awakened by Dias opening the front of their little tent.

"The sun is up, señors, and it is a fine morning after the storm. Maria has got coffee ready, baked some cakes, and fried some slices of meat."

"All right, Dias! we will be out directly. We will first run up the bank a short distance, and have a dip."

"You won't be able to swim, señor. The bed of the torrent is full, and no swimmer could breast the water."

"All right! we will be careful."

Throwing on their ponchos, they went down to the stream and ran along the bank.

"The water is coming down like a race-horse, Bert, but just ahead it has overflowed its banks. We can have a bath there safely, though it is not deep enough for swimming."

After ten minutes' absence they returned to the camp, completed their dressing, and sat down to breakfast.

"What were all those frightful noises, Dias? Were they pumas or jaguars?"

"They were both, señor. You can easily tell the difference in the sounds they make. The jaguar's is between a roar and a snarl, while the puma's is a sort of a hissing roar."

As soon as breakfast was over, the tents were packed up and the mules and llamas laden. Dias had given them a feed all round an hour before. The course they should take had been already agreed upon; they must descend to the plain, for it would be next to impossible to cross the ravines on the mountain-side.

"Each stream coming down from the hills," Dias said, "must be followed nearly up to its source, but for the next seventy or eighty miles the search need not be so careful as it must be afterwards. The place cannot be far from Tinta, but somewhere this side of it. We need not hurry, for there are two months to spare."

"How do you mean, Dias?"

"On a day that answers to the 21st of March, Coyllur—that is a star—will rise at midnight in a cleft in a peak. It can be seen only in the valley in which the stream that contains the gold runs down. This is what my father taught me; therefore there must be mountains to the south-east, and this can only be where the Cordilleras run east, which is the case at Tinta."

"That is excellent as far as it goes, if we happen to be in the right valley at the time, Dias, but it would not help us in the slightest if we were in any other valley. And we should have to wait a year before trying in another place."

"Yes, señor, but there are marks on the rocks of a particular kind. There are marks on rocks in other valleys, so that these should not be distinguished by Spaniards searching for the place. I should know the marks when I saw them."

"Then in that case, Dias, the star would not be of much use to us."

"I know not how that might be, señor, but as these instructions have been handed down from the time when the Spaniards arrived, it must surely in some way be useful, but in what way I cannot say."

"At any rate, Dias, what with those marks you speak of, and the star, it will be hard if we cannot find it. I suppose you are sure that the place is rich if we do light upon it?"

"Of that there can be no doubt, señor. Tradition says that it was the richest spot in the mountains, and was only worked when the king had need of gold, either for equipping an army or on some special occasion. At such a time it would be worked for one month, and then closed until gold was again required. However, as we go that way we shall explore other valleys. Gold is found more or less in all of them. Possibly we may find some rich spot which we can fall back upon if we fail in our search."

"But I hardly see how we can fail, with the star and those marks on the rocks to aid us."

"The marks may have disappeared, señor, and in that case we may not be in the right spot when the star rises; or again, the Incas may have closed the approach in some way to make the matter sure. I cannot promise that we shall find the gold; but I shall do my best with the knowledge that has come down to me. If I fail, we must try in other directions. When the Spaniards came, forty thousand of the Incas' people left Cuzco and the neighbouring towns, and journeyed away down the mountains and out to the west. Since then no reliable news concerning them has been heard, but rumours have from time to time come from that direction to the effect that there is a great and wealthy city there. I say not that if we failed here we should attempt to find it. The dangers from the savages would be too great. There would be great forests to traverse, many rivers to be crossed. We might travel for years without ever finding their city. When we got there, we might be seized and put to death, and if we were spared we might not be able to make off with the treasure. I mention it to show that gold may be found in many other places besides this valley we are seeking."

"I quite agree with you, Dias, that unless we could get some indication of the position of this city, if it now exists, it would be madness to attempt to search for it. I want gold badly, but I do not propose that we should all throw away our lives in what would be almost a hopeless adventure. Even if I were ready to risk my own life on such a mad enterprise, I would not ask others to do the same."

Crossing the stream, they made their way down through the forest. It was toilsome work, as they often had to clear a way with axes through the undergrowth and tangle of creepers. But at noon they reached level ground. The heat was now intense, even under the trees, and the air close and oppressive. On the way down Harry shot a wild turkey. When they halted, this was cut up and broiled over a fire, and after it had been eaten all lay down and slept for two or three hours.

"Ought we not to set a guard?" Harry had asked.

"No, señor, I do not think it necessary. José will lie down by the side of the llamas, and even if the mules should not give us a warning of any man or beast approaching, the llamas will do so. They are the shyest and most timid of creatures, and would detect the slightest movement."

For the next three weeks they continued their way. During this time five or six ravines were investigated as far as they could be ascended. Samples were frequently taken from sand and gravel and washed, but though particles of gold were frequently found, they were not in sufficient quantity to promise good results from washing.

"If we had a band of natives with us," Dias said, "we should no doubt get enough to pay well—that is to say, to cover all expenses and leave an ounce or two of profit to every eight or ten men engaged—but as matters stand we should only be wasting time by remaining here."

They had no difficulty in obtaining sufficient food; turkeys and pheasants were occasionally shot; a tapir was once killed, and, as they had brought hooks and lines with them, fish were frequently caught in the streams. These were of small size, but very good eating. But, as Dias said, they could not hope to find larger species, except far out in the plains, where the rivers were deep and sluggish.

The work was hard, but they were now accustomed to it. They often had to go a considerable distance before they could find trees available for bridging the torrents, but, on the other hand, they sometimes came upon some of much smaller girth than those they had first tackled. The labour in getting these down was comparatively slight. Sometimes these stood a little way from the stream, but after they were felled two mules could easily drag them to the site of the bridge. When on the march, Harry and his brother carried their double-barrelled guns, each with one barrel charged with shot suitable for pheasants or other birds, the other with buck-shot. Dias carried a rifle. Very seldom did they mount their mules, the ground being so rough and broken, and the boughs of the trees so thick, that it was less trouble to walk at the heads of their animals than to ride.

CHAPTER VII — AN INDIAN ATTACK

One day when they returned from exploring a valley, Harry and his brother, taking their rifles, strolled down an open glade, while Dias and José unpacked the animals. They had gone but a hundred yards when they heard a sound that was new to them. It sounded like the grunting of a number of pigs. Dias was attending to the mules. Harry and Bertie caught up their guns. Presently a small pig made its appearance from among some trees. Harry was on the point of raising his gun to his shoulder when Dias shouted, "Stop, do not shoot!"

"What is the matter, Dias?" he asked in surprise, as the latter ran up.

"That is a peccary."

"Well, it is a sort of pig, isn't it?"

"Yes, señor. But if you were to kill it, we might all be torn in pieces. They travel through the forests in great herds, and if one is injured or wounded, the rest will rush upon its assailants. You may shoot down dozens of them, but that only redoubles their fury. The only hope of escape is to climb a tree; but they will keep watch there, regardless of how many are shot, until hunger obliges them to retire. They are the bravest beasts of the forests, and will attack and kill even a lion or a tiger if it has seized one of their number. I beg you to stroll back quietly, and then sit down. I will go to the head of the mules. If the herd see that we pay no attention to them, they may go on without interfering with us. If we see them approaching us, and evidently intending to attack, we must take to the trees and try to keep them from attacking the mules; but there would be small chance of our succeeding in doing so."

He and José at once went up to the mules, and stood perfectly quiet at their head. Harry and Bertie moved closely up, laid their double-barrelled guns beside them, and then sat down. By this time forty or fifty of the peccaries had issued from the trees; some were rooting among the herbage, others stood perfectly quiet, staring at the group on the rise above them. Seeing no movement among them nor any sign of hostility, they joined the others in their search for food, and in a quarter of an hour the whole herd had moved off along the edge of the forest.

"Praise be to the saints!" Dias said, taking off his hat and crossing himself. "We have escaped a great danger. A hunter would rather meet a couple of lions or tigers than a herd of peccaries. These little animals are always ready to give battle, and once they begin, fight till they die. The more that are killed the more furious do the others become. Even in a tree there is no safety. Many a hunter has been besieged in a tree until, overpowered by thirst, he fell to the ground and was torn to pieces."

"What do they eat?" Harry asked.

"They will eat anything they kill, but their chief food is roots. They kill great numbers of snakes. Even the largest python is no match for a herd of peccaries if they catch him before he can take refuge in a tree."

"Well, then, it is very lucky that you stopped us before we fired."

"Fortunate indeed, señor. By taking to the trees we might have saved our lives, but we should certainly have lost our mules. Both pumas and tigers kill the little beasts when they come across stragglers. And it is well that they do, for otherwise the woods would be full of them, though fortunately they do not multiply as fast as our pigs, having only two or three in a litter. They are good eating, but it is seldom that a hunter can shoot one, for if he only wounds it, its shrieks will call together all its companions within a mile round."

"Then we must give up the idea of having pork while we are among the mountains."

"Now, are you going to keep me here all day, Dias?" Maria called suddenly. "It seems to me that you have forgotten me altogether."

Harry and Bertie could not help laughing.

Dias had, on returning to the mules, taken his wife and seated her on a branch six feet from the ground, in order that, should the peccaries attack them, he might be ready at once to snatch up his rifle and join in the fight without having first to think of the safety of his wife. He now lifted her down.

"DO YOU SEE THEM?" MARIA WHISPEREL

The action did even more than what Dias had said to convince Harry of the seriousness of the danger to which they had been exposed, for as a rule Donna Maria had scoffed at any offers of aid, even in the most difficult places, and with her light springy step had taxed the power of the others to keep up with her. These offers had not come from Dias, who showed his confidence in his wife's powers by paying no attention whatever, and a grim smile had often played on his lips when Harry or his brother had offered her a hand. That his first thought had been of her now showed that he considered the crisis a serious one.

"I thought Dias had gone mad," she said, as she regained her feet. "I could not think what was the matter when he began to shout and ran towards you. I saw nothing but a little pig. Then, when he came slowly back with you and suddenly seized me and jerked me up on to that bough, I felt quite sure of it, especially when he told me to hold my tongue and not say a word. Was it that little pig? I saw lots more of them afterwards."

"Yes; and if they had taken it into their heads to come this way you would have seen a good deal more of them than would be pleasant," Dias said. "With our rifles we could have faced four lions or tigers with a better hope of success than those little pigs you saw. They were peccaries, a sort of wild pig, and the most savage little beasts in the forest. They would have chased us all up into the trees and killed all the mules."

"Who would have thought it!" she said. "Why, when I was a girl I have often gone in among a herd of little pigs quite as big as those things, and never felt the least afraid of them. I must have been braver than I thought I was."

"You are a good deal sillier than you think you are, Maria," Dias said shortly. "There is as much difference between our pig and a peccary as there is between a quiet Indian cultivator on the Sierra and one of those savage Indians of the woods."

"I suppose I can light a fire now, Dias. There is no fear of those creatures coming back again, is there?"

"No, I should think not. Fortunately they are going in the opposite direction, otherwise I should have said that we had better stop here for a day or two in case they should attack us if we came upon them again."

The next day, as they were journeying through the forest, at the foot of the slopes José gave a sudden exclamation.

"What is it?" Dias asked.

"I saw a naked Indian standing in front of that tree; he has gone now."

"Are you sure, José?"

"Quite sure. He was standing perfectly still, looking at us, but when I called to you he must have slipped round the tree. I only took my eyes off him for a moment; when I looked again he was gone."

"Then we are in for trouble," Dias said gravely. "Of course it was one of the Chincas. No doubt he was alone, but you may be sure that he has made off to tell his companions he has seen us. He will know exactly how many we are, and how many animals we have. It may be twenty-four hours, it may be three or four days, before he makes his appearance again; but it is certain that, sooner or later, we shall hear of him. Hunters as they are, they can follow a track where I should see nothing; and so crafty are they, that they can traverse the country without leaving the slightest sign of their passage. The forest might be full of them, and yet the keenest white hunter would see no footprint or other mark that would indicate their presence."

"What had we better do, Dias?"

"We shall probably come to another stream before nightfall, señor. This we will follow up until we get to some ravine bare of trees. There we can fight them; in the forest we should have no chance. They would lie in ambush for us, climb into the trees and hide among the foliage, and the first we should know of their presence would be a shower of arrows; and as they are excellent marksmen, we should probably be all riddled at the first volley. There can be no sauntering now, we must push the animals forward at their best speed. I will lead the way. Do you, señor, bring up the rear and urge the mules forward. I shall try and pick the ground where the trees are thinnest, and the mules can then go at a trot. They cannot do so here, for they would always be knocking their loads off."

It was evening before they arrived at a stream. Here they made a short halt while they gave a double handful of grain to each of the animals, then they pushed on again until it was too dark to go farther.

"Will it be safe to light a fire, Dias?"

"Yes, that will make no difference. They are not likely to attack us at night. Savages seldom travel after dark, partly because they are afraid of demons, partly because they would be liable to be pounced upon by wild beasts. But I do not think there is any chance of their overtaking us until tomorrow. The man José saw may have had companions close at hand, but they will know that we are well armed, and will do nothing until they have gathered a large number and feel sure that they can overpower us. They will probably take up the track to-morrow at daylight; but we have made a long march, and can calculate that we shall find some defensible position before they overtake us. José and I will keep watch to-night."

"We will take turns with you, Dias."

"No, señor; my ears are accustomed to the sounds of the forests, yours are not. If you were watching I should still have no sleep."

The night passed without an alarm.

An hour before daylight Dias gave all the animals a good feed of corn, and as soon as it was light they again started. They were already some distance up the mountain, and after eight hours' travelling they arrived at a gorge that suited their purpose. For two hundred yards the rocks rose perpendicularly on each side of the stream, which was but some thirty feet wide. No rain had fallen for some days, and the water was shallow enough at the foot of the cliff for the mules to make their way among the fallen rocks, through which it rushed impetuously. At the upper end the cliffs widened out into a basin some fifty yards across.

"We cannot do better than halt here," Dias said. "In two or three hours we can form a strong breast-work on the rocks nearly out to the middle of the stream, where the current is too swift for anyone to make his way up against it."

"Are they likely to besiege us long, Dias?"

"That I cannot say; but I do not think they will give it up easily. Savages learn to be patient when roaming the forest in search of game. Their time is of no value to them; besides, they are sure to lose many if they attack, and will therefore try to get their revenge."

"They may have to give it up from want of food."

Dias shook his head.

"There are sure to be plenty of fish in the river, and they will poison some pool and get an abundance. With their bows and arrows they can bring down monkeys from the trees, and can snare small animals. However, señor, we can talk over these things to-morrow. We had best begin the breast-work at once while Maria is cooking dinner, which we need badly enough, for we have had nothing but the maize cakes we ate before starting."

Working hard till it was dark, they piled up rocks and stones till they formed a breast-work four feet high on both sides. Some twelve feet in the centre were open. They had chosen a spot where so many fallen rocks lay in the stream that it needed comparatively little labour to fill up the gaps between them.

"I thought wood-chopping bad enough," Bertie said as they threw themselves down on the ground after completing their labour, "but it is a joke to this. My back is fairly broken, my arms feel as if they were pulled out of the sockets, my hands are cut, I have nearly squeezed two nails off."

"It has been hard work," Harry agreed; "still, we have made ourselves fairly safe, and we will get the walls a couple of feet higher in the morning. We shall only want to add to them on the lower face in order to form a sort of parapet that will shelter us as we lie down to fire, so it won't be anything like such hard work. Then we will fill in the rocks behind with small stones and sand to lie down upon."

"They will never be able to fight their way up to it," Dias said.

"We need have no fear on that score. The question is, can they get down into this valley behind us; the rocks look very steep and in most places almost perpendicular."

"They are steep, señor; but trees grow on them in many places, and these savages are like monkeys. We shall have to examine them very carefully when we have finished the wall. If we find that it is possible for anyone to get down, we must go up the next gorge and see if we can find a better position."

"I suppose you think we are safe for to-night, Dias?'

"I don't think they will try to come up through the stream. They have keen eyes, but it would be so dark down there that even a cat could not see. They will guess that we have stopped here, and will certainly want to find out our position before they attack. One or two may come up as scouts, and in that case they may attack at daybreak. Of course two of us will keep watch; we can change every three hours. I will take the first watch with your brother, and you and José can take the next."

"José had better sleep," Maria put in; "he watched all last night. My eyes are as good as his, and I will watch with Don Harry."

Harry would have protested, but Dias said quietly:

"That will be well, Maria, but you will have to keep your tongue quiet. These savages have ears like those of wild animals, and if you were to raise your voice you might get an arrow in the brain."

"I can be silent when I like, Dias."

"It is possible," Dias said dryly; "but I don't remember in all these years we have been married that I have known you like to do so."

"I take that as a compliment," she said quietly, "for it shows at least that I am never sulky. Well, Don Harry, do you accept me as a fellow watcher?"

"Certainly I shall be very glad to have you with me; and I don't think that you need be forbidden to talk in a low tone, for the roar of the water among the rocks would prevent the sound of voices from being heard two or three yards away."

Accordingly, as soon as it became dark Dias went to the wall with Bertie. José, after a last look at the mules, wrapped himself in a blanket and lay down.

"I think I had better turn in to the tent," Harry said; "we have had two days' hard work, and the building of that wall has pretty nearly finished me, so if I don't get two or three hours' sleep to-night I am afraid I shall not be a very useful sentinel."

Five minutes later he was sound asleep, and when his brother roused him he could hardly believe that it was time for him to go on duty.

"Dias is waiting there. Will you come down?" the latter said. "You were sleeping like a top; I had to pull at your leg three times before you woke."

"I am coming," Harry said as he crawled out. "I feel more sleepy than when I lay down, and will just run down to the stream and sluice my head, that will wake me up in earnest, for the water is almost as cold as ice."

When he came back he was joined by Donna Maria, and, taking both his shot-gun and rifle, he went forward with her to the barricade.

"So you have neither seen nor heard anything, Dias?"

"Nothing whatever, señor."

"I have had a good sleep, Dias; we will watch for the next four hours. It is eleven o'clock now, so you will be able at three to take it on till daylight."

"I will send and call you again an hour before that," Dias said. "If they attack, as I expect they will as soon as the dawn breaks, we had better have our whole force ready to meet them."

So saying Dias went off.

"This is scarcely woman's work, Donna Maria."

"It is woman's work to help defend her life, señor, as long as she can. If I found that the savages were beating us I should stab myself. They would kill you, but they might carry me away with them, which would be a thousand times worse than death."

"I don't think there is any fear of their beating us," Harry said; "certainly not here. We ought properly to be one on each side, but really I shirk the thought of wading through the river waist-deep at that shallow place we found a hundred yards up; it would be bad enough to go through it, worse still to lie for four hours in wet clothes."

"Besides, we could not talk then, señor," Maria said with a little laugh, "and that would be very dull."

"Very dull. Even now we must only talk occasionally; we shall have to keep our eyes and ears open."

"I don't think either of them will be much good," she said; "I can see the white water but nothing else, and I am sure I could not hear a naked footstep on the rocks."

"It is a good thing the water is white, because we can make out the rocks that rise above the surface. When our eyes get quite accustomed to the dark we should certainly be able to see any figures stepping upon them or wading in the water."

"I could see that now, señor. I think it will be of advantage to talk, for I am sure if I were to lie with my eyes straining, and thinking of nothing else, they would soon begin to close."

Talking occasionally in low tones, but keeping up a vigilant watch, they were altogether hidden from the view of anyone coming up the stream, for they exposed only their eyes and the top of their heads above the rough parapet. No attempt had been made to fill up the spaces between the stones, so that, except for the rounded shape, it would be next to impossible to make them out between the rough rocks of the crest. Harry had laid his double-barrelled gun on the parapet in front of him. He had loaded both barrels with buck-shot, feeling that in the darkness he was far more likely to do execution with that weapon than with a rifle.

They had been some two hours on watch when Donna Maria touched his arm significantly. He gazed earnestly but could see nothing. A minute later, however, a rock about fifteen yards away seemed to change its shape. Before, it had been pointed, but just on one side of the top there was now a bulge.

"Do you see them?" Maria whispered. "I can make out one above the rocks; the other is standing against the wall."

[Image: AN INDIAN SPIES THE EXPEDITION.]

There was no movement for two or three minutes, and Harry had no doubt that they were examining the two black lines of stones between which the water was rushing.

"There are two others on this side, señor," Maria whispered.

The pause was broken by the sharp tap of two arrows striking on the stones a few inches below their heads.

"Well, you have begun it," Harry muttered.

He had already sighted his gun at the head half-hidden by the rock. He now pulled the trigger, and then, turning, he fired the other barrel, aiming along the side of the canyon where the two men seen by his companion must be standing. The head disappeared, and loud cries broke from the other side. The stillness that had reigned in the valley was broken by a chorus of shrieks and roars, and the air overhead thrilled with the sound of innumerable wings. Harry on firing had laid down the fowling-piece and snatched up his rifle.

"Do you see any others?"

"Two have run away; the one against the rocks on the other side was wounded, for I saw him throw up his arms, and it was he who screamed. The man by him dropped where he stood; the one behind the rock is killed, I saw his body carried away in the white water."

Half a minute later Dias and Bertie came up.

"So they have come, señor?"

"Yes, there were four of them. Your wife saw them, though I could only make out one. They shot two arrows at us, and I answered them. The man I saw was killed, and Donna Maria said that one on the other side also fell, and another was wounded."

"That was a good beginning," Dias said. "After such a lesson they will attempt nothing more to-night, and I doubt whether they will come down in the morning. They can get sight of the barricades from that bend a hundred yards down, and I don't think they will dare come up when they see how ready we are for them."

"Well, we will work out our watch anyhow, Dias. Now that I see how sharp Donna Maria's eyes are I have not the least fear of being surprised."

"I will stop with you," Bertie said; "I shall have no chance of going off to sleep again after being wakened up like that."

"If you are going to stop, Bertie, you had better go back and fetch a blanket, it is chilly here; then if you like you can doze off again till your watch comes."

"There is no fear of that, Harry. I have been eight-and-forty hours on deck more than once. I will warrant myself not to go to sleep."

In spite of this, however, in less than ten minutes after his return Bertie's regular breathing showed that he was sound asleep. Harry and Maria continued their watch, but no longer with the same intentness as before. They were sure that Dias would not have lain down unless he felt perfectly certain that the Chincas would make no fresh move until the morning, and they chatted gaily until, at two o'clock, Dias came up.

"Everything is quiet here, Dias. My brother is fast asleep, but I will wake him now that you have come up."

"Do not do so, señor; he worked very hard building the walls today. If I see anything suspicious I will rouse him. We may have work tomorrow, and it is much better that he should sleep on."

"Thank you, Dias! the fatigue has told on him more than on us; his figure is not set yet, and he feels it more."

He walked back to the tents with Maria.

"If you wake just as daylight breaks please rouse me," he said.

"I shall wake, señor; I generally get up at daybreak. That is the best time for work down in the plain, and I generally contrive to get everything done before breakfast at seven."

Harry slept soundly until he was called.

"The sky is just beginning to get light, señor."

He turned out at once. José was already feeding the mules.

"You had better come along with me, José, and bring that gun of yours with you. If the savages do attack, it will be well to make a forcible impression on them."

Greatly pleased with the permission, José took up the old musket he carried and accompanied Harry.

"What have you got in that gun, José?"

"The charge of buck-shot that you gave me the other day, señor."

"All right! but don't fire unless they get close. The shot will not carry far like a bullet; but if fired when they are close it is better than any bullet, for you might hit half a dozen of them at once."

José had been allowed to practise at their halting-places, and though he could not be called a good shot, he could shoot well enough to do good execution at thirty or forty yards.

Bertie was still asleep.

"Everything quiet, Dias?"

"I have seen nothing moving since I came out."

"Now, Bertie," Harry said, stirring his brother up with his foot. "All hands on deck!"

Bertie sat up and opened his eyes. "What is up now?" he said. "Ay, what, is it you, Harry, and José too? I must have been asleep!"

"Been asleep! Why, you went off in the middle of my watch, and Dias has been on the look-out for over three hours."

"Oh, confound it! You don't mean to say that I have slept for over five hours? Why didn't you wake me, Dias?" he asked angrily.

"Two eyes were quite enough to keep watch," Dias said. "I should have waked you if I had seen anything of the savages. Besides, Don Harry said you might as well go on sleeping if nothing happened, and I thought so too."

"I feel beastly ashamed of myself," Bertie said. "I don't want to be treated like a child, Harry."

"No, Bertie, and I should not think of treating you so; but you had had very hard work, and were completely knocked up, which was not wonderful; and you may want all your strength to-day. Besides, you know, you would have been of no use had you been awake, for you could have seen nothing. Donna Maria's eyes were a good deal sharper than mine, and I am quite sure that, tired as you were, Dias would have seen them coming long before you would. We had better lie down again, for it will be light enough soon for them to make us out. How far do their arrows fly, Dias?"

"They can shoot very straight up to forty or fifty yards, but beyond that their arrows are of very little use."

"Well, then, we shall be able to stop them before they get to that ravine."

Presently, as it became light, a figure showed itself at the turn of the ravine.

"Don't fire at him," Harry said; "it is better that they should think that our guns won't reach them. Besides, if the beggars will leave us alone, I have no wish to harm them."

In a minute or two the figure disappeared behind the bend and two or three others came out. "They think that our guns won't carry so far, or we should have shot the first man."

For a quarter of an hour there were frequent changes, until at least fifty men had taken a look at them.

"Now there will be a council," Harry said as the last disappeared. "They see what they have got before them, and I have no doubt they don't like it."

"I don't think they will try it, señor," Dias said. "At any rate they will not do so until they have tried every other means of getting at us."

Half an hour passed, and then Harry said. "I will stop here with my brother, Dias, and you and José had better examine the hillsides and ascertain whether there is any place where they can come down. You know a great deal better than I where active naked-footed men could clamber down. They might be able to descend with ease at a place that would look quite impossible to me."

Without a word Dias shouldered his rifle and walked away, followed by José. He returned in two hours.

"There are several places where I am sure the savages could come down. Now, señors, breakfast is ready; I will leave José here, and we will go and talk matters over while we eat. The tents are only a hundred yards away, so that if José shouts, we can be back here long before the savages get up, for they could not come fast through that torrent."

"It seems to me," Harry said after they had finished the meal, "that if there are only one or two points by which they could climb down we could prevent their doing so by picking them off; but if there are more, and they really come on in earnest, we could not stop them."

"There are many more than that," Dias replied. "I made out certainly four points on the right-hand side and three on the left where I could make my way down; there are probably twice as many where they could descend."

"Then I should say that the first thing to do is to go up through the gorge above and see whether there is any place that could be better defended than this. If we find such a spot, of course we could move to it; if not, we shall have to settle whether to go up the gorge till we get to some place where the mules can climb out of it, or stay here and fight it out. By camping on the stream at a point where it could not be forded, and making a breast-work with the bales, stones, and so on, I think we could certainly beat off any attack by daylight, but I admit that we should have no chance if they should make a rush during the night."

"I will go at once," said Dias, "and examine the river higher up. If I can find no place where the mules can climb, I am sure to be able to find some spot where we could do so. But that would mean the failure of our expedition, for we certainly could not go up the mountains, purchase fresh animals, food, and tools, and get down to the place we are looking for until too late."

"That would be serious, Dias, but cannot be counted against our lives. If there is no other way of escape from these savages, we must certainly abandon the animals and make our way back as best we can. In that case we must give up all idea of finding this gold stream. The star would not be in the same place again for another year, and even then we might not find it; so we must make up our minds to do our best in some other direction. That point we must consider as settled. I should not feel justified in risking my brother's life, yours, your wife's, and your nephew's, by remaining here to fight we know not how many savages—for there may be many more than the fifty we saw this morning, and they may in a day or two be joined by many others of their tribe."

"I should not like to lose all the animals and go back empty-handed," Dias said after a silence of two or three minutes, "unless it were a last resource."

"Nor should I, Dias; but you see, if we linger too long we may find it impossible to retire, we may be so hemmed in that there would be no chance of our getting through. For the day of course we are safe. The savages will have to decide among themselves whether to give the matter up, seeing that they are sure to lose many lives before they overpower us.

Then, if they determine to attack us, they will have to settle how it is to be done. Numbers of them will go up to the top of the hills on both sides and try to find a point at which they can make their way down; others, perhaps —which would be still more serious—may go farther up into the hills to find a spot where they could come down and issue out by the upper gorge, and then our retreat would be altogether cut off. All this will take time, so we may feel sure that no attack will be made to-day."

"I will start up the river at once, señor. Certainly the first point to be settled is whether we can find a more defensible spot than this, the second whether there is any way by which the animals can be taken up."

"There must surely be many points higher up where this can be done."

"Yes, señor, if we could get to them. But you saw we had difficulty in making our way through this gorge; there may be others higher up where it would be impossible either for us or the animals to pass."

"I did not think of that. Yes, that must be so. Well, you had certainly better go at once. My brother will relieve José, and after the boy has breakfasted he can return to his post, and Bertie can join me. I think if I see the savages trying to find a path I will open fire upon them. I don't say I should be able to hit them, for the top of those hills must be eight or nine hundred yards' range, and it is not easy to hit an object very much above or very much below you; but it is important that they should know that our weapons carry as far as that; when they hear bullets strike close to them they will hesitate about coming lower down, and unless they do come within two or three hundred feet from the bottom they cannot be sure of getting down."

Dias nodded. "That is a very good idea. Another cause of delay will be that those at the top cannot see far down the rock on their own side, so they will have to start by guess-work. Each party must fix upon the easiest places on the opposite side, and then go back again and change sides. I don't suppose they know any more of this place than we do. They always keep down in the plains, and it is only because they met us down there that they have followed us so far. I believe they will follow on as long as they think there is a chance of destroying us, for they are so jealous of any white man coming into what they regard as their country that they would spare no pains to kill anyone who ventured there. Now I will go, señor. You will keep near this end of the valley, in case there should be an alarm that they are coming up the stream."

"Certainly; and my brother shall remain with José. With his rifle and the two double-barrelled guns and José's musket they could hold the ravine against anything but a rush of the whole tribe."

An hour later Harry saw a number of figures appear against the sky-line on both sides. As they were clustered together, and would afford a far better mark than a single Indian, he took a steady aim at the party on the southern hill and fired. He had aimed above rather than below them, as, had the ball struck much below, they might not hear it, whereas, if it went over their heads, they would certainly do so. A couple of seconds after firing he saw a sudden movement among the savages, and a moment later not one was to be seen. Donna Maria, who was standing close by him watching them, clapped her hands. "Your ball must have gone close to them," she said, "but I don't think you hit anyone."

"I did not try to do so," he said. "I wanted the ball to go just over their heads, so that they should know that even at that distance they were not safe. I have no doubt that astonishment as much as fear made them bolt. They'll be very careful how far they come down the side of the hill after that. Now for the fellows on the other side."

But these too had disappeared, having evidently noticed the effect produced upon the others. After a pause heads appeared here and there at the edge of the crests. Evidently the lesson had impressed them with the necessity for precaution, as they no longer kept together, and they had apparently crawled up to continue their investigations. Beyond keeping a watch to see that none had attempted to descend the slope Harry did not interfere with them. At times he strolled to the breast-work, but no movement had been seen in that direction. In two hours Dias returned.

"The gorge above is a quarter of a mile through, and very difficult to pass. It is half-blocked with great rocks in two or three places, and there would be immense difficulty in getting the mules over. Beyond that it widens again, but the extent is not more than half what it is here. The walls are almost perpendicular, and I do not think that it would be possible to climb them at any point. Farther up there is another ravine. It is very narrow—not half so wide as this—and the stream rushes with great velocity along it. Two hundred yards from the entrance the rocks close in completely, and there is a fall of water sixty or seventy feet high."

"Well, that settles the point, Dias. We cannot get the animals out except by the way they came in. As for ourselves, we might climb up at some point in this ravine, but not in the others."

"That is so, señor," Dias said. "The outlook is a bad one—that is to say, we may now be unable to reach the gold river in time—but so long as we stay here we may be safe. We have plenty of provisions, we can catch fish in the stream, and no doubt shall find birds in the bushes at the lower part of the slopes. I doubt whether the natives will dare come down those precipices at night. If they try to descend by day, we can very well defend ourselves."

"The only question is, How long will it take to tire them out?"

"That I cannot tell. We know so little of the Chincas that we have nothing to go upon. Some savages have patience enough to wait for any time to carry out their revenge or slay an enemy; others are fickle, and though they may be fierce in attack, soon tire of waiting, and are eager to return to their homes again. I cannot think that they will speedily leave. They have assembled, many of them perhaps from considerable distances; they have had two days' march up here, and have lost at least two of their comrades. I think they will certainly not leave until absolutely convinced that they cannot get at us, but whether they may come to that decision in two days or a month I cannot say."

CHAPTER VIII — DEFEAT OF THE NATIVES

Bertie, who had joined Harry when he saw Dias approaching, had listened silently to their talk, then said:

"Don't you think that, by loading the mules and moving towards the mouth of the next gorge just as it is getting dark, we might induce the Chincas to think that we are going that way, and so to follow along the top of the hills. We might, as soon as night has fallen, come back again and go down the stream. Of course there may be some of them left to watch the mouth of the ravine, but we could drive them off easily enough, and get a long start before the fellows on the hills know what has happened."

None of the others spoke immediately; then Harry said:

"The idea is a good one as far as it goes. But you see at present we are in a very strong position. If we leave this and they overtake us in the woods, we shall not have the advantages that we have here."

"Yes, I see that, Harry; but almost anything is better than having to wait here and lose our chance of finding that gold."

"We can't help that, Bertie. You know how much that gold would be to me, but, as I said this morning, I will run no desperate risks to obtain it. When I started upon this expedition I knew that the chances of success were extremely slight, and that there might be a certain amount of danger to encounter from wild beasts and perhaps brigands; but I had never calculated upon such a risk as this, and certainly I am not prepared to accept the responsibility of leading others into it."

There was again silence, which was broken at last by Dias.

"The proposal of the young señor is a very bold one; but, as you say, Don Harry, after leaving our position we should be followed and surrounded. In the forest that would be very bad. I should say let us wait for at least a week; that will still give us time to reach the gold valley. By then the savages may have left, and some other plan may have occurred to us; at any rate, at the end of a week we shall see how things go. The Indians may have made an attack, and may lose heart after they are repulsed. They may find difficulty in procuring food, though I hardly think that is probable. Still, many things may occur in a week. If at the end of that time they are still here, we can decide whether to try some such plan as the young señor has thought of, or whether to wait until the Indians leave, and then return to Cuzco; for I feel certain that the place cannot be found except by the help of the star."

"Well, then," Bertie said, "could we not hit upon some plan to frighten them?"

"What sort of plan, Bertie?"

"Well, of course we could not make a balloon—I mean a fire-balloon—because we have no paper to make it with. If we could, and could let it up at night, with some red and blue fires to go off when it got up high, I should think it would scare them horribly."

"Yes; but it would be still better, Bertie, if we could make a balloon big enough to carry us and the mules and everything else out of this place, and drop us somewhere about the spot we want to get to."

"Oh, it is all very well to laugh, Harry! I said, I knew we could not make a fire-balloon; I only gave that as an example. If we had powder enough we might make some rockets, and I should think that would scare them pretty badly."

"Yes, but we haven't got powder, Bertie. We have plenty of cartridges for sporting purposes, or for fighting; but a rocket is a thing that wants a lot of powder, besides saltpetre and charcoal, and so on."

"Yes, yes, I know that," Bertie said testily. "My suggestion was that we might frighten them somehow, and I still don't see why we shouldn't be able to do it. Let us try to hit upon something else."

"There is a good deal in what the young señor says," Dias said gravely. "All the Indians are very superstitious, and think anything they don't understand is magic. It is worth thinking over: but before we do anything else we might find out how many of them there are at the other end of the ravine. Only a few may be left, or possibly the whole tribe may be gathered there at nightfall. To-night nothing will be settled, but to-morrow night I will go down the torrent with José. I will carry your double-barrelled guns with me, señor, if you will let me have them. When we get to the other end I will take up my station there. José is small and active. He could crawl forward and ascertain how many of them there are. If he should be discovered, which is not likely, he would run back to me. I should have four barrels ready to pour into them. That would stop them, for they would think we were all there and were going to attack them, and before they could recover from their alarm we should be back here again."

"That seems a good plan, Dias; but I do not see why Bertie and I should not go down with you."

"It would be better not, señor. In the first place, they may have men posted at their end of the ravine, and though two of us might crawl down without being seen, just as they crawled up here, they would be more likely to see four; in the next place, they might chance to crawl down the hillside above just as we were going down the ravine, and Maria and the animals would be at their mercy."

"They are hardly likely to choose the exact moment when we are to be away, but I quite agree with you that the risk must not be run."

"Well," Bertie said, returning to his former idea, "if Dias can go down there, I still think that somehow we might get up a scare."

Harry laughed.

"Well, you think it over, Bertie. If you can suggest anything, I promise you that Dias and I will do our best to carry it out."

"Very well," Bertie replied gravely, "I will think it over."

"Now," Harry said, "we had better sleep in watches at night; one must be at the breast-work, and one must listen for noises on the cliffs. It would be hardly possible for a number of men to crawl down without exciting suspicion or putting in motion some small stones."

"I do not think, señor," Dias said, "that it will be necessary to keep that watch, for, as we knew from the noise when you fired last night, there are numbers of birds and at least one beast—I fancy it is a bear from the sound of its roar—up there, and it would be strange if a number of men making their way down did not disturb some of them; indeed, if one bird gave the alarm, it would put them all in motion; besides, there are certainly monkeys, for I heard their cries and chattering when the birds flew up. Still, it is perhaps as well that one of us should watch. Shall we divide, as we did last night? only, of course, José takes his place with you."

"I quite agree with you, Dias. Bertie, you had better get three hours' sleep at once, and then after dinner we will sit by the fire here, smoke, and listen, and Dias will watch the gorge and keep one ear open in this direction too. It is a comfort to know that if we cannot get away by going up the stream, the Indians cannot get down to attack us from that direction."

Two nights and days passed. The Indians were still on the hills, and once or twice men came down some distance, but a shot from Harry's rifle sent them speedily back again. The third night Bertie was on watch; he saw nothing, but suddenly there came three sharp taps. He discharged one barrel of his gun at random down the ravine, and then held himself ready to fire the other as soon as he saw anyone approaching. It was an anxious minute for him before the other three ran up.

"What is it, Bertie; have you seen anything?"

"No, but three arrows tapped against the wall, so I fired one barrel to call you up, and have been looking out for someone to take a shot at with the other; but I have not seen anyone, though, as you may imagine, I looked out sharply."

"It is probable that after the lesson they got the other night they did not come so near, and that they merely shot their arrows to see if we were still on guard. However, we may as well stay here for a bit to see if anything comes of it."

Nothing happened, however, and they returned to the tents. Next morning Bertie said to his brother:

"Look here, Harry, I have been thinking over that plan of mine. I really think there is something to be done with it."

"Well, tell us your plan."

"In the first place, how much powder can you spare?"

"There is that great powder-horn José drags about with him to charge his musket with. It will contain about a couple of pounds, I should say."

"That ought to do, I think."

"Well, what is your plan, Bertie?"

"In the first place, do you think that burned wood would do for charcoal?"

"It depends on what purpose you want it for."

"I want it to prevent the powder from going off with a bang."

"Oh, well, I should think that burned wood ground to a powder would be just as good as charcoal. So you are still thinking of rockets? Your two pounds of powder won't make many of them—not above two fair-sized ones, and the betting is they would not go up."

"No, I am not thinking of rockets, but of squibs and crackers. I know when I was at school I made a lot of these, and they worked very well. My idea is that if we could crawl up close to where the Indians are assembled, each carrying a dozen squibs and as many crackers, we could light a lot of the crackers first and chuck them among them, and then send the squibs whirling about over their heads, with a good bang at the end. It would set them off running, and they would never stop till they were back in their own forests."

"Well, I really do think that that is a fine idea—a splendid idea! The only drawback is, that in order to carry it out we should want a lot of strong cartridge-paper, and we have no paper except our note-books."

"I have thought of that, Harry, though it bothered me for a good long time. You see, the cases are only to hold the powder and to burn regularly as the powder does. At first I thought we might find some wood like elder and get the pith out, just as we used to do for pop-guns, but that unfortunately would not burn. We might, however, make them of linen."

"But we have no linen."

"No, but our leather bed-bags are lined with that coarse sort of stuff they cover mattresses with."

"Tick, you mean?"

"Yes, tick. Now, it struck me that this would do for the crackers. We should have to cut it in strips three or four times the width of the cracker. Then we could get Maria to make us some stiff paste; starch would be better, but of course we have none. Then, taking a strip of the cloth, we would turn over one side of it an inch from the edge to make a sort of trough, pour in the gunpowder, carefully paste all the rest of it and fold it over and over, and then, when it begins to dry, double it up and tie it with string. We should then only have to add touch-paper, which, of course, we could make out of anything, and put into the end fold. We could break up a few of the cartridges, soak them in wetted powder, and then cut them up into small pieces and stick them into the ends of the crackers. I think that would do first-rate. I have made dozens of crackers, and feel sure that I could turn out a good lot of them now. The squibs will be easier; we should only have to paste one side of the strips and roll them up so as to form suitable cases. When these are dry we should put a thimbleful of powder into each, and then fill them up with powder and charcoal. In order to make sure of a loud bang we could undo a piece of rope and wind the strands round each case for an inch and a half from the bottom. Of course, when we had ground down the burned wood we would mix it with powder and try one or two of the squibs, so as to find the proportions of charcoal to be used."

"You have evidently thought it all out well, and I think it does you no end of credit. I authorize you to begin the experiment at once. The first thing, of course, will be to get some wood and char it. I should think that you would require at least two pounds of that to two pounds of powder; but you had better only do a little at first—just enough to make an experiment. You know it will require ramming down well."

When Dias, who was on watch, returned he found Bertie at work burning pieces of wood and scraping off the charred surface. Harry explained the plan to him. As he had frequently seen fireworks at Lima, Dias quickly grasped the idea.

"It is splendid, señor; those things will frighten them far more than guns. They will think so many devils have got among them, and we will heighten the effect by discharging every piece that we can among them. In their confusion they will think it is the fireworks that are killing them. That would be necessary, for otherwise when they recovered from the panic and found that no one had been hurt, they might summon up courage to return."

At noon the next day Bertie with assistance had four squibs and two crackers ready for trial. The squibs contained respectively one, two, three, and four parts of charcoal to one of powder.

"Don't hold them in your hand while you are trying the experiment, Bertie. Lay them down on that stone one by one and touch them off with a burning brand from the fire, and take care that you have a good long one."

All, with the exception of José who was on watch, gathered round. The first squib exploded with a bang, the second did the same, but with less violence, the third went off in an explosive spurt, the fourth burned as a squib should do, though a little fiercely, and gave a good bang at the end.

"They go off rather too rapidly, Bertie," Harry said; "we should want them to whiz about in a lively way as long as possible. I should put in five parts of that burned wood next time."

"I will try at once," Bertie said. "I have got lots of cases made, and enough burned stuff to make eight or ten more."

The mixture was soon made and another case charged, Bertie ramming down the mixture with a stick which he had cut to fit exactly, and a heavy stone as a hammer. This was done after each half-spoonful of the mixture was poured in. Then he inserted a strip of his touch-paper.

"I will take this in my hand," he said, "there is no fear of its exploding. I want to throw it into the air and see how it burns there."

The touch-paper was lit, and when the mixture started burning Bertie waved the squib high above his head and threw it into the air. It flew along some fifteen yards and then exploded.

"I don't think you can better that, Bertie. But you might make the cases a bit stronger; it burned out a little too quickly. We shall probably not be able to get very close to them."

The cracker was equally satisfactory, except that they agreed that a somewhat larger charge of powder should be used to increase the noise of the explosion.

"Now, Bertie," Harry said, "we will put all hands on to the business. Donna Maria shall make a good stock of paste, and cut the tick into strips for both widths. You shall make the cases for the squibs. Dias and I will take charge of the manufacture of charcoal. That will be a long job, for as you have two pounds of gunpowder we shall want ten of this charred wood."

"Not quite as much as that, Harry, because we shall want the powder alone for the crackers and the bangs of the squibs, and also for making the touch-paper for all of them."

"Well, we will say ten pounds, anyhow. We have a big stock of cartridges, and can spare a few of them for so good a purpose."

They were soon at work. By night the cases were all made and drying, and were left near the fire so as to be ready for filling in the morning.

Dias then said: "José will go down to-night, señor. Of course I shall go with him. We must find out, in the first place, how near the mouth of the ravine the savages are gathered, whether they keep any watch, and what force they have. It will be well not to make ourselves known to them until at least the greater part are gathered there. If we were only to scare a small party, the others, when they came down, would know nothing of the panic, and might take up the pursuit."

"I wish we had some means of driving them off the top of the hill, Dias."

"I don't see how that can be done, señor. But probably in another day or two they will all go down of their own accord. They must by this time have satisfied themselves that there is no getting at us from above, and that it would be too dangerous to attempt a descent here under the fire of our guns. They will be very likely, instead, to go down to-morrow or next day to hold a general council, and in that case they may decide either to risk climbing down at night, or to make a grand assault on the breast-work. Or, if they cannot bring themselves to that, they may decide to leave half a dozen men to watch the entrance, while the rest scatter themselves over the forests. In that case the watchers would only have to go off and summon them when we started again. As they might well imagine that we should not find another position like this again, I expect that is what they will do. If there are a hundred of them, they will find it difficult to feed themselves long. Certainly the men on the hills will get little to eat up there."

"Well, Dias, be sure you warn José to be careful. They may be posting sentries at the mouth of the ravine, just as they are keeping them at this end."

"They may be, but I do not think it is likely; they will know that we could not abandon our animals, and that if we passed through they would have no difficulty in over-taking us, and would then have us at their mercy. The last thing they would want is to prevent us from leaving this position. They certainly would not fear an attack from us, knowing that there are but four of us and a woman. Therefore, I think it probable that they will keep at some little distance from the entrance, so as to tempt us to come out."

"I hope it is so, Dias. Still, José will have to be very careful."

"He will be careful, señor. He knows his own life will depend upon his crawling along as noiselessly as a snake. If he is seen, of course he will come at all speed back to me; and, unless he is hit by a chance arrow, he will not run much risk, for by the time they are ready to shoot he will be out of sight on such dark nights as these, and in the shade of the mountains and trees. I shall be ready to send four barrels of buck-shot among them when they come up. That is sure to stop them long enough to allow us to get under the cover of your rifles before they can overtake us.

"I don't think that you need be at all uneasy about him, señor. We will start in an hour's time, so that José can get near them before they go to sleep. They will probably have a fire burning, but if not the only guide to their position will be the sound of their talking. He will strip before he leaves me, so that if they catch sight of him, they will suppose that he is one of themselves."

Bertie now relieved José, who came back and had a long talk with Dias.

"We are ready now, señor."

"Here is my fowling-piece. It is already loaded with buck-shot. Bertie has taken down his rifle and gun, and will give you the latter as you pass. I suppose José will take no weapons?"

"Only a long knife, señor, that may be useful if he comes upon one of them suddenly."

At the barricade José stripped, retaining only a pair of sandals. These were as noiseless as his bare feet, and would be needed, as in the dark he might tread upon a thorny creeper, or strike against a projecting rock.

"Good-bye, José!" Harry said. "Now, be careful. It would be a great grief to us if anything happened to you."

"I will be careful, señor. The Indians won't catch me, never fear."

Harry and Bertie both shook hands with him, and then he and Dias stepped into the water, and, keeping close along by the wall of rock, started on their perilous expedition.

"I don't like it, Bert," Harry said as they lost sight of them. "It seems a cowardly thing to let that lad go into danger while we are doing nothing."

"That is just what I feel, Harry. I would have volunteered willingly, but he will do it a great deal better than either you or I could."

"There is no doubt about that," Harry agreed. "Of course when he is out with the mules he often travels at night, and certainly both he and Dias can see in the dark a good deal better than we can."

There was suddenly a slight movement behind them, and they turned sharply round. "It is I, señor. I am anxious about Dias, and I didn't like staying there by myself. I thought you would not mind if I came up and sat by you."

"Certainly not," Harry said. "Sit down and make yourself comfortable. I do not think there is any fear for Dias. He cannot be taken by surprise, for he will hear by their shouting if they discover José, and you may be quite sure that he will bring them to a stand with the four shots he will fire among them as they come near, and so will get a good start. They might run faster than he can in the forest, but will scarcely be better able to make their way up the torrent."

When Dias had been gone twenty minutes their conversation ceased, and they sat listening intently. In another ten minutes, which seemed an hour to them, Harry said, "The savages can keep no watch at their end of the torrent, and José must have got safely away."

Very slowly the time passed.

"They must have been gone an hour," Bertie said at last.

"Quite that, I should think, Bertie. At any rate, we may feel assured that all has gone well so far. For, though we might not hear the yells of the savages over the rustle and roar of the torrent, we should certainly hear gunshots."

Another half-hour passed, and then to their relief they heard Dias call out, "All is well!" some little distance down. In three or four minutes they could see the two figures approaching. "Give me your guns, Dias," Harry said, "and then I will help you up the rocks. They might go off if you were to make a slip. Now, while José is putting on his clothes, tell me what he has found out."

"I have not heard much, señor. As soon as he rejoined me we started off, and, coming up the torrent, we had not much chance of talking. He told me that there were many of them, and that they were camped at some little distance from the stream, just as I thought they would be."

"I will stay here, Harry," Bertie said. "You can hear the news and then come and tell me."

"Very well. I will be back before long."

Dias, his wife, and Harry walked down towards the tent, and Bertie chatted with José while the latter was dressing.

"You must feel horribly cold, José," he said.

"I am cold, now I think of it. I did not notice it while I was watching the savages. When I took to the water again I did feel it. Maria will make me a cup of hot coffee, and then I shall be all right again. It was good fun to look at them, and know that they had no idea that I was so close. If I could have understood their language, I should have learned something worth telling. I felt inclined to scare them by giving a tremendous yell, and I know I could have got away all right. They were sitting round a big fire and would not have been able to see in the dark. I should have done it, only I thought Dias would have blamed me for letting them know that one of us had come down the cañon."

"He would have been angry, José, and so would my brother, for they would certainly have set a watch afterwards, which would have spoilt all our plans. Now run along, your teeth are chattering, and the sooner you get something warm and wrap yourself up in your blankets the better."

The fire had burnt low when the others returned, but an armful of sticks was thrown upon it at once. The kettle had been left in the embers at its edge by Maria when she started, so that after it had hung in the blaze for two or three minutes it began to boil, and coffee was soon ready. At this point José ran in, and after he had drunk a large mugful he told them what he had learned.

"When I left Dias at the mouth of the ravine," he said, "everything seemed quiet. I walked along the edge of the stream for fifty yards, keeping my ears open, you may be sure, and I saw a light glow close under the rocks some distance on the other side of the river. I followed the stream down till I came to a place where there was a quiet pool, and there I swam across, then very carefully I made my way to where I could see the light. It was quite three hundred yards from the river. As I got near I could hear talking; I crawled along like a cat, and took good care not to disturb a leaf, or to put a hand or a knee upon a dried stick, for I could not tell whether they had anyone on watch near the fire. I perceived no one, and at last came to a point where I could see the flame. It was in an opening running a hundred feet into the mountains, and perhaps forty feet across at the mouth.

"In this were sixty or seventy savages sitting or standing round a fire, which had evidently been made there so that anyone coming down to the mouth of the ravine should not see it. The fire was not a very large one, and a good many of the men were gathered outside the little hollow. Some of them were talking loudly, and it seemed to me that they were quarrelling over something. Sometimes they pointed up to the top of the hills, sometimes towards the mouth of our ravine. I would have got close if I had understood their language. Presently I saw some of them lying down, so that I could see that the quarrel, whatever it was about, was coming to an end, and that they were going to lie down for the night. As I could learn nothing further I crawled away and went down to the place where I had swum the river before, and then crept quietly up to Dias, who was on the look-out; for although I had seen no one as I had passed before, there might still have been some of them on the watch."

"You have done very well, José," Harry said. "We have learned two things. First, that they are not keeping watch at the mouth of the ravine, either because they feel sure that we will not try to escape, or because they wish us to leave and are giving us the opportunity of doing so. In the second place, you have learned what force they have got down there, their exact position, and the fact that they were evidently arguing how they had best attack us. Well, from what you say there is every chance that we shall be able to come upon them without being noticed till we are close enough to throw our fireworks among them. Really the only thing for us to learn is whether many of them are still at the top of the hill."

"I hardly think there can be many; only a few have shown themselves to-day. They must know very well that we would not venture to climb up during the day, and that it would be next to impossible for us to do so in the dark, even if we made up our minds to abandon the animals and all our stores."

"Well, I should say, Dias, there is no reason why we should put the matter off. It will not take us long to load all the squibs to-morrow. My opinion is that at dusk we had better saddle the mules and pack everything on them in readiness for a start; then at ten o'clock we can go down and attack the savages. The best moment for doing so will be when they are just lying down. When we have sent them flying we will come up the torrent again, and start with the mules as soon as it is daylight. It would be next to impossible to get them down in the dark, as they might very easily break their legs, or by rubbing against the wall shift their packs and tumble them into the water."

"It would be a pity to waste time, señor. I will get some torches made to-morrow. Some of the trees have resin, and by melting this I can make torches that would do very well. By their aid we could get the mules down without waiting for daylight. As they have already come up the torrent, they will have less fear in going down, for the stream will help them instead of keeping them back. I will go first with José and his mule; she is as steady as a rock, and where she goes the others will follow; and with five torches along the line they will be able to see well enough."

"Four torches, Dias. Your wife rode coming up, and she had better ride going down."

"She can hold a torch as she sits; it does not matter to us if we get wet to the waist, but it would be very uncomfortable for her. We shall have to put the largest burdens on to the mules. One of the riding mules could carry the two llamas, or if you think that that is too much, we can tie each across a separate mule. They were more trouble coming up than all the mules put together. We had pretty nearly to carry them through the deep places, though at other points they leapt from rock to rock cleverly enough."

"I am not going to be left behind if you are going to the fight, señor," Donna Maria said, "if you will give me one of your pistols."

"We could manage that, I should think," Harry said. "We can put you on one of the steadiest mules when we first go down, and with one at each side of you we can manage it very well. José must go on a hundred yards ahead to see whether any of the savages are on the watch at their end, and if so, you must wait till we have cleared them out. You see, we shall have no hesitation in shooting any of them if necessary, and though that would bring the rest of them down on us, yet when our squibs and crackers begin to fly among them, you may be sure they won't face us for an instant."

Dias grumbled that his wife had better stay where she was till they went back for the mules; but Harry said: "I do think, Dias, that she had better go with us. It would be cruel to leave her now that we are going into a fight—leave her all alone to tremble for our lives, with a knowledge that if things should go wrong with us the savages will soon be up here."

"Well, señor, if you think so, there is no more to be said."

"I am not going to be made a trouble of," Maria said. "I shall go down on foot like the rest of you. I will take some other clothes with me, so that when you all come back for the mules I can change into them."

"Perhaps that would be the best plan," Harry agreed. "Now I will go back and take Bertie's place. It is my turn to be on watch, and he will be wanting to hear the news."

"Well, Harry, is it all right?" Bertie asked as he heard his brother coming up to him.

"It couldn't be better! There are sixty or seventy of them in a sort of little ravine three hundred yards away, on the left-hand side of the river. They don't seem to be keeping guard at all, and if they are not more careful to-morrow night we shall take them completely by surprise. We are going to saddle all the mules directly it gets too dark for any of the fellows on the hills to see us, then we must set to work and pull down enough of the barricade here to allow them to pass. We ourselves, when we go down, will cross at that shallow place above here, and go down the river at that side, otherwise we sha'n't be able to cross it except at some distance beyond the other end of the torrent. Of course the mules must go down this side, as we shall want to turn to the right when we get off. We shall make our attack about ten o'clock."

Bertie went off, and three hours later Dias relieved Harry. As soon as it was light the next morning Bertie and José set to work to fill the cases—there were a hundred squibs and fifty large crackers.

Donna Maria after breakfast went out and returned with a number of flexible sticks of about half an inch in diameter; these she carried into her tent, where she shut herself up for the forenoon. When, at one o'clock, she came out with the result of her work, it resembled a chair without legs and with a back about a foot wide and three feet high.

"What in the world have you got there, Donna Maria?" Bertie asked.

"Don't you know?"

"No, I have never seen a thing like it before."

"This is the thing the porters use for carrying weights, and sometimes people, over the Cordilleras. You see that strap near the top goes round the man's forehead, and when there is a weight in the chair these other straps pass over his shoulders and under his arms, and then round whatever is on the seat."

"But what is going to be on the seat?"

"I am," she laughed. "Dias is so overbearing. It had all been arranged nicely, as you know; and then when he spoke to me afterwards he said, 'The first thing to-morrow morning, Maria, you will set to work to make a porter's chair, and I shall carry you down the stream. No words about it, but do as you are told.' Generally Dias lets me have my own way, señor, but when he talks like that, I know that it is useless to argue with him. And perhaps it is best after all, for, as he said to me afterwards, it is a nasty place for men to get along, but for a woman, with her petticoats dragging and trailing round her, it would be almost impossible for her to keep her footing."

"Well, I thought the same thing myself when we were talking about it yesterday," Bertie said. "Of course I did not say anything, but I am sure Dias is right. I found it very hard work to keep my footing, and I really don't believe that I could have done it if I had been dressed as a woman. And Dias can carry you like that?"

"Carry me, señor! he could carry three times that weight. He has cut himself a staff seven or eight feet long this morning to steady himself, but I don't think there was any need for it. Why, it is a common thing for people to be carried over the Cordilleras so, and Dias is stronger a great deal than many of the men who do it. As he said, if I had been going through on foot you would all have been bothering about me. And it is not as if two people could go abreast, and one help the other. There is often only room between the rocks for one to pass through, and it is just there where the rush of the water is strongest."

CHAPTER IX — THE SIGNAL STAR

During the afternoon Dias, who had been keeping a careful look-out at the cliffs, said to Harry: "I think, señor, that the savages are leaving the hills. An hour ago I saw a man walking along where we generally see them; he was going straight along as if for some fixed purpose, and I thought at once that he might be bringing them some message from the people below us. I lost sight of him after a bit, but presently I could make out some men moving in the other direction. They were keeping back from the edge, but I several times caught sight of their heads against the sky-line when there happened to be some little irregularity in the ground. They were not running, but seemed to me to be going at a steady pace. Since then I have been watching carefully, and have seen no one on the other side. I think they have all been sent for, and will be assembled this afternoon at the mouth of the torrent."

"I am very glad to hear it, Dias; that is just what we wanted."

"In one way—yes," Dias said. "It would be a great thing for us to catch them all together, for I have no fear that they will stand when these fireworks begin to go off among them."

"What is the drawback, then?"

"It is, señor, that they have either been collected because they have given up the hope of catching us at present, and are going to scatter and hunt till we venture out, which would be the worst thing possible; or they have made up their minds to make a rush upon us."

"Don't you think that we can beat them back?"

"Not if they are determined, señor. You see, we can't make them out till they are within twenty or thirty yards of us. At most you and your brother could fire four shots, then you would take up your rifles. We shall have then only four shots left. If they continue their rush where shall we be? There would be two of us on one wall and two on the other. There would be four shots to fire from one side and four from the other. Then the end would come. Two on each side would not be able to keep back the rush of two or three score. In two minutes it would be all over."

"Yes, Dias, I see that if they were determined to storm the place and take us alive they could do it; but we have the fireworks."

"I did not think of that. Yes; but having once worked themselves up and being mad with excitement, even that might not stop them, though I should think it would. Yes, I believe we might feel assured that we should beat them back, and if so, we should hear no more of them."

"If I knew that they would come," Harry said, "I would certainly say we had best stay and defend ourselves; but we can't be sure that that is their motive for assembling. They may, as you say, be going to move off, leaving perhaps half a dozen men to watch the entrance and report if we attempt to escape. That would be fatal, and our only chance would be to leave everything behind and endeavour to climb up one side or the other; and even that might not avail us, as there may be one or two men up there to see if we make off that way. I am more inclined to think that this is the course that they will take rather than risk a heavy loss of life. They must have a good idea of what it would cost them to take the place."

"What do you think we had better do, then, señor?"

"I think we had better attack them as soon as possible after nightfall. It is likely that they will do nothing before morning; as you say, they do not like moving at night, and if they attack it will not be until shortly before daybreak. There is sure to be a palaver when the men who have been on the hills come down. It will be too late then for them to go back before night, so that I think we are pretty sure to find them all in the ravine this evening. If, when we get there, we find the place empty, we must come to a decision as to what our best course will be. In that case I think we ought to climb the hills and make our way up the mountains as rapidly as possible. We could calculate on eight or ten hours' start, and by keeping as much as possible on the rocks, might hope to get so high among the mountains that they would not be able to follow our traces and overtake us before we reach a point where they would not dare follow us. In that case, of course we should have to give up all hope of finding the gold valley, and lose the mules with all our belongings, which would cripple us terribly."

"Very well, señor; I think that is the best plan."

"Then we will settle to start at nine o'clock, Dias."

They then discussed the arrangements for the attack. Each was to carry a glowing brand, and when he got there, was to sling his gun behind him and hold twelve squibs in one hand and the brand in the other. When they approached within throwing distance of the savages, they were to lay their guns down beside them, and then Harry was to put the ends of his squibs against his brand, and hurl the whole of them among the Indians. A few seconds later Bertie was to do the same, while Harry fired one barrel of buck-shot. Bertie was to fire as Dias threw a dozen crackers, and then José was to throw his squibs. Then all were to throw squibs and crackers as far as they could go; and the other two barrels of buck-shot and José's musket were to be poured in. By this time they calculated the savages would be in full flight, and the three rifles could then be used.

Harry was to hand his rifle to Dias before the firing began, and he and Bertie were to slip fresh cartridges into these guns and recap them before sending off the last batch of their fireworks, so as to have them in readiness either to empty their contents into the flying Indians, or to cover their retreat should the fireworks fail to effect the panic they hoped for. Their pistols were also to be reserved until the Indians fled. Donna Maria was to stay by the water, and start at once on her way back if Dias shouted to her to do so. Every step of the plan settled upon was repeated again and again, until there was no possibility of any mistake being made. Maria had not attended the council; her confidence in her two white friends was unbounded, and Bertie's invention of the fireworks had placed him on a level with his brother in her estimation. She therefore quietly went on with her preparations for dinner without concerning herself as to the details of the affair.

As soon as it was dark and the meal eaten, the tents were struck, the baggage all rolled up and packed on the animals, and the fireworks divided. When everything was in readiness they went together and made a breach in the breast-work wide enough for the mules to pass. At nine o'clock Maria was seated in the carrying-chair, and strapped on to her husband's back; then four brands were taken from the fire and the party started. When within fifty yards of the lower end of the ravine José went forward, and, returning in a few minutes, reported that no savages were on guard. A fire was burning outside the mouth of the ravine where he had seen them on the evening before, and from the reflection on the rock he believed that another fire was alight inside. His report caused a general feeling of relief, for their great fear had been that the natives might have made off before their arrival.

When they stepped out from the water Dias set Maria down. "You understand, Maria," he said: "the moment I call, you are to start up the river."

"I understand," she said. "I have my knife, and if you do not rejoin me I shall know how to use it."

"We shall rejoin you, Maria," Dias said confidently. "I believe that at the first volley of fireworks they will be off. They must be more than human if they are not scared, as they never can have heard of such things before."

Keeping close to the rock wall, they went along in single file until within forty or fifty yards of the fire; then, going down on their hands and knees, they crawled up a slight rise, from the top of which they could see a hundred or more natives gathered round a fire. One was addressing the others, who were seated listening attentively. Laying the guns down to be ready for instant action, and keeping themselves concealed in the herbage, Harry took his bundle of squibs from his pocket. They were but lightly tied together; slipping off the string he applied the ends to the brand. There was a sudden roar of fire, and waving them once round his head he hurled them into the midst of the assembly. There was a yell of astonishment as the missiles flew hither and thither, exploding with loud reports. The last had not exploded when Bertie's handful flew among them; then came the parcel from Dias, and at the same moment Harry poured a barrel of buck-shot among them, followed by a volley of crackers, while almost simultaneously Harry threw his squibs and Bertie fired a volley of buck-shot. For a moment the savages were paralysed, then many of them threw themselves on their faces in terror of these fiery demons, while others started in headlong flight.

"Send them off as quick as you can!" Harry shouted, as he discharged his second barrel into the flying natives. Bertie followed suit, and then both paused to reload while Dias and José hurled their remaining fireworks. By this time the last of the natives had leapt up and fled. José's musket and the three rifles cracked out, and then the little party rose to their feet and joined in a wild "Hip, hip, hurrah!"

"You can come up, Maria; they have all gone!" Dias cried out; and Maria joined them a minute later. More than a score of natives lay dead or badly wounded round their fire.

"What are we to do with the wounded?" Bertie asked.

"We can only leave them where they are," Harry said. "Some of the savages may have wandered away, or not have come down from the hills, and will return here unaware of what has happened, or one or two of the boldest may venture back again to look after their comrades. At any rate, we can do nothing for them."

"It would be better to shoot them, señor," Dias said.

"No, I could not bring myself to do that," Harry said. "Buck-shot, unless they strike in a body, are not likely to kill. I expect they are more frightened than hurt. After we have gone many of them will be able to crawl down to the river. Savages frequently recover from wounds that would kill white men; and even if no others come down, those who are but slightly wounded will help the more incapable. We have cleared the way for ourselves, which was all we wanted, and have taught them a lesson they are not likely to forget for many years to come. Let us go back at once and bring down the mules. I suppose you will sit down by the stream, and wait till we come back, Maria?"

"Yes," she said, "there is nothing to be afraid of now; but you can leave me one of your pistols in case one of these savages may be shamming dead."

"José will wait with her," Dias said. "Now, José, you strike up a song. You are generally at it, and as long as they hear you they will know that some of us are still here, and will not venture to move."

"You take my gun, José; it is loaded," Harry said. "If any of them should move and try to crawl away, don't fire at them; but if they look about and seem inclined to make mischief, shoot at once."

Coming down with the animals the three men carried torches in each hand. The mules reached the mouth of the torrent without accident, and the llamas were then lifted off the baggage mules which had carried them, and all were turned loose to graze on the rich grass near the edge of the river. José and Dias went to the fire in the ravine, and returned laden with burning brands, and a fire was soon blazing near the water. Two of them kept watch by turns at the spot from which they had fired, lest any of the wounded Indians should, on recovering, try to avenge their loss by sending arrows down amongst the party. During the night four of the fallen Indians, after first looking round cautiously, crawled away, and the watchers could hear them running fast through the bushes till they were beyond the light of the fire.

At dawn a start was made. The river was crossed at the pool where José had swum over. Dias, on examination, found that the water, even in the deepest part, was not more than breast-high. Accordingly he returned; Maria, kneeling on one of his shoulders and one of Harry's, was carried across without being wetted. Then they joined the animals, which were grazing a short distance away, and set off without delay. Although they kept a sharp look-out they saw no more of the Indians. They ascended several more streams unobserved. Rough carvings on the face of several of the rocks led them to carry their excursions farther than usual, but beyond a few ounces of gold, washed from the stream, they found nothing.

"They must have been put here for some purpose," said Dias.

"I have been thinking it over, Dias, and I should not be surprised if, as you thought, they were done to deceive searchers. You told me there were some marks by which you would be directed in the gold valley; it is quite likely that other marks might have been placed in the valleys so that the real ones would not be particularly noticed."

"That is possible, señor; they would certainly do everything they could to prevent anyone not in the secret from knowing. The mark I have to look for first is a serpent. It is carved on a rock at the end of a valley."

"In that case the indication of the star would not be necessary, Dias."

"That may be, señor; but the valley may be a large one, and the hiding-place very difficult to find, so that even when the valley was known, it would need the guidance of the star to take us to the right place."

"That might be so, Dias, if it were a hidden treasure that we were looking for; but as, according to your account, it is simply an extraordinarily rich deposit in the river, I hardly see why the guidance of the star should be necessary when once the valley was known."

"That I cannot tell you, señor; but I am sure that it must be difficult to find, for the Spaniards searched everywhere for gold, and although the records of most of their discoveries still exist, there is no mention of such a find, nor is there is any word of it among the Indian traditions."

A week before the appointed date they found themselves in the neighbourhood where they felt sure the cleft must lie. Mount Tinta was twenty miles in front of them, and from that point a range of mountains trended off almost at right angles to that which they were following. One lofty peak some thirty miles to the south-east rose above another.

"I believe that that is the peak," Dias said.

"I don't see any signs of a cleft in it, Dias."

"No, señor; it is a very narrow one."

The next day they halted at the mouth of another valley, and as they unloaded the mules, Harry exclaimed: "See, Dias, there is a cleft in that peak! From here it looks as if it were a mere thread, and as if some giant had struck a mighty sword-cut into it."

"That is right. Sure enough, señor, this must be the valley. Now, let us look about for the serpent."

The search did not take them long. An isolated rock rose a quarter of a mile from the mouth, and on this was a rude representation of a serpent. The next morning they explored the valley thoroughly to a point where, five miles higher, it ceased abruptly, the rocks closing in on either side, and the stream coming down in a perpendicular fall from a point some eighty feet above them. Going down the river, they washed the gravel again and again, but without obtaining even as much gold as they had found several times before.

"I cannot understand it," Harry said, as they sat down to their meal at dusk. "Your tradition says nothing about hidden treasure, and yet there does not seem to be gold in the stream."

"It may be higher up, señor. We must ascend the hills on each side of the valley, and come down upon the river higher up."

Harry was on watch that night, and at one o'clock he roused the others up. "See!" he exclaimed later on; "there is a bright star apparently about a foot above the peak. I should think that must be the star. No doubt that will rise in exact line behind the cleft on the 21st, that is four days from now; probably it can only be seen when we are exactly in the line with the cleft and the position of the gold. This cleft is undoubtedly very narrow—no doubt the result of an earthquake. It certainly goes straight through, and very likely it is some hundred yards across, so that unless we are exactly in the line we sha'n't see it. As soon as it is dark on the 21st we will all go some distance up the valley, where it is only about four or five hundred yards across. We will station ourselves fifty yards apart across it, then one of us is sure to see the star through the cleft. We had each better take two sticks with us. Whoever sees the star will fix one in the ground and then go backwards for a hundred yards, keeping the star in sight, and plant the other; then the line between those two sticks ought to lead us to the spot."

Each night the star rose nearer to the cleft. "There is no doubt we shall see it in the proper position to-morrow night," Harry said on the 20th of the month. "That certainly is strong proof that the tradition handed down to you, Dias, is correct."

They employed the next day in again searching for some indication that might assist them, but in vain. Dias and José both asserted that the tiny rift in the rocky peak looked wider from the middle of the valley than at any other point, and even Harry and his brother admitted that it could scarcely be seen from the foot of the hills on either side, and therefore it was agreed that Dias, Harry, and José should take their places only some forty yards apart across the centre; Maria and Bertie going farther, near the sides of the hills. When midnight approached they took their stations. Suddenly Harry, who was standing by the side of the rivulet, exclaimed, "I see it!" It was more than a minute later before Dias saw it, while it was three or four minutes before José spoke, by which time Harry had crossed the streamlet and fixed his second rod some distance on the other side. Dias and José did the same. Bertie did not catch sight of it for some time after José, and Maria did not see it at all. Then they went back to their camping place.

"It is curious that I should have seen it before either of you, when you were standing so close to me," Harry said. "It was lower than I expected, and it is evident that the cleft must continue much farther down than we thought, and that it must be extremely narrow at the bottom. It is certainly a splendid guide, and there can be no mistaking it. Unless I had been standing on the exact line, I should not have noticed the star till later, and the crack is so much wider towards the top that it could probably be seen on a line half a mile across. It will be strange if we cannot find the place in the morning. Certainly we searched in the stream just where I was standing, and found nothing. But, of course, it is possible that in all this time it may have changed its course considerably."

Dias shook his head. "It can hardly be that, señor, because, in that case, anyone who had examined the valley could have found it. I begin to think that it must have been a mistake about its being merely a rich place in the river, and that it must be some vast treasure, perhaps hidden by the people before the Incas, and kept by them as a certain resource when needed. We shall have to search, I think, for some walled-up cave in the rocks. We have already looked for it, but not seriously; and besides, there are many boulders that have fallen, and formed a bank at the foot of the cliff."

"Well, we shall know in a few hours. I feel absolutely certain that the line between those two sticks will lead us to it."

None attempted to sleep, and as soon as it became light they took picks and shovels and started up the valley. Harry gave an exclamation of surprise as, standing behind the first stick, he looked towards the second. "The line goes to the middle of that waterfall," he said.

This was so; for the stream made two or three sharp bends between the spot where he had crossed it and the foot of the falls.

"'Tis strange!" Dias said; "we have examined that spot more than once. There are great stones and boulders at the foot of the fall, and a large deep pool. Can a treasure be buried in that? If so, it will be hard indeed to get it."

Harry did not reply; his face was white with excitement. He walked forward slowly till he reached the edge of the pool. It was some fifteen yards across, and the colour of the water showed that it was very deep.

"I will dive, Harry," Bertie said; "I have gone down more than once in five fathoms of water to pick up an egg that has been thrown overboard." He stripped and swam out to the middle of the pool and dived. He was down about a minute, and on coming up swam to the shore. "I could find no bottom, Harry," he panted. "I am sure I must have gone down seven fathoms."

"Thank you, Bertie," Harry said quietly; "we will make up our minds that if it is there, we sha'n't get it at present. The foot of the valley is so flat that it would need a cut at least a mile long to let the water off, and we should therefore require either an army of men or a regular diving apparatus, which there would be no getting this side of England. However, it may not be there. Let us search now behind the fall."

There were some four or five feet clear between the sheet of water and the rock. At times, as Harry pointed out, there would be an even wider space, for the weather had been dry for the past two months, and the quantity of water coming down was but small, while in the wet season a mighty flood would shoot far out from the rock. The width of the stream in the wet season was shown by the broad bed of what was now but a rivulet. Looking upwards as they stood, the wall actually overhung them, and they could see the edge where the water poured over unbroken.

"There may be a cave here," Harry went on, "and it may be covered by these rocks piled up for the purpose. On the other hand, they may have fallen. I think that is the most likely explanation, for as the top projects beyond the bottom it is possible that some time or other there was a big fall."

They searched every foot of the rock within reach, but there were no signs of any man's handiwork. The rock was solid, thickly covered with dripping moss and ferns which had flourished in the mist and spray that rose from the foot of the fall. This they had ruthlessly scraped off with their picks. Silently they went out again at the end, and stood hopelessly looking at the fall. It was some time before Harry said, "We must move some of those stones now. Let us go at once and cut down some young trees, for we can do nothing with our hands alone, but must use levers. For that purpose we shall want straight wood, and strong. We had better get half a dozen, in case some of them break; make them about ten feet long, and from four to six inches thick, and sharpened slightly at the lower end."

In an hour the levers were ready.

"We had better breakfast before we begin, Dias. Your wife went off to prepare it when we came out from the waterfall. I dare say it is ready by this time."

In half an hour they were back again. They chose the central spot behind the fall, and then set to work. Some of the rocks were dislodged without much difficulty, but to move others, it was necessary to first get out the smaller ones, on which they rested. So they toiled on, stopping for half an hour in the middle of the day for food, and then renewing their work. By evening they had made an opening four or five feet wide at the top, and six feet deep, close to the wall. It was now getting dark, and all were fagged and weary with their work, the light was fading, and they were glad to return to camp. Maria came out to meet them. She asked no questions, but said cheerfully, "I have a good olla ready, I am sure you must want it."

"I feel almost too tired to eat," Bertie said.

"You will feel better when you have had some coffee. I have fed the mules, José, and taken them down to water."

"I think," Bertie said, when they had finished their meal, "that we might splice the main brace."

"I do think we might," Harry laughed. "We have not opened a bottle since we started, and certainly we have worked like niggers since seven o'clock this morning. I will open the case; it is screwed down, and I have a screwdriver in the handle of my knife;" and he rose to his feet.

"What does Don Bertie want?" Dias said. "I will get it, señor. I do not understand what he said."

"It is a sea expression, Dias. After a hard day's work the captain orders that the main brace shall be spliced, which means that the crew shall have a glass of grog—that is, a glass of spirits and water—to cheer and warm them after their exertions. José, will you bring a blazing brand with you? I shall want it to see the screws."

In a few minutes he returned.

"This is brandy, Dias. I don't suppose you have ever tasted a glass of good brandy. Is your kettle boiling still, señora? We shall want hot water, sugar, and five of the tin mugs. Have you any of those limes we picked the other day?"

"Yes, señor."

"That is good. Just a slice each will be an improvement." Harry mixed four mugs, and a half one for Maria. "There, Dias!" he said. "You will allow that that is a considerable improvement on pulque."

He and his brother had already lighted their pipes. The other three had made cigarettes. Dias and José were loud in their commendations of the new beverage. Donna Maria had at first protested that she never touched pulque, and this must be the same sort of thing. However, after sipping daintily, she finished her portion with evident satisfaction. They did not sit up long, and as soon as they had finished their first smoke all retired to bed, leaving for once the llamas and mules to act as sentries. As soon as it was fairly daylight, they drank a cup of coffee and started again to work. Harry went first into the hole they had made, and, kneeling down, struck a match to enable him to see the rock more thoroughly. He gave a slight exclamation, then said: "Open your knife, Bertie, and come in here and strike another match. I want both my hands."

"I have a torch here, señor,"

"That is best; then light it, Bertie."

There was just room at the bottom for Bertie to stand by the side of his brother, who was lying down.

"Hold the torches as low as you can, Bertie."

Harry picked away with the point of his knife for a minute or two and then sat up.

"That is the top of a cave," he said. "Do you see, this crack along here is a straight one. That, I fancy, was the top of the entrance to the cave. That stone under it has a rough face, but on the top and sides it is straight. It is fitted in with cement, or something of that sort, and is soft for some distance in, and then becomes quite hard. I can just see that there are two stones underneath, also regularly cut."

He made room for Bertie to lie down, and held the torch for him. "I think you are right, Harry. Those three stones would never fit together so closely if they had not been cut by hand, though, looking at the face, no one could tell them from the rock above them."

Dias next examined the stones.

"There is no doubt that that is the entrance to a cave, señor," he said as he joined them; and the three went out beyond the fall, for the noise of the water was too great for them to converse without difficulty behind the veil of water. José stayed behind to examine.

"Well, Dias, we have found the place where the treasure is hidden, but I don't think that we are much nearer. Certainly we have not strength sufficient to clear away those fallen stones, and probably the cave is blocked by a wall several feet thick. We should want tools and blasting-powder to get through it. No doubt it is a natural cave, and it seems to me probable that they altered the course of the stream above, so that it should fall directly over the entrance. I think before we talk further about it we will go up there and take a look at it. If we find that the course has been changed that will settle the matter."

It took them an hour to climb the hill and make their way down to the gorge through which the river ran. They examined it carefully.

"It must always have come along here," Dias said. "There is no other possible channel; but there are marks of tools on the rocks on each side of the fall, and the water goes over so regularly that I think the rock must have been cut away at the bottom."

"It certainly looks like it, Dias. The rocks widen out too, so that however strong the rush of water may be it will always go over in a regular sheet. Let us follow it along a little way."

Fifty yards farther on, the gorge widened out suddenly, and they paused with an exclamation of astonishment. Before them was a wide valley, filled to the spot where they were standing with a placid sheet of water four or five hundred yards wide, and extending to another gorge fully a mile away. Bertie was the first to find his voice.

"Here's a go! Who would have thought of finding a lake up in the hills here?"

"I did not know there was one," Dias said. "I have never heard of it. But that is not strange, for no one who came up the valley would dream that there was anything beyond that fall."

Harry had sat down and thought for some minutes, looking over the lake without speaking.

"I am afraid, Dias," he said at last, "that your tradition was a true one after all, and that the gold lay in the bed of a stream in the valley we now see filled up."

"But it must always have been a lake, señor," Dias said after thinking for a minute, "and could not have been shallower, for there is no other escape than the waterfall; and however heavy the rains it could not have risen higher, except a few feet, as one can see by the face of the rock."

"It may have had some other way out," Harry said.

Dias looked carefully round the side of the valley. "There is no break in the hills that I can see, señor."

"No; but my firm conviction is that the top of that cave that we found behind the fall is really the top of a natural tunnel through which the stream originally flowed. There are two or three reasons for this. In the first place, it is certainly remarkable that there should be a cave immediately behind that fall. I thought at first that the stream above might have been diverted to hide it, but the ravine is so narrow that that could not be possible. In the next place, your tradition has proved absolutely true in the matter of the star, and in the hour of its appearance in the exact line to the mouth of that cave. How correctly the details have been handed down from generation to generation! If they are right on that point it is hardly likely that they can be inaccurate on other points, and that the tale of an extraordinarily rich treasure could have been converted into one of an exceptional deposit of gold in the bed of a river.

"I think that the passage was probably closed by the old people when they were first threatened by the invasion of the Incas. No doubt they would choose a season when the stream was almost dry. They had, as the remains of their vast buildings will show, an unlimited supply of labour. They would first partially block up the tunnel, perhaps for the first fifty yards in, leaving only a small passage for the water to run through. They might then close the farther end with sacks of sand, and having the other stones all cut, and any number of hands, build it up behind the sacks, and then go on with the work till it was solid; then no doubt they would heap stones and boulders against the face of the wall. By the time the Incas had conquered the country the valley would be a lake many feet deep. The Incas, having gained an abundant supply of treasure elsewhere, would take no steps towards opening the tunnel, which in any case would have been a terrible business, for the pressure of water would drive everything before it. Having plenty of slave labour at their disposal, they knew that it could be done at any time in case of great necessity, when the loss of the lives of those concerned in it would be nothing to them. When the valley became full the water began to pour out through this gap, which perhaps happened to be immediately over the mouth of the tunnel, or it may have been altered by a few yards to suit, for they were, as we know from some of their buildings, such good workmen that they could fit slabs of the hardest stone so perfectly together that it is hardly possible to see the joints. Therefore they would only have to widen the mouth of the gorge a little, and fit rocks in on either side so that they would seem to have been there for all time; and indeed the natural growth of ferns and mosses would soon hide the joints, even if they had been roughly done."

"And that all means, Harry—?" Bertie asked.

"That all means that we have no more chance of getting at the gold than if it were lying in the deepest soundings in the Pacific."

Bertie sat down with a gasp.

"There is no way of getting that water out," Harry went on quietly, "except by either cutting a channel here as deep as the bottom of the lake, or by blasting the stone in the tunnel. The one would require years of work, with two or three hundred experienced miners, and ten times as many labourers. The other would need twenty or thirty miners, and a hundred or two labourers. There is possibly another way; but as that would require an immense iron siphon going down to the bottom of the lake, along one side of this ravine, and down into the bottom of the pool, with a powerful engine to exhaust the air in the first place and set it going, it is as impracticable, as far as we are concerned, as the other two.

"In the same way I have no doubt that, with a thousand-horse-power engine, the lake could be pumped dry in time; but to transport the plant for such an engine and its boiler across the mountains would be an enormous undertaking; and even were it here, and put up and going, the difficulty of supplying it with fuel would be enormous. Certainly one could not get up a company with capital enough to carry out any one of the schemes merely on the strength of an Indian tradition; and with the uncertainty, even if they believed the tradition, whether the amount of gold recovered would be sufficient to repay the cost incurred.

"Well, we may as well go down to dinner."

He shouldered his pick and led the way back. Scarce a word was spoken on the way. Bertie tried to follow the example of his brother, and take the matter coolly. Dias walked with his head down and the air of a criminal going to execution. The disappointment to him was terrible. He had all along felt so confident that they should be successful, and that he should be enabled to enrich those he considered as the preservers of his life, that he was utterly broken down with the total failure of his hopes.

CHAPTER X — A FRESH START

Not until he got to the camp did Harry look round. When he caught a glimpse of the guide's face he went up to him and held out his hand.

"You must not take it to heart, Dias; it has been unfortunate, but that cannot be helped. You have done everything you could in the matter, and brought us to the right spot, and no one could tell that when we got within half a mile of the gold river we should find the valley turned into a deep lake. We can only say, 'Better luck next time'. We would say in England, 'There are as good fish in the sea as ever came out of it'. I have never felt very sanguine myself about this; it has all along seemed too good to be true. Of course we are disappointed, but we may have better luck next time."

"But I don't know, señor, with certainty of any other place. No one was ever entrusted with more than one secret, so that if the Spanish tortures wrung it out of him two treasures would not be lost."

"We need not talk any more about this place, Dias. I see your wife has got some of the fish that we caught yesterday fizzling on the fire. Now I think of it, I am very hungry, for it is six hours since we had our coffee this morning. After we have had our meal we can discuss what our next move had better be."

While they were speaking, José had been rapidly telling Maria the misfortune which had befallen them, and the tears were running down the woman's cheeks.

"You must not feel so badly about it, Maria," Harry said cheerfully; "you see my brother and I are quite cheerful. At any rate, no one is to blame. It would have been an enormous piece of luck if we had succeeded, but we never looked on it as a certainty. Anything might have happened between the time the gold was shut up and now, though we certainly never expected to find what we did. We only thought it possible that we might have the luck to find the treasure. Now you had better look to those fish, or we shall lose our breakfast as we have lost our gold, and this time by our own fault. We are as hungry as hunters all of us; and in fact we are hunters, although we have not brought any game with us this time."

The woman wiped away her tears hastily, and, taking off the fish which she had put on when they were coming down the hill, she laid them on plates with some freshly-baked cakes. The fish were excellent, and Bertie, as they ate, made several jokes which set them all laughing, so that the meal passed off cheerfully.

"Now for the great consoler," Harry said, as he took out his pipe. "When we have all lighted up, the council shall begin. Never mind clearing away the plates now, Maria; just sit down with us, there is wisdom in many counsellors. Now, Dias, what do you think is the best course for us to adopt at present?"

"Unless you wish to stay here and make further search?"

"By no means, Dias," Harry said; "for the present, I have seen enough of this side of the mountains. We will get back to Cuzco and make a fresh start from there."

"In that case, señor, there is no doubt as to the best route. There is a pass over the mountains just on the other side of Mount Tinta; it leads to the town of Ayapata, which lies somewhere at the foot of that peak. I have never been there, but I know its situation. It is a very steep pass, but as it is used for mule traffic it cannot be very bad. Once we have passed over it on to the plateau we shall not be more than seventy or eighty miles from Cuzco."

"That is quite satisfactory. We will set off to-morrow."

"We had better catch some more fish, for we have had no time for hunting lately," Maria said. "The meat we ate yesterday was the last we had with us. If we cut the fish open and lay them flat on the rocks, which are so hot one can scarcely hold one's hand on them, they will be sufficiently dry by sunset to keep for two or three days, and before that you are sure to shoot something."

The river was full of fish, and in half an hour they had caught an abundance, having fifteen averaging eight pounds apiece. These were at once cut open, cleaned, and laid down to dry.

"The fishing on this river would let for a handsome sum in England," Harry laughed; "and I think the fish are quite as good as trout of the same size. The only objection is that they are so tame, and take the bait so greedily, that, good as the stream is, they would soon be exterminated."

That evening there was a slight stir among the animals which had just lain down. José leapt up and walked towards them.

"There is something the matter, Dias," he cried; "the llamas are standing up with their ears forward. They see or hear something."

"It may be pumas or jaguars," Dias said. "Take your gun, señor."

He picked up his rifle, and Harry and Bertie followed suit, and further armed themselves with their shot-guns.

"You had best come with us, Maria," her husband said. "There is no saying where the beasts may be. See! the mules are standing up now and pulling at their head-ropes. Let us go among them, señors, our presence will pacify them."

They all moved towards the mules, which were standing huddled together. Dias and José spoke to them and patted them.

"You stand at their heads, Maria," the former said, "and keep on talking to them. We must see if we can discover the beasts. There is one of them!" he exclaimed, but in a low tone. "Do you see the two bright points of light? That is the reflection of the fire in his eyes."

"Shall I fire?"

"No, señor, not yet. If we were only to wound him he would charge us; let us wait till he gets closer. Probably there are two of them, male and female, they generally go about in pairs."

Even as he spoke the seeming sparks disappeared.

"He has moved," Dias said; "he will probably walk round us two or three times before he makes up his mind to attack."

"If he would go near the fire we could get a fair shot at him, Dias."

"He won't do that, señor; he will most likely go backwards and forwards in a semicircle, getting perhaps a little closer each time."

Ten minutes passed and then Maria said:

"There are two of them. I can see their outlines distinctly."

"Do you think, if we were to fire a gun, they would move off, Dias?"

"They might for a time, señor, but the probability is that they would come back again. They have smelt the mules, and are probably hungry. It is better to let them attack us at once and have done with it."

A minute or two later there was a snarling growl.

"They are jaguars," Dias said.

Again and again the threatening sound was heard, and in spite of Maria's efforts the mules were almost mad with fright.

"We had better lie down beyond them," Dias said. "There is no doubt the beasts will come from that side. If we posted ourselves behind them the mules might break loose and knock us over just as we were taking aim."

They lay down side by side on the grass with their rifles at their shoulders.

"I can see them now, Dias," Harry whispered, "not more than fifty yards away. I think we could hardly miss them now."

"You could not if it were daylight, señor; but in the dark, when you can't see the end of your rifle, you can never be certain about shooting."

The beasts had now apparently made up their minds to attack. They crouched low, almost dragging their bellies on the ground, and one was somewhat in advance of the other.

"That is the male ahead," Dias whispered. "Do you and your brother take aim. I will take the female, and José will hold his fire of buck-shot till she is within a length of us."

"How shall I know when it is going to spring?"

"When it stops, señor. It is sure to stop before it springs."

"Aim between the eyes, Bertie, and fire when I do," Harry whispered to his brother, who was lying next to him.

When within twelve yards the jaguar halted.

"Now!" Harry said, and they discharged their rifles at the same moment, and, dropping them, grasped the shot-guns.

The jaguar fell over on one side, clawing the air, and then recovered himself. As he did so two charges of buck-shot struck him on the head, and he rolled over and remained motionless.

Dias had fired at the same moment, but he had not stopped the second jaguar. José, instead of waiting, hastily discharged his gun, and in another instant a dark body bounded over their heads on to the back of one of the mules, which it struck to the ground.

Harry and Bertie leapt to their feet, and discharged their second barrels into the jaguar's body. It turned suddenly round and attempted to spring, but its hindquarters were paralysed; and Bertie, pulling out his pistol, fired both barrels into its head. The brute at once fell over dead, and the lad gave a shout of triumph.

"Thank goodness that is over without accident!" Harry said. "They are formidable beasts, Dias."

"In the daytime, when one can see to aim, they can be killed easily enough, señor; at night their presence is to be dreaded."

"I am afraid we have lost a mule."

"I think not, señor. He was knocked down by the shock, but he had his saddle on, and the brute had no time to carry him off."

The mule rose to its feet as they spoke; José ran and brought a flaming brand from the fire. Blood was streaming from both the animal's shoulders.

"It stuck its claws in, señor, but has not made long gashes. I should say that these wounds were caused by the contraction of the claws when you finished her with your pistol. The animal will be all right in a day or two; and as our stores have diminished, we need not put any load on it for a time."

"I hope you were not frightened, Maria?" Bertie said

A MIDNIGHT SURPRISE

"I was a little frightened," she said, "when the mule came tumbling down close to me, and I could see the jaguar's eyes within a few yards of me, but I had my dagger ready."

"It would not have been much good," Dias said, "if the beast had attacked you."

"I think you showed no end of pluck," Bertie said. "If he had come close to me, and I had got nothing but that little dagger in my hand, I should have bolted like a shot."

"I am sure that you would not, señor," she said. "You are a great deal too brave for that."

Bertie laughed.

"It is all very well to be brave with a rifle in your hand and another gun ready, to say nothing of the pistols. By the way, I thought Harry had given you one of his?

"So he did, but I had forgotten all about it. If I had thought of it I should have used it."

"It is just as well that you did not," Harry said. "If you had done so, the brute would have made for you instead of turning round to attack us."

"Now, señor," Dias put in, "we had better drag the jaguars away; the mules will never get quiet with the bodies so close to them."

It needed all his strength and that of his companions to drag each of the bodies fifty yards away.

"Now, José," Dias said when they returned, "you had better give the animals a feed of maize all round. They will settle down after that. I shall keep watch to-night, señor. It is not likely that any more of these beasts are in the neighbourhood; but it is as well to be careful, and I don't think any of us would sleep if someone were not on the look-out."

"I will relieve you at two o'clock," Harry said.

"No, señor, I have not been on the watch for the past two nights. I would rather sit up by the fire to-night."

Two days later they arrived at the foot of the pass. Just as they gained it they met two muleteers coming down it. Dias entered into conversation with them, while the others erected tents, preparing to camp.

"What is the news, Dias?" Harry asked as he returned.

"The men say, señor, that the pass is very unsafe. Many robberies have taken place in it, and several men, who endeavoured to defend themselves against the brigands, have been killed. They were questioned by four armed men as they came down, and the goods they were carrying down to Ayapata were taken from them. They say that traffic has almost ceased on the road."

"That is bad, Dias."

"Very bad, señor. We need not be afraid of brigands if they meet us as we travel along the foot of the hills, but it would be another thing in the passes. There are many places where the mules would have to go in single file, and if we were caught in such a spot by men on the heights, we might be shot down without any chance of defending ourselves successfully."

"That is awkward, Dias. It is a scandal that these brigands are not rooted out."

"People are thinking too much of fighting each other or their neighbours to care anything about the complaints of a few muleteers, señor."

"Is there no other way of crossing the mountains than by this pass?"

"There is a pass, señor, between Ayapata and Crucero, but it is a very bad one."

"And where should we be then, Dias?"

"Well, señor, it would take us along the other side of the mountains to Macari. From that place there is an easy path to La Raya; there we are on the plateau again, and have only to travel by the road through Sicuani to Cuzco."

"In fact, it would double the length of our journey to Cuzco?"

"Yes, señor; but if you liked, from Crucero you might go down to Lake Titicaca. There are certainly good mines in the mountains there."

"Yes, but is there any chance of our finding them?"

"I can't say that, señor, but I fear that the chance would be very small."

"Then it is of no use trying, Dias. We saw at the last place what pains the old people took to hide places where gold could be found, and if there had been rich mines among these mountains you speak of, no doubt they would have hidden them just as carefully. The question is, shall we go up this pass as we intended, and take our chance, or shall we go by this roundabout way?"

By this time José had lit a fire, and they had seated themselves by it.

"One hates turning back, but we are not pressed for time. As far as I can see, my only chance is the feeble one of finding treasure in the place you spoke of up the coast above Callao. It is now four months since we left Lima. Travelling straight to that place would take us how long?"

"Well, señor, if we go round by Ayapata to Crucero, and then to Macari, it would be nearly a thousand miles."

"Quite a thousand, I should think. That is three months' steady work. By the time we get there it will be about a year from the time we left England. I have seen quite enough of the mountains to know that our chance of finding anything among them is so small that it is not worth thinking of. It seems to me, therefore, Dias, that we might just as well, instead of going south over these difficult passes, return by the foot of the mountains as we have come, going through Paucartambo, crossing the rivers that flow north and fall somewhere or other into the Amazon, and keeping along it till we come to Cerro de Pasco. There we should be nearly in a line with this place you know of, and can keep due west—that is to say, as nearly due west as the mountains will allow. It would be three or four hundred miles shorter than by taking the pass at Ayapata. We should have a good deal of sport by the way, and should certainly have no trouble with the brigands till we got to Cerro. Of course it is possible that we might fall in with savages again, but at any rate they are not so formidable as brigands in the passes. What do you say to that?"

"It is certainly shorter, señor; and, as you say, we should have no trouble with the brigands, and we should also escape the troubles that have been going on for some years, and are likely, as far as anyone can see, to go on for ever. We were very fortunate in not meeting any of the armies that are always marching about."

CHAPTER XI — BRIGANDS

Three months were spent in the journey to the foot of the pass leading up to Cerro. They had good shooting, and found no difficulty in providing themselves with food. Fish were plentiful in the streams, and in some of the long-deserted plantations they found bananas, grapes, and other fruits in abundance, together with sugar-canes, tomatoes, maize growing wild, and potatoes which were reverting to the wild type. They met neither with alligators nor large serpents, for they kept on the lower slopes of the foot-hills, as much as possible avoiding the low forest lands, where they might come in contact with the savages. For the same reason, they had no opportunity of taking any of the great fish found in the sluggish rivers, but had an abundance of smaller fish in the bright mountain streams. They killed two tapirs and several pumas and jaguars. Their two llamas, having one night wandered away from the mules, were killed by these beasts. But as the stores were a good deal lighter than when they started, this was no great misfortune. Occasionally they followed streams up into the hills, and did a little washing for gold when they halted for a day or two there.

"We have had a good time of it," Harry said as they sat round the fire, "and I am almost sorry that it is over, and that this is our last day of wandering where we like, shooting and fishing, and above all, camping in pleasant places. We have been very fortunate in not meeting any of the savages since the fight we had with them four or five months ago. It is a splendid country for sport, and except that we should like it a bit cooler, and could have done without some of the thunder-storms, it is a grand life. For a time now we are going back to a sort of civilization, filthy inns, swarms of fleas, and fifteenth-rate cooking."

"It is not so much the fault of the cooking," Maria said, "as of the meat. Here we get fish fresh out of the stream, and birds shot an hour or two before they are eaten. We pick our fruit from the trees, instead of buying it after it has been carried miles and miles to the market. We have a capital stock of coffee, tea, and sugar. Among the old plantations we pick cocoa and pound it fresh, and boil it. As we brought plenty of pepper and spices, it would be hard indeed if one could not turn out a good meal. And then, señors, you always come to eat it with a good appetite, which is all in favour of the cook."

"Yes, I grant that you have had all those advantages, Maria, but it is not everybody who makes the best of them. I can safely say that since we started we have never sat down to a bad breakfast or dinner. Now, for a bit, we are going to lead a different sort of life. We shall be on beaten tracks. We shall meet lots of people. It is strange to think that, except for those peasant muleteers we met at the foot of the pass by the Tinta volcano, we have not seen a soul except the savages—who have souls, I suppose—since we left Paucartambo more than six months ago; and yet somehow we do not seem to have missed them. I wonder what we shall find when we get up to Cerro, and who will be president then."

"I wonder what they are doing in Europe!" Bertie said. "We have heard no later news than what we had when we went on board a ship sixteen months ago. There may have been great wars all over Europe."

"I don't think there is much chance of that, Bertie. India was the only place where there was any fighting going on, and it seemed as if, since Napoleon was crushed, Europe would become permanently pacific. Still, I do hope that when we are at Lima we shall get hold of a pile of English newspapers. The consul is sure to have them."

"I don't suppose we shall want to stay there many days, Harry, for we shall be eager to start the search for the enchanted castle Dias has told us of. We saw quite enough of Lima during the ten days that we were there."

"Is the pass a bad one up to Cerro, Dias?"

"There are some very bad points, señor. It never was a good one, but as nothing has been done to the roads for at least a hundred years, it must have got into a very bad state. I have been down it twice with travellers, the second time ten years ago, and it was bad enough then. It is likely to be worse now."

"Well, as the road is used so little, Dias," Harry said, "there is no fear of brigands."

"I hope not, señor; but there may be some, though they would not be there in the hope of plundering travellers. But desperate men are always to be found in the mountains—men who have committed murders and fled from justice. They are able to live on what they can shoot, and of course they can get fish in the streams, and when they are tired of that can come down here, where they will find plenty of turkeys, and pheasants, and other game, besides the maize, and fruits, and other things in the old plantations. Sometimes they will take a little plunder from the small villages. Anyhow, they do not fare altogether badly. Therefore one can never feel certain that one is safe from them, even when travelling over tracks where travellers seldom pass. Still, we may very well hope that we shall not have the bad luck to fall in with them."

"I hope so, Dias. We did not come out here to fight. So far we have been very fortunate, and have not had to fire a shot, except at those wretched savages."

The next day's journey took them far up into the hills, and they camped that night at the upper end of a deep ravine. It had been a hard day's work, for at several points the mules had to be unloaded and taken up singly, and the loads then carried up. Fortunately, the packs were now very light, and were carried or hauled up without much difficulty.

In the morning they again started. They were just issuing from the ravine when a party of ten armed men made their appearance from amongst some rocks, and shouted to them to halt. Dias rode in front.

"You speak to them, Dias. Keep them for a minute in talk if you can, and then take shelter behind that boulder."

Then Harry ran back to José, who was walking with a leading mule twenty paces behind.

"Turn them back again, José. Halt a little way down, and then come up; there are some brigands ahead. Bertie, bring up your rifle and the two shot-guns. Tell Maria to remain with the mules."

Then he ran back again just as a shot rang out, and, dodging among the fallen rocks, he took shelter behind one abreast with Dias. "Was it you who fired?" he asked.

"No, one of the brigands. The ball went through the brim of my sombrero. I think they are talking to each other, they know there is no hurry."

"Hail them again, Dias, but don't show yourself above the rock."

"What do you want? Why did you fire at me?"

"We want everything you have got," a voice came back—"your mules and their burdens, and your arms. If you will give them up without resistance, we will let you up the pass without hindering you."

"Tell them that you must talk it over with the others, Dias."

"Well, we will give you five minutes," the man called back. "If you do not accept our terms, we will cut your throats."

Dias stood up, and walked quietly down the rugged pass. At the point where the mules stopped, the rock rose almost perpendicularly on each side.

"Maria," he said, "do you and José take off the saddles and bags and fill up the spaces between these rocks on each side. Get the animals in behind them. You stop with them, Maria. I have got five minutes, and will help you."

"You had better go up at once, señor," he went on to Bertie, "and help your brother, so that they may not get sight of you. However, I am afraid they know how many we are. It was foolish to light that fire yesterday evening, I expect they were somewhere near and caught sight of us, and no doubt one of them crept quietly down to find out what our force was. Seeing there were but four of us, they thought they could take us all easily here in the morning without firing a shot. But as your brother and I happened to be going on first, they thought they would parley. They would be sure that if they attacked us, we should kill two or three of them at least before we had finished with them. And as they reckoned that we should gladly accept their terms, they would get all they wanted without trouble, and could shoot us afterwards if they felt inclined."

Bertie had by this time got the guns unstrapped, and had filled his pockets with cartridges. He now went forward, and as he kept among the rocks he was able to get within four or five yards of his brother without being seen, as the mouth of the pass was almost blocked with great boulders.

"I cannot get any nearer without running the risk of being seen. I have loaded the double-barrelled guns."

"Stay where you are then, Bertie. I don't think they will make a rush, and if they do, you can use them as well as your rifle. Of course I have my pistols and you have yours. I don't believe they will venture to attack in daylight, our trouble will be after dark."

"Now, then, the five minutes are up!" the brigand shouted.

"I am coming!" Dias shouted back.

As he approached, Harry said: "Stand by the side of a rock, Dias, so as to be able to shelter as soon as you have given them the answer; they are likely enough to fire a volley."

"We will give you nothing," Dias shouted. "Anything you want you had better come and take."

Three men raised their heads above the rocks and fired. Almost at the same instant Harry's rifle and Bertie's cracked out, the heads disappeared, and a fierce yell of rage showed that one, if not both of the shots had found their mark.

"You had better clear off," Harry shouted. "There are four of us, and we have eight barrels between us, to say nothing of two brace of pistols."

A volley of curses was hurled back in reply.

"Now, Dias, what do you think is our best move?"

"I don't know, señor. I fancy there are only eight of them now. You and your brother could hardly miss marks like their heads at thirty paces." "If I were quite sure that there are no more of them I should say that, as soon as it becomes dark, we had better creep forward and fight them. It would be better to do that than wait for them to attack us. But there may be, and very likely are, more of these bands among the hills. Besides, Dias, we don't want to lose one of our number, and we could hardly hope to get through unscathed, for if we were to try to push on they would have us at a tremendous advantage. They would hide among the rocks and shoot us down before we had time to level a gun at them. Now that we have killed one, if not two of their number, they will certainly try to get their revenge, and will harass us all the way up the pass."

"It is not only that, señor; it is the booty they expect to take."

"They could not expect much booty," Harry said, "for our baggage animals only carry small loads."

"Gold does not take up a large bulk, señor; and I have not the least doubt that they believe we have been gold-hunting, and have probably a big amount of gold dust among the baggage."

"I did not think of that, Dias. If they believe we have gold we will take it as granted that they will do their best to get it. Well, do you think it would be a good thing to make a rush?"

"No, señor, it would be throwing away our lives. They will guess that we shall probably attempt such a thing, and I have no doubt that they will move away, if they haven't done so already, and hide themselves among other rocks. Then if we dashed forward to the place where they had been, they would pour a volley into us and finish us at once; for if they were lying twenty yards away they ought certainly to hit every one of us, as they have eight shots to fire. At present I have no doubt they are talking, and I think we can safely get back to where we piled up the saddles and bales. We can defend ourselves better there than here. We can then talk matters over quietly."

"That will be the best plan, Dias, certainly."

Keeping under cover as well as they could they retired to the barricade, thirty yards lower. José, aided by Maria, had completed the defence. They had not, however, attempted to block the passage between two great rocks. It was but three feet wide; the rocks lay about six feet from the cliffs on either side, and these spaces were partly filled by smaller fragments. Wherever there were open spaces the blankets had been thrust in from behind. Dias had done the greater part of the work before he went up to answer the demands of the bandits, but the others had laboured very hard to finish it.

"Well done!" Harry said as they passed through the entrance.

"I told them not to close the path," Dias said. "We can do that now we are all together. Most of the rocks are too heavy for José and Maria to lift. Shall we build it up now, señor? I am sure they cannot force their way through while we four are holding the barricade."

"Certainly not, Dias, and I have no fear of their attempting it. But I think it would be as well for us to close it, otherwise we could not cross from one side to the other without exposing ourselves."

It took them two hours' hard work—the harder because the stones had to be thrown into the passage from the sides, as the brigands might be crouching among the rocks higher up waiting for an opportunity to get a shot. At the end of the two hours the gap was filled up to the height of six feet.

"Now we can talk matters over quietly, Dias," Harry said. "We may take it that, whether they attack by day or by night, we can beat them off. There is a little rill of water that trickles down along the centre, so we need not fear being driven out by thirst, and we have food enough to last us a fortnight. That is settled; but they may stay there for any time, and without exposing ourselves to sudden death we cannot find out whether they are still hanging about or not. Of course one very important question is, are they going to be joined by others?"

"I think they certainly will be, señor. As many of these fellows are hiding among the hills as would make a good-sized regiment, and they have only to send off two or three of their number with the news that a party of gold-diggers with five laden mules are shut up in this ravine to gather any number of them. They would come as quickly as vultures to a dead horse. It must be a long time since they had any really valuable plunder, and the fact that we have five baggage mules besides the three riding ones would show that we had probably been a very long time away, and might therefore possess a lot of gold."

"Are there any other passes near?"

"The nearest, señor, is on the other branch of the Palcazu—the river we followed till we entered the passes—and is about thirty miles to the north. The pass starts from a spot about fifteen miles above the junction, and goes up to Huaca, a place that is little more than ten miles south of Huanuco. From Huaca we could either follow the road to Cerro, or strike across the Western Cordilleras to Aguamiro."

"Then I think, Dias, that our best plan will be to go down again into the valley we left yesterday morning, and then strike across for the mouth of this pass you speak of. You know the direction?"

"I know the general direction, although I have never been along there."

"Well, Dias, you must be the guide. I should say the sooner we start the better. My idea is this: If you with your wife and José will start at once, so as to be down the pass before it gets dark, my brother and I will remain here. You will leave our riding mules at the point where the track is good enough for us to gallop on."

"We should not like to leave you, señor," Maria said.

"I have not the least fear of their attacking us, and with our rifles and double-barrelled guns and pistols we could beat them off if they did. I can't see any better way of getting out of this scrape, and am quite willing to adopt this plan."

"I don't see any other way, señor," Dias said. "The plan is a good one; but I wish I could stay here with you."

"But that would be impossible, Dias, for there would be no chance of our finding the mouth of this pass by ourselves."

"Why could we not all go together?" Maria asked.

"Because if there were no one here the brigands might discover that we had gone, within an hour or so of our starting. They might fire a shot or two, and, finding that we did not answer, crawl gradually down till they got here, for it must seem possible to them that we should return down the pass; and as there is no getting the baggage mules to go fast, we might very well be overtaken—I don't mean by those eight men, but by a considerable number."

"But how are you to find your way, señor?" Dias said.

"We shall follow the valley down till we come to the spot where you have struck off. You can fasten a white handkerchief to a stick and put it in some bare place where we are sure to see it. I want you to halt when you get to the river somewhere opposite the mouth of the pass. We will ride nearly due north, and when we strike the river will follow it down till we reach you."

"We can't halt opposite the mouth of the pass, for the river there is already some size, and we could not cross it. I shall keep along near the foot of the hills—the water there is shallow enough to ford. Then I will follow it down until, as you say, near the entrance to the pass, and there stop on the bank till you come."

"That will do very well. In that case it won't matter much where we strike the stream, as our mules can swim across easily enough—they have had plenty of practice during the past six months. However, we will turn off north where we can see your signal."

"When will you leave, señor?"

"To-morrow morning. I have no fear of their attacking during the night, for they can hardly bring other bands down here before morning. As soon as it gets dark we will light two torches and put them down at the foot of the barricade, so that we shall be in the shadow. These will show them that we are still here, and they won't care to venture down into the circle of light. We have let them know what a formidable amount of firearms we have, and have given them a lesson that we can shoot straight."

"They certainly would not come, señor, as long as your torches are burning, but three hours are as much as you can reckon upon their burning."

"Well, we have a dozen left now, Dias, and when they burn out we must light two more and throw them over and trust to their burning as they lie among the stones. Of course we should not think of going down to stick them upright, for the scoundrels will probably be watching us as closely as we are watching them. However, I shall manage to keep the lights going till daybreak, and shall start a good hour before that. We shall have to go down cautiously, and I should like to be well away with the mules before they discover that we have left. Now, the sooner you are off the better. Breakfast has been ready for the past hour. You had better eat it and get under weigh as soon as you can. After you have gone one of us will keep watch while the other eats. I have no doubt there will be plenty left for our supper."

"Yes, señor, and enough cakes to carry you on till you join us."

Half an hour later the party started, Dias having muffled the mules' hoofs, so that the clatter, as they passed over the rocks, might not be heard above.

"Now, Bertie, you go down to breakfast. When you have done come up and relieve me. You have no occasion to hurry, for it is absolutely certain that they won't dare to attack till they get reinforcements."

When Bertie returned he said, "Here is a lot of food, Harry, they have hardly eaten anything. There is plenty for us to-day and to-morrow."

"That is just like them, Bertie; but I daresay they will camp in five or six hours. It feels quite lonely without them."

"That it does. It is really the first time we have been alone since we left Lima, except, of course, when we were out shooting together."

"Be sure you don't show your head above the barricade, Bertie. You must do as I have been doing, sit down here and look out through this peep-hole between these rocks Shove your rifle through it, so that, if you see a head looking out from between the rocks up there, you can fire at once."

In half an hour Harry came back and sat down by his brother, and, lighting their pipes, they chatted over the events of their journey and the prospect before them.

"I am afraid, Harry, the journey will be a failure, except that we have had a very jolly time."

"Well, so far it has not turned out much; but, somehow or other, I have great faith in this haunted castle. Of course the demons Dias is so afraid of are probably Indians, who are placed there to frighten intruders away, and they would not keep watch unless they had something to guard. I cannot understand how it has escaped the notice of the Spaniards all these years. I had not much faith in their stories until we found how true they were in all particulars as to what they call the golden river. There is one satisfaction, however: if the place is really a castle, it can hardly have disappeared under the lake. Of course if it is in ruins we may have a lot of difficulty in getting at the vaults, or wherever else treasure may have been buried; but unless it is a very big place, which is hardly probable, the work would be nothing compared with the draining of the lake."

"We have got nearly a year in hand, Harry, and can do a lot of work in that time, especially if we use powder."

"Yes; but, you see, we ought to allow at least five months for getting home. Still, no doubt if I felt justified in writing to ask for another three or four months, saying I had great hopes of finding something very good in a short time, she would stand out against her father a little longer. I shall write directly we get to Lima to say that, although I have so far failed, I do not give up hope, and am just starting on another enterprise that promises well." Bertie held up his finger. "I think I heard somebody move. It sounded like a stone being turned over." For two or three minutes he lay motionless, with his finger on the trigger. Then he fired.

"What was it, Bertie?"

"It was a man's leg. I suddenly saw it below that rift behind the rock. I expect he had no idea that his foot showed there. I am pretty sure I hit it, for I had time to take a steady aim, and the foot disappeared the instant I fired. If he did not know it was exposed, there was no reason why he should have moved at all if he hadn't been hit."

"It was better to hit his foot than his head, Bertie. It is equally good as a lesson, if not better, for though we don't mean to let them kill us, I don't want to take life unless it is absolutely necessary. Well, after that proof of the sharpness of our watch they are not likely to make any fresh move."

The day passed slowly. They took it by turns to keep watch, and just before dusk Harry said, "I think, Bertie, that we might pull out the leaves and bush that Dias shoved into one of these gaps when he took the blankets and things out. I could push the torch through and fix it there, that would save having to cross the barricade. It is quite possible that one of those fellows may be keeping as sharp a look-out as we are doing, and it is as well not to set one's self up as a mark. If I put it through now it won't show much, while if I wait till darkness falls it will be an easy object to fire at. You keep a sharp lookout while I am doing this, and if you see either a head or a gun try to hit it."

Harry accomplished the operation without drawing a shot, and as soon as he had fixed the torch he again stopped the hole up behind it.

"It is evident that they are not watching us very closely," he said. "If they have not sent for help, they have gone off. With two of their men killed and two disabled, the fight must have been taken out of them. We will watch by turns to-night. It is six o'clock now; will you sit up till eleven, or shall I?"

"I don't care a bit. Which would you rather take?"

"I don't care;—however, I may as well take the first watch. We will start at five, so rouse me at four. If they come at all, which is possible, but not probable, it will be between four and five."

At ten o'clock Harry could see a glow of light at some distance from the mouth of the ravine, and in the stillness could occasionally catch the sound of voices. When he woke Bertie at twelve the lad looked at his watch and said, "You are an hour late in calling me, Harry."

"Yes, I had no inclination for sleep. The fellows have been reinforced. Of course I don't know to what extent, but I should say pretty strongly. They have lit a big fire some distance from the ravine. They would not have dared to light one if they had not felt themselves strong enough to fight us. No doubt they have half a dozen men on watch where we first saw them, and these would give notice if we were coming. I think we may as well fire a couple of shots, it will show them that we are here and on guard. They will suppose we thought we heard someone coming down to reconnoitre our position."

They both fired over the top of the barricade.

"I see you have renewed the torch, Harry," Bertie said as they reloaded.

"Yes, I have done so twice. I was very careful, however, as I feared they might be watching. I did not wait for the lighted one to burn out, but passed the other one out, putting the end of my poncho round my hand and arm, so that they could hardly be noticed even by anyone within ten yards, and certainly could not be seen from up there. As I pushed it through I lighted it at the stump of the old torch and then withdrew my hand like a shot. I did the same thing again an hour ago with equal success, so it is evident that they are not keeping a very sharp look-out above, and have no fear of our making a sortie, hampered as we are by our animals."

The torch was changed again at four o'clock, and a little later Bertie heard a slight noise.

"I think they are coming, Harry," he said quietly.

Harry was at once on his feet. "Use your rifle first, Bertie, and sling it over your shoulder before you give them the two barrels of buck-shot, so that you can start to run at once if we don't stop them."

"Yes, I am certain they are coming," he said, after listening for two or three minutes. "We have got two or three torches left, and I will give them the benefit of them."

He went back to the embers of the fire, lighted the torches, and, returning to the barrier, threw them twenty or thirty yards up the ravine. There was a hoarse shout of anger, and then a dozen shots were fired. Bertie's rifle cracked out in return, and Harry's followed almost immediately. A dark group of some twenty or thirty men were rushing forward, and had just reached the line where the torches were burning, when four barrels of buck-shot were poured into them. Three or four fell, the rest fled at once, and the cries and oaths showed that many of them were wounded.

"They won't venture again for the present," Harry said. "You may be sure they will hold a council of war, so load again and then we will be off."

Two minutes later they were making their way carefully down the rocky passage, Harry carrying the bundle they had made up of the unconsumed provisions. As they had to exercise great care in climbing over the rocks, the day was just breaking when they came upon two mules that had been left behind for them. They rode cautiously until they were quite out of the ravine, and then started down the valley at a gallop. In an hour Bertie exclaimed, "There is the flag!" They rode to it and then turned off to the north, slackening their pace to a trot. The animals were in good condition, as they had of late been making short marches, and at eleven o'clock they came upon the river. Here they waited for an hour, gave a couple of cakes to each animal, and ate the rest themselves. The river was some fifty yards across, but the mules only needed to swim about half this distance. The brothers kept beside them, placing one elbow on the saddles and holding their rifles and ammunition well above the water. They were soon across, and, mounting, followed the river down, letting the animals go their own pace, and sometimes walking beside them, as they wished to keep them fresh for the next day's work. At five in the afternoon they saw smoke ahead of them, and, riding faster now, soon joined their companions, who hailed their arrival with shouts of joy.

"We have been terribly anxious about you, señors," Dias said, "and regretted deeply that we deserted you."

"It was not desertion, Dias; you were obeying orders, and were on duty guarding the baggage. There was really no cause for uneasiness; we were certain that we could beat them off if they ventured to attack us."

"And did they do so?"

"They made a feeble attack this morning at four o'clock, but we were ready for them. They might have carried the barricade had we only had our rifles, but buck-shot was too much for them. Of course we brought down two with our rifles; but there must have been over a score of them, and the four barrels of buck-shot did heavy execution. Some of them fell, and I fancy most of the others got a dose of shot, as they were all in a close body. I will tell you all about it after we have had supper."

"I have got it ready," Maria said. "We have been expecting you for the past hour, and I was sure you would have good appetites when you arrived."

After the story had been told Dias said: "That was a capital plan of keeping the torches burning all night, and especially of throwing two of them up the ravine when you heard the fellows coming. Of course they calculated on getting within fifteen yards or so before you saw them. Well, there is no fear of our hearing any more of them. I expect you must have been gone hours before they found out that you had left."

"I should not be surprised if, after they had recovered from their defeat, half of them made a big circuit over the hills—no doubt they know every foot of them—and, coming down at the bottom of the ravine, built a strong barricade, making up their minds to guard both ends until we were obliged to surrender from want of food. Having suffered so heavily, they would do everything in their power to prevent any of us from getting out alive."

"In that case they must have been prepared to wait for some time, Dias, for they knew we had eight animals to eat."

"They would not have lasted long, señor, for we have only a few handfuls of grain left, and there is not enough forage in the ravine to last them a couple of days."

"I expect they would have tried to get us to surrender, by offering to let us pass if we would give them half of the gold they thought we had with us. There is no chance of our being followed, I suppose, Dias?"

"Not the slightest. When at last they discover that we have gone, they will come down the pass and find where the mules were left standing. They will then see that only two of us had remained at the barricade, and will guess at once that the rest left hours before. They will therefore conclude that, being on foot, they have no chance of overtaking us, even if they could find the track."

"No, I expect by this time they are dancing with rage, and as likely as not quarrelling furiously among themselves. How far do you think we have ridden to-day?"

"Nearer sixty miles than fifty, señor."

"Yes, I suppose we have. And if we had come straight here?"

"It would have been nearly fifteen miles shorter. But if they pursued they would not come that way, because they would not be able to get across. I think they would have to go round and ford the river some miles higher than you did. They could never swim across with their guns and ammunition to carry."

"I should not count on that, Dias. They might come straight here, as they would guess that we had made for this pass, and they might make bundles of reeds to carry their guns and ammunition across, and swim over."

"That would be possible," Dias admitted reluctantly, "and if they knew that the five mules were all loaded with gold they might be tempted to follow; but that they could only guess. I have no doubt, too, that many of them had been walking for hours across the mountains before the attack, and as you fired into the thick of them, a fair share must have been too much wounded to start on a forty-miles' tramp.

"No, señor. I do not think there is any chance whatever of their pursuing us. Besides, I chose a spot where the ground was hard and rocky to plant that flag. And they would have a good deal of difficulty in ascertaining in what direction we went from there."

"We pulled up the flag-staff and threw it away among the bushes a mile and a half farther, and of course brought the handkerchief with us."

"I don't think we need give another thought to them, señor. At the same time, it would be as well to keep one on watch all night. José and I will be on guard by turns. Neither of you slept a wink last night, so you must not keep watch this time."

"I sha'n't be sorry for a good sleep, for the meal we have eaten has made me drowsy. However, if you hear the least noise, wake us at once."

"That I will do, señor. It is a great deal more likely to be made by a wild beast than by a brigand."

The brothers were sound asleep in a few minutes, and did not wake till Dias called them, and said that Maria had coffee ready.

"What sort of a pass is it to-day, Dias?"

"Not a very bad one, señor. The one we tried yesterday hadn't been used for very many years, there is regular traffic up and down this; not valuable traffic, for Pozuco is a small place. They send up fruit and dried fish, and the oil they get from the fish; and bring back cloth, and such things as are required in the village."

"So there is nothing to tempt brigands to infest the pass and rob travellers!"

"No, señor. When I last went through it I heard no talk of them at all. They are more likely to infest the hills beyond Cerro, for near that place really valuable captures can be made."

"That accounts for their being able to gather so many men to attack us."

The journey up the pass occupied two days. They met three or four small parties of men with donkeys or mules, but all these when questioned said that the pass was perfectly open, and that it was a very rare thing indeed for anyone to be robbed on the way. Late in the evening of the second day they arrived at Huaca, and were advised to go to the priest's house, as the accommodation at the inn was so bad. The man who directed them there was the head man of the place, and they gladly accepted his offer to guide them to the priest's house.

"It would be the best way, señor," Dias said. "I know a man here who would willingly put us up, and who has a yard where the mules could pass the night."

"Very well, Dias. Be sure you buy a good stock of grain. They have scarce had any for the last three days."

The priest—a cheery, hearty man—received Harry and Bertie cordially when they were introduced as English travellers, especially when he found that they could both speak Spanish fluently.

"It is a pleasure to receive British travellers," he said. "Cochrane and Miller have done more for us than any of our own countrymen. It is not often that travellers come this way. I have heard of two or three going to Cuzco, but they never come farther north than Cerro. I shall be delighted if you will stay two or three days here, señors. We get so little news of the world that it would be a great pleasure to us to hear what is going on outside this unfortunate country."

"We can give you but little news, for it is more than a year since we left England, and we have heard nothing of what is doing in Europe, as we have been travelling and shooting at the foot of the mountains between the bottom of this pass and Tinta volcano."

"And gold seeking?" the priest asked with a twinkle in his eye.

"We have occasionally washed the sands in the streams, but have not found enough to repay our work. The amount we have gathered is only about twenty ounces."

"Well, gentlemen, I shall be delighted to have you as my guests as long as you are willing to stay."

"We are greatly obliged to you," Harry said, "and will gladly be your guests. To-morrow the animals need a rest, and we shall enjoy one too. Next morning we must be going on, as we have been away longer than we ought, and want to get down to Lima quickly."

They had great difficulty in getting away from Huaca, where the good priest made them extremely comfortable, and was very loath to let them go. However, at dawn on the second day they started for Cerro, and arrived there forty-eight hours later after a rough journey through the Mils.

"We never know in Peru, when we go to bed, who will be president when we wake," Dias said that evening. "There have been a dozen of them in the past five years. Lamar, Gamarra, La Fuente, Orbegozo, Bermudes, and Salaverry succeeded one another; then Santa Cruz became master. Nieto had the upper hand for a bit, and at that time there was no travelling on the roads, they were so infested by robbers; one band was master of Lima for some time. Then the Chilians occupied Lima; Santa Cruz was defeated, and Gamarra came in again. None of these men was ever supreme over the whole country. Generals mutinied with the troops under them, other leaders sprang up, and altogether there has been trouble and civil war ever since the Spaniards left. That is why the country is so full of robbers. When an army was defeated, those who escaped took to the hills and lived by plunder until some other chief revolted, then they would go down and join him; and so it has gone on."

"Who composed those armies? because the fields seem to have been well cultivated, and the peasants are quiet enough."

"Yes, señor, for the most part they take no part in these affairs. The men who compose the armies were in the first place the remains of those who fought against the Spaniards. When the Spaniards left the country these men had nothing to do, and were ready to enlist under anyone who raised a flag and promised them pay. Of bourse there are many men in the towns who are too lazy to work, and who help to keep up the supply of armed men. The good God only knows when these things will come to an end. A few of those who have come into power really loved their country, and hoped to establish order and do away with all the abuses caused by the men who were appointed to offices by one or another of those tyrants; but most of them were ambitious soldiers, who led mutineers against the chief of the moment. If Heaven would but destroy or strike with blindness the soldiers —and above all, every official in Peru—the country might hope for peace and good government. The best man who has ever fought out here since Lord Cochrane left the place was General Miller, your countryman, who was splendidly brave. He was always true to his word, never allowed his soldiers to plunder, and never ill-treated those captured in battle. Ah! they should have made him president, but it would never have done. As the Chilians were jealous of Lord Cochrane, the Peruvians were jealous of Miller, first because he was a foreigner, secondly because his uprightness and fidelity were a reproach to their ambition and treachery, their greed, and their cruelty. Besides, he understood them too well, and if all Peru had asked him to be president, he knew well enough that conspiracies against him would begin the next morning. Ah, he was a great man!

"Well, señor, I think that before we start it will be well that I at least should go on to Ayapata and find out what is doing. That would only delay us two days, and we might be better able to judge as to which route to take. They may be fighting in the north, and we do not want to get mixed up in any way in their quarrels."

"I think that would be a very good plan, Dias. You start in the morning, and we will stay quietly here till you come back with the news. If many brigands are in the pass they might get to hear of us from someone going over from this side, and take it into their heads to come down. I would certainly rather not have to fight with you away."

Accordingly next morning Dias went on ahead. On the following evening he rejoined them.

"There is fresh trouble in the south, señor. Colonel Vivancohidas has declared himself Regenerator of Peru, and is now marching against Gamarra, and General Castilla is advancing against him. The fighting will be somewhere near Arequipa. Whichever wins will presently cross the mountains and make for Cuzco."

"Then that settles it, Dias. Certainly I have heard nothing in Gamarra's favour, but a great deal against him, since I landed, and I care nothing about either side; but I hope the new man will win, because I think that any change from Gamarra will be an improvement."

CHAPTER XII — PRISONERS

When they arrived at Cerro de Pasco they found that the division of Gamarra's army stationed in the district had mutinied and had declared for Vivancohidas, and were killing all those known as adherents of Gamarra. All traffic was at a stand-still. Numbers of the soldiers who did not choose to join in the mutiny had taken to the hills, and were pillaging convoys and peaceful travellers alike.

"I think, señor," Dias said, "that instead of crossing the Cordilleras to the west, as we had intended, it will be better for us to go south, skirt the lake of Junin, and make for Oroya. That is the route generally taken, for the passes west are terribly difficult. I have traversed this route many times, and when going with merchandise I always go through Oroya, though in returning from Cerro I take the shorter route."

"Very well, Dias, you are the best judge of that. It is a great nuisance that this rising should have taken place just as we want to traverse the country, but it can't be helped. I will go to the head-quarters of Quinda—he is established at the mayor's house here—and get a pass from him.

"It would be well, perhaps, if you were to go with me, Dias, to confirm my statement that we have been shooting and hunting. I hope he will give us a pass, so that we shall not be interfered with by his men gathered at different points on the road to Oroya. I hear that a considerable portion of his force have already marched forward."

The Peruvian colonel questioned Harry closely as to his motives for travelling there.

"I suppose," he said, "you have been searching for gold. We are sorely in need of funds, and I shall feel myself obliged to borrow any gold that you may have collected for the use of my army, giving you an order on the treasury at Lima, which will, of course, be honoured as soon as the authority of President Vivancohidas is established."

"I do not doubt the goodness of the security," Harry said quietly, "although possibly I might have to wait some time before the order was cashed; but while hunting I have not come upon any treasure. We have occasionally, when halting at streams, amused ourselves by doing a little gold-washing, but when I tell you that during the eight months since we started from Cuzco we have only collected about twenty ounces of gold, you may well suppose that no good fortune has attended us."

"Is that all, señor?"

"I give you my word of honour that is all, señor; and as I shall have to lay in a store of provisions and so on for my journey down to Lima, you may well imagine that it would be a serious inconvenience to me to part with it."

"Quite so, señor; so small a sum as that would not go far among the four thousand men under my command. However, I shall have pleasure in giving you the pass that you ask. You have had good sport, I hope?"

"As good as I expected. We kept ourselves in food, and have seen a splendid country, which I hope some time will again be cultivated, and add to the wealth of your country."

After a further exchange of compliments Harry returned to the inn where they had put up.

Next morning, after purchasing some coffee and other stores that were needed, they set out.

"Now we are all right, Dias," Harry said as they started.

"I hope so, señor; but from what I heard yesterday evening several strong bands of disaffected soldiers are in the hills between this and Oroya. Quinda's troops have by no means all joined him, and several companies that broke off have stationed themselves in the hills along this road. They have stopped and robbed more than one mule train with silver from the mines there. They have not meddled, as far as I hear, with Quinda's troops, but have simply seized the opportunity of perpetrating brigandage on a large scale."

"Well, we must take our chance, Dias. Fortunately we have money enough at Lima to replace the animals. We have pretty well finished all our stores, and beyond the tents and the bedding, which would be a matter of a hundred dollars, there is nothing worth thinking of; still, certainly I do not want to lose it. I hope we sha'n't fall in with any of those scoundrels."

"I hope not, señor. Perhaps we had better put our gold dust and money in José's boots. They are less likely to examine him than they are us.

"You had better put half in his boots, and give the other half to my wife to hide about her clothes. We shall want some money, if we are robbed, to take us down to Lima. With the gold dust we could get a couple of mules and enough provisions to take us down there. We should be in a very awkward position if we found ourselves penniless."

They stopped for the night at a little village close to the lake. There was but one small room at the inn, but at the other end of the straggling village there was a yard where the mules could stand, and a loft where Dias, Maria, and José could sleep.

Harry and his brother had lain down but an hour on their blankets when there was a shouting in the street, and two or three shots were fired. They leapt up.

"We had better hide our rifles and pistols," Harry said, "under that ragged bed that we did not care about sleeping on. We may possibly get them again even if we are robbed of everything else."

A minute later four or five men with a lantern rushed into the room. They were all armed with muskets, and one carried a torch.

"Who are you?" this man asked.

"We are English sportsmen," Harry said. "We have been shooting for some months at the foot of the hills, and are now returning to Lima. There are our guns, you see."

"We will take you before the captain," the man said. "Bring those guns along, Pedro and Juan."

The village was in an uproar. Some fifty men were occupied in searching the houses and in appropriating everything they thought useful. One house had been set on fire, and near this a man in an officer's uniform was standing. He heard the report of Harry's and Bertie's capture.

"English sportsmen, eh! How long have you been shooting?" he asked.

"Eight months."

"Eight months! Then guard them securely, Montes; they are doubtless rich Englishmen, and we shall get a good ransom for them. English señors who come out here to shoot must be men with plenty of money; but likely enough they are not sportsmen, but gold-seekers. However, it matters little."

"I protest against this," Harry said. "Our consul at Lima will demand satisfaction from the government."

The other laughed.

"Government!" he said, "there is no government; and if there were, they would have no power up in the hills."

So saying he turned away.

Plunder that had been collected was brought in and divided among the party, four of the men with muskets keeping guard over the prisoners.

"I don't see anything of Dias and the mules," Bertie said in English.

"No, I have been expecting to see them brought up every minute. Now I am beginning to hope that they have got safely off. I think the fellows began their attack at our end of the village.

"You know how watchful Dias is. Very likely he or José were up, and you may be sure that the moment they heard the uproar they would drive the mules out and be off. You see only two of them are laden, and they could have thrown the things on to their backs and been off at once. He would know that it was useless to wait for us. I expect he would turn them off the road at once and make down towards the lake. If these fellows had caught him and the mules they would certainly have brought them up here before this."

"I hope he got off—not so much because of the mules, as because I am sure that, if he gets fairly away, he will do what he can to help us."

"I am sure he will, Bertie. We must make the best of it. There is one thing, we have got a good month before us. It will take them all that time to go down to Lima about our ransom and return; and it is hard if we don't give them the slip before that."

A quarter of an hour later the band started with their booty and prisoners for the hills.

"I don't suppose they will go far," Harry said. "Quinda has got his hands full, and will be wanting to start as soon as he can to join Vivancohidas. He won't lose time in hunting the scoundrel who has caught us, so I expect the band make their head-quarters in some village at the foot of the hills."

This turned out to be so. After a march of four hours the band halted in a village in a valley running up into the hills. The prisoners were thrust into an empty hut, and four men with muskets told off as their guard. Next morning the captain of the band came in.

"I shall require a hundred thousand dollars for your ransom," he said.

"We could never pay such a sum," Harry said. "We are not rich men. I am a lieutenant on half-pay in the English navy, and, having nothing to do at home, came out with my brother for a year's sport. I could not pay a tenth of that sum."

"That we shall see," the man said. "If you cannot pay, your government can. You will at once write to your consul at Lima, telling him that if this hundred thousand dollars are not handed over to my messenger within four days of his arrival there, you will both have your throats cut."

"I will write the letter if you wish," Harry replied quietly, "but you won't get the money. If you like to say ten thousand dollars, I dare say the consul will do his best to raise that amount."

"One hundred thousand is the smallest sum," the man said angrily. "He can get it out of the government there. They will not choose to risk having trouble with your country for the sake of such a sum."

"Gamarra is away," Harry said, "and it is pretty certain that he will not have left a hundred thousand dollars in the treasury; and even if he has, you maybe sure that his people there would not give it up, for he wants every penny for his war expenses."

The man shrugged his shoulders.

"So much the worse for you. Write as I told you; here is paper, pen, and ink. Do not write in English. I will come back in a quarter of an hour for it."

"This is awkward, Bertie. It is evident that I must write. As to their paying twenty thousand pounds, the thing is absurd; if he had mentioned two thousand they might have considered the matter. What I hope is that they will not send up anything. I feel certain that we shall be able to get away from here within a month; and if they were to send up one or two thousand pounds, we should probably miss the fellow on the way. In that case we should have to repay the money when we got to Lima, which I certainly should not see my way to do—anyhow, until I got to England, when I could, of course, sell out some of my stock. There is nothing here that we could use as invisible ink. If there were, I would risk writing a message with it; but even then it is fifty to one against their bringing it to light. Well, here goes!" and he wrote in Spanish the required message.

The robber on his return read it through, turned the paper over to see that nothing was written on the back, and held it up to the light.

"That will do," he said. "Now let me warn you, don't attempt to escape. You won't succeed if you do, and the sentries have orders to shoot you down should you attempt it."

The time passed slowly. The brigand was evidently determined to give them no chance of escaping, and four sentries remained round the hut, one at each corner. In the daytime the prisoners were allowed to sit at the door of the hut, but they were shut up at nightfall. The guards were not allowed to speak to them, and there was therefore no chance of offering them a bribe. On the evening of the fifth day they had, as usual, been shut up, and were chatting over the situation.

"If they continue to guard us like this, Bertie, I really don't see a shadow of a chance of getting away. We calculated on there being one, or perhaps two sentries at the door, and thought we could have cut a hole through that adobe wall at the back and crept out through it; but as there is a guard at each corner, I don't see a chance of it. The fellows are evidently afraid of their captain, and each keeps to his corner, and sits there and smokes and drones out songs, but they never move till they are relieved. Of course we must make the attempt if we see no other way of escaping. But I have still great hope that Dias will somehow or other try to get us out, though how he can do it I don't know."

THEY SAW APPROACHING A PEASANT WOMAN SITTING ON A MULE

They observed that the sentries were not changed in any military way. Five minutes before sunset the four men who were to relieve those on guard came sauntering up. The former guard ordered the captives into the hut and bolted the door, and then after a short chat with the others went off, the new sentries having already taken their posts at the corners of the hut. On the fifth evening after their capture they saw approaching a peasant woman sitting on a mule. A man was walking beside her. Behind the woman was a small barrel, and two packs and two small wine-skins hung on each side.

"Harry," Bertie exclaimed, "I believe that is Dias and Maria!"

"It is," Harry said. "Thank God they have found us! Twenty to one they will get us out. What have they got with them, I wonder?"

They stopped in the road opposite the house, which was the end one in the village.

"You are not to come nearer," one of the sentries shouted.

"I am sure I don't want to come nearer," the woman said pertly. "You don't think you are so handsome that I want to get a better sight of your face?"

"What have you got there?" the man asked. "We shall be coming off duty in ten minutes."

"Well, we have got a little of everything," she said. "As pretty sashes as there are in the country, beautiful silk neckerchiefs, silver brooches for your sweethearts, and for those who purchase freely a glass of the best pisco spirit."

"Well, wait, and I dare say we shall lay out a dollar or two."

A minute or two later four other men sauntered up, and began to talk to Maria, who slipped off her mule. The guards, fearful that the best bargains would be sold before they could get forward, hurried the prisoners into the hut and bolted the door. The brothers heard a great deal of talking and arguing, and ten minutes later the sentries came up to their usual post.

"I would not mind betting odds," Bertie said with delight, "that Dias has drugged that spirit."

"I expect so, Bertie. He would be sure that they could not resist it, for it is the best spirit there is in Peru."

For a time the sentries talked, saying that the pedlars' goods were cheap and the spirit as good as any they had ever tasted. "We had great difficulty in getting her to sell us a second glass each; and she was right, for she had not much of it, and it must help her rarely to sell her goods. The husband seemed a surly sort of chap. I wonder such a pretty little woman would marry such a fellow."

"I suppose he was well-to-do and she was poor," another said; "such is generally the case when you see a marriage like that. I dare say he makes a good thing of it; the goods are as cheap, though, as they would be in Lima."

Gradually the talking ceased, and within an hour there was perfect quiet outside the hut. Half an hour later they heard footsteps coming quietly up to the door. They held their breath; but instead of, as they expected, hearing the bolt drawn, they heard the new-comers going round the hut, pausing a minute at each corner. Then they again stopped at the door; the two bolts were shot back, and the door opened.

"Come, señors," Dias said; "it is quite safe. We have put them all to sleep. Here are their muskets and pistols. You had better take them, in case we are pursued, which is not likely. At any rate, should one of them wake the want of a gun will mean delay in raising the alarm.

"Don't speak, señors; it is as well to keep quiet till we are fairly off." He shut the door and rebolted it, and then led the way down into the road.

Not a word was spoken till they had gone a hundred yards, and then Harry said: "You have done us another good turn, Dias; we did not see any possible way of getting out; but we both agreed that if you could find us you would."

"Of course, señors, you could not suppose that Maria and I would go quietly off."

"How did you manage to get away, Dias?"

"It was easy enough. After what we had heard of these brigands I made up my mind that I would not unsaddle the mules, nor take the packs off the two loaded ones. The burdens were not heavy, for we have little but our bedding and the tents left, and I thought they might as well stay where they were, and in the morning we could shift them on to the others. I told José to watch about half the night; but I was standing talking to him, and smoking my last cigarette, when he said suddenly, 'I can hear a noise at the other end of the village.'

"The evening was still, and I could also hear the sound of many footsteps, so I ran and pulled down the bar at the back of the yard, called Maria, and told her and José to take the mules straight down to the lake, and then to follow the bank. Then I ran to warn you; but before I got half-way I heard shouts and firing, and knew that I was too late, so I ran back to the lake, where I overtook the mules, and we mounted and went off at a trot. When I got a quarter of a mile away I told the others to go on to Junin, which we knew was twenty miles away, and put up there till I joined them. Then I ran back to the village, and, keeping myself well behind a house, watched them getting ready to start, and saw you. There was nothing to do but to follow you. I did so, and observed where they had shut you up, and I waited about for some hours, so as to see how you were guarded.

"I saw their captain go into your hut twice. When he came out the second time he had a paper in his hand. He went to the house he has taken possession of, and I kept a good watch over that. Presently two lieutenants came out, talking together. They entered another house, and ten minutes afterwards issued out again, dressed in ordinary clothes, such as a muleteer or a cultivator fairly well off would wear, and returned to the captain's house, and stayed there for a good half-hour before they came out again. Two horses had been brought round to the door. The captain came out with them, and was evidently giving them some last instructions. Then they rode off, saying good-bye to some of the men as they passed through the village.

"Knowing the ways of these bandits, I had no doubt the paper I saw their captain bring out of the hut where you were was a letter he had compelled you to write to request a large sum of money to be sent in exchange for you; and as I felt certain that we should rescue you somehow, I thought it was a pity that this letter should go down, so I started at once to follow them. They had not got more than a quarter of an hour's start of me, and by the line they had taken I saw that they intended to go to Junin. I did not think it likely that they would enter the place, because they would be sure to meet some of Quinda's men there; but would probably sleep at some small village near it, and then make a circuit to strike the road beyond the town.

"Fortunately I had some money in my pocket, and at the first farm I came to I bought a mule. You see, señor, I had not lain down the night before, and had done a fair day's work before I started to follow your captors. I had walked twenty miles with them, and had been busy all the morning. I knew it could not be much less than thirty miles to Junin, and that if I could not find them there I should have to push on after them again the next morning, so I gave the farmer what he asked for his mule, and started at once on it barebacked. It turned out to be a good animal, and I rode hard, for I wanted to get down to Junin before the two men. I reckoned I should do that, because, as they were going a very long journey, they would not want to press their horses, and besides would prefer that it should be dark before they stopped for the night.

"When I got to Junin I found Maria and José, who had put up the mules at the only inn there. I set Maria to watch on the road leading into the town, and went out with José to a little village a mile back, where I made sure the fellows would stop. I was not long in finding out that they had arrived about half an hour after I had ridden through, and had put up at the priest's. That was good enough for me. We went back to the town. I had some supper, which I can tell you I wanted badly, for I had been afraid of going into the brigand's village to buy anything, as, being a stranger, I might have been asked questions, so I had had nothing since the night before. I had found that there was a road from the place where they had stopped, by which they could ride along by the lake without going into the town; so José and I ambushed there an hour before daylight, thinking that they would be off early. We were right; for in a quarter of an hour they came along. Day was just breaking, so we could make out their figures easily enough, and as they were not five yards away as they passed, we were not likely to miss them. Well, I found the paper you had written in the coat-pocket of one of them, together with two hundred dollars, no doubt for the expenses of his journey. We hid the two bodies under a heap of stones."

"Then you killed them, Dias?" Harry said, in a tone of surprise.

"Of course! what else would one do with them? They were brigands, and they had attacked a peaceable village and killed several people. Even if I had not wanted to get your paper it would have been a very meritorious action."

"Oh, I am not blaming you, Dias, at all! There was no other way of getting the paper, and it may be regarded as an act of necessity. And what did you do with their horses?"

"José went on with them, and I returned to the town again and started with Maria and the mules. We journeyed to a village half-way to Oroya. Of course we overtook José a mile or two after we had left Junin. There we put up at a quiet place and talked over the situation. We knew that there was no particular hurry, for we read your letter, and knew that no harm would come to you for a long time. It would be a month at least before they would expect the men back with the money. There was another letter, addressed to Don Mariano Carratala, whom I know to be a busy politician in Lima. The money was to be paid to him; at least he was to receive it from the two men immediately they left the British consul's house, and he was to hold it for Valdez, which is the name of the brigand."

"I thought he would not trust the men to bring up a sum like that."

"It would be enough to tempt the most incorruptible Peruvian, and certainly the men he sent down would have taken good care never to come to this part of the country again if they had got the money into their possession. I don't think either it would have been safe in the hands of Carratala, if he did not know that sooner or later he would get a knife between his shoulders if he kept it. Next morning Maria and I started back, bringing with us four mules, the fastest we had. We rode on two and led the others. I knew some people at Junin, for I have often passed through the town when I have been bringing down silver from Cerro, and one managed to get for us that little barrel of pisco. I was sure that no soldier would refuse a glass; but it was almost a sin to give such liquor to the dogs. Then we bought peasants' clothes, and a parcel of goods such as travelling hawkers carry.

"You know how we succeeded. Of course we had drugged the pisco heavily, and knew that two glasses would send any man off to sleep in half an hour. As soon as it was dark, Maria went on with the mule. We shall find her half a mile from here at a deserted hut where we left the other three mules."

"Well, Dias, you have assuredly saved our lives. Guarded as we were, there was not the slightest chance of our getting away by ourselves; and as the British consul certainly could not have raised the sum they demanded, we should have had our throats cut when the messengers returned empty-handed. Valdez is not the man to go back from his word in that respect."

"It is a pity you have lost your arms, señor."

"Yes, we have certainly lost our double-barrelled guns, but our rifles and pistols are hidden in the straw of the bed in the room where we slept. We had just time to hide them before the brigands burst into the room."

"Then we can recover them, señor. Of course I intended to ride straight to Junin, but it won't make very much difference. We will ride to the village, get the rifles and pistols, and then follow the road by the lake. It is now only nine o'clock; we can be there by one easily, and reach Junin by morning. It will be perfectly safe to rest there. I suppose your guards will be relieved about twelve o'clock?"

"Yes, that was the time we heard them changed."

"They will most likely discover that you have gone then. When they find the four guards sound asleep, they are sure to unbolt the door and see if you are there, then of course they will give the alarm at once. But I hardly think they will even attempt to pursue. They are infantry, and none of them are mounted but the officers, which means that at present only Valdez himself has a horse. They would know that you had been assisted, and that probably horses were waiting for you somewhere. There is the hut, señors."

Maria ran out as they came up.

"The saints be praised," she exclaimed, "that you are with us again, señors!"

"The saints are no doubt to be praised," Harry said, "but we feel at present a good deal more indebted to Dias and yourself than to them. We are indeed grateful to you both, and you managed it splendidly. My brother and I felt so confident that you would do something to get us out, that we were not in the least surprised when we recognized you and Diaz got up as travelling hawkers."

"You did not tell them that we were with you?"

"No. Fortunately they asked no questions at all, and took us for Englishmen travelling by ourselves. They may have thought of it afterwards, but in the hurry of carrying off their booty they apparently gave the matter no attention. If they had done so they would probably have sent a party out in pursuit of the mules. Even if they had not done so, they would have been sure to look with some suspicion at two hawkers arriving at such an out-of-the-way village at such a time."

"Well, we had better be moving at once," Dias said. "We are going down to the village where they were captured, Maria. They hid their rifles and pistols there when they found the place was in the hands of the brigands."

Three minutes later they started. There was a full moon, so they were able to ride fast, and it was just midnight when they arrived at the village. When they knocked at the house where their rifles had been left, the proprietor looked out from the upper window in great dismay, fearing that the brigands might have returned. However, as soon as he recognized the party he came down and opened the door. The arms were found where they had been hidden, and in five minutes they were again on their way, and arrived at Junin at five o'clock. It was necessary to wait here twenty-four hours to rest the animals. The next morning they started as soon as it was light, and picked up José and the convoy. The brothers mounted the two horses, and Dias and Maria rode on one mule, and led three behind them. José rode another and led four. The horses and the mule Dias had bought were sold at Oroya, and after purchasing enough provisions for the rest of their journey they started for Lima, having concluded that it would be better, now that they were on the main track, to follow it instead of striking across the hills.

CHAPTER XIII — LETTERS FROM HOME

There was some little discussion over the amount of supplies that it would be necessary to purchase.

"Travelling quietly, the journey will not occupy over fourteen days," Harry said. "Do not get anything more than is absolutely necessary. It is evident that the whole country is in a disturbed state, and it is as well to have nothing to lose. We can buy nearly everything we want in the way of meat and flour at villages we pass through. Therefore, if we have enough tea, coffee, and sugar there will be really no occasion to buy anything more. We have still two or three bottles of spirits left, and you can buy pulque everywhere. There is a proverb two or three thousand years old, 'The empty traveller can sing before the robber'. We are reduced to that condition, except for our tents, bedding, and blankets, and they have done good service and would not cost much to replace. There remain, then, only the animals. They would certainly be a serious loss to us."

"Brigands would not want to take them. They would not be of the least use to them in the mountains. I would not say the same of parties of disbanded soldiers making their way down to Lima or Callao, who might prefer riding to travelling all that distance."

"The brigands might take our rifles and pistols, Dias."

"Yes, they would be sure to do that, señor. But we have had more than our share of bad luck already, what with the brigands in the Cerro pass, and these rascals we have just had to do with. I will enquire when the last silver convoy went down. If one has gone during the past five or six days, we could overtake it soon, for we can do two days' journey to its one. If no convoy has gone forward later, and there is one starting shortly, it might be worth our while to wait for it, for by all accounts the road down to Lima is infested by discharged soldiers, and ruffians of all kinds from Callao and Lima."

"Have the convoys an escort?"

"Yes, señors. The silver mines have always a considerable force in their pay. They used to have troops from the division stationed here, but what with the constant revolutions, and the fact that more than once the escort, instead of protecting the convoys, mutinied and seized them, they found it better to raise a force themselves. They do not take Creoles, preferring pure-bred Indians, who are just as brave as the Creoles, if not braver, and can be relied upon to be faithful to their trust. The consequence is that, in spite of the disturbed state of the country, it is a long time now since one of their escorts has been attacked, especially as the robbers would find great difficulty in disposing of the silver, as each ingot is marked with the name of the mine it comes from.

"They might, of course, melt it up again; but even then there would be a difficulty, as the law is very strict as to the sale of silver, and a certificate has to be obtained from the local authorities in every case, stating where it was obtained. This is hard upon the natives, for many of the little mines are worked among the mountains, and the rascals, to whom all official positions are given in reward for services done to the party which happens to be in power for the time, take good care to fleece the Indians heavily before they will give them the necessary documents. Nothing can be done here, señors, without greasing the palms of two or three people, and the grease has to be pretty heavily laid on."

Dias went out and made enquiries. "There will be no convoy for another fortnight. One went down ten days ago."

"I certainly shall not wait another fortnight, Dias. As to an escort, less than a dozen men would be useless, and as they would be a fortnight at least going down, and as much returning, even if you could get twelve men who could be relied upon, it would be a very expensive job. We might as well risk losing our baggage, and even our guns. The great thing will be to reduce the weight as much as possible. Four cotton beds take up a lot of space, and I think in any case I should have bought new ones at Lima; at any rate they can go. The blankets and ponchos we could, of course, carry behind us. So that practically there are only the two tents, cooking utensils, and the stores, which will not weigh many pounds, to carry, and with our clothes the whole will make a ridiculously small load even for one mule. We had better get rid of the pickaxes and shovels, they would fetch pretty nearly as much here as we should give for new ones at Lima.

"Thus, then, with Donna Maria riding one of the mules, there would be our five selves and three led mules, of which only one would be laden. That would offer no great temptation to plunderers; and as we shall all have guns across our shoulders, they would see that it would not be worth while to interfere on the very slight chance that the one laden mule might be carrying anything valuable."

"I agree with you, señor. Our appearance would be that of a party of travellers who have been exploring the old ruins, or, as has been done before, endeavouring to ascertain whether the rivers on the east are navigable down to the Amazon. Besides, the bulk of the people here do not forget what they owe to Englishmen, and the fact that you are of that nation would in itself secure good treatment for you among all except desperate men."

Accordingly they started the next morning. Maria rode, in Amazon fashion, on a mule between her husband and Harry. Bertie followed with José, to whose saddle the three baggage mules were attached in single file. They were undisturbed on their journey. Three or four times they were hailed by men on the rocks above as they went through difficult points of the pass. The reply of Dias, that the two gentlemen with him were Englishmen who had been exploring the ruins and doing a little shooting among the hills, generally satisfied them. One or two, however, who enquired what the mule was carrying, were invited by him to come down and see, though at the same time they were informed that the load contained nothing but blankets and cooking vessels, and enough provisions to last them on the way.

When, within two days' journey from Lima, a party of rough men came down into the road, Dias rode forward to meet them and repeated his usual story. "You can examine the mule if you like," he said, "but I warn you not to interfere with us; the English señors are not men to be meddled with. They are armed with rifles, and each carries a brace of double-barrelled pistols. They are dead shots, too, and you may reckon that it will cost you over a dozen lives were you to interfere with them. Moreover, the other muleteer and myself could give a fair account of ourselves. Rather than have trouble, however, two of you can come forward and see that my statement as to what the mule carries is correct. Its burden would not fetch fifty dollars at Lima."

Two of the men came forward and examined the mule's burden, and felt the saddles of the others to see that nothing was concealed there. When they rejoined their party one who appeared to be their leader came forward.

"Señors," he said, "I regret that we have stopped you; but we are poor men, and are obliged to take to the road to live. Perhaps your honours would not mind giving us ten dollars to buy food at the next village."

[Image: THEY SAW APPROACHING A PEASANT WOMAN SITTING ON A MULE.]

"I have not many dollars left," Harry said, "but if you really need food you are welcome to ten of them, for we shall need nothing more than what we carry till we arrive at Lima." He handed him the ten dollars, and then, showing him his purse, said, "You see there are but five others."

With many thanks the man retired, and he and his companions took off their hats as Harry and his party rode through them.

"Another such stoppage," Harry said with a laugh, "and we shall have to fall back upon our little stock of gold-dust."

However, they met with no more trouble, and on the following evening rode into Lima and took up their quarters at the hotel. Dias asked that he might go on with the mules to his home.

"In the first place, señor, we want to know how things have gone on in our absence. We had arranged with neighbours to look after the garden and the house. They were glad to do so, as the garden was a fruitful one. They were to take all they could raise and keep it well planted, so that whenever we might return we should find our usual supply of fruits and vegetables. In the next place, Maria is nervous about my staying here after what happened last time. We may take it as certain that the friends of the men we hurt will take the chance of paying off the score if they can find an opportunity. I shall come in each day to see if you have any orders for me."

"There will be no occasion for that, Dias. We have quite made up our minds to wait here for a week before starting on our next expedition, so if you will come over in four days that will be quite soon enough. You can overhaul the blankets and bags, and see that those good enough to keep are put in good repair, and those worn out replaced. We shall want quite as many stores as those we took last time, for there are very few villages except on the sea-shore, and we shall find difficulty in replenishing our stock. We shall have to buy double-barrelled guns in place of those we lost, but that we shall do ourselves. We have plenty of ammunition and cartridges for the rifles and pistols, but we had only a few shot cartridges left when we lost the guns."

As soon as Dias had gone on with the mules Harry went to the British consul's and found three letters waiting there for him, two from Miss Fortescue and one from Mr. Barnett. He put the former into his pocket to be read and enjoyed privately, but opened that of Mr. Barnett at once. It was in answer to that Harry had written at Cuzco.

"My dear Harry," he said,

"Your first letter was quite satisfactory. I was glad to find that you had reached Lima without encountering more than a stiffish gale, which was as well as you could have expected. I was still more glad that you had found

Dias alive and willing to accompany you. Your letter from Cuzco has now reached me. I think you were extremely lucky to get through that street broil without any damage to either of you. It was certainly a hazardous business to interfere in an affair of that kind without having any weapons except the sticks you carried. Still, I can well understand that, as you would certainly have lost the services of Dias had you not done so, it was worth running a good deal of risk; and, as you say, it had the natural effect of binding him to you heart and soul.

"I feel very uneasy about you both, and have blamed myself many a time for suggesting this scheme to you. I can only say that it is really the only possible way in which it seemed to me you could carry out the task set you. In fairy stories it is, so far as I can remember, a not uncommon thing for a king to set some task, that appears absolutely hopeless, to the suitors for his daughter's hand, and the hero always accomplishes the impossible. But this is always done with the assistance of some good fairy, and unfortunately good fairies are not to be met with in the present day. I have great faith in Dias, but fear that he is a very poor substitute for a fairy godmother. Still, I am convinced that he will do all in his power, and will even strain his conscience severely, by conducting you to places where his traditions lead him to believe that gold, either in the shape of mines or hidden treasure, is to be found.

"Your search will not improbably lead you into places where the Indians have won back their own from the civilization introduced by the Spaniards, and I have always heard that on the eastern side of the Cordilleras the natives entertain a deadly hatred for whites, and attack all who endeavour to penetrate into the forest. Don't be too rash, lad. Remember that it will not add to your lady-love's happiness to learn that you have been massacred in your attempt to carry out your knight-errant adventure, and if you are careless about your own life, don't forget that its loss will probably entail the loss of your brother's also. Dangers, of course, you must meet and face, but remember that prudence is a valuable aid to bravery.

"I am glad to know that Dias has taken his wife with him. A woman is a very useful adjunct to an expedition such as yours. Of course in some ways she is necessarily a trouble, and always a responsibility. Still, if, as you say is the case with her, she is a good cook, this makes a wonderful difference in your comfort, and certainly adds to the chance of your preserving your health. And in the next place, should you fall ill, or be mauled by a tiger or puma, she will make a far better nurse than Dias himself would be. Now that you are cutting yourself adrift from civilization, I shall not expect to hear from you again for a long time. I shall try and not be uneasy; but really, Harry, I do feel that I have incurred a very heavy responsibility, and may, with the best intentions in the world, have sent you and Bertie to your death.

I have, as you directed me, addressed this to the care of our consul, and it must be many months before you receive it, many months more before I again hear from you. Should you require more money, draw upon me. I have always a good balance standing at the bank, therefore do not hesitate to draw, in case the amount sent out to you quarterly does not prove sufficient to carry out any scheme you may have in hand.

"With all good wishes for your own and Bertie's welfare,

"I remain,

"Your affectionate guardian,

"JAMES BARNETT."

When he returned to the hotel he handed Mr. Barnett's letter to Bertie to read, and said:

"Stop down here in the patio, Bertie; I have two letters that I want to read quietly."

Bertie laughed.

"All right, Harry; take your time over them; I won't disturb you."

It was dusk now, and when Harry went to his room he lit a couple of candles and seated himself in a large cane arm-chair and opened his letters.

The first one consisted chiefly of expressions of pleasure at his arrival at Callao, of remarks upon the voyage, of complaints as to the long time that had passed without news of him, and of assurances of affection.

The second was, like Mr. Barnett's, in reply to his letter from Cuzco.

"My dearest Harry,

"After reading your letter I have been more and more impressed with my heartlessness in allowing you to undertake such a journey as you have before you. I ought to have been braver. I ought to have refused absolutely to allow you to go. The prospect of your being able to overcome my father's objections really amounts to nothing, and I ought to have said that I would not accept the sacrifice, and would not allow you to run such risks; that it would be better and kinder for both of us to accept the inevitable, and not enter upon such a struggle with fate.

"Do not think that I am already growing weary of waiting, and that my heart is in any way changed. It is not that. It is anxiety about you, and the feeling how wrong I was to let you go. Were there even a shadow of chance of your success I would wait patiently for years. I do not say that my life is a pleasant one. It is not. My father is still bitterly angry with me for, as he says, throwing away my chances; that is to say, of marrying a man I do not care for, simply because he is rich. But I can bear that. Mother is very very good, and does all in her power to cheer me; but, as you know, she has never been much more than a cipher, accustomed always to submit to my father's will, and it is wonderful to me that in our matter she has ventured, not openly to oppose him, but to give me what strength and comfort she can.

"I hardly know how I should have got on without her comfort. My father hardly speaks to me. He treats me as if I had been convicted of some deadly sin, and is only restrained from punishing me in some way because, by some blunder or other, contumacy against the will of a father has been omitted from the penal code. Seriously, Harry, it makes me unhappy, not only for myself but for him. Until I was unable to give in to him in this question he has always been the kindest of fathers. I am sure he feels this estrangement between us almost as much as I do, but believes that he is acting for my good; and it is a great pain to him that I cannot see the matter in the same light as he does. Of course to me it is most ridiculous that he should suppose that my happiness depends upon having a title, and cutting a figure at court, and that sort of thing; but there is no arguing over it, and I am as thoroughly convinced that my view is the correct one as he is that it is utter folly.

"However, I am almost as sorry for him as for myself, and would do almost anything short of giving you up to make him happy. However, do not think that I am very miserable, because I am not. Somehow, though I can't give any good reason for my belief, I do think you will succeed. I do not say that I think for a moment you are likely to come home with the sum my father named as necessary; that seems to be quite hopeless. But I think somehow you may succeed in doing well; and though some people might consider that he was justified in refusing his consent to what he might think was a bad match, he could not do so with any justice were I to determine upon marrying a gentleman with some fortune. He thinks a great deal of public opinion, and would know that even chat would be against him. But Indeed, Harry, I am beginning to doubt whether in the end I shall be able to sacrifice my life to his unfortunate mania, that I must marry what he calls well. I love you, and told him that if at the end of two years you were not in a position to claim my hand, I would give in to my father's wishes. I will keep my promise so far, that I will not run away with you or marry you in defiance of his command. But as I have agreed to wait for two years for you, I may ask you to wait another two years for me.

"When I think of you going through all sorts of dangers and hardships for my sake, I feel that it would be downright wickedness to turn against you if you find that you cannot perform an impossible task. Instead of this separation making you less dear to me, it is affecting me in quite the other way. My thoughts are always with you. How could it be otherwise? I have worked myself up to such a pitch that I have almost resolved that, when the two years are up, I will say to my father: 'I shall ask Harry to release me from my promise to him, and for two years, Father, I will go about and allow men a fair chance of winning my love. If at the end of that time I have met no one to whom I can give my heart, I will then go my own way, and if Harry will take me I will marry him.' It will require a great deal of courage to say so; but you are doing so much to try and win me, that it would be hard indeed if I were to shrink from doing a little on my part.

"Still, it would make it easier for me if you should have the good fortune to bring home something; not because, as I have told you many times, I should shrink for a moment from renouncing all the luxuries in which I have been brought up, and for which I care so little, but because it would, in his eyes, be a proof of how earnestly you have striven to do what you could to meet his requirements. I did not mean to say this when I began my letter, but it seems to me that it will give you heart and strength in your work, and that you will see from it that I, too, have taken my courage in my hand, and show you that your love and faithfulness shall some day have the reward they deserve.

"God bless you and keep you, dearest,

"Your loving HILDA."

Harry read the letter through again and again, and at last Bertie came in.

"What! at it still, Harry?" he said with a laugh. "You must have got your letters by heart by this time. I have been sitting in the patio by myself for two mortal hours expecting you to come down. At last I said to myself, 'This sort of thing will bring on madness. When a healthy sailor forgets that his brother is waiting for supper, to say nothing of himself, it is clear that there is something radically wrong.'"

"It is evident, Bertie, that at present you know nothing of human nature. If there had been anything radically wrong in this letter I should probably have been down long ago. It is just the contrary. Hilda says that if I don't succeed here, she will give herself, or rather her father, two years, and at the end of that time, if she doesn't find someone she likes better, she will marry me, whether he likes it or not—at least, that is what it comes to."

"I congratulate you, old boy. At the same time, it is evident that she would not have been worth her salt if she had arrived at any other conclusion. Now, having settled that comfortably, let us go and have something to eat. You appear to forget altogether that you have had nothing since breakfast, and it is now past eight o'clock."

"You boys think of nothing but eating," Harry grumbled.

"Well, up till now, Harry, from the time we started, I have observed that you have a very healthy appetite yourself, and I can tell you it has cost me half a dollar in bribing the cook to stay on beyond his usual hour. I did not like to tell him that you were engaged in reading a love-letter fifty times, so I put it delicately and said that you were engaged in business of importance. It went against my conscience to tell such a buster."

"There, come on, Bertie. I had begun to hope that you were growing into a sensible fellow, but I am afraid that there is no chance of that now, and that you will continue to be a donkey to the end of your life."

Harry had told Dias that they had better take two or three days at home before they came into Lima again, but to his surprise the muleteer came in at ten o'clock next morning.

"Well, Dias, I did not expect to see you again so soon. You have found everything right at home, I hope?"

"No, señor, I am sorry to say I did not. Three days after we left here our house was burnt down."

"Burnt down, Dias! I am sorry indeed to hear that. How did it happen? I thought you said that you had locked it up, and left no one there."

"That was so, señor. The people who took over the garden were to go into the house once a week to see that everything was in order; but as this fire broke out only three days after I left, they had not entered it. Everyone says that it must have been fired on purpose, for the flames seem to have burst out in all parts at once. No one in the town thought that I had an enemy in the world, and all have been wondering who could have had a grudge against me. Of course we need not go very far to guess who was at the bottom of it."

"I suppose not, Dias. It must have been those scoundrels we gave such a thrashing to."

"There is no doubt of that, señor. But this time they have got the best of me, for they know very well that I have no proof against them, and that it would be useless to lodge any complaint."

"I am afraid it would, Dias. Is it quite burnt down?"

"The walls are standing, señor. It takes a good deal to burn adobe."

"What do you suppose it would cost to put it in the same condition as before, with the furniture and everything?"

"No great thing, señor; two hundred or two hundred and fifty dollars. It would not be as much as that if it hadn't been that Maria had left her festa dresses and her silver trinkets behind. There was not much furniture in the house; but I think I could replace everything for about two hundred dollars, and I have a good deal more than that laid by."

"I shall certainly make that up to you, Dias. It was entirely your kindness in deciding to take us on Mr. Barnett's recommendation, and to undertake this journey, that brought the ill-will of these scoundrels upon you. Of course it is of no use doing anything now, but when our search is over I shall certainly see that you are not in any way the loser."

"No, señor; if I could not replace it myself I might accept your kind offer, but I can do it without breaking very heavily into my savings. And indeed their attack on me was the outcome of an old grudge. I have been long regarded as a fortunate man, and truly I have been so. If there was a job for five mules, and I was disengaged, I always had the first offer."

"But that was not fortune, Dias; that was because you were known to be wholly trustworthy."

"There are few muleteers who are not so, señor; it is rarely indeed that muleteers are false to their trust. I can scarce remember an instance. We Indians have our faults, but we are honest."

"Well, perhaps your getting the first job to go with foreign travellers may have been a piece of good fortune, but it is because these were so well satisfied with you that others engaged you. Trustworthiness is not the only thing wanted in a muleteer; willingness, cheerfulness, and a readiness to oblige are almost as important for the comfort of travellers. Well, do you think these fellows will try and play you another trick, Dias?"

"I hope they will," Dias said savagely, "that is, if they don't have too much odds against me. I owe them a big score now, for twice they have got the better of me. I should like to get even with them."

"Well, Dias, I hope they won't try anything of the sort. If anything should happen to you, I should not only be extremely sorry for your sake and your wife's, but it would destroy the last chance I have of carrying out my search for treasure. Do you think that if I were to go to the consul and lay a complaint against them, on the ground, in the first place, of their attack on you, and now of burning your house, it would have any effect?"

"If you were to make a complaint it might do, señor; it certainly would not were I to do so. A little bribe would, of course, be necessary; you cannot do anything without that. The officials here are all Gamarra's men, and there is not one of them who would not take a bribe. But would it be worth while, as we are only going to stay here a week? And if you got them imprisoned they would be out again before I came back, and would be more anxious than ever to get rid of me."

"There is a good deal in that, Dias. As, of course, we shall be away, and starting for home again as soon as we return here, their spite would be directed entirely against you."

"I hope, señors, that while you stop here you will never go out without your pistols. It is against you they have a grudge now more than me; it was owing to you that they failed in killing me."

"We will do so; and we won't carry sticks this time, so that if they see us going along they will think we are unarmed."

Whenever they went out after dark, indeed, Harry and Bertie had an idea that they were followed, and on their way home each invariably carried a cocked pistol in his pocket, ready for instant use. It was well that they did so, for on returning late one evening from Señor Pasquez, four men suddenly sprang out upon them.

They were on their guard, and their arms went up in an instant, and two shots were fired. As the pistols were almost touching the men's heads when the trigger was pulled, both the assailants dropped dead, and the others at once took to their heels.

"There are two of Dias's enemies wiped out," Harry said quietly. "I hope the others will give us a chance before we leave. Well, let us walk on before the watch comes along. It would ruin our plans altogether if we were kept here for an indefinite time while enquiries are being made."

The next morning they heard from their waiter at breakfast that two men had been found dead in the street.

"They are muleteers," he said, "but are known to be bad characters, and are suspected of having been concerned in several murders. It is evident that they made a mistake this time, and have got what they deserved. They are known to be associated with others. There were five of them; one was killed in a knife fight some months ago, and a search has been made for the others, but it is not likely that they will be caught. They were probably concerned in the affair, and knowing that they would be suspected of having a hand in this, and that their character will go against them, I expect they went off at once to the foot of the hills, and won't be heard of again for some time to come."

"I think it a pity they were not all shot. It is a shame that in a town like this people cannot walk in the streets after dark without the risk of being assassinated."

Dias was very pleased when, on coming up that morning, he heard of what had happened. He quite agreed that the other men would almost certainly have taken to the mountains.

"Even if they have not, señor, you are safe from another attack. Now they know that you carry pistols, and are prepared for them, they will let you alone."

"When we come back here, Dias, we will give you a brace of our pistols, and I trust you will carry them in your pocket ready for use after dark, whether you are in Lima or at Miraflores."

"Thank you, señor. I do not think they are likely to show their faces here again for a long time; but at any rate I will be on my guard, and will gratefully accept your offer of the pistols. Now, señors, I must set to work to-day to get in our stores for the next journey. I have made a list of what we shall want."

"Well, I have plenty of money, Dias, for I find two remittances from home awaiting me here. We have already bought two double-barrelled guns and a stock of ammunition, principally buck-shot, for we shall not be doing much big game shooting. We can always buy food at the sea-side villages."

Three days later all was in readiness. The mules were brought up from Miraflores by José, accompanied by Maria, and an early start was made on the following morning.

CHAPTER XIV — THE CASTLE OF THE DEMONS

"To-morrow, señor," Dias said, "you will see the spot I was telling you about, where, as the traditions say, the spirits of our ancestors inhabit the ruins of a building so old, that it was ancient when the Incas first came here. They are still there, and men who have been rash enough to approach the spot have been found torn to pieces as if by wild beasts; but none go near now."

"Did the Spaniards never go there?"

"I know not, sir; but 'tis likely they never even heard of it. The country is all dry and barren, and there were no mines to tempt them. The Indians never speak of it; those who were alive when the Spaniards came had some reasons for not doing so; and even now you could go to the nearest village, which lies more than twenty miles away, and ask the people about it, but they would only say that they had never heard of it, that no such place existed, for they believe that even to speak of it would bring dire disaster. We Indians are Christians; the Spaniards made us so. We make the sign of the cross, and we bow before their images and pictures, and once a year we go to their churches; but among the tribes east of the mountains that is all. We believe in the traditions of our fathers and in the demons of the forest; and though on this side of the hills, where the Spaniards held a tight grip upon us, the people have well-nigh forgotten their old faith, they still believe in many of the tales they have learned from their fathers, and this of the Castle of the Demons, as it is called, is as strong as ever in these parts."

"Have you ever seen the castle, Dias?"

"I have seen it, señor. There is only one point from which it is visible. We shall go there to-morrow, it is ten miles from here. The castle lies in a rift of the rock. I should say that in ancient times this opened to the sea, but the building closed the entrance. Whatever it may have been, it does not rise above the summit of the cliff, which goes down as straight as a wall for miles on the sea-face. The rift on the land side of the castle seems to have a width of about fifty feet, and I could see openings which were, I suppose, windows. The rocks on each side are higher than the castle itself, so that anyone coming along would not see it until he looked down upon it."

"But of course it is visible from the sea, Dias?"

"It would have been visible in the old days without a doubt, señor, but it cannot be seen now. The stones are the colour of the rocks beside them. They are stained and broken, and unless a boat went along within a very short distance none would dream that there was a break in the cliff there. I heard that from a fisherman whose boat was driven in by a gale and well-nigh lost. He said that he could see that the stones, which are very large—much larger than any of those in the remains of the buildings of the Incas—were not in regular lines."

"It is very strange that anyone should have taken the trouble to build a place in such a singular position. Is there not any legend as to its construction?"

"There is a tradition, señor, that it was built as a prison, by the king of those times, a thousand years before the Spaniards came, and even before the people whom the Incas conquered came into the land, and that it was a place of imprisonment, some say of a wife, others of a son, who had rebelled against him. Some say that it was built by the demons, but as it happened long before our people came here, none can know."

"Well, Dias, it seems to me that this old place is very likely to have been used as a hiding-place for treasure. As to these tales about demons, of course they are ridiculous. I took your advice when we were being opposed by fierce Indians, but when it is a question of demons, I can trust to my revolvers and rifles against a legion of them."

"Well, señor, you are the master. I have led you here as I promised. There may be treasure here or there may not. If you will go, you must; but I pray you not to command me to go with you. I would have followed you to the death through the swamps and forests on the other side, but I dare not risk being torn to death by demons and being left without burial."

"I do not press you to go, Dias. I respect your convictions, though I do not share in them. I have had a year of travel with you, and we have had many adventures together. This will be my last before I return home. Here at least there seems to me a chance of finding treasure, an infinitely better chance than any we have had, except in the gold valley. Here is a mysterious castle, of whose very existence the Spaniards seem never to have heard. It is just the place where treasure might be hidden. If it has guardians, they must be human, and also there can be but few. The urgent necessity for secrecy was so great, that it must, like all the other secrets, have been confided to a few only. Maybe but one or two old men are there, of whom certainly I need not be afraid. I have told you why I came here, and why I feel so anxious to find a valuable mine, or part of the lost treasures of the Incas. So far I have failed altogether, and I should be a fool as well as a coward were I not ready to run some slight risk in searching this mysterious castle."

"So be it, señor. I say not that you may not succeed. It may be that the demons have no power over white men. If you go and return safely I will go with you, and, should you find treasure, aid you to carry it away. I will lead you to within two miles of it, and will wait three days for your return. If you come not then, I will return to my place and mourn for you."

"Very well, Dias, you may count upon my return long before the three days are up. Now, in the first place, take me to the point from which I can have a view of the castle."

"We have had a long journey to-day, señor, and it is two hours' journey from here. We had better rest and go in the morning."

Harry nodded.

"We will be off early. You say it is ten miles from the spot where we shall see it. If we start at daybreak I can be there before noon, which will give me plenty of time for a first look round the place. We have got some torches left. I shall want them, for possibly there may be some chambers underground into which we shall have to penetrate. We may take it as certain that, whether the old people hid a great treasure from the Incas, or the Incas hid one from the Spaniards, they did not leave it about in rooms, but stowed it away in vaults like those we saw at Pachacamac, and these will certainly want a lot of looking for."

"I will help you look, señor, and will work there as long as you like in the search, if you return and tell me that you have seen and heard nothing of the demons that are said to be there. I am not afraid of danger when I know that it is men that we have to do with. But I dread being strangled and torn, as the legends say that all who have ventured here have been."

"But according to your own account, Dias," Bertie laughed, "that was long, long ago, and the demons may have got tired of guarding a place that no one came near, and have gone elsewhere in search of victims."

Dias shook his head gravely. In spite of his life as a muleteer, and his acquaintance with Englishmen, he was as superstitious as the rest of his countrymen. The nominal Christianity enforced by the Spaniards upon the natives was but skin-deep, and thus they clung with undying fidelity to the superstitions and traditions that had been handed down from generation to generation, and had been preserved with a tenacity that even the tortures of the Spaniards had failed to shake. The failure to obtain the gold which they confidently expected to find in the valley had still further strengthened his belief that it was destined that these treasures should never be discovered; and although when there he had listened gravely to Harry's explanations of the manner in which the lake had been formed, his own conviction that all this was the work of demons had been unshaken. If, then, a spot, which even the tradition handed down to him had in no way connected with the guardianship of demons, was so firmly watched, how much more must this be so at a spot which all legends agreed was inhabited by demons, and had been the scene of so many executions by them of those who had ventured near.

As Bertie and his brother sat together by the fire that evening after the others had retired to rest, they talked long over the matter; for just as when they had approached the gold valley, their excitement had increased with every day's journey. Harry felt that this was his last chance, his only hope of gaining the object for which he had left England.

"It is strange, Harry," Bertie said, "that the natives should believe these absurd stories about demons. Dias seems, in every other way, as sensible a fellow as one can want to meet, but in this respect he is as bad as any of them."

"It is not extraordinary, Bertie, if you remember that it is not so very long ago since people at home believed in witches who sailed through the air to take part in diabolic ceremonies, and brought about the death of anyone by sticking pins into a little waxen image, and that even now the peasantry in out-of-the-way parts of the country still hold that some old women bewitch cows, and prevent milk turning into butter however long they may continue churning. Fairy superstitions have not quite disappeared, and the belief in ghosts is very wide-spread.

"When you think of that it is not surprising that these poor ignorant natives still have implicit faith in the traditions of their ancestors. It is possible that this old place is still inhabited by Indians, who have been its guardians for ages, and if not now, may have had charge of it long after the Spaniards came here, and murdered any who ventured to approach the place. We know that the tradition of the gold valley has been faithfully maintained in the family of Dias; this may also be the case in the family to which the guardianship of this old place was entrusted, but to my mind it is less likely. In the case of the gold valley there was nothing for those in the secret to do but to hold their tongues; but to supply guardians to this place from generation to generation must have been a much more irksome task, and it may have been abandoned, either from the dislike of those who had to spend their lives in such a monotonous business, or by their families dying out. I certainly don't want to have a fight with men who are only following orders passed down to them for hundreds of years. If they attack us, we shall have to fight; but I sincerely trust that we may find the place deserted, for, fight or no fight, I mean to get the treasure if it is there."

"I should think so," Bertie agreed. "The treasure is absolutely of no use to them, and may be no end of use to you."

"To both of us, Bertie. If there is a treasure, you may be sure it is a large one, ample for both of us, and to spare. Of course we shall have trouble in getting it away—the gold would be invaluable to any of these rascally adventurers who are a curse to Peru. I really want to see the place, even putting aside the question of the treasure, for it must have been extraordinarily well hidden if the Spaniards never came upon it; and I think there can be no doubt whatever that in this respect the traditions must be true. The whole thing would have been upset if the Spaniards had once paid a visit there, for, from what we saw at Pachacamac and Cuzco, they spared no exertions whatever to root out likely hiding-places. The treasure, if there is one, will be difficult to find, but I have got nearly a year yet, and if necessary I will spend the whole of it in digging. Dias could go and get provisions for us. Of course he must not always go to the same place. Sometimes he can go up to Huaura, sometimes down to Chancay or Ancon. This place, he has told me, lies a mile or two south of the Salinas promontory, which would partly account for its escaping notice, for the road from Huaura, as we see on the map, skirts the foot of the hill, and goes straight on to Chancay and Ancon, and there is no earthly reason why anyone should go out to the promontory. People here don't leave the roads and travel eight or ten miles merely to look at the ocean, especially when by following the straight line they would see it without trouble. Well, we have both had hard work during the past year, what with felling trees to make bridges, chopping logs for fires, making roads practicable by moving rocks out of the way, occasionally using our picks where Dias thought that there was a lode, and carrying mules' burdens up and down steep places.

"Altogether it has been a sort of backwoodsman's life, and if there are treasure-vaults in this place I think we shall be able to get at them, however thick and heavy the stones may be on the top of them."

"I am game," Bertie said. "There is a lot more excitement in working when possibly a treasure lies under your feet than in chopping away at trees, some of which are so hard as almost to turn the edge of an axe. The place cannot be very large, so it won't take us very long if we are obliged to tear up every foot of it. I suppose there cannot be above three feet of stone over the mouths of any of these vaults."

"I think, Bertie, that when we have once investigated the place and settled on our plans, we had better send Dias and José down to Callao to get three or four kegs of powder and some boring tools, besides a supply of provisions. We should get on a lot faster with these than with only pickaxes. We shall want a couple of strong iron crowbars for lifting slabs of stone, and of course some fuse for the mines."

"We should have to be careful not to put too much powder in, so as not to bring the whole thing down about our ears."

"Oh, we should not want to make a mine of that sort, but only to blast the stone as they do in quarries and mines. We should have to make a hole to begin with, by means of our picks and crowbars, in one corner of the room, two or three feet wide; then we must make a couple of holes the size of the boring tool, a foot or so away, according to the hardness of the ground, put in charges and fire them, and in that way blow down the rock into the hole we had made; and so we should go on until we had done the whole floor. Of course, the bigger the hole we first make—that is to say, the wider the face it has—the easier we shall blow the stone down afterwards. I have watched them blasting stone at Portland, and at some galleries they were making at Gibraltar, and I know pretty well how it is done. Of course it is hard work driving the borers down, for that we shall want two or three sledges of different weights. It will make our arms ache at first, but after a week or two we shall be able to stick to it fairly well. Now we had better turn in. We shall start at daybreak tomorrow. It will take us two hours to reach the spot from which Dias said we could see the place, and another three hours to get to the castle. That will give us a long afternoon to take our first look over it."

"There, señor," Dias said, when at eight o'clock in the morning they stopped on a projecting spur of the hill, "that is the castle!"

From where they stood they could see that the ground fell away into what was at first a mere depression, but gradually deepened into a valley half a mile wide. Still farther down the sides became more precipitous, and in the distance the valley was closed in by rock walls, and appeared to come to an end. That it did not do so was evident from a streak of bright green in the centre of the valley, showing that a small stream must run down it. From the point at which they stood they could see the level line of the plateau near the cliff facing the sea, and on the surface of this a dark zigzag line marked the course of the ravine. Then, when apparently close to the termination of the flat land by the cliffs, the dark streak widened out somewhat. Through a small but powerful telescope which Harry carried he could make out distinctly the upper part of what might be a house.

"It is a strange-looking place for a castle to be built," he said, "but it quite answers to your description, Dias. There are certainly some openings, which may have been windows. I am sure no one looking from here, and ignorant that such a place existed, would notice it, and of course from the valley it could not be seen at all. Even from this height I do not think I can see more than ten or twelve feet of the upper part. But surely it must be noticeable to anyone coming along the cliffs?"

"It may be, señor, but I cannot say. Certainly no native would go along there even in the daytime. Still, it does seem likely that in the Spanish time some must have ridden along the top of the cliffs, and if they had seen the castle it would certainly have been searched. Assuredly it has not been so. I have been at Ancon and Salinas many times, and have talked with the people there. They would never speak on the subject to one of white blood, but knowing that I was of native blood, and belonged to one of the families to whom the secret could be strictly trusted, they were ready enough to talk about the Castle of Demons. Had the Spaniards ever searched it they would have known, and the place would no longer be feared; but all say that from the time of the conquest by the Spaniards no living being has, as far as is known, entered it."

"Then the Incas knew of it, Dias?"

"I think so, señor, though I have not heard that any of them ever lived there; but tradition says that the vessel in which a great store of treasure was sent away from Pachacamac, and which, as is proved by Spanish writings, was never heard of afterwards, and doubtless was sunk in a great storm that came on two or three days after it sailed, was intended to be landed and hidden in this castle, which they thought might well escape the observation of the Spaniards."

"And even among your traditions there is no allusion to what became of this treasure ship?"

"No, señor; all traditions say that it was never heard of from the day it sailed. Had it landed at that castle the secret would have been handed down to some of the native families, just as that of the golden valley and of other hidden treasures has been. But there can be no doubt that the ship was lost with all her treasure."

"Well, we need not talk any more about it now, Dias; we shall learn nothing more, however long we stay here and stare at it."

They stopped half an hour for breakfast and then rode down the valley. When they got near the spot where it closed in Harry saw by the pallor on the native's face that he was beginning to be greatly alarmed.

"You had better stop here, Dias. My brother and I will go on and explore this ravine and have a look at the place. We will take some ropes with us, for the ravine may be blocked by falls of rocks, and we may have to let ourselves down. Evidently the water gets to the sea, or this valley would be a lake like that in the golden ravine, for although it is but a mere driblet of water now, you can see by the banks that a considerable amount comes down in the wet season. How it gets past the castle I don't know; I can only suppose that there is a passage for it underneath the building. We will take both our guns, Bertie, and our pistols. That there are no demons we are quite sure, but the place may have been used as a hiding-place for outlaws and brigands, who could find no better spot, as there was no fear whatever of its being discovered. We will take some bread and meat in our haversacks and a flask of spirits. Perhaps we shall be away longer than we expect, Dias, but at any rate we will not stop there after dark."

Tears were in the Indian's eyes as Harry and Bertie said good-bye to him and started, and when he saw them enter the ravine he sat down with his elbows on his knees and cried unrestrainedly. His wife went up to him and put her hand on his shoulder.

"Do not sorrow, Dias; as for me, I have no fear, though I love them as well as you do. I do not say that there may not be demons in the castle—everyone says there are;—but though these may strangle our people who break the orders that were given that none should go near, I do not believe they can hurt our white friends. You saw that they had no fear; you know how brave they are, and how they laughed at the idea of the demons having any power over them. Do you think I could smile and talk if I thought they were in danger? Still, as there is no need to prepare dinner yet, I will tell my beads over and over again. We shall know if any harm comes to them if we hear them fire their guns, for it is certain that they would do so. Even if a legion of demons attacked them they would never run away, but would fight till the last."

"I love them," Dias said; "I love them as my own sons. At first, when they came to me from Señor Barriett, it was for his sake that I consented to accompany and aid them; but from that night when they saved my life by rushing, with no weapons save their sticks, into the midst of five men with drawn knives, I felt how noble they were, and I loved them not only for the sake of my life, but for their bravery. Since then my feelings have grown every day. Have they not treated us as equals, as they would do people of their own race—us who, by every Peruvian with white blood in his veins, are looked down upon?"

"It is true, Dias. They have laughed and joked with us, and have treated me with as much respect as if I had been of pure Spanish blood, and have always done everything they could to make things easy for me. I will not believe God and the Holy Virgin can permit them to be overpowered by the evil ones. Should it be otherwise, should they never return, I should be inconsolable. It would be to me as if you yourself had died, and I should be ready to stab myself to the heart at the thought that we had brought them here."

"I could not live after it either, Maria; but, as you say, I will trust that God will protect them."

He cut down two rods and fastened them together in the form of a cross, and then he and his wife knelt before it and repeated innumerable paternosters and Ave Marias, crossing themselves as they did so.

José, as soon as he had removed the burdens from the mules and turned them out to graze at the edge of the streamlet, came and joined them in their supplications, occasionally breaking off from the repetition of the only prayers he knew, and in his native language imploring the saints to protect their friends.

"There is no humbug about Dias," Bertie said as they left the others. "He is really in a blue funk."

"Yes, he is quite in earnest; and we know that he is no coward in other matters."

"Certainly not. He showed any amount of pluck in the affair with the Indians. But he seems such a bright, sensible sort of chap, that it is quite funny to hear him going on about his demons. I should not be surprised at anything the ordinary peasant might believe, but it is different with a man like Dias."

"You know, Bertie," Harry said, coming to a sudden stop, "I think we are making a mistake going on into this ravine. I have no belief that the place is inhabited; still, there may be desperadoes, and perhaps a few fanatics. It is quite possible that a certain number of families bound themselves to keep watch here, and formed a little community that has lasted to the present day."

"But how could they have lived?"

"We will talk that over, Bertie, if we find any of them there. Now we must turn back. It is not more than a mile at the outside to the place where we can climb the hillside. In that way we shall be able to look down into this ravine, and take a general view of the place. We shall know what we are doing then, whereas if we were to go on through the gorge without knowing anything about it, we might find ourselves caught in a trap. It won't make half an hour's difference, for the ground up there will be as good walking as it is here, while we might find all sorts of obstacles in this ravine, and with two guns apiece, ammunition, pistols, coils of rope, food, and so on, we should find it awkward work climbing among heaps of rocks.

"You were saying, How could a group of people exist here for centuries without any communication with the outside world? Well, I don't suppose they could. They might get water from the stream, and possibly there may be some way of getting down to the sea-shore; anyhow, this stream must find a passage when it is in flood. They might have been able to get enough fish for their wants; but a fish-and-water diet would scarcely be sufficient.

"At the same time we are by no means sure that they could have had no communication with the outside, for just as some families may have been ordered to live here, others may have been instructed to supply them with food. The watchers may have had a store of gold-dust sufficient to last them all this time, and their friends outside may have brought them a sheep or two, and corn and other articles of necessity once a week. There could have been no difficulty in doing so. The stories of demons, and probably the murder of inquisitive people who tried to pry into what was going on, created such a dread of the place that those in the secret would come and go without the slightest difficulty. Conceivably, young men may from time to time have gone out for a year into the world and brought back wives with them, or girls may have been sent by the people in league with them outside, and obtained husbands, which is less likely. I should think it was more probable that young boys and girls would be kidnapped, and brought in here from time to time. All this is pure guesswork, of course, but nevertheless there may be people here, and it is just as well to take a look round from above before we trust ourselves inside the place."

On gaining the plateau they followed the crest of the valley until they came to a spot where the ravine appeared to end. They found that in fact it made a sharp turn. It was here only some ten feet wide, but soon broadened out to thirty. Fifty yards farther there was another sharp bend, the ravine narrowed to twenty feet, and the sides became absolutely perpendicular. Twenty yards farther still they saw something like a wall about thirty or forty feet high stretching across the gorge, which was here some seventy feet deep. About twenty feet from the foot there was a steep ascent of rocks, such as might have fallen there by a slip from one side or the other. Above these a perpendicular wall rose for another twenty-five feet. Harry and his brother looked at it in surprise from the height at which they stood. Its appearance was precisely that of the wall-precipices on each side. It was rough and uneven, and they could see no signs of any joints.

"It looks as if it were natural," Bertie said, "but it can't be."

"No, it must certainly be artificial, but it is a wonderful imitation, and certainly anyone coming up the ravine would suppose that bank of rocks at the foot had fallen from its face; but we know that it can't be that, for the water makes its way through. Besides, you see it is only three feet wide at the top, and then there is a narrow ledge a couple of feet wide, which was evidently made for the garrison to stand upon and shoot their arrows at anyone attempting to come up the ravine. Behind the slope is all rough rocks, except just below our feet, where there is a narrow stone staircase of regularly-cut steps. It is so narrow that it could not be noticed by anyone standing here, unless they bent over to look straight down as I am doing. Well, it is just as well that we made the circuit, for we certainly could not have climbed over there."

Another sharp turn, and the ravine ran straight towards the castle. They hurried on, and when they had gone fifty yards stood at the edge of a roughly circular pit. It was seventy or eighty feet across, narrowing at each end. At one end was the ravine at whose mouth they were standing, and directly opposite, in what might be called the neck of the bottle, stood the Castle of the Demons. It was some fifty feet in width, and as it stood back about forty feet up the neck it could hardly be seen at any point except that at which they were standing. There was no door or other opening at less than some twenty-five feet from the ground. At that height was a broad aperture about four feet high and twelve wide. Above this were several smaller openings about four feet square. The singular point in the structure was a rough arch of rock, which extended above it and formed its roof. This arch projected thirty or forty feet in front of the building, so that the latter had the appearance of standing in a great cave.

"What an extraordinary-looking place!" Bertie said in a low voice.

"Extraordinary, but how splendidly chosen for concealment! You see the top of the rock above it is level with the ground on either side. This would perfectly well account for people riding along the line of the cliffs, and passing over without dreaming that there was a house below them. Even if they went to the edge on this side, they would simply see this deep pit and the ravine beyond, but could not by any possibility obtain a sight of the house unless they came round to nearly where we are standing, which they could have no possible motive for doing. Besides, you see, all the way we have been passing through a thick bush; and I have no doubt that in the old time a wood stood here, possibly planted by the builders of the house. Of course the arch existed before the house was built. The stratum below was probably softer, and the stream gradually trickled through, and perhaps in some great flood, when this basin was full, burst its way out, after which the rock gradually fell until it formed that great natural arch."

"Well, let us go round and have a look at the other side."

They found that the width of the arch to the sea cliff was a hundred and fifty feet.

"If the castle extends to this face, Bertie, it is a hundred feet across, but from here we can't see whether it does so. It is probably built flush, however, as Dias said that it was not noticeable from the sea, and had the arch projected beyond it it could certainly have been seen."

"Well, Harry, if you will tie a rope round my waist you can let me down, and I will have a look at it. You can hold me easily enough if you stand twenty feet back from the edge, and you won't have to pull me up, because I can easily climb up the rope by myself. I need not go down more than thirty or forty feet, and I can do that easily enough."

"Oh, I could pull you up, Bertie."

"Well, you could do that if by any chance I should get tired; then I could give a shout, and you could haul on the rope."

"There are lots of stumps of trees here, Bertie, and I can take half a turn round one of them and so let you down easily; then when you shout I will fasten the rope there and come to the edge, and I can hear whether you want me to haul or not. Of course it must depend whether there are any jagged rocks sticking out. If so, it would be better for you to climb, as the rope might chafe against them if I pulled."

"I understand." Bertie laid down his weapons and water-flask, made a loop at the end of one of the ropes they had brought large enough for him to sit in, then he looked for a spot where the short grass extended to the very edge. "This is a good place, and the rope won't chafe as it runs over that. Now I am ready. If you will go back to that stump fifteen feet away and let it out gradually, I will be off."

He knelt down, and putting the rope over his head took a firm hold of it just above the loop, and then crawled backwards, his brother keeping the rope taut. "Slack it out gradually now," Bertie said; "I am just over."

Directly afterwards his shoulders disappeared. Harry let the rope slowly out until he calculated that fifty feet were over the cliff, then he fastened it very securely round the stump and went forward to the edge.

"Are you all right, Bertie?" he shouted.

"Quite right."

The face of the rock was very even, and there was nothing for the rope to chafe against. Harry lay down at the edge, keeping a firm hold of the rope to prevent himself from slipping over, and was able to look down on Bertie.

"Well, Bertie, what is it?"

"It is the wall of the house, I have no doubt, but it is so cleverly built that I can scarcely see where the arch ends and the house begins. Looking quite close I can see where the stones join, but their face has been left rough; and as it is just the same colour as the rocks, and lines have been cut down its face, and cracks made across it answering to the lines in the rock on both sides, I am sure I should not have known it was built up unless I had examined it. It is much narrower on this side than on the other—not more than twenty-five feet, I should say. There seem to be some irregularly-shaped holes in what looks like a fissure in the middle. I suppose they are to light the rooms on this side of the house, but they are certainly too small to be noticed from the sea."

"Does the sea come right up to the foot of the cliff?"

It was a minute before the answer came. "The water comes to the foot, but there is a line of rocks running along forty or fifty feet farther out. Some of them seem to be thirty feet out of the water; at one end they touch the cliff, and at the other there is a free passage. The water is very clear, but as far as I can judge I should say there is a depth of a fathom or a fathom and a half between the rocks and the cliff. Certainly a boat could row in to a position underneath where I am."

"Is there anything more?"

"No."

"You don't see an entrance down here?"

"No."

"All right! Then you may as well come up again. Can you climb up?"

"Easily."

"Well, hail me if you want me to haul."

Harry went back to the stump, unwound the rope until it was only half a turn round it, and then, holding it firmly, stood ready to haul up.

CHAPTER XV — INVESTIGATIONS

Harry was relieved when, a few minutes later, Bertie's head appeared above the edge, and directly afterwards he crawled over. "My arms have strengthened ever so much with our work. I could have done it before, but it would have been hard work."

"Well, so far so good, Bertie. There is no doubt that it is one of the best hiding-places in the world, and I am not a bit surprised that the Spaniards never found it. Now we will go back to the edge of the ravine and have a good look from that side."

As they went along he said, "Let us have a look at these bushes, Bertie. The soil is very thin about here, and I wonder that the trees grew."

"These are pines," Bertie said, "and in the mountains we often saw pines growing among rocks where there did not seem a handful of soil for them."

On examining they found several old stumps, and thrusting a ramrod down Harry found, to his surprise, that the soil was from three to four feet deep. He tried again a little farther off, and found that it was two feet; further still, it was only one.

"The tree must have stood in a hole in the rock," he said. "Try another one, Bertie." The same results were obtained. "That explains it, Bert. Evidently when they planted the trees to prevent this place from being seen from the hills, they cut away the rock in circles about twelve feet across and made cup-shaped holes, which they filled up with earth. When they planted the young trees I dare say at first they watered them. They could easily enough fetch water up from the stream. When the trees got fairly rooted they would be able to leave them alone, perhaps giving them a good watering once every two or three months. Whenever the rains came they would be able to give up watering altogether, for in these basins the earth would keep moist for a very long time. It would be a big job, but no doubt the king who built the place had all his tribe at work on it. It is probable that the Incas had established themselves at Cuzco for many years before they came down to this place, and the trees may not have been planted till their coming was first heard of. In that case there would be plenty of time to hide the place before they came down and searched the shore. We know that the Chimoos resisted them for a considerable time before they were finally conquered. Well, for whatever purpose this place was built it is one in which either the Chimoos or the Incas, if they ever found the place, would be likely to hide treasure, which is satisfactory. Now we will sit down here for a short time and watch both windows. You look at the two top lines, Bertie, and I will look at the two lower lines. I certainly do not see any signs of life. That is how the water gets out," and he pointed to a roughly-shaped arch about twelve feet wide and as many high. Through this the little stream disappeared. "I expect there is a similar passage at the other end."

"There may have been," Bertie said. "I was hanging so close to the wall that there may very well have been one without my being able to see it. But it looks pitch-dark in there. If there were much of an opening we ought to see the light, for, as we agreed, it can't be more than a hundred feet long."

[Image: HARRY DROPPED THE BARREL OF HIS RIFLE INTO THE PALM OF HIS LEFT HAND.]

"That is the first place we will investigate, Bertie. The question of how we are to get into the house wants some thinking over. That lowest window is a good twenty-five feet above the ground."

"Of course if we had a grapnel we could fasten it to the end of a rope and chuck it in."

"We shall have to make something of that sort. If the window had been on the other side instead of this it would have been easy enough, because I could have lowered you and slipped down the rope afterwards, but that arch sticking out so far on this side makes it impossible. All that we can do now is, as far as I can see, to lower ourselves down on to the top of that wall in the ravine, then go and examine the tunnel. We have got plenty of rope to lower ourselves from here on to the wall."

They watched the building for another twenty minutes. "I am convinced that no one is there," Harry said. "I have not seen as much as a shadow pass any of the windows since. If people did live in it they would naturally be on this side of the house, because the rooms here are better lighted and more cheerful, and no doubt they are the principal rooms, as the house narrows so much at the other end."

"Well, let us try it," Bertie said. "If there is a strong force here we should only have to make a bolt back to that narrow staircase. We could hold that against a whole tribe."

They rose and walked along the edge of the ravine till they were above the wall, then, fastening the rope to a stump, they slid down on to it.

"So far so good," Harry said, as, holding their rifles in their hands, they went down the steps. Then he suddenly stopped. "Hullo," he exclaimed, "here are two skeletons!"

They were not quite skeletons, for the bones were covered by a parchment-like skin, and there were still remains of the short skirt each had worn in life. A spear lay beside each. With difficulty the brothers passed down without treading upon them.

"They must have been here a long time, Harry," Bertie said when they got to the bottom.

"Any time," the other said. "In the dry air of these low lands there is scarce any decay. You remember those mummies we saw. I believe iron or steel will lie here for years without rusting. They may have been here for a couple of hundred years or more."

"I wonder what killed them, Harry?"

"I have no idea. You see, one was lying almost on the other with his arms round his body, as if he had died trying to lift him up. If they had been shot by arrows they would still be sticking into them; if they had been killed by people pursuing them they would probably be lying upon their backs, for they would naturally have faced round at the last moment to resist their pursuers, whereas there are no signs of injury. This settles the point that there is no one in the house. Had it been inhabited, the bodies would have been removed from the path, for it is by this that people would go out and return. There may have been a ladder down from the wall; the only other way they could have got out would have been through that passage to the sea. A boat may have been kept there; but even if that had been so, we should scarcely have found those bodies on the steps. Well, we shall have plenty of time to talk over that."

They walked across the open space until they approached the building. For a height of twenty feet it was constructed of stone, above that it appeared to be made of the great adobe bricks which had been so largely used at Pachacamac, and in others of the old ruins they had seen.

"There is no question that it must have been built by the Chimoos or some race before them," Harry said; "the Incas could have had no possible reason for erecting such a place. Well, now for the tunnel."

The little stream only occupied two feet of the passage. They were therefore enabled to walk down dry-foot.

"We ought to have brought a torch with us," Bertie said.

"I don't think we shall want that; there is a sort of thin blue light, the reflection of the light upon the water outside, though I don't know why it should be so blue."

The reason was soon manifest. The passage sloped downwards, and when they had gone some fifty feet their progress was arrested by water which appeared of a deep-blue colour.

"That is it," Harry said. "You see the roof comes down into the water twenty feet off, and the light has come up under it. They sloped this passage to make the water flow out below the surface of the sea, so that the opening could not be seen from without. By the light I should not say that the opening is more than six inches under the water. I don't know how the tides are, but if it is high tide now, the top of the opening would be eighteen inches out of water at low tide, for, as you know, the tide only rises about two feet on this coast. In that case a boat would be able to come in and out at low tide, but of course a man wanting to come in or go out could easily dive under at any time. Well, that settles that point for the present. It was a clever plan; any amount of water could flow out in flood time, and yet no one who took the trouble to come behind that ledge of rocks we saw would have any idea that there was an opening. I think now that we had better go back, Bertie; in the first place because we can do nothing until we have manufactured a grapnel of some sort, and in the next place because every moment we delay will add to the anxiety of our friends in camp. We must have been away three hours, I should say."

They ascended the steps, fastened the short rope round a block at the top of the wall across the ravine, and lowered themselves down. They had to proceed with great care while making their way down the slope composed of rough and jagged rocks, Once at the bottom of the ravine, however, they walked briskly on. They had scarcely issued from the entrance when they saw a stir in the camp in the distance and heard a shout of delight, and then Dias dashed off to meet them at the top of his speed.

"Thanks to all the saints, señor, that you are safe! You do not know how we have suffered. We have prayed ever since you started, all of us. Once or twice I threw myself down in despair, but Maria chided me for having so little faith in God to keep you from evil, and cheered me by saying that had harm come to you we should assuredly have heard the sound of your guns. Have you been in the castle?"

"No, Dias, we have not been in—for the good reason that we could not get in, because the only entrance is fully twenty-five feet from the ground. We cannot enter until we have made some contrivance by which a rope can be fixed there, or manufactured a ladder, which would be the best way and save a lot of trouble, if we could get a couple of poles long enough. We thought that we would come back when we had seen all there was to be seen outside the place."

The Indian's face fell. "Then you do not know what is in the house, señor?"

"No; but we are certain that there is no one there, and that probably no one has been there for the past two hundred years, and perhaps a good deal longer."

"And the demons have not interfered with you?"

"The demons knew better," Bertie laughed.

"They may not be powerful in the daytime," Dias said in an awed tone. "It is at night that they would be terrible."

"Well, Dias," Bertie said, "everyone knows that the demons cannot withstand the sign of the cross. All you have to do is to make a small cross, hold it up in front of you and say, '*Vade retro, Satanas!*' and they will fly howling away."

"Seriously," Harry said, "you know it is all bosh about demons, Dias."

"But the church exorcises evil spirits. I have seen a priest go with candles and incense to a haunted house, and drive out the evil spirits there."

"That is to say, Dias, no spirits were ever seen there afterwards, and we may be very certain that no spirits were ever seen there before, though cowardly people might have fancied they saw them. However, to-morrow we shall get inside, and Bertie and I will stop there all night, and if we neither see nor hear anything of them you may be quite sure that there are none there."

"But the traditions say they have strangled many and torn them, señor; their bodies have been found in the daytime and carried off."

"It is quite possible that they were strangled and torn there, but you may be sure that it was the work not of demons, but of the men who were set to guard the place from intruders. Well, those men have gone. We found two skeletons, which must have been there at least a hundred years, perhaps a great deal more. They were lying on the stairs, the only way of getting into the place, and they would have been removed long ago if anyone had been passing in or out."

By this time they had arrived at the camp. "I knew you would come back all safe, señors," Donna Maria said triumphantly; "I told Dias so over and over again. But what have you seen?"

"I see something now—or rather I don't see something now that I should like to see," Bertie laughed. "I thought you would have got a good dinner ready for me, but I do not see any signs of its being even begun."

The woman laughed. "I have been too busy praying, señor, and have been keeping up Dias's spirits. I never knew him faint-hearted before, and it really almost frightened me; but I will set about getting dinner at once."

"No, no," Harry said; "we are really not hungry. We had a good meal before we started. So do you three sit down and I will tell you all we have seen."

The three natives listened with intense interest. When he had done, Maria clapped her hands. "It must be a wonderful place," she said. "I wish I had gone with you, I will go to-morrow if you will take me."

"Certainly we will take you, Maria; and I have no doubt that Dias will go too."

"I will go as far as the place," said Dias, "but I will not promise to go in."

"I won't press you, Dias. When we have slept there a night I have no doubt you will become convinced that it is quite safe. And now about the ladder. We shall really want two to be comfortable—one for getting up to the window, that must be made of wood; the other, which will be used for getting up and down the wall in the ravine, may be made of ropes. But I think that that had best be hung from the top of the ravine above it, so as to avoid having to climb over those rough stones at the foot, which are really very awkward. One might very well twist one's ankle among them."

"I will go at once, señor, and get the poles," Dias said. "You may as well come with me, José. We passed a wood in the valley about five miles off; there we can cut down a couple of young trees. If we put the saddles on two of the riding mules, when we have got the poles clear we can fasten the ends to ropes and trail them behind us."

"We shall also want some of the branches you cut off, Dias. You had better say thirty lengths of about two feet long, so that we may place the rungs nine inches apart. You had better get poles thirty feet long, for we may not have just the height by a couple of feet."

The two natives at once rode off, and the brothers set to work to collect sticks for the fire.

"It is too bad, señors, that this should not have been done while you were away, but we thought of nothing but your danger."

"You were perfectly right, Maria; if we were in peril, you did the best thing of all to obtain help for us. As to the dinner, there is no hurry whatever for it. What have you got to eat?"

"There is nothing, señor, but a few of the fish we fried two days ago, and the ham that we smoked of that bear."

"I will take the line, then, and go down and try to catch some fresh fish," Bertie said. "There is a good-sized pool about half-way between here and the ravine. I might get some fish there."

"I will take my gun, Bertie, and go up to the bushes by the ravine, and see if I can get a bird or two. There is no other shelter anywhere about here."

In half an hour the lad brought a dozen fish into the camp. None of them were above half a pound, but they were nearly of a size.

"These will be very nice," the woman said with a smile as he handed them to her. "I have thrown away the others. I do not think we dried them enough; they were certainly going bad. I have heard your brother fire several times, and as he does not often miss, I have no doubt he will bring us something."

Twenty minutes later Harry was seen coming along. When he arrived he threw down a large bunch of wild pigeons.

"There are ten brace," he said. "That will give us four apiece. I found nothing in the bushes, but I suddenly remembered that when we went across from the ravine to the house, lots of wild pigeons rose from the sides of the rocks. We did not give them a thought at the time, our attention being fixed upon the building. But when I got nothing above, I suddenly remembered them, and concluded that they had their nests in the crannies of the rocks. So I walked along to the top, and as I did so numbers of them flew up. I shot a couple; most of the others soon settled again, but some kept flying round and round, and in ten minutes I got as many as I wanted. Then of course I had to go down into the ravine by the rope and the steps to gather them up. I returned the way we did, by the rope we had left hanging from the top of the wall."

Maria was already at work on the birds. Taking them by the legs, she dipped them for a minute into a pot of boiling water, and as she took them out Bertie pulled off the feathers. Then she cut off the heads and feet, cleaned them, and spitted them on José's ramrod, and, raking out a line of embers from the fire, laid the ends of the ramrod on two forked twigs while she attended to the fish.

"But they will be done before the others arrive," Bertie said.

"No, señor; there they come! They will be here in a quarter of an hour. The cakes are ready and hot, so we will lay the pigeons on them, and they will be nicely flavoured by the time that we have eaten the fish and are ready for them."

Dias and José soon arrived at a gallop, with the long poles trailing behind them and a fagot of short sticks fastened to each saddle.

"Those are capital poles, Dias," Harry said as he examined them—"strong enough for anything. We will chop notches in them for the rungs to lie in. There will be no fear then of their shifting, which they might do if the lashings stretched. Now, we have got a capital dinner just done to a turn, so you see we have not been lazy while you were away.

"You see," he said, after they had finished breakfast, "my shooting has quite settled the point that no Indians are in the castle. If there had been they would certainly have come to the windows to see who was firing. I kept an eye on the castle between each shot, and saw no signs of any movement. It is a capital thing that so many pigeons live among the rocks. If we content ourselves with say five brace a day, they will last us a long time, and will be a change from salt and dried meat, which we should otherwise have to depend upon, for we cannot be sending away for fresh meat two or three times a week. We can get fish, though I don't suppose that will last very long, for the pool will soon be fished out, and I don't think that there is water enough in other places for fish of that size."

"We can get them from the sea, Harry. We have got plenty of large hooks and lines, which we used on the other side of the mountains. If any of the window openings on that side are large enough, we can let down the lines from there. If not, we can do it from the top where I went down."

"I should not like that," Harry said. "One might slip on that short grass."

"Well, one could dive out through the passage and sit on that ledge of rocks, and fish either inside them or in the sea outside."

"Yes, we might do that, Bertie, and certainly it would be a first-rate thing if we could get plenty of fish. It would keep us in good health and make a nice change. I think to-morrow morning, Dias, we had better fix our camp close up to the mouth of the ravine. Out here in the open valley we can be seen from the hills, and if anyone caught sight of the animals, it would very soon get talked about, and we should have a party down here to see who we were and what we were about."

"Yes, señor, that would be much better. I should not have liked to go nearer this morning; but now that you have been there twice, and have returned safely, I am ready to move."

"It would certainly be better; besides, it would save us a couple of miles' walk each time we wanted a meal. However, when we once set to work I have no doubt we shall establish ourselves in the castle. Of course one of us will come down morning and evening to see to the animals."

As soon as the meal was finished they set to work to make the ladder. A short stick was cut as a guide to the space that was to be left between the rungs. Bertie and José marked off the distances on the two poles, and Dias and Harry with their axes cut the grooves in which the sticks were to lie. Then the poles were laid a foot apart, and the work of pressing the sticks into their places began. They agreed that the ropes should not be cut up, as they would be wanted for fastening on the loads whenever the mules went to fetch food or powder. Two of the head-ropes were used on each side, and a firm job was made.

"When you go, Dias, for the powder and so on, you must get another supply of rope. We shall want a longer ladder than this in the ravine, and also a rope to lift powder and firewood and so on into the castle, and perhaps for other things that one does not think of at present. Tomorrow we will unfasten the cord by which we descended to the wall, as we shall not want to use that in future. I think to-morrow, when we go to the castle, as you and José do not mean to accompany us, you might take your axes and cut down a lot of those stumps among the brushwood, split them up, and pitch them into the courtyard of the castle. It would be well to lay in a good stock of firewood. We shall want it for cooking and lighting of an evening. We have only one or two torches left, and we shall want a cheerful fire."

"I may go with you to-morrow, may I not?" Maria said.

"Certainly you may, if you wish."

"I should like to," she said. "In your company I sha'n't be a bit afraid of demons; and I want to see the place."

"That is right, Maria, and it shows at any rate that your curiosity is stronger than your superstition."

"If Maria goes I will go," Dias said. "I don't like it; but if she went and I didn't I should never hear the last of it."

"Very well," Harry said with a laugh, "I do think she would have the better of you in the future if you didn't. So you see you will be both conquering your superstitions—she, because her curiosity is greater; you, because you are more afraid of her tongue than you are of the demons."

"A woman never forgets, señor; if she once has something to throw up in a man's teeth it comes out whenever she is angry."

"I suppose so, Dias. Bertie and I have had no experience that way, but we will take your word for it."

The next morning they moved the mules and all their belongings to the extreme end of the valley. Then they had an early breakfast. José took up his axe and the others their arms; the former turned back for the point where he could climb the hill. Dias and Harry took the heavy end of the ladder, Bertie the light one, and they started up the ravine. Maria followed with a store of bread that she had baked the day before. It was hard work carrying the ladder up the rocks at the foot of the wall. When it was securely fastened there, they mounted and dragged it up to them.

When they came out into the open space there was a pause. "It is, as you said, a strange place, señor."

"It is, Dias, an extraordinary place; and if the people who built it wanted, as I suppose they did, to avoid observation, they could not have chosen a better. When those trees were growing it would have been impossible to catch sight of them without coming down the ravine."

"It looks very still," Dias said in a doubtful voice.

"That is generally the case when a place is empty, Dias, Now let us go on at once and get the ladder up."

As soon as the ladder was in position Harry mounted, closely followed by Bertie. Dias hesitated; but a merry laugh from his wife settled the point, and he followed with an expression of grave determination on his face. As soon as he was on the ladder his wife followed him with a light step.

As Harry reached the top, he found that the sill of the window was two feet and a half above the floor of the apartment. He stepped down and then looked round. The room occupied the whole width of the house, and was some twenty feet wide. Four rows of pillars ran across it, supporting the roof above. the ends of the room were in semi-darkness. It was not above ten feet in height. There were rude carvings on the pillars and the walls.

By the time he had made these observations the others had joined him. "I see people there," Dias said, in an awed voice, pointing to one end of the room. Harry dropped the barrel of his rifle into the palm of his left hand. After gazing two seconds he placed it on his shoulder, saying, "There are people, Dias, but they won't do us any harm;" and he walked in that direction. Two figures lay on the ground; four others were in a sitting position, close to each other, against the end wall. Some bows and arrows and spears lay near them. All were dressed in a garment of rough cloth. Harry walked up to one and touched it on the head with the muzzle of his gun. As he did so it crumbled away; the bones rattled on the stone floor as they fell. Donna Maria gave a little cry.

"They are dead!" she exclaimed. "They must have been dead years and years ago."

"Two or three hundred, I should think. Your legends are evidently true, Dias. There was a party left here to keep strangers from entering this place. Now, before we go farther, let us think this out. We will sit down on the ledge of the window. But before we do so, take a good look at their arms and skulls, Dias. You have often been with travellers to the ruins; let us hear what you say."

Dias, who was now assured that he had only to deal with human beings, examined them carefully, looking at the ornaments that still hung round their necks, and then said: "They are not the old people, señor; these were Incas."

"That is an important point; now let us see how this is to be explained. Now," he said, as they sat down, "it is clear that the Incas did know this building. They may have discovered treasures here or they may not; but it would certainly seem that they were as anxious as the Chimoos had been to keep its existence a secret, and it is certain that they must have had some interest in doing so. We have reason to believe that the Spaniards at least did not know of it. There is no doubt whatever that these men were not killed in fight; on the contrary, their sitting position proves that they died quietly, and probably at the same time. We see no signs of food; we may find some as we search the place. If we do not, we must take it that they either died from an outbreak of some epidemic or from hunger. And it is quite probable that the two skeletons on the steps were two of their companions who were going out to seek for food, and that they fell from weakness; one clearly died in the act of trying to lift the other. What do you think of that, Dias?"

HARRY DROPPED THE BARREL OF HIS RIFLE INTO THE PALM OF HIS LEFT HAND

"I think that what you say is likely. But why should they have died from hunger?"

"It is probable that others were in the secret, and were in the habit of bringing provisions to them, and perhaps of relieving them at certain periods. We know that there were fierce battles in the early times of the Spaniards. In one of these battles the whole of those who were acquainted with the secret may have fallen. Or it may have been earlier after the conquest had been completed, when the Spaniards drove tens of thousands of men to work as slaves in the mines. The people here may have remained at their post, hoping for relief until it was too late. Two of the strongest may have started at last, but have been too weak to climb the steps, and died there. Their comrades may have never known their fate, but have sat down to die here, as you see. I should think it probable that the second of my suggestions is likely to be the right one, and that this did not take place until perhaps a hundred years after the arrival of the Spaniards, otherwise those legends of men who came near this place being killed would never have been handed down. If all this is as I suggest, either the Incas knew that the Chimoos had buried treasure here, or they themselves buried some, although, as you say, there is no tradition of treasure having been taken here. But it is possible that that treasure ship, which undoubtedly sailed from some place along the coast and was never again heard of, really came here; that her treasure was landed, and the vessel then destroyed. In either case, there is strong reason for hope that there is treasure somewhere in this castle if we can but find it."

"We will find it," Bertie said confidently. "What you say must be true. These Indians would never have been fools enough to sit here and die without some good reason for it. Well, I vote that before we do anything else we clear these bones out."

"We can do that the first thing to-morrow morning, Bertie. We can't just throw them out of the window. The bones are of men who died doing their duty to their country. We will leave them as they are to-day, and to-morrow we will bring up one of the big leather bags, place the bones in it, and take them down into the valley and bury them."

"Then you won't sleep here to-night, Harry?"

"No; I have not a shadow of superstition, but I do not think it would be lively here with those things at the end of the room. Now, let us look about a bit.

"This was evidently the great hall of the place; do you not think so, Dias?"

"Yes, señor; the house gets narrower as it nears the sea. This is by far the best lighted room on this side. No doubt the rooms on this floor were the abode of the chief who built it, and his principal followers; the others would be above."

"Well, we will light the two torches. Yes, there is no doubt that this was the room. You see there are brackets against all the pillars for holding torches. Before we go farther we will see what they are made of."

He took his knife out of his pocket and went up to one of the brackets, which consisted of bars of metal an inch and a half square and eighteen inches long. They widened out at the end, and here was a round hole about two inches in diameter, evidently intended to put the torch in. The metal was black with age. He scraped a few inches off one of them with his knife. "Silver!" he exclaimed. "It would have been better if they had been gold. But as there are four on each pillar, and twelve pillars, they would make a tidy weight. That is a good beginning, Bertie. If they are the same in all the rooms there would be several tons of it."

There was but one door to the room; through this they passed. Dias, now that there was some explanation for what he considered the work of the demons, had a more assured air. One passage led straight on; two others ran parallel to the wall of the room they had left.

"We will examine these first," Harry said. "It is likely enough they lead to the stairs to the lower room. There must be two floors below us, one above the level of the top of the tunnel, the other below that must be divided in two by it."

As they advanced into the passage there was a strange and sudden clamour, a roaring sound mingled with sharp shrieks and strange little piping squeaks. Maria ran back with a shriek of alarm, and there was a strange rush overhead. The torches were both extinguished, and Harry and his brother discharged their rifles almost at the same moment. Dias burst into a shout of laughter as they both dropped their weapons and swung their double-barrelled guns forward. "What on earth is it, Dias?"

"It is bats and birds, señor. I have seen them come out of caves that way many times. I dare say the place is full of bats. The birds would only come into rooms where there is some light."

Turning round they saw quite a cloud of bats flying out through the door.

"Confound it!" Harry said. "They have given me the worst fright I ever had in my life."

They went back to the room, they had left. Both Harry and Bertie had lost every tinge of colour from their faces.

"I am very glad, Harry," Bertie said, with an attempt at a laugh, "that you were frightened. I was scared almost out of my life."

Maria had thrown herself down on her face.

"Ah, señors," Dias said triumphantly, "you thought they were demons!"

"I did not think they were demons, Dias, but what they were I could not tell you. I never heard any such sound before. I am not ashamed to say that I did feel badly frightened. Now, see to your wife, Dias."

"There is nothing to be afraid of, Maria. What are you lying there for?"

The woman raised herself slightly. "Are you alive?" she said in a dazed way.

"Alive? of course I am! You don't suppose I am going to be frightened at a lot of bats? There, look at them, they are still streaming out."

"It is all right, Maria," Harry said. "You have had a fright; and so have Bertie and I, so you need not be ashamed of yourself. It is all very well for Dias to laugh, but he says he has seen such things before."

"If you were afraid, señor, I need not be ashamed that I was; I really did think it was the demons."

"There is no such thing, Maria; but it was as good an imitation of them as you are ever likely to see."

"I was in a horrible funk, Maria," Bertie said, "and I am only just getting over it; I feel I am quite as pale as you. What are you looking so pleased about, Dias?" he asked almost angrily.

"I am pleased, señor, now I have got even with Maria. The first time she says to me 'demons', I shall say to her 'bats'."

"Now, let us start again," Harry said as they all laughed. "But instead of going down, we will go upstairs. I have not pulled myself quite together yet, and I don't suppose you have."

"No, my knees are quite wobbling about, and if I saw anything, I certainly could not aim straight just at present. And it's rum; we had the main-mast struck by lightning off the Cape one voyage I made, and I did not feel a bit like this."

"I dare say not, Bertie. We all feel brave in dangers that we are accustomed to; it is what we don't know that frightens us. We will sit here on the window-sill for another five minutes before we move again. José, you have got some pulque in your gourd, I suppose?"

"Yes, señor."

"Then we will all take a drink of it. I don't like the stuff, but just at present I feel that it won't come amiss at all."

Some of the spirit was poured into a tin mug they had with them, and mixed with water, with which they had filled their water-bottles from the stream before starting.

CHAPTER XVI — THE SEARCH BEGINS

In a few minutes all were ready to go on again. Harry had asked Maria if she would like to go down the ladder and wait till they returned.

"No, señor, I should not like it at all. I don't care how full of bats the rooms are, now that I know what they are. As for Dias, I have no doubt that the first time he heard them he was just as frightened."

"No, I was not; but I dare say I should have been if the man I was with—I was then only about José's age—had not told me that the cavern was full of bats. There was a great storm coming on, and he proposed that we should take shelter there. We brought the mules into the mouth of the cave, and he said, 'Now, we will light a torch and go in a bit farther, and then you will be astonished. It is a bat cavern, and I have no doubt there are thousands of them here. They won't hurt us, though they may knock out our torch, and the noise they make is enough to scare one out of one's senses, if one does not know what it is.' Though I did know, I own I was frightened a bit; but since then I have been into several such caves, so I knew in a moment what it was. I ought to have warned the señors, for an old house like this, where there is very little light, is just the place for them."

"But there were birds too, Dias."

"Yes, I expect they were nearer. Perhaps some of them were in the other rooms, where they would be close to the openings. But they were probably scared too by the noise of the bats, and as the windows behind were too small for them all to fly out together, they made for the light instead."

"Well, now, let us start," Harry said, getting up. They again lit their torches, and this time found everything perfectly quiet in the passage. Two or three yards beyond the spot at which they had before arrived they saw a staircase to the left. It was faintly lighted from above, and, mounting it, they found themselves in a room extending over the whole width and depth of the house. The roof at the eastern end was not supported by pillars, but by walls three feet wide and seven or eight feet apart. The first line of these was evidently over the wall of the room they had left. There were four lines of similar supports erected, they had no doubt, over the walls of rooms below. The light from the four windows in front, and from an irregular opening at the other end some three feet high and six inches wide, afforded sufficient light for them to move about without difficulty. There were many signs of human habitation here. Along the sides were the remains of mats, which had apparently divided spaces six feet wide into small apartments. Turning these over they found many trifles—arrow-heads, bead-necklaces, fragments of pots, and even a child's doll.

"I expect this is the room where the married troops lived and slept," Harry said; "there is not much to see here."

The two stories above were exactly similar, except that there were no remains of dividing mats nor of female ornaments. They walked to the narrow end. Here the opening for light was of a different shape from those in the rooms below. It had apparently been originally of the same shape, but had been altered. In the middle it was, like the others, three feet high and six inches wide, but a foot from the bottom there was a wide cut, a foot high and three feet wide. As they approached it Dias gave an exclamation of surprise. Two skeletons lay below it. "They must have been on watch here, señor, when they died," he said as they came up to them.

"It is a rum place to watch," Bertie said, "for you cannot see out."

"You are right, Bertie, it is a curious hole."

The wall was over two feet thick; all the other openings had been driven straight through it, and, as they had noticed, were doubtless made in the stones before they were placed there, for inside they were cleanly cut, and it was only within three inches of the outer face that the edges had been left rough. This opening was of quite a different character. It sloped at a sharp angle, and no view of the open sea could be obtained, but only one of the line of rocks at the foot of the cliffs. It was roughly made, and by the marks of tools, probably of hardened copper, it had evidently been cut from the inside.

Harry stood looking for some time. "I cannot understand their cutting the hole like this. It could not be noticed from the sea that there was an opening at all; that is plain enough. But why make the hole at all when you can see nothing from it? And yet a watch has been placed here, while there was none at the other places where they could make out any passing ship."

"Perhaps," Bertie said, "it was done in order that if from the other places boats were seen approaching, they could chuck big stones down from here and sink any boat that might row inside the rocks into the entrance to the passage, which, as this is in the middle of the room, must be just under us."

"In that case they would have kept a supply of big stones here. I have no doubt whatever that it was made some time after the castle was built, and I should say, judging by its unfinished state, the work was done in haste. But what for, goodness only knows. Well now, having made no discoveries whatever on the upper floor, we will go down. It is certain that there can be no great treasure hidden under any of these floors, there is not depth enough for hiding-places. I counted the steps as we came upstairs, and there cannot be much more than two feet between the floor of one room and the ceiling in the next. I fancy that this is of single stones, each the flooring length of the space between the half-walls. You see that there is a long beam of stone running on the top of the dividing wall, and the ends of these stones appear to rest on it. It is below that we must look for hiding-places."

They descended to the first floor. They found that the space behind the great room was divided into a number of chambers. All of these, with the exception of the small one on the sea-face, were necessarily in absolute darkness, and in all were brackets for torches, similar to those in the principal chamber. Bertie counted them, and found that, including those first met with, they numbered one hundred and twenty-three.

"How much do you think they weigh apiece?" he asked Harry when the tour was finished.

"I have not the slightest idea, Bertie. I should think about fifteen pounds, but it may be five pounds less than that. They would certainly give a very nasty knock on the head."

"Oh, I was not thinking of knocks on the head. If there are a hundred bars at fifteen pounds apiece, it is a big amount of silver; if they are only ten pounds each—and really I think that is nearer the mark—they weigh a thousand pounds. What is silver worth a pound?"

"It varies. You can put it at five shillings an ounce; that would be three pounds sterling for one of silver—three thousand pounds in a rough calculation for the lot."

"Well, that is not a bad beginning, Harry; it would pay all the expenses and leave a couple of thousand over."

Harry shrugged his shoulders. "A drop in the ocean as far as I am concerned, Bertie. Still, it is a beginning; and you may be sure that they did not take all this trouble to guard this castle for the sake of three thousand pounds' worth of silver."

They now went down to the next floor. Here there were two staircases, and the space was divided into two parts by a wall along the centre. There were no openings whatever for light. One half had evidently been devoted to arms. Here still lay hundreds of spear-shafts, tens of thousands of arrows, piles of hide shields, and caps of the same material.

"This store must have been larger than was required for the garrison of the place," Harry said, "it must have been a reserve for re-arming a whole tribe."

Besides the arms there were great bales of rough cloth and piles of skins, all in a marvellous state of preservation owing to the dryness of the air. After thoroughly examining the room they went up the stairs leading into it and descended those into the adjoining chamber. This was divided into compartments by transverse walls four feet shorter than the width, thereby leaving a passage through from end to end. Here in confusion—for the most part turned inside out—were sacks of matting and bags of leather. One of the compartments was filled with great jars arranged in tiers. Some of the compartments were quite empty.

"I think, señor, that these were stores of loose grain, probably maize. I do not see a single grain left."

They looked carefully round with the torches. "This carries out our idea, Dias, that the people upstairs died of hunger. I have no doubt, as you say, that the sacks did contain grain. If these had been cleared in the ordinary way there would certainly remain a good deal loosely scattered about. They might have been full or half-full at the time the place was left as we found it. Possibly, instead of ten men, the garrison may have been ten times as strong at first, but in the fifty or hundred years before the last survivors died they may have dwindled to a tenth of that number. However, it is plain that, as you say, the store of food was not carried away, but was consumed to the last grain. In the same way you can see, by the way the sacks and bags are tumbled about and turned inside out, how careful was the search for any remnant that might have been overlooked when they were first emptied. It all points to starvation."

Three of the largest divisions bore evident traces that at some time or other, animals, probably llamas or vicuñas, had been closely penned there. Another had been occupied by a store of hay, some of which still remained. When they had thoroughly examined this room, Harry looked at his watch and said, "It is late in the afternoon—our torches are nearly finished; however, there is time for a casual look round at the cellars below. To-morrow we will begin a regular search there."

They descended by the staircase to the basement.

"How narrow this place is!" Bertie exclaimed. "It is not much more than half the width of the room above."

"Of course it is not; the two rooms above occupied the whole width of the house, these only occupy the width between the passage and the rock-wall on each side. You see, the tunnel is twelve feet wide, and we may take it that these walls are at least three feet thick—it is not as if they had been built of brick, or even of stones cut to shape. They knew nothing of the arch, and, as you saw outside, this came up nearly to a point. The stones were longer and longer with each course, each projecting over the one below it, until, when they were within two feet of joining, a very long slab was laid across them. The stones may be three feet wide at the bottom and ten feet at the top, and you see the wall extends over here in the same way—as of course it must have done, otherwise the whole thing would have overbalanced and fallen in before that slab at the top was added. So, you see, there is the width of the tunnel, twelve feet, and the two walls, say six feet more, to be taken off the fifty feet. So the cellars by the side of the passage can only be about sixteen feet and a half at this end, which is what they seem to be, and will go away to nothing at the other end, as we shall see presently."

The first thing they saw was a sunken tank in the floor. This was full of water. It was about four feet square, and on sounding it with one of the ramrods, they found it was about the same in depth, the water coming to within a foot of the top. It was against the wall facing the ravine.

"This must have some connection with the stream. Otherwise it would have been dry long ago."

"We did not see any hole when we went down the passage," Bertie said.

"No. Most likely a hole something like this was cut in the rock outside, and a pipe driven to the bottom of this cistern. They would only have to fill the one in the tunnel with cut blocks to within a foot of the surface, and with smaller stones to the same level as the bed of the stream; then the water in the cistern would always be level with that outside. They put it in this end so as to be well out of reach of the salt water farther in. They were no fools who built this place. However closely they were besieged, and even if the enemy occupied the space in front of the house, their water-supply was secure."

"But in time of floods, Harry, if the water rose a foot in the passage—and we saw it did more than that—it would flood the whole of this basement."

"That is so, Bertie; but you may be sure that there was some provision against that. They would have some valve that they could shut, or possibly there was a block of wood covered with leather that they could push into the pipe at the bottom of this cistern."

Beyond a considerable store of firewood, in large and small blocks, nothing could be seen in the chamber.

"I expect these two places were used as prisons," Harry said, "though in case a very large force were assembled some may have slept here. At ordinary times the upper rooms would be quite sufficient. But you see they had to build the whole height of the rocky arch, and they wanted the entrance to the place to be so far above the ground-level that it would be extremely difficult for an enemy to climb into it. A hostile force could only have come in at that entrance, and a small body of determined men might have held it against a host. These lower chambers were simply cellars; the store-rooms were above them, and the habitable part of the castle. Now let us look at the chamber on the other side; no doubt we shall find it just like this."

This proved to be the case. There were another cistern and more piles of firewood, otherwise it was empty. After a short survey they returned to the main chamber, bringing up with them two of the empty leather bags. In these they placed the bones of the dead, the remains all crumbling when touched, as the first skeleton had done. The bags were lowered to the ground, and the four searchers descended and carried them to the mouth of the ravine. In a spare bag which they brought with them they placed the bones of the two skeletons on the steps, and then carried them all out to the open valley.

"We will bury them when we move the camp down here to-morrow morning," Harry said. "We forgot the two up at that window. That is no matter, we can throw them out to-morrow; they will lie as well at the bottom of the sea as in the earth here."

Not much was said as they returned to the castle. They had been a very silent party all day. The gloom and darkness, the way in which their voices echoed in the empty hall, had exercised a depressing effect on them; and Donna Maria, generally the most talkative of the party, had not quite recovered from the shock which the exit of the bats had given her. It was not until she had cooked a meal, and they all sat down to it, that they quite recovered their spirits. They had found José awaiting their return. He had a blazing fire, having brought down as much firewood as he could carry, and Dias had briefly told him the result of their explorations.

"Well, Harry, what do you think altogether?" Bertie asked after the meal was over.

"I think we ought to be very well satisfied," he replied. "Everything has borne out the ideas we had. The castle may have been built as a fortress by some great chief, certainly before the time of the Incas, or it may have been used for a prison. The ornaments and things we found showed that it was known to the Incas. They would have had no occasion to use it when they were undisputed masters of the country, but when the troubles came with the Spaniards a garrison was placed here, and possibly some of their chiefs took refuge in the place. Then came the time when all opposition to the invaders ceased, and only a small body of men were left here to guard the secret, and the treasure if there were any. Generations may have passed before the last of the garrison died of hunger, and probably all others who were in the secret fell in some insurrection or died in the mines. All this seems plain enough, except that possibly there was no treasure. That left by the Chimoos may have been discovered by the Incas. I should think it extremely likely that the ship Dias mentioned as setting out with a large amount of treasure was intended to land its stores here.

"It may have done so, or it may have sunk at sea. I am inclined to think that it was lost, because the traditions concerning these hidden treasures seem to be extremely accurate; and yet, as Dias says, none tell of any Inca treasure being concealed here. However, it is quite possible that the treasure did come here and was landed, and that the ship was then broken up, so that it might be supposed she was lost at sea, and that this was kept so profound a secret by the men here, that the news was never generally known even among the natives. So far our search to-day has been successful, but I see that a hunt for the treasure will be a very difficult one. Certainly in the upper chambers there doesn't appear any possibility of such a hiding-place existing. The whole space is accounted for. The walls are all of solid stone, and have no special thickness. If the roofs had been arched there might be empty spaces on each side of the spring of the arch, but they are supported by pillars or walls, with only just space between the floors for the beams of solid stone. Of course it is in the lowest room that one would expect to find hiding-places like those we saw at Pachacamac." He paused.

"Well, why should they not be there, Harry?"

"Because, as we saw, the floor is at most twelve inches above the water-level. How is it possible that they could have constructed chambers below that level, that is in the bed of a torrent? It is probable that the solid rock lies many feet below the bed of the stream. A portion of that great arch must from time to time have fallen into it; and it may be that the river once ran forty or fifty feet below its present level. In all the places that we have seen these treasure chambers were formed in solid adobe foundations, as the temples always stood on artificial terraces. With all our appliances at the present time it would be next to impossible to sink in a stratum of great rock fragments below the water level, and I do not believe that the old people here could have done so even had it been a solid rock. The difficulties of excavating chambers in it would have been enormous. They could split rocks with the grain, and all the stone walls we have seen were made of regular pieces, and evidently formed of stone so split. They were able to give them a sort of facing with great labour, but the tools they had were not made of material hard enough to work in solid rock, and the labour of excavating such chambers would have been stupendous. Therefore I am at a loss to imagine where any such chambers can be in that castle."

Dias nodded gravely. He had been with travellers who had done a great deal of excavation, and he was able to understand Harry's argument. Maria, who was listening attentively, also understood it. José simply rolled cigarettes and smoked them. It was a matter for his elders, and he did not even try to follow what Harry was saying. There was some minutes' silence, and then Bertie said, "But the floors are all even."

"What do you mean, Bertie?" Harry asked in a puzzled tone.

"I mean, Harry, that they run straight along. There is no dip in them."

"Of course there isn't. Who ever heard of building floors on the slope?"

"Yes, that is what I mean. We know that the tunnel slopes down its own height. It is twelve feet high at the entrance, and at the lower end it is some inches below the level, so it falls twelve feet at least. At the end where the cistern is, the floor of the basement is only a few inches above the bottom of the passage; therefore at the other end it must be twelve feet above the water-level."

"You are right, Bertie!" Harry exclaimed. "What a fool I was not to think of it! There must be a space underneath it a hundred feet long, sloping from nothing down to twelve feet. There is room for a dozen chambers such as those we saw on each side of the tunnel. Well done, Bertie! you have given me fresh hope. It would be a splendid hiding-place, for any searchers who came down and saw the water in the cistern would believe at once that, as neither the Chimoos nor the Incas could have known how to build under water, there was no use in searching for hidden chambers under this floor. You see, neither of them had any knowledge of cement or mortar. All their bricks and stones are laid without anything of the sort; and whatever amount of labour was available no chamber could be made under water, for as fast as holes were dug the water would come in, and even if they could line it with stone-work the water would penetrate through the cracks. Now, Dias, that we see with certainty where we have to dig, we can make our preparations. I will write down a list of the things we decided the other day we should want:—Six kegs of powder, two hundred feet of fuse, four boring-tools, six steel wedges, the smallest smith's fire you can buy—for we shall have to sharpen the tools,—six borers, a large bundle of torches, four sledge-hammers—we have enough pickaxes and shovels,—and another fifty fathoms, that is a hundred yards, of rope. I don't know anything else that we shall want in the mining way.

"You and your wife had better settle what provisions you must get. We shall certainly need a good supply of flour—a couple of sacks, I should think—tea, coffee, and sugar, dried or salted meat. And you might get a supply of smoked fish. I have no doubt that we shall catch fresh fish here in the sea, but we shall all be too busy to spend much time on that. You had better get three or four gallons of pulque; one cannot be always drinking coffee. We have still got a good stock of whisky and brandy. Your wife will certainly want a good supply of red pepper and other things for her stews. It would not be a bad thing to have a couple of crates of poultry. Don't pack them too closely, or half of them will be smothered before you get them here. Dead meat would be of no use, for it won't keep in this heat. We can turn them all out in the courtyard in front of the castle, and they can pick up their living there among the lower slopes of the cliffs. We can give them a few handfuls of grain a day. Don't get too many cocks, and let the hens be young ones. They ought to supply us with plenty of eggs and some broods of chickens. You must calculate what the weight will be, and take the mules accordingly."

"Very well, señor. I need not be away more than three days at most. It is only about twenty miles to Ancon."

"You might take the two llamas down with you and sell them there. They have done good work, and I should not like to kill and eat them. So mind you sell them to someone who wants them for carriage work. We shall not require them any more for that purpose. Will you want to take José with you?"

"I think not, señor, for I should say that four baggage mules will be ample, and I can lead them myself; and certainly you will find José useful here."

Dias and his wife then withdrew a short distance from the fire, and engaged in an animated conversation as to the things she required.

"Don't stint matters," Harry said, raising his voice. "We may be here for the next two or three months, and the less frequently you have to go down to buy things the better. It would be easy to account for your first purchases by saying that you were going on an expedition to the mountains, but you could not go to the place with the same story again."

"There are other places I can go to, señor; but I will get a good store of everything this time."

Dias started at daybreak with four mules and the two llamas. The others rolled up the tent-beds and the remaining stores, loaded up the other mules, and moved down to the mouth of the ravine. Here they pitched the little tents again.

"They will form a central point for the mules to come to," Harry said. "We will leave the sacks of maize here, but give the animals a good feed now. They will be sure to keep close to the spot. All the other things we will carry into the castle; but before we start we will bury these bags of bones."

When this was done, and the saddles taken off and piled together against the rocks, the other things were made up in portable packets, and they started up the ravine. They made three journeys before everything was brought to the foot of the ladder leading up to the window. Then the two brothers mounted, and hauled the things up with a rope which José, who remained below, fastened to them. When the last was up he went to the foot of the rock and brought several armfuls of the wood he had thrown down on the previous day. This was also hauled up.

"You had better fetch some more, José. We mean to keep a big fire burning here night and day; it will make the place cheerful. I will have a fire also burning where we are at work below. Now, señora, we will rig up some blankets on a line between the pillars at the end of the room opposite to that in which we found the skeletons, so as to make a special apartment for you and Dias. We will spread our beds at night near the fire."

The screen was soon made. A cord was run from the wall to the pillar next to it, some five feet above the floor, and three blankets were sufficient to fill the space.

Harry was about to make another line from the pillar, when Maria said:

"I would rather not, señor; I am not a bit afraid. This screen is quite large enough, and it will be more cheerful not to be shut up altogether, as then, when I am lying down, I can see the reflection of the fire on the walls, and it will be much more cheerful."

Then a blazing fire was lit. The wood was almost as dry as tinder, and burnt without smoke. It was built almost touching the back wall, in which, some five feet above the fire, Harry with a pick made a hole four inches deep.

While he was doing this, José went down and cut a sapling four inches in diameter, growing in a cleft on the rock, and from this cut off two six-foot lengths and brought them up. One end of the thickest of these was driven into the hole and tightly wedged in there, the other end was lashed securely to an upright beam.

"There, Maria," he said when it was finished, "you will be able to hang your pots and kettles from that at any height you like above the fire. Now, you can set to work as soon as you like, to get breakfast for us. We have been at work for four or five hours, and have good appetites."

"I have the cakes ready to bake, señor, and I sha'n't be long before I get an olla ready for you."

"Well, José, what do you think of the place?" Harry asked.

"I should like it better if it were not so big," the lad said. "I shall want a broom, señor, to sweep out the dust."

"It is three inches deep," Maria said.

"I should not bother about that, Maria; it would be a tremendous job to sweep such a big room, and the dust is so fine that it would settle again and cover everything. Besides, it will be a good deal softer to lay our beds on than the stones would be, so I think you had better let it remain as it is, especially as you are fond of going about without your shoes. I think I will rig up a blanket against the doorway. It will make the place look a good deal more snug, and will keep the bats from returning."

"I am not afraid of the bats, now I know what they are; but I should be constantly expecting them to rush out again."

"I expect a good many went back last night," Harry said. "We won't put the blankets up till after dark. They are sure to come out again; then, as soon as they have gone, we will close it, and they won't be able to get in when they come back before daybreak."

Harry's expectations were fulfilled. At dusk a stream of bats rushed out again, but this time quite noiselessly. The rush lasted for three or four minutes. As soon as they had gone, the blankets were hung up, and fastened across the doorway.

"They will be puzzled when they come back."

"Yes, señor," Maria said; "but when they find that they can't get in here, they will come in through the openings above."

"So they will; I did not think of that. But when they once find that they cannot get out here in the evening, they will go out where they came in, and we shall have no more trouble with them. I don't know whether they are good to eat?"

Maria gave a little cry of horror.

"Oh, señor! I could not eat such horrible things!"

"Their appearance is against them, Maria; but when people eat alligators, frogs, snakes, and even rats, I don't see why a bat should be bad. However, we won't touch them unless we are threatened by starvation."

"I should indeed be starving before I could touch bats' flesh, señor."

"Well," Harry said, "if people eat monkeys, rats, and squirrels—and it seems to me that a bat is something of a mixture of the three—one might certainly eat bats, and if we are driven to it I should not mind trying; but I promise you that I won't ask you to cook them."

They chatted for another hour, and then Maria went off to her corner. The brothers spread their beds by the fire, and José had his blanket and poncho, and it was arranged that any of them who woke should put fresh logs on the fire.

They were all roused just before dawn by a squeaking and twittering noise. They threw on fresh logs, and as these blazed up they could see a cloud of bats flying overhead. They kept on going to the doorway, and when they found they could not get through they retired with angry squeaks. The light was gradually breaking, and in a few minutes all had flown out through the opening. Harry and his brother followed them, and could see them flitting about the upper windows. Presently, as if by a common impulse, they poured in through the various openings.

"I don't suppose we shall see any more of them," Harry said, "and I own that I shall be glad. There is something very weird in their noiseless flitting about, and in the shadows the fire casts on the ceiling."

"They are a great deal larger than any bats I have seen," Bertie said.

"I have seen as large, or larger, at Bombay and some of the towns on the coast."

"They bite people's toes when they are asleep, don't they?"

"Yes, the great vampire bat does, but I have never heard of any others doing so. They live on insects, and some of them are, I believe, vegetarian."

"Are vampire bats found here?"

"I do not think so; I fancy that they inhabit Java and other islands in the Malay Archipelago. However, they are certainly rare, wherever they come from, and you can dismiss them altogether from your mind."

"I was glad when I heard your voices, señors," Maria said when she appeared a quarter of an hour later. "I knew they would not hurt me; but I was horribly frightened, and wrapped myself up in my blanket and lay there till I heard you talking, and I heard the logs thrown on the fire; then I felt that it was all right."

"I don't suppose they will come again, Maria."

After drinking a cup of coffee, with a small piece of maize cake, Bertie said:

"What is the programme for to-day?"

"We can't do much till Dias comes back. We may as well go down and have a look at the lower rooms. I don't think there is much dust on the floor there, but while José is away looking after the mules we will cut enough bushes to make a couple of brooms. We shall want the place swept as clean as possible, so that we can look about, but I don't think there is the least chance of our being able to move the stones. Before we do anything we will go down to the pool and have a swim, and dive out through the entrance and have a look at those rocks."

"That is right," Bertie said. "I was longing for one yesterday morning, but of course the first thing to be done was to examine this place."

"Would it be safe for me to bathe, señor?"

"Quite safe, Maria; the slope is very gradual, and you need have no fear of getting out of your depth suddenly. We will be off at once, Bertie."

CHAPTER XVII — AT WORK

Harry and his brother went to the edge of the pool, where they undressed and waded out. They found that the bottom of the passage sloped more gradually at the edge of the water than it did higher up, and they were able to walk out till they came to the point where the roof dipped into the water. They dived, and in a few strokes came up beyond the roof.

"This is glorious!" Bertie said. "We have often bathed in pools, but this is a different thing altogether. It is more than a year since we had our last dip in the sea, the day we arrived at Callao."

Although there was little or no wind, the rollers were breaking on the line of rocks outside, pouring over the lower points in volumes of foam, and coming in broken waves up the passage.

"We mustn't go beyond the point, Bertie, or we may be dashed against the foot of the cliff. We will climb up that rock to the left; it is not too steep, and I think we can manage it. From there we shall get a good view of this side of the house and of the situation in general."

It required considerable care to climb the rocks, and more than once they hurt their feet on sharp projections. The top of the rock, however, was smooth by the action of time and sea, and they were able to sit down on it in comfort.

"The castle is just as you described it, Bertie; and certainly no one sailing past, however close he came outside these rocks, would be able to detect it. No doubt the stone of which it is built is the same as that of the cliffs. Most likely it was taken from the ravine where the passage now is, and had fallen from the arch above. It might have been more noticeable at first, but now it is weathered into exactly the same tint as the cliffs. The openings are very dodgily placed, and a stranger would not dream that they went many inches in. Now, from where we stand we can look up into that curious opening on the top story. I have been puzzling over that ever since I saw it, but can't think of any possible reason for its having been cut like that, except to enable them to throw stones on to any boat that came into this passage behind the rocks; and yet that can hardly have been the case, for, as I remarked, there are no stones piled up there. Certainly they had a very large number of arrows, but stones would be very much more useful than arrows against a boat almost under their feet. However, that does not concern us now. This line of rocks must greatly aid in hiding the house from the sea. They are higher than you thought they were, looking down at them from above. We are quite thirty feet above the water, and at two or three points they are at least ten or twelve feet higher. Of course a short way out no one would be able to see that they were detached from the cliff, or that there was any passage whatever behind them.

"Besides, they break the force of the waves. If it was not for them it would be impossible for any boat to come up close to the face of the house, and a heavy storm might even break down the wall altogether. A tremendous sea would roll in here in a westerly gale; and if it hadn't been for these rocks it would have been necessary to build the lower part of the house absolutely solid to resist the sea. It is possible that the rocks were higher than they now are when the place was first constructed, in which case the house might have been almost entirely hidden from sight. Well, we may as well go back again, Bertie; we know all there is to be known about this side."

They swam back into the tunnel, dressed, and went out.

"We have come out, Maria," Bertie called. "The coast is clear for you. The water is not so deep as we thought it was, and you can walk out to the point where the roof comes down on to the water without getting out of your depth."

It did not take them long to cut a number of switches to serve as brooms, and a couple of handles. They carried them up into the house, and lashed the switches firmly on to the handles. The work was rough, but the brooms when completed were large, and, although not strong enough for heavy work, would do well to sweep aside the thin layer of almost impalpable dust on the floor below.

"Shall we take wood down there, Harry?"

"No; I think a fire would be a drawback rather than an assistance. It would be very valuable if we were working at one spot, but it could give no general light in a place a hundred feet long. We will take a torch down, and hold it and sweep by turns. We shall only want, to begin with, to make a clear path a couple of feet wide down the middle. Of course later on we shall clear it all. That will be sufficient to enable us to see how the floor is constructed, whether with big blocks or small ones, how closely they are fitted together, and so on. It is certainly unlikely that we shall find any indication as to where chambers exist."

It took but a very short time to clear the path; the dust was so light that one sweep of the broom cleared it away. When they got to the farther end they returned to examine the floor. For four or five feet from the cistern the rock had been evidently untouched, except to cut off any projecting points. Then there was a clear line running across the path. Bertie held the torch down close to it. Harry knelt down and examined it.

"This is a clean cut, Bertie. It is evidently solid above this, but the stone is not quite the same colour on each side of it, and it looks as if they had cut away the rock here and begun to build so as to keep the floor level. The cut may be six inches deep and it may be a foot, that doesn't matter. The face of this stone is very smooth, but it is not cut; it is, I think, the face of the natural fracture. Move the torch along and let us see where the next join is. Ah, here it is!"

The slab was four feet across.

"You had better sweep the dust off both ways, Bertie, so that we may see what size it is."

It was, they found, about eight feet long.

"It has straight edges, Harry, almost as straight as if it had been sawn."

"Very likely it was sawn, Bertie; They could have had no tools that would cut a hard stone like this regularly, but as they were certainly clever builders they must have employed some means to do it. Possibly they used a saw without teeth, for however much they might have hardened the copper, the teeth could not have stood, but if they had a hard copper band fixed like the saw some masons use, and kept the stone moistened with fine sand, they might have cut into it. Of course it would have been a slow process; but they would not have needed to go far into the stone, for when they got down two or three inches they might have broken it through by dropping a heavy weight on the end. It would not have mattered if the fracture had not been straight below the cut, for only on the surface would they have wanted to fit accurately to the next stone. In another way they might have got a straight edge, that is, by driving very dry wedges into the cut made by the saw, and then moistening them. I know that great stones can be split in that way. They may have used both methods. However, it doesn't matter to us much how they did it. It is clear that they could in some way or other cut stones. As they took the trouble to do so here, we may conclude that they were anxious to have a smooth floor that would be extremely difficult to get up.

"They would never have taken all this trouble if they had merely been making a floor for a cellar. For that purpose it would only have been necessary to throw rocks and stones of all sizes into the vacant space below, and when it was nearly full, to level it with small stones and sand. That they chose to undertake such tremendous labour as the making of so regular a floor as this must have been, shows that they had some very strong motive for doing so."

Going carefully along the track they had cleared, they found that the stones were of different sizes; some were but two feet wide, others as much as ten, but all fitted so closely together that it was difficult to see the joints.

"It is going to be a hard job to get these out, Bertie," Harry said, when they had completed their examination, "and it is lucky for us that the room gradually narrows from sixteen feet wide to two at the other end, and when we stepped it we made it eighty feet long. We need not take up the stones near the rock wall, for the ravine would naturally narrow as it went lower, and the depth would be greatest by the side of the wall of the tunnel."

"Well, we shall soon blow up the stones when we have got the powder."

"I hope so, Bertie; but I see that we shall have difficulty unless these top stones are extraordinarily thick."

Bertie looked surprised. "Why, I should have thought the thicker they were the more difficult to break up."

"Beyond a certain point that would be so. But suppose they are six inches thick, you may take it for granted that underneath there will be rubble, loose stuff, except where any chambers may be built. If we were to bore a hole through this top layer the powder, instead of splitting the stones up, would expend its force among the loose stuff beneath it; and besides, instead of remaining in its place, it might get scattered, and we would then get no explosion at all."

"Then we should only have to make the hole four inches deep, Harry?"

"As a result of which there would only be two inches of tamping over the powder, and this would blow right out, as if from a little mortar, and would have no effect whatever upon the stone. I have no doubt that we shall find some way to get over these difficulties, but it is evident that the work will not be all clear sailing."

"Of course we shall manage it somehow, Harry, even if we have to smash up all the stones with the sledge-hammers Dias will bring us."

"Is breakfast nearly ready, señora? That swim in the sea has given us a prodigious appetite. Did you enjoy it?"

Maria nodded.

"It is very nice, señor; but I should have liked it better if the water had not been so blue. It seems so strange bathing in blue water."

"You will soon get accustomed to it," Bertie laughed. "There are no pools except that one two miles up the valley. Besides, it is much nicer to have a great bathing chamber all to yourself. Here comes José!"

"Well, José, are the mules all right?" he shouted.

"Yes, but I had difficulty in catching them. They had evidently been frightened by something, and were three miles up the valley with their coats all staring. It must have been either a puma or a jaguar. Of course they must have got wind of him in time; but as, fortunately, they were not tethered, they were able to get away from him."

"I should think he must be up somewhere among the bushes, José," Harry said. "We had better go down tonight and see if he returns again. We shall be losing some of the mules if we don't put a stop to his marauding. Besides, it will be very dangerous for you, José, cutting the wood up there, if he is lurking somewhere. It is fortunate that you escaped yesterday."

"I expect he was on the other side of the ravine, señor; and even if he had not been, the sound of the chopping would have scared him. They will not often attack in the daytime."

When they had finished their breakfast José asked what he should do next.

"There is nothing else to do, so it would be as well to take our pickaxes and get some of those brackets out of the walls. We will begin with the other rooms of this floor and leave these here till the last."

"I will come and hold a torch for you, señors," Maria said. "I like to be doing something. I will wash up first, and then I shall have nothing to do till it is time to get ready for dinner. Now I know there is a savage beast about I should not like to go down the ladder."

"There is very little chance of his coming down the rocks," Harry said. "He is more likely to be lying somewhere on the other side watching the mules."

No move was made until the woman was ready to start. Then they lit two torches. She took one and Bertie the other, while José and Harry took two picks. It was hard work, for the brackets were driven far into the pillars and walls. It was necessary to knock away the stones round them to a depth of two or three inches before they could be got out. They worked one at each side of a bracket, relieving each other by turns, and after four hours' work only eighteen brackets had been got out. As far as they could tell by lifting them, the weight was somewhat greater than they had at first supposed. Harry could hold one out in each hand for a minute and a half, Bertie and José for a little over half a minute, and they agreed that they must be about twenty pounds each.

By this time their shoulders ached, and it was agreed that they had done a good day's work. For the rest of the day they did nothing but sit on the sill of the window and smoke quietly. The next day's work was similar, and twenty more brackets were got out. Late in the afternoon they saw Dias coming down the steps, and at once went down the ladder to meet him.

"Have you got everything, Dias?"

"I think so, señor, and I can tell you that the mules have had a pretty heavy load to bring back."

"Well, we will go with you at once, Dias, and bring some of the things up. I expect you have had nothing to eat since the morning. Before you do anything else you had better go in. Your wife has been keeping a dish hot for you, as she did not know when you might arrive."

"I shall not be long before I come and help you, señor. I have unsaddled the mules and turned them out to graze."

"It is just as well, Dias, for there is a beast somewhere about that gave them a fright last night. We will get all the eatables up to-night, the powder and drills and hammers we can very well leave till to-morrow morning."

It took them four trips to bring the provisions over, for it required two of them to carry each sack of flour, and indeed all had to give their aid in getting them up the rocky slope at the foot of the wall.

"No one seemed to think it unusual, your taking so large a load, I hope, Dias?" Harry said as they sat down to their evening meal.

"No, señor. The man I bought the powder of was a little surprised at the amount I wanted; but I said that I might be absent many weeks in the mountains, and might want to drive a level in any lode that I might discover. I led him to believe that I had seen a spot in the mountains that gave good indications, and that two of my comrades were waiting there for my return to begin work at it. I sold the llamas to a man who carries goods from Ancon up to Canta, and got the same price that you gave for them."

Harry then told him the work on which he had been engaged since he had been away.

"Of course there is no hurry about the brackets, but as we could do nothing else without the powder and drills, it was just as well to get them out, as otherwise we might have been delayed when we had done our other work. We think that they weigh twenty pounds each, so that altogether they will be worth nearly four thousand pounds. Not a bad start. I am afraid we sha'n't make such quick work down below."

"We shall see," Dias said cheerfully, for now that his fear of the demons had passed he was as eager as Harry himself to begin the search for the treasure.

"Has Maria seen any more bats?"

"Yes, she has seen some more bats," his wife said, "but no demons. Dias, what do you think? Don Harry suggested that we might eat the bats."

"I have heard of their being eaten," Dias said, "and a man who ate them raw told me that he had never enjoyed anything more. But I should not like to try it myself, unless I were driven to it as he was."

"How was that, Dias?"

"He was a muleteer, señor, and was up in the mountains. He had a cargo of silver on his mule, and during the day he had seen some men who he doubted not were brigands on the top of the ravine he passed through. He knew of a cavern where he had once taken refuge with the animals during a storm. It lay on the hillside some twenty or thirty yards away from the road. The entrance was hidden by bushes, and he had first noticed it by seeing a bear come out as he was passing along. He had his pistols, and thought that it was better to risk meeting a bear than a brigand. He arrived opposite the cave just as it became dark, and at once led the mules up there. He first lighted a torch—the muleteers always carry these with them—and then went in with his pistols ready, but there were no signs of a bear anywhere near the entrance.

"He drove the mules in and put out his torch. The entrance had been only wide enough for the laden animals to pass, but it widened out a great deal inside. He took off the loads, piled them up in the narrow part to make a barricade, and then sat down at the entrance and listened. He soon heard five or six men come down the road talking. They were walking fast, and one was saying that he could not be more than half a mile ahead, and that they should soon catch him. When they had gone, he went some distance in the cave and relighted his torch. He went on and on. The cave was a very large one, and when he had gone, as he thought, four or five hundred yards, it branched off into three. He took the middle one, and followed it for a long way. At last it opened into a large chamber from which there were several passages. Here he found a large number of things that had evidently been stolen from muleteers. There were at least a dozen mule loads of silver; goods of all kinds that had been brought up from the coast; the ashes of fires, and a great many bones and skins of llamas, and some sacks of flour.

"He thought he would now return to the mules; but apparently he entered the wrong passage, for he went on till he felt sure he ought to be in the chamber where he had left the animals, and he was turning to go back when he tripped over a stone and fell, and his torch went out. Then he felt in his pocket for his box of matches, and to his horror found that it had gone. It must have dropped out when he was examining the passages. He did not think much of it at first, but he had passed several openings on his way, and in the dark he probably turned down one of these. At any rate he lost his way somehow, and wandered about, he thinks, for hours; but it might have been much less, for he told me that he quite lost his head. At last he came out into a place where he could only feel the rock on one side of him, and knew that he must be in a large chamber.

"Looking up he saw, to his joy, a faint light, and moving a little, caught sight of a star. He was utterly worn out, and threw himself down. He was awakened by a strange rustling sound, and looking up saw that daylight was breaking, and that a stream of bats was pouring in through a hole, which was about three feet wide. He made several efforts to climb up to it, but failed. The bats hung thickly from every projecting point in the rocks. He hurt himself badly in one of the attempts to get up, and twisted his foot. All day he lay there. Then the idea struck him that he would kill a bat, cut it open, and use it as a poultice to his foot. The creatures did not move when he touched them, and he cut off the head of one of them and split it open. He did this three or four times during the day, and felt that the application was easing the pain of his ankle.

"When it became dusk the bats flew out again, and he knew his only chance was to keep his ankle perfectly rested. In the morning he killed some more bats. He was by this time tortured with thirst, and sucked the blood of one of them, and in the afternoon ate one raw. Another night passed, and in the morning he felt so much better that he could make another trial. He ate another bat to give him strength, and in the middle of the day made a fresh attempt. He had while lying there carefully examined the wall of rock, at the top of which was the opening, and had made up his mind at what point would be best to try. This time he succeeded. He made his way down the hillside, and found that he was a quarter of a mile higher up the pass than the spot at which he had left the mules. He hobbled down, and to his delight found his animals still in the cavern.

"He had when he first got there opened their sack of grain in order to ensure their keeping quiet. There was still some remaining at the bottom. He lost no time in loading them and leading them out, and made his way down the pass without seeing anything of the robbers. Afterwards he went back there with a good supply of torches, found his way to the cave, and brought down two mule-loads of silver. Gradually he brought the rest of the goods down, and today he is a rich man."

"Well, I think under those circumstances, Dias, I would have eaten bats myself. It was certainly a clever idea of his to convert them into poultices, though the general opinion is that cold bandages are the best for a sprained ankle."

Then they discussed their plans for the next day. "I know nothing about blasting, señor. You give me instructions, and I will do my best to carry them out; but it is useless for me to talk of what I know nothing about."

"There is a lot of common sense in that, and yet in every work, Dias, sometimes while a skilled man is puzzling how to do a thing a looker-on will suggest a satisfactory plan. That treasure has been buried there I have no doubt whatever. They would never have gone to the labour of paving those cellars as carefully as they have done unless for some special purpose. The floor was undoubtedly made when the house was built, and if we find treasure-chambers there they will be those of the old people. Of course they may have been discovered by the Incas, and when they in turn wanted to bury treasure this place might occur to them as being particularly well fitted to escape search by Spaniards. However, to-morrow we shall learn something more about them. The first thing to do in the morning, when we have brought up the rest of the goods, is to sweep the floors of those chambers carefully. When we have done that we will determine where to set to work."

Two trips brought up the powder and instruments.

"We will take one of the kegs of powder down with us," said Harry, "and leave the other five in the empty room behind this. It is just as well not to have them in this room; the sparks fly about, and some things might catch fire. I don't think there is any real danger, but, at the same time, it is best to be on the safe side."

"There are a dozen pounds of candles in this bundle, señor. You did not tell me to get them, but I thought they might be useful."

"Thank you, Dias! they certainly will be useful. What are they?—tallow?"

"Yes, señor."

"Then before we go down we will get a couple of pieces of flat wood, and drive a peg into each, sharpened at the upper end. Candles stuck on these will stand upright, and we can put them down close to where we are working. They will give a better light than a torch, and leave us all free to use the tools. Did you think of buying some more tinder?"

"Yes, señor, I have five boxes, and half a dozen more flints."

They carried the keg of powder, the sledges, drills, and wedges downstairs, and then Dias and José set to work to sweep out the two chambers. The work was easy, but they were obliged to stop several times, being almost choked with the light dust. Harry and Bertie offered to take their turn, but the others would not hear of it, and they were glad to go up to what they called their drawing-room until the work was done and the dust had settled a little. Then they examined the pavement carefully with their torches. They had hoped that they might find either copper rings, or at least holes where rings had been fastened, but there were no signs whatever of such things in either of the chambers.

"We will begin to work half-way down," Harry said. "Of course the treasure may lie near the cistern end, but the depth below the floor would be very shallow there. More likely the chambers would be at the deep end. If we begin in the middle we may be pretty sure that we have not passed them. We will begin rather nearer the passage wall than the other, as the depth there will be greater. It does not matter which stone we take, one is as likely as another. Step ten paces from the cistern, Bertie, and the stone you stop on we will try first."

When Bertie came to a stand-still they carefully examined the pavement. "You are standing on one of the cracks, Bertie; I will stay there while you all bring the tools along."

"Shall I open the powder?" Bertie asked.

"No. It is no good doing that until we have quite decided what we are going to do. The wedges certainly won't go into this crack. I think our best plan will be to sink a bore-hole about two inches from the crack. We will drive it in in a slanting direction towards the edge, and in that way it will have more chance of blowing a piece out. First of all, we must make a slight indentation with a pick, otherwise we sha'n't get the bore to work. I will begin."

He took a pick and struck several blows.

"It is very hard stone," he said. "I have scarcely made a mark upon it."

He worked for some time, and then let Bertie take the pick. The lad struck a blow with all his strength, and then dropped the pick with a loud cry, wringing his hands as he did so.

"You have jarred your hands, Bertie; you should not hold the haft so tightly."

"It did sting!" Bertie said. "I feel as if I had taken hold of a red-hot poker. It has jarred my arm up to the shoulder; I can't go on at present."

"You try, Dias."

Dias went more carefully to work, knelt down on one knee, and proceeded to give a number of what seemed light blows.

"That is better than I did, Dias. The stone is crumbling into dust, and we shall be able to use the borer in a short time. Perhaps it will be better after all to drive the hole down straight. It will be easier to begin with; when we see how thick the stone is we shall know better how to proceed."

In ten minutes Dias had made a hole a quarter of an inch deep.

"Now, give me one of the borers—that one about two and a half feet long. I will hold it, and you strike to begin with, Dias, only mind my fingers. Keep your eye fixed on the top of the borer, and take one or two gentle strokes to begin with; then, when you know the distance you have to stand from it, do your best. You needn't really be afraid of striking my fingers. I shall hold the drill at least a foot from the top."

Dias began very carefully, gradually adding to the strength of the blows as he got the right distance, and was soon striking hard. After each blow Harry turned the borer a slight distance round. When he heard the native's breath coming fast he told José to take a turn. The lad was nervous; the first blow he struck only grazed the top of the borer, and narrowly missed Harry's fingers. José dropped the sledge. "I can't do it, señor; I am afraid of hitting your fingers. I will sit down and hold it; it does not matter if you hit me."

"It would matter a good deal, José. No, no; you have got to learn."

"Would it not be well, señor," Dias said, "to take the borers and three hammers outside, and try them in soft ground? We could work them there till we all got accustomed always to hit them fair. There would be no occasion for them to be held, and we should get confident. I could have hit twice as hard as I did, if I hadn't been afraid of missing it."

"I think that is a very good plan, Dias. The loss of a day or two will make no difference. We shall make up for it afterwards."

Accordingly the drills and hammers were all taken up, and they were soon at work. Two or three gentle taps were given to the borers, to make them stand upright, and then all four began work. At first they often either missed the heads of the borers or struck them unevenly.

"It is well, Dias, that we carried out your suggestion, as I see I should have had an uncommonly good chance of getting my fingers smashed, or a wrist broken. I have missed as often as any of you."

They stopped frequently for breath, and at the end of an hour were glad to lay down their hammers. Dias was comparatively fresh; his practice as a woodsman now did him good service.

"I should have thought from the number of trees that I have helped to cut down," Bertie said, "that I could hit pretty hard, but this is a great deal stiffer work. I should say that this hammer is at least twice the weight of the axe, and it is the lightest of the four. I ache a good deal worse than I did when I first chopped that tree down."

"So do I, Bertie. We will stick at this till we get accustomed to the work. By doing so we shall gain strength as well as skill."

"I will get some grease, señor, from Maria, and then I will rub your shoulders, and arms; that will do you a great deal of good."

"Thank you, Dias! It would be a good plan."

Dias did this to José as well as to the brothers, and then José in turn rubbed him.

They waited half an hour, and then Harry said: "Let us have another spell." This time a quarter of an hour sufficed. "It is of no use, Harry; I can't go on any longer," Bertie said. "I feel as if my shoulders were broken."

"I am beginning to feel the same, Bertie. However, we are all hitting straighter now. We will go up into the shade and take it quietly for two or three hours; then we will have a spell again."

However, after the rest, they all agreed that it would be useless to try again, for they could not lift their arms over their heads without feeling acute pain. Three days were spent at this exercise, and at the end of that time they had gained confidence, and the heads of the drills were no longer missed.

After the first day they only worked for a quarter of an hour at a time, taking an hour's rest. The pain in their arms had begun to abate. On the following day they practised striking alternately, three standing round one borer. They found this at first awkward, but by the end of the day they were able to strike in regular order, the blows falling faster after each other on to the drill.

"I think we shall do now," said Bertie. "No doubt we shall hit harder with a fortnight's practice, and shall be able to keep it up longer. However, I think that even now we have sufficient confidence in striking to be able to hold the borer without any fear of an accident."

The next day they began work early in the cellar. José volunteered to take the first turn to hold the drill.

"You understand, José, you must turn it round a little after each stroke, and in that way it will cut the hole regularly."

Harry took his place on one side of José, who sat with a leg on each side of the drill. Dias stood facing Harry, Bertie behind José holding the torch so that its light fell strongly on the head of the drill. At first the two men struck gently, but gradually, as they grew confident, increased the weight of their strokes until they were hitting with their full power. After ten minutes they stopped. "Let us look at the hole," Harry said. "How far has it got down?"

José moved his position and Harry examined the hole. "About an eighth of an inch," he said. "Let us scrape the dust out of it."

"Shall we take a spell now, Harry?" Bertie said.

"No, we will wait five minutes and then go on again, and after that we will change places with you, relieving each other every twenty minutes."

The work went on, and at the end of two hours the hole was three inches deep. Another hour and a half and the drill suddenly went down.

"We are through it," Bertie said, "and I am not sorry."

"Now I will lift the drill up gently, Bertie; do you kneel down, and when I stop, take hold of it close to the floor, so that we may see the thickness of the stone."

"Five inches," he said as he measured it. "Now put on a little grease, Dias. I will lower it again, and we shall be perhaps able then to get some idea of what is underneath."

He lowered the drill and turned it round two or three times, and then carefully raised it. Some sand and little stones were sticking to it.

"Sand and gravel," he said. "That settles that point. Now we have done a good morning's work, and let us go up and have breakfast."

Maria looked enquiringly at them. "I was just coming down for you. Well, what have you done?"

"We have drilled one hole, Maria, and none of us have got our fingers smashed, so I think we have every reason to be satisfied with our first experience at the work."

As they breakfasted they talked matters over. Harry said that he was certain that the thickness of the stone was not sufficient for them to break it up by blasting. "We shall have to try some other plan. It is equally certain that we cannot smash the stone with the sledge-hammers, and I don't think that the wedges would break it. Of course if we got one stone out it would be comparatively easy to lift the next, as we could put the crowbars under it. If we can do it in no other way, we must drill a line of holes close to each other right across the stone, and we might then break off the piece between them and the crack and get our crowbars under the slab. It might be worth while to drill holes a foot apart, from the point where we have begun to the other end of the room. Of course if we found that gravel and stones were everywhere under the slabs we should learn nothing; but the opening to the chambers is probably covered by another stone, and if we found that, we could put in one or two more holes so as to be sure that it was flat, in which case we might smash it somehow. Of course, if we don't come upon a flat stone we shall conclude that they put a layer of sand and fine gravel over the slabs covering the vaults, and must then, as I say, get up one stone and gradually lift all the rest, clearing out the gravel as we go to the depth of a foot or so. In that way we shall make sure that we shall not miss any chamber there may be.

"I think that would certainly be the best plan. At present we are groping altogether in the dark, and it will take us a fortnight at least to make that row of holes close to each other, as you propose."

CHAPTER XVIII — DISAPPOINTMENT

Six more days were spent in driving holes according to Harry's plan. The result was in all cases the same. Sand and small stones were brought up attached to the grease. They had now sunk the holes at a much more rapid rate than at first, for they were accustomed to the work, their muscles had hardened, and they were able to strike more frequently and with greater force. They would have got on still more quickly had it not been for the trouble in sharpening the drills. These were heated in the small blacksmith's fire Dias had brought. They were first placed in the fire, but this was not sufficiently hot to raise them beyond a dull red glow. When this was done a shovelful of glowing fragments was taken from the fire and placed on the hearth, and among these the small bellows raised the ends of the drills to a white heat, when of course they were easily worked. At first they had some difficulty in tempering them. Sometimes, when cooled, the points were too soft, at other times too brittle; but at the end of a week they had arrived at the proper medium. But one of the party had to work steadily to keep the drills in good order.

Bertie was daily employed at this work, as José generally failed to give the proper temper to the tools. Bertie, however, generally managed to get in two or three hours' work below. Although perfectly ready to do his share, he was by no means sorry to be otherwise employed for a part of the day, and as he was now able to talk Spanish with perfect fluency he and Donna Maria maintained a lively conversation whenever they were together. All the party, however, were glad when Sunday came round and gave them a day of complete rest; then they would bathe, fish, shoot pigeons, or lie in the shade, each according to his fancy, and recommence work with fresh vigour the next morning.

Just a fortnight after they had begun work they were about to begin a hole in a fresh stone. Talking it over, they had come to the conclusion that this was the most likely spot in the cellar for the situation of an underground chamber. Farther on there would scarce be width for one, for it was here but eight feet across. Where they had already tried there would scarcely have been depth enough. This seemed to them to be the happy medium.

Before setting to work Dias passed his torch over the stone. Presently he stopped. "Will you light two of the candles, señor; the torch flickers too much to see very plainly."

Somewhat surprised, for no such close examination had been made before, the candles were lighted and handed to him. Dias knelt down, and, with his face close to the stone, moved about carefully, examining it for some minutes without speaking.

"This stone, señor, is broken," he said at last, "broken into a dozen pieces, and they have been so carefully fitted together again that the dust that settled upon it quite prevented our seeing it till we swept it again just now, and it was only because there was a tiny chip out where I first looked that I noticed it."

Harry knelt down and also examined the stone. Like all the others, it had not been faced with tools. Consequently, although roughly even, there were slight irregularities in the surface. Now, as Dias pointed them out to him, he saw that there were lines running through it here and there.

"Look here, señor. The stone has been struck here. Here are some dents."

These were scarcely noticeable. The surface had taken the same colour as the rest of the stone. They were of irregular size, and from a quarter of an inch to an inch in diameter, and nearly in the centre of the stone, from which point several of the cracks started.

"It certainly looks as if the stone had been struck with something heavy," Harry said. "I should think, by the appearance, some very heavy piece of rock must have been dropped upon it."

"Yes, señor, very heavy rock—so heavy that there must have been many men to lift it."

"It must have been heavy indeed to break up this slab."

"Perhaps it is not so thick as the others," Dias suggested.

"I don't like it, Dias. Well, let us set to work. We will try the wedges there. They were no use against the solid stone, but they might move these pieces. Put one of the borers just at the place from which these cracks start—at least, I suppose they are cracks—and let us drive it in for an inch. You hold it, José. Don't turn it, we want it to go in just in a line with this crack. I know we cannot drive it in far, but at least we may make it go deep enough to give a wedge a hold in it."

Five such small holes were made in a crack that seemed to form a rough circle, then the wedges were put in, and they began to work with sledges. In ten minutes Harry, examining the place carefully, said: "The bit of stone is breaking up. There are lines running across it from the wedges. Give me the heaviest sledge." He swung it round his head and brought it down half a dozen times in the centre of the wedges. The cracks opened so far that he could see them without stooping.

"Now we will try with the crowbars," he said.

In ten minutes a fragment of the stone was got up; then they hammered on the wedges again, and a piece of rock, which was roughly seven or eight inches in diameter, broke completely off.

"It is only about two and a half inches thick," Harry said as he drew one of the fragments out. And, holding the candle to the hole, he went on: "And there is another slab underneath. That settles it. We are at the top of one of these vaults. The question is, is it empty? I am afraid it is. This stone has evidently been broken up and fitted in again with wonderful care."

"Why should it be fitted in carefully if they emptied the chamber?"

"That I can't tell you, Dias, and it is of no use trying to guess now. First of all, we will get the rest of the stone up. It won't be difficult, for now that we have made a start we can use our crowbars. José, run up and tell my brother to come down. We shall want him to help with the crowbar; and besides, he would, of course, wish to be here, now that we are on the point of making a discovery one way or the other."

In a minute Bertie came down with José, and Donna Maria followed. "José tells me you have broken a hole in one of the stones," Bertie exclaimed as he ran up.

"We have got a bit out of a broken stone, Bertie. This stone had been broken before, and evidently not by accident. It is only half the thickness of the others, and, as you can see, there is another slab underneath."

"Who can have broken it, Harry?"

"That question we cannot decide, but I should say probably the Incas. We agreed that it was very possible they discovered the hidden treasures of the Chimoos. They must have learned, as the Spaniards did, how cleverly these places were hidden, and it must have been as evident to them as it is to us, that if there was a hiding-place here, this must be the spot."

When one or two more pieces of the stone had been got out by the aid of crowbars, the rest was removed without the least difficulty. Another slab two feet square was exposed. In the middle of this was a copper ring, and the slab fitted, into a stone casing about eighteen inches wide. As soon as this casing was cleared, Dias and José took their places on one side, the two brothers on the other. A crowbar was thrust through the ring, and all of them, taking hold of the ends, lifted with all their strength. At first the stone did not move, but at the second effort it lifted suddenly. It was the same thickness as the one they had broken, and, on being moved, was easily handled. The torches were thrust down, and all peered eagerly into the vault. So far as they could see it was empty.

"Shall I jump down, señor?'

"No, the air may be bad, José. Run up and bring down a short length of rope, twenty feet will be ample. Now, let your torch drop down, Dias. If it burns, it will be safe for us to go down; if not, we must keep on dropping blazing brands into it till they burn."

As, however, the torch burnt brightly, Harry lay down, and, saying, "Hold my legs, Bertie!" looked down into the vault. Eighteen inches below the surface, the hole widened out suddenly. A minute later Harry's head appeared above the surface again.

"It is empty," he said in as cheerful a voice as he could manage. "Of course it is a disappointment," he went on, "but I felt certain that it would be so directly we found the stone was cracked. The only hope was that the first finders of the treasure afterwards used the place for the same purpose. That they thought it possible they might do so is clear by the care with which they fitted the stones together."

None of the others spoke. The disappointment was a heavy one. Bertie broke the silence by saying; "Well, better luck next time. They may have found out this place, but there may be others which they did not find."

"Quite so, Bertie. Now we have got up one stone, It will be comparatively easy work getting up the others. We will take up every stone to the end, and then work back till we get to a place where there is not more than a couple of feet between the bottom of the stone and the top of the rock."

At this moment José ran into the room with the rope. Harry took it, and dropped one end until it nearly touched the floor below. "Hold on," he said, "and I will slip down first." Half a minute later he stood at the bottom of the chamber, beside the torch, which was still burning.

"It is only about three feet across at the bottom," he said; "the wall by the passage goes straight up, on the other side it is the bare rock, so it is almost wedge-shaped. It is twenty feet long, and five feet high up to its roof, that makes it nearly seven to the upper part of the mouth." The vault was absolutely empty. He moved about for a minute and then said: "Gold has been stored here. There are particles of gold at the bottom, and there is gold-dust in the cracks of the broken face of the rock. Now I will come up again. Hold the rope tight; I will climb about a yard, and then I can get my fingers on the ledge."

He was soon up. "Now, do any of you want to go down?" Dias and José shook their heads; and Bertie grumbled, "I don't want to look at the beastly hole; it has been trouble enough to get at it."

"Well, I think we will not do any more to-day, Dias. It has rather taken the heart out of one. Still, we could not expect to hit upon the treasure for the first time. We will go up and talk it over, and when we have smoked a pipe or two we shall be more inclined to take a cheerful view of the matter. We won't talk about it till we have got to the end of our second pipe."

The tobacco did its usual work, and it was with quite a cheerful voice that Bertie broke the silence: "The Incas must have been pretty sharp fellows to find that hole, Harry?"

"Well, very likely they heard that the Chimoos had treasure there. Indeed they must have known, because, you see, not one of the other stones is broken, so they evidently knew where that chamber was situated."

"Yes, I suppose that was it. Well, we are in fine working order now, and we sha'n't be very long getting the other stones up."

"Not very long this side anyhow, Bertie. We shall want some short blocks of wood to put under the stones as we raise them. I expect they are all five inches thick, and they must be a very big weight. Evidently it is going to be a longish job. As we have been a fortnight without fresh meat, Dias had better go off and buy half a dozen sheep. We won't have dead meat this time. He can bring them slung over the mules, and we can kill them as we want them."

"We have not had fresh meat, but we have not done badly, Harry; we have generally had a good many eggs and some pigeons, and José has brought us in fish from that pool. But they have dwindled down lately. He only brought in a couple of fish yesterday evening."

"Well, the pigeons are getting scarcer too, Bertie. We have killed a good many, but the rest are getting very shy, and I think most of them must have gone off and settled in new places on the face of the rocks above the ravine. While Dias is away, we will try and lay in a stock of sea-fish. We can swim out and sit on the rocks during the day, and lay our lines at night. We have worked very hard for a fortnight, and we deserve a holiday."

Dias, when he was spoken to, said he would start at once with four mules for Huacha. "It is not above fifteen miles," he said, "and I can get there this evening. I should think that I could buy the sheep there; if not, I must go on to Huaura. Each mule will bring two sheep. Of course I could drive them, but that would seem more singular."

"You had certainly better take the mules, Dias. Tie the sheep carefully on them, so that they will not be hurt."

"I will take eight of the leather bags, señor. The sheep are not large, and I will sling one on each side of the mules."

"Yes, it would be as well, while you are about it, to bring eight. You may as well get some more coffee. We drink a lot of that, and like it strong. If your wife thinks we shall want more sugar, or anything else, by all means get some."

As soon as Dias started, the lines were got ready. They cut a couple of saplings to serve as rods, and José, digging among the rocks, found plenty of worms, beetles, and grubs for bait. In addition, they took a cake or two of maize, to break up and throw in to attract the fish.

"We had better swim out in our flannel shirts and trousers," Harry said. "They will soon dry, and they will keep off the sun. If we were to sit there without them, we should get blistered from head to foot."

"Shall we fish outside the rocks, or inside, Harry?"

"We will try both; but I think we are likelier to catch most inside. I should think a back-water like that would attract them."

They met with equal success on both sides of the rocks, and by evening had caught over forty fish, at least half of which weighed over four pounds. Then they set the long lines, each carrying forty hooks, and returned to the castle with as many fish as they could possibly carry. Maria was delighted with the addition to her larder, and she and José set to work at once to clean and split them. In the morning they were hung in strings from the broad window. Maria said they would get the benefit of the heat from the walls, and any air there might be would be able to pass round them.

By means of the night-lines they caught almost as many fish as they had done with their rods, and that day they had the satisfaction of bringing in more than they could carry in one journey.

"We have got plenty now to keep us going for another three weeks," Harry said, "and we can always replenish our stock when we choose."

Dias returned at sunset carrying one sheep over his shoulders.

"I have left the others out there, señor; I don't think there is any fear of their straying. There is no fresh grass anywhere except near the stream, and moreover, being strange to the valley, they will naturally keep near the mules."

Another month passed in continuous labour. The stones had all been taken up in the basement they had first visited, but no other chamber had been found. The parallel chamber had given them much trouble at starting, as no stone had been found showing any cracks upon it, and they had had to blast one stone to pieces before they could begin to cut up the others. No chamber whatever had been discovered until they were within six feet of the farther end. Then one was found, but it showed no signs whatever of having ever been used. "So far so bad," Harry said when the supper had been eaten almost in silence; "but that is no reason why we should be disheartened. If the Incas buried a treasure they may have thought it prudent to choose some other spot than that used by the old people."

"But where could it be, Harry? You agreed that there was not sufficient depth between the floors for any place of concealment."

"That is so, Bertie, of course. I have been thinking of it a lot during the past few days, when the chances of our finding a treasure under the basement were nearly extinguished. There are still the side walls."

"The side walls!" Bertie repeated. "Surely they are built against the rock?"

"Yes, but we don't know how straight the wall of rock is. You see, they did not build against it at all in the basement, but above that the side walls begin. The rock must have been irregular, and as the walls were built the space behind may have been filled in or may not. When they came to build they may have found that there was a cavern or caverns in the rock—nothing is more likely—and they may have left some sort of entrance to these caverns, either as a place of refuge to the garrison if the place were taken, or as a hiding-place. They might have thought it more secure for this purpose than the underground chamber, which was their general hiding-place. At any rate it is possible, and to-morrow I vote that we have a thorough inspection of the walls of the storeroom below this. That would be the most likely place, for near the sea-level the chances of finding caverns would be much greater than higher up."

Bertie's face brightened as Harry proceeded.

"It certainly seems possible, Harry. Of course the other place seemed so much more likely to us that we have never given the side walls a thought. We may find something there after all. I do hope we may, old boy. I cannot believe that after things have gone altogether so well with us, and we have been twice so near finding treasure, that we should fail after all. Which side shall we begin on?"

"We will have a look at them before we decide, Bertie. We have not really examined them since the first day; I really forget what stores we found in the two side-rooms."

An examination in the morning showed that the passage near the entrance to the rock on the left-hand side had been used for fuel, that on the other side was filled at the upper end with skins for some distance, and spears and sheaves of arrows were piled against the outer wall along the rest of the distance.

"Which do you think is the most likely hiding-place?"

"I should say the right-hand passage. The other with the fire-wood in it might be visited every day, but the spears and arrows would only be wanted in case of any attacks upon the castle, or to arm a large force going out to give battle there. They would naturally put anything they wanted to hide in the passage less likely to be visited."

"That does seem probable," Bertie agreed; "therefore, hurrah for the right-hand side!"

"I still think, señor," Dias said, "that there must be treasure concealed somewhere. I should not think a guard would have been placed here, and remained here so many years still keeping watch, as we find they did at that big loophole on the top floor, unless there was something to watch."

"Quite so, Dias. I have thought that over in every way, and I can see no possible motive for their being here except to prevent the place from being examined. That was needless if there was nothing to guard, and nothing to take away, except these silver brackets, which in those days would scarcely have been worth the trouble of getting out and carrying away. There must be treasure somewhere. We know now that it is not in the basement, and we will try these side walls, even if we have to blow half of them in; there is no doubt that the stones are at least as thick as those at the end, but they will not be difficult to manage. I noticed in the upper story that they had not taken the trouble to fit them nearly so accurately as they did those of the outer walls. I don't say that they didn't fit well, but the stones were of irregular sizes, and I have no doubt that in many places we could prize them out with a crowbar. Once an opening is made, there will be no difficulty in getting a lot of them out, as the old people did not use cement or mortar. Well, to-morrow morning we will move all the spears and arrows across to the other side of that passage and have a good look at the stones, but we will go up first and look at the side walls of all the other rooms and see if they are of the same build. There may be some difference which we have not noticed. You see all the side walls of this room are built like those in front. I didn't notice whether it was the same in the other rooms."

"I will look at once," Dias said, lighting a torch at the fire.

"No, señor," he said, when in ten minutes he returned; "none of the walls on this floor are built of stone like this. This was the grand chamber, the stones are all nearly one size, and so well fitted that you can hardly see where they join each other. In the other rooms they are not so, but the stones are, as you noticed above, irregular in size, and although they fit closely, there is no attempt to conceal the cracks."

"Thank you, Dias! Well, we won't look any more to-night; we shall see in the morning if the room below us is built in the same way. I have no doubt it is. At any rate we have done enough for to-day. There is some whisky left in that bottle, Bertie, and we may as well make ourselves a glass of grog. Maria, you had better get down that jar of pulque. We will drink to better luck next time."

The woman smiled faintly. She did not often do so now, her spirits had gradually gone down as the hopes of success faded.

"Now, Maria," Harry said, "you had better take a glass of pulque for yourself. I know you don't often touch it, but you have been working so of late that I think you want it more than any of us."

"I cannot help feeling low-spirited, señor," she said. "I have so hoped that you would find the treasure you wanted, and marry this lady you love, and it would be such joy for us to have in some small way repaid the service you rendered us, that I felt quite broken down. I know I ought not to have been, when you and your brother bear the disappointment so bravely."

"'It is of no use crying over spilt milk', which is an English saying, Maria. Besides, it is possible that the milk may not be spilt yet, and until lately your good spirits have helped us greatly to keep ours up. If I were once convinced that we had failed, I have no doubt I should feel hard hit; but I am a long way from giving up hope yet. There is treasure here, and if I have to blow up the whole of the old place I will find it. I have got six months yet, and in six months one can do wonders. Anyhow, these brackets will pay us very well for our work. I certainly should not have earned half the sum in any other way in the same time. And even if I fail in my great object, I shall have the satisfaction of knowing that I have done all in my power to gain it. She will know that I have done my best. I have always told her, when I have written, how much I owe to you and Dias, how faithfully you have served me, and how you have always been so bright and pleasant. I have no doubt it has cheered her up as well as me."

Maria was wiping her eyes now. "You are too good, señor; it is so little I can do, or Dias either, to show our gratitude."

"Nonsense! You show it in every way, even in the matter-of-fact way of always giving us excellent food, which is by no means unimportant. Now we will all turn in, and make a fresh start to-morrow morning."

They were up at daybreak, and after taking their usual cup of coffee lit the torches and descended the stairs to the floor below.

As soon as they reached the right-hand wall, Harry exclaimed: "Why, this is built in the same way as the one we have left! The stones are squared and fitted together as closely as those in the drawing-room. Then why should that be, except in that one room? The side walls all the way up are roughly built. Why should they have taken the trouble on this floor to build these, which are only meant as store-rooms, when even in the rooms above, which were meant for the habitation of the chief and his family, the rough work was deemed sufficiently good? There must have been some motive for this, Dias."

"There must have been, señor; it is certainly strange."

"First of all, let us clear the wall and take a general view of it. Guessing won't help us; but I have the strongest hopes that behind one of these stones lies a cavern. By the way, Dias, take a torch and go into the next chamber and see if the stones are solid there."

"They are just the same as those here," Dias said when he returned.

"I would rather that it had been the other way," Harry said, "for then I should have been more sure that there was some special reason for their building them in this way here."

It took them all half an hour's work to move the spears and arrows to the other side.

"Do you think, Harry, if we were to tap the stones we should be able to find whether there is a hollow behind any of them?"

Harry shook his head.

"Not in the least. I have no doubt these stones are two or three feet thick, and there could be no difference in the sound they would make if struck, whether they were filled in solid behind or had no backing. To begin with, we will make a careful examination of the walls. Possibly we shall see some signs of a stone having been moved. It would be very much more difficult to take one of the great blocks out and put it in again than it would be to get up one of the paving-stones."

When they had gone about half-way along, examining each stone with the greatest care, Bertie, who was ahead of the rest, and passing the candle he held along the edge of every joint, said, "Look here! this stone projects nearly half an inch beyond the rest."

The others gathered round him. The stone was of unusual size, being fully two and a half feet wide and four feet long, the bottom joint being two feet above the floor.

Bertie moved along to let the others look at the edge. He was keeping his finger on the joint, and they had scarcely come up when he said, "The other end of the stone's sunk in about as much as this end projects."

"Something certainly occurred to shift this stone a little," Harry said, examining it carefully. "It is curious. If others had been displaced, one would have put it down to the shock of an earthquake—a common enough occurrence here—but both above and below it the stones are level with the others, and nowhere about the house have we seen such another displacement. Look! there is a heap of rubbish along the foot of the wall here. Stir it up, Dias, and let us see what it is."

"It is sand and small stones, and some chips that look like chips of rock."

"Yes, these bits look, as you say, as if they had been chipped off a rock, not like water-worn stones. Though how they got here, where everywhere else things are perfectly tidy, I cannot say. However, we can think that over afterwards. Now for the stone! Let us all put our weight against this projecting end. I don't in the least expect that we can move it, but at any rate we can try."

They all pushed together.

"I think it moved a little," Harry said, and looked at the edge.

"Yes, it is not above half as far out now as it was."

"That is curious, for if it is as thick as we took it to be, it would weigh at least a couple of tons. We won't try to push it in any farther. I am sorry we pushed it at all. Now, give me that heavy sledge, José, possibly there may be a hollow sound to it. I will hit at the other end, for I don't want this to go in any farther."

He went to the stone beyond it first and struck two or three blows with all his strength. Then he did the same with the stone that they were examining.

"I don't think it gives such a dead sound," he said.

The others were all of the same opinion.

"Good! This is another piece of luck," he said. "We have certainly hit on something out of the way."

"Your hammering has brought this end out again, Harry," Bertie said.

"So it has, and it has pushed this end in a little. Let us try again." But although all took turns with the sledges, they could make no further impression on the stone.

"Well, we will try the drills," Harry said. "In the first place, we will find out how thick it is."

They at once set to work with the drill. Progress was slower than it had been before, because, instead of striking down on the head of the drill, they had now to swing the hammer sideways and lost the advantage of its weight; and they were obliged to work very carefully, as a miss would have seriously damaged the one holding the drill. It took them four hours' steady work to get the hole in three inches. Ten minutes later, to their astonishment, the drill suddenly disappeared. Dias, who was striking, nearly fell, for instead of the resistance he had expected, the drill shot forward; the hammer hit José, who had this time been holding the drill, a heavy blow on the arm, causing him to utter a shout of pain.

Harry, who was sitting down having breakfast, having just handed his hammer to Bertie, jumped to his feet.

"How did you manage that, Dias? I suppose it slipped off the head. You must have hit José a very heavy blow."

"I have hit him a heavy blow, señor, and nearly tumbled down myself; but I struck the drill fairly enough, and it has gone."

"Gone where, Dias?"

"I think it must have gone right through the hole, señor."

"Then there is an empty space behind!" Harry shouted joyfully. "However," he went on in changed tones, "we must see to José first. That blow may have fractured his arm. Let me look, José. No, I don't think anything is broken, but there is a nasty cut on the wrist. It is fortunate that you were not striking straight down, Dias, for I am sure we have not put anything approaching the strength into our blows, now we are hitting sideways, that we exerted before. You had better go up to Maria, José, and get her to bathe your wrist with cold water, and put on a bandage."

"Now, señor, what shall we do next?"

"Well, now that we know that its weight cannot be anything very great, and that certainly to some extent it can be moved, we will try hammering again at that end. Do you stand three or four feet beyond it, so as to be able to bring your sledge down with all your strength just on the lower corner. I will face you and strike six or eight inches above where you hit. Of course we must both bring our hammers down at the same instant. We shall be able to do that after two or three trials. Stand at the other end of the stone, Bertie, and tell us if it moves at all."

After one or two attempts the two men got to swing their hammers so as to strike precisely at the same moment, and when half a dozen blows had fallen, Bertie said: "It comes out a little at each blow. It is not much, but it comes."

Three or four minutes later he reported, "It is an inch and a half out now, and there is room to get the end of a crowbar in here."

"That is curious," Harry said as he lowered his sledgehammer, and, taking up the candle, examined the end where he had been striking.

"This is sunk about the same distance, Bertie. The stone must work somehow on a pivot."

They now put a crowbar into the end Bertie had been watching, and all three threw their weight on the lever. Slowly the stone yielded to the pressure, and moved farther and farther out. It was pushed open until the crowbar could act no longer as a lever, but they could now get a hold of the inside edge. It was only very slowly and with repeated efforts that they could turn the stone round, and at last it stood fairly at right angles to the wall, dividing the opening into equal parts about two feet four each.

"There is a pivot under it; that is quite evident. It may be a copper ball in the stone below, or it may be that a knob of the upper stone projects into a hole in the lower. However, it does not matter how it works. Here is an opening into something. Dias, will you go upstairs and tell your wife and José to come down? They had better bring half a dozen more torches. Our stock here is getting low, and we shall want as much light as possible. It is only fair that we should all share in the discovery."

Dias went off.

"Now, Bertie, we must not let our hopes grow too high. I think it is more likely than not that we shall find nothing here."

"Why do you think so, Harry? I made sure we had as good as got the treasure."

"I think, if there had been treasure," Harry went on, "that this stone would have been closed with the greatest care. They would hardly have left it so carelessly closed that anyone who examined the wall would have noticed it, just as we did. We found the other places most carefully closed, though there was nothing in them."

"Perhaps there was something that prevented them from shutting—a little stone or something."

"But we know that that wasn't so, Bertie, because the stone yielded to our weight; and if it did so now, it could have been shut with the greatest ease originally, when no doubt the pivot was kept oiled, and the whole worked perfectly smoothly. It is almost certain that they were able in some way to fasten it securely when it was shut. What is that piece of square stone lying there?"

"It fell down from above just as the slab opened."

Harry took it up. It was about six inches long by two inches square.

"It is a very hard stone," he said—"granite, I should say. I expect you will find that it fits into a hole in the stone above."

"Yes, there is a hole here," Bertie said, feeling it; "the stone goes right in."

"Well, I think, Bertie, you will find a hole in that end of the stone we moved that it will fit."

Bertie crept in, and felt along the top of the stone.

"Yes, there is a hole here about the same size as the stone, but it is not more than three inches deep."

"Then, that stone was the bolt, Bertie. You see it was pushed up, and the door then closed; and when the stone was exactly in its place, it would drop into the hole and keep it from moving, and nothing short of breaking up the bolt would give an entrance. It is lucky that we did not push it quite to; another quarter of an inch and that bolt would have fallen, and we could not have moved it unless by smashing the whole thing into bits. That was why they did not quite close the stone; they wanted to get in again."

"Here come the others!"

Maria had been washing some clothes in the stream, and they had therefore been longer in coming than if she had been in the room. They all looked greatly excited.

"So you have found it, señor!" Dias exclaimed in delight.

"We have found an entrance into somewhere, but I am afraid it will be as empty as the other chambers."

"Why do you think so, señor?" Dias asked in dismay.

Harry repeated the reasons he had given Bertie for his belief that the stone must have been left in such a position as to be easily opened when required.

"Why should it have been left so?"

"Because the treasure they expected had never arrived. It is possible that when the Incas discovered the treasure in that chamber we searched, they may also have found this entrance. It may have been shown to them by one of the prisoners, and they may have broken the stone here into pieces as they broke that over the chamber afterwards. Seeing what a splendid hiding-place it was, they may have, when the Spaniards first arrived, made another stone to fit, with the intention of using it for a hiding-place themselves. The fact that the stone was left so that it could be at once opened is conclusive proof to my mind that the treasure never came. That heap of sand, small stones, and chips of rock is another proof that they were ready to receive treasure, and it was probably swept out of the chamber that is behind here, and would, of course, have been removed when the treasure was put in and the door closed; but as the treasure never did come, it was left where it lay. However, we will now go and see. I have only kept you waiting because I did not want you to be disappointed."

One by one they crept through the opening. For four feet in, the passage was the same width as the stone, but two feet deeper; then it at once opened into a large cavern.

"This wall was four feet thick, you see, Dias. Apparently squared stone was only used for the facing, as the stones are of irregular shape on the back. This would be a natural cavern, and a splendid hiding-place it makes. No doubt its existence was one of the reasons for building this castle."

The cavern was some twelve feet wide and thirty feet high at the mouth; the floor sloped up sharply, and the sides contracted, and met forty feet from the mouth. The floor had been cut into steps two feet wide, running across the cave and extending to the back. These steps were faced with a perfectly flat slab of stone. The cave was empty.

The natives uttered loud exclamations of disappointment and regret.

Harry had so thoroughly made up his mind that nothing would be found there that he surveyed the place calmly and in silence. Bertie imitated his example with some difficulty, for he too was bitterly disappointed.

"You see, Dias," Harry went on quietly, "this place was prepared to receive treasure. The steps have all been swept perfectly clean. You see, the gold could be piled up, and no doubt the steps were cut and faced with stone to prevent any gold-dust that might fall from the bags, in which, no doubt, it would be brought, and small nuggets, from falling into the cracks and crevices of the rock. I should say that in all probability they expected that treasure ship that was lost, and had everything in readiness for hiding the cargo here directly it came. It never did come. The door was shut as far as it could be without the bolt falling down and fastening it; then they waited for the ship; and if it did not arrive, other treasure might be brought by land. Well, it cannot be helped. So far we have failed. There may still be treasure hidden somewhere. We cannot say that we have searched the place thoroughly yet."

For another six weeks they worked hard. The wall was broken through in several places, but no signs of the existence of any other cavern or hiding-place was discovered.

"I should give it up," Harry said, when at the end of that time they were sitting gloomily round the fire, "but for one thing: I can see no possible explanation why a party of men should have been left here, and a guard kept, for perhaps a hundred years, perhaps more, and the stories about demons been circulated, and people who ventured to approach been murdered, unless there had been some good reason for it. That reason could only have been, as far as I can see, that there was a treasure hidden here. I have turned it over and over in my mind a thousand times, and I can think of no other reason. Can you, Bertie, or you, Dias?"

"No," Bertie replied. "I have often thought about it; but, as you say, there must have been some good reason, for no people in their senses would have spent their lives in this old place, and starved here, unless they had some cause for it."

Dias made no reply beyond shaking his head.

"You see," Harry went on, "they kept up their watch to the end. There were those two skeletons of men who had died at their post at that curious window where nothing could be seen. I hate to give up the search, and yet we seem to have tried every point where there was a possibility of a hiding-place existing."

CHAPTER XIX — THE TREASURE

The next morning Harry said:

"I will go upstairs to that look-out place again. I have been up there pretty nearly every day, and stared down. I can't get it out of my mind that the key of the mystery lies there, and that that hole was made for some other purpose than merely throwing stones out on to any of those who might go in behind the rocks. I have puzzled and worried over it."

"Shall I come up with you, Harry?"

"No, I would rather you didn't. I will go up by myself and spend the morning there; some idea may occur to me. You may as well all have a quiet day of it."

He lit his pipe and went upstairs. José went off to the mules, and Bertie descended the ladder, and strolled round what they called the courtyard, looking for eggs among the rocks and in the tufts of grass growing higher up. Dias scattered a few handfuls of maize to the chickens and then assisted Maria to catch two of them; after which he descended the ladder and sat down gloomily upon a stone. He had become more and more depressed in spirits as the search became daily more hopeless; and although he worked as hard as anyone, he seldom spoke, while Harry and his brother often joked, and showed no outward signs of disappointment. An hour passed, and then Harry appeared suddenly at the window.

"Bertie, Dias, come up at once, I have an idea!"

They ran to the ladder and climbed up. The excitement with which he spoke showed that the idea was an important one. "Now, Dias," he broke out as they joined him, "we know, don't we, that a part of the Incas' treasure was sent off by boat, and the belief of the Indians was that it was never heard of again."

"That is so, señor. There was certainly a storm the day after it started, and, as I have told you, it was never heard of again. Had it been, a report of it would surely have come down."

"I believe, Dias, that the boat was dashed to pieces against that line of rocks outside the entrance to the passage. We have reason to believe that the people here were expecting the treasure to arrive, and had the entrance to the cave in readiness to receive it. Certainly no better place could have been chosen for concealment. The boat may have been coming here when the storm broke and drove them towards the shore. They probably attempted to gain the mouth of the cove, but missed it, and were dashed to pieces against the rocks. The Indians on guard here no doubt saw it, and would be sure that the heavy sacks or boxes containing the gold would sink to the bottom. They would lie perfectly secure there, even more secure than if they had been removed and placed in the cave, and could always be recovered when the Spaniards left, so they were content to leave them there. Still, they obeyed the orders they had received to keep watch for ever over the treasure, and to do so knocked that strange hole through the wall and always kept two men on guard there.

"So it must have gone on. They and those who succeeded them never wavered. Doubtless they received food from their friends outside, or some of them went out, as you have done, to fetch it in. Then came a time when, for some reason or other—doubtless, as I supposed before, when the Spaniards swept pretty nearly all the natives up to work in the mines, and they themselves dared not issue out—the attempt to get food was made, when too late, by the men whose skeletons we found on the steps when we first came here; and the rest were all too feeble to repeat the experiment, and died—the two sentinels at their post, the rest in the room where we found them."

"Hurrah!" Bertie shouted, "I have no doubt you have hit it, Harry. I believe, after all, that we are going to find it. That is splendid! I shall dance at your wedding, Harry, which I had begun to think I never should do."

"Don't be a young ass, Bertie. It is only an idea, and we have had several ideas before, but nothing has come of them."

"Something is going to come of this, I am convinced; I would bet any money on it. Well, shall we go and have a trial at once?"

"What do you think, Dias?" Harry said, paying no attention to Bertie's last remark.

"I think it is quite possible, señor. Certainly, if the Indians had been told to guard the treasure, they would do so always. You know how they kept the secrets entrusted to them whatever tortures they were put to. If the gold had been, as you say, lost amongst the rocks, I do think they would have still watched the place. I thought it strange that they should have made that hole, but when you said that they might have made it to throw stones down it seemed to me to be likely enough; but the other suggestion is more probable. Well, señor, I am ready to try it, but I am not a very good swimmer."

"My brother and I are both good swimmers, and we will do that part of the work. The hardest part will be getting it up, and you will be able to give us your help at that."

"Well, let us be off," Bertie said; "I am all on thorns to begin. We shall soon find it out. If it is there, it is almost certain to be at the foot of the rocks, though, of course, it is possible that the boat sank before striking them. At any rate, I feel sure she went down somewhere within the area that can be seen through that hole. It won't take many days' diving to search every yard of the bottom."

They hastily descended the ladder, and, divesting themselves of their clothes, swam out through the opening. Dias climbed up on the rocks, the others swam round by the ends of the barrier. The water was so warm that they would be able to remain in it for any time without inconvenience.

"We need not begin here, Bertie; we are outside the line of sight. From that hole I could not see the end of these rocks. We will start at the middle, and work in opposite directions."

On arriving off the centre of the wall both dived. The depth was about twelve feet, and as the water was perfectly clear, Harry could see four or five feet round him. He was obliged to swim carefully, for the bottom was covered with rocks, for the most part rounded by the action of the sea. For an hour he continued his search, by which time he had reached nearly the end of the line of rocks. Then he landed on a ledge of rock and sat down, calling to Bertie to join him.

"We will rest for a quarter of an hour," he said, "and then begin again. This time we will keep twenty or thirty feet farther out; it is more likely to be there than close in. If the boat struck, the next wave would sweep over her, and she would probably go down stern first, and her cargo would fall out that way."

After their rest they started again, swam out a few strokes, and then dived. Harry had gone down five or six times, when, on his coming to the surface, he heard a shout, and saw Bertie swimming towards him.

"I have found them, Harry! There are a number of ingots, but they were so heavy that I could not bring one of them to the surface."

As Harry reached him the lad turned round and swam back. "There they are, just opposite that cleft in the rock! I looked directly I came up so as to know the exact spot."

Harry trod water for half a minute, then took a long breath and dived.

It was as Bertie had said. Scattered among the rocks were a score of ingots. They had lost their brilliancy, but shone with a dull copperish hue, with bright gleams here and there where rocks had grated against them. Putting one hand on a block of rock he lifted one of them with the other.

"About twenty pounds," he said to himself. "Thank God, Hilda is as good as won!" Then he rose to the surface. "Shake hands, Bertie; there is enough there to make us all rich for life. Now we will get back again. We have to think matters over, and see how they are to be got ashore. There is no hurry; they have lain there for three hundred years, and would lie there as much longer if we did not take them. We have found them, Dias!" he shouted; and the latter gave a yell of delight. "Swim ashore, and we will join you there."

Not another word was spoken until they had dressed and walked out.

"I am too excited even to think," Harry broke out. "It is time for dinner. When we have had that and smoked a pipe I shall be able to talk calmly over it."

Maria was wild with delight at the news, and laughed and cried by turns. Even José, who was accustomed to take all things quietly, was almost as excited. The woman was only called to herself when Harry said, laughing, "Maria, for the first time since we started from Lima, you are letting the dinner burn."

"To think of it!" she cried. "It is your fault, señor; you should not have told me about it till we sat down."

"You won't have to cook much longer, Maria. You will be able now to have a servant, and a house as big as you like, and a beautiful garden."

"I should not like that, señor; what should I do all day with myself?"

"I am glad, señor, glad for your sake," Dias said gravely. "To us it will make no difference. You said there was enough there to make us rich. Assuredly that is so; but not one peso of it will we touch. No man with Indian blood in his veins, not even the poorest in Peru, would have aught to do with an ounce of the Incas' treasures. When they were buried, a curse was laid upon any who betrayed their hiding-place or who ever touched the gold. It has brought a curse upon Spain. At the time the Spaniards landed here they were a great nation. Now their glory has departed; they no longer own the land they tyrannized over for three hundred years, and we have heard that their power in Europe has altogether gone. It must be the curse of the gold, or they would never have allowed your great Englishman, Cochrane, with but two or three ships, to conquer them here. My mind is easy as to the finding of the treasure. You came here in spite of my prayers that you would not do so. It is you who have made the discovery, not me. But I will take no share in the gold. From the day I took it I should be a cursed man; my flesh would melt away, I should suffer tortures, and should die a miserable death."

"Well, Dias, I will not try to persuade you. I know that, Christian though you be, your native belief still clings to you, and I will not argue against it; but I have money of my own, and from that I will give you enough to make you comfortable for life, and that you can take without feeling that you have incurred any curse from the finding of this treasure."

"I thank you heartily," Dias said gratefully; "I thank you with all my heart. I have ever been a wanderer, and now I will gladly settle down. I do not desire wealth, but enough to live on in comfort with my wife, and only to travel when it pleases me."

"You shall have enough for that and more, Dias."

After some more meat had been cooked and eaten, and he had smoked a pipe, Harry said: "A boat would, of course, be the best thing, but there are difficulties connected with it. There is no spot, as far as I know, where we could land for fifteen miles on either side, and there would only be small villages where everything we did would be seen and talked about. There is no place where we could keep a boat here, for if even a slight breeze sprang up the swell coming in round the passage between the rocks and the cliff would smash her up in no time."

"That is so, señor."

Harry was silent again for some time, and then said: "The only plan I can think of is to get some strong leather bags. Then we could take one down with us when we dive, with a strong cord tied to it, put a couple of the ingots into it, and you could haul it up on to the rocks, and so on until we have finished a day's work. Then we could carry them to this side of the rocks; there you could put them, three or four at a time, into the bag, and drop them down in the water. We would swim up the tunnel and haul them in, and then bring the bag back again. We sha'n't be able to get anything approaching all the ingots, for a great many of them must have gone in between the crevices of the rocks, and unless we broke it up with powder, which would be next to impossible without a diving-dress and air-pumps and all sorts of things, which cannot be bought in this country, we could not get at them. However, we have only just begun to look for them yet; we may come across a pile. Heavy as the sea must be on this coast in a gale, I hardly think it would much affect a pile of ingots; their weight would keep them steady even were big rocks rolled about.

"I think the best thing, Dias, would be for you to go off with two or three mules. We shall soon be running short of provisions, and you had better get enough flour and dried meat to last us for a month. I don't suppose we shall be as long as that, but it is as well to have a good store so as not to have to make the journey again. Then you had better get twenty leather bags, such as those in which they bring the ore down from the mountains. We have plenty of stout rope, but we shall want some thin cord for tying the necks of the bags. You may as well bring another keg of spirits, brandy if you can get it, a bag of coffee, and some sugar, and anything else you think of. Now I am a millionaire we can afford to be comfortable. By the way, we might as well this afternoon get the rest of those silver brackets out. These are not a part of the Incas' treasure, and you can take them as your share without fear of the curse. It would be best for you to smelt them down; I know all of you natives can do that."

"Do you think that they are not part of the Incas' treasure, señor?" Dias said doubtfully.

"Certainly not; they were undoubtedly here before the Incas' time. But even had they been put there by Incas, you could not call them hidden treasure. They might be part of the Incas' property, but certainly not part of the treasures they hid."

"But it is altogether too much, señor; it is noble of you to offer it me."

"Not at all; we owe everything we find to you, and it would be only fair that you should have at least a third of the gold. But still, if you won't touch that, you must take the silver."

"But I heard you say that it was worth four thousand pounds."

"Well, if we are lucky we shall get twenty times as much, Dias."

"Certainly we will take it, señor, and grateful we shall both be to you," Maria said; "and so will José, who will inherit it all some day, as he is the only relative we have. I agree with Dias about the gold. I have heard so often about the curse on it that I should be afraid."

"Well, Maria, you see there is a lot of nonsense in all your superstitions. You know it was one of them that this place was guarded by demons. Now you have seen for yourself that it was all humbug. If you are afraid about the silver, I will take it to England and sell it there and send you the money it fetches; but that would give a great deal of trouble. It will be difficult to get the gold safely away, without being bothered with all this silver.

"You had better buy some bags of charcoal, Dias. I suppose you will use that small hearth we have?"

"No, señor, it would take an immense time to do it in that. I will load one of the mules with hard bricks."

"You will want two mules to carry a hundred, Dias—I think they weigh about four pounds and a half each. Will that be enough?"

"Plenty, señor; but I shall want another bellows. José and I can work the two of them, and that will make a great heat. We can melt two or three hundred pounds a day. I have helped to make many a furnace up in the mountains, and I know very well all about the way to build and work them."

"Very well, then, that is settled. You had better start to-morrow morning with José, and we will spend the day in finding out a little more about the gold."

Dias started the next morning, and the two brothers were in the water most of the day. Harry found, as he had expected, that a great deal of the treasure had sunk out of reach between the rocks; but he came upon one pile, which had apparently been originally packed in sacks or skins, lying in a heap a little farther out than they had before searched. He had no doubt that this was the point where the stern of the boat had sunk, and a considerable portion of the contents had been shot out, while the rest had been scattered about as the boat broke up, and as the skins rotted their contents had fallen between the rocks. There were, as nearly as he could calculate, two hundred and fifty to three hundred ingots in the pile.

"I need not trouble about the rest," he laughed to himself. "Each ingot, if it weighs twenty pounds, is worth a thousand. Two hundred of them would make me as rich as any man can want to be. I can hardly believe in my luck; it is stupendous. Fancy a half-pay lieutenant with two hundred thousand pounds! Old Fortescue will become one of the most complaisant of fathers-in-law."

The evening before Dias left, Harry had written a letter for him to post at Callao, telling Hilda to keep up a brave heart, for that he hoped to be at home before the end of the second year with money enough to satisfy her father.

"I should not tell you so unless I felt certain of what I am saying. I told you before I left that it was almost a forlorn hope that I was undertaking, and that the chances were ten thousand to one against me. I think now that the one chance has turned up, and I hope to be home within two months of the time that you receive this letter."

He did not say more; but even now he could scarcely believe that the good fortune had befallen him, and feared that some unlucky fate might interfere between him and the fulfilment of his hopes. When Dias returned after two days' absence the work began. Each morning they worked together at bringing up the gold and piling the ingots on the rock. It was slower work than Harry had expected, for on hauling the bag to the rocks it was often caught by the boulders, and he and Bertie sometimes had to dive four or five times before they could free it and get it ashore. The gold was piled in the tunnel just beyond the water. In a fortnight the last ingot they could get at was stored with its fellows—two hundred and eighty-two in all.

They had repeatedly talked over the best plan of getting the gold away, and finally concluded that it would be risking too much to take it into a town, and that the best plan would be for Harry to buy a boat at Callao, which, as a naval officer, would be natural enough. They decided to procure three times as many bags as the ingots would really require, and that they should put in each bag three ingots only, filling it up with pieces of stone, so that the weight should not exceed what it would have been were the contents heavy ore. Harry arranged that he would go down to Callao, buy a large boat, and after having made several excursions, to accustom the officials at Callao to seeing him going about, he would make a bargain with the captains of two ships about to sail to England, to carry about two tons each of ore, which he could put on board them after dark, so as to avoid the extortion he would have to submit to before the port officials and others would allow him to ship it. The question that puzzled them most was the best way of taking the bags into the boat. Dias was in favour of their being carried on the mules to a point lower down the coast, at which they could be loaded into the boat.

"It would be only necessary to carry the gold," he said, "the stones to fill the bags could be put in there."

The objection to this was that they might be observed at work, and that at most points it would be difficult both to run the boat up and to get her off again through the rollers. If the boat were brought round into the inlet she could be loaded there comfortably. The only fear was of being caught in a gale. But as gales were by no means frequent the risk was small; and should a sudden storm come on when she was lying there, and she were broken up, it would be easy to recover the gold from the shallow water behind the rocks. This was therefore settled. Only half the treasure was to be taken away at once, and not till this had been got on board a ship and the vessel had sailed would the boat come back for the rest of their treasure.

Dias was at once to start with the mules and carry the silver, in two journeys, to a safe place among the mountains. There he could bury it in three or four hiding-places, to be fetched out as he might require it, only taking some fifty pounds to Lima. Here he was to dispose of a portion of it to one of the dealers who made it his business to buy up silver from the natives. As many of these worked small mines, and sent down the produce once a month to Lima, there would be nothing suspicious in its being offered for sale, especially as it would be known that Dias had been away for a very long time among the mountains. It was necessary that the sale should be effected at once, because Harry's stock of money was running very low, and he would have to pay for the passages of Bertie and himself to England, and for the freight of the gold. Dias was to dispose later on of all the remaining stores, the powder and tools, and the three riding mules.

Two days later the last of the silver brackets had been melted, and Dias and Harry started with the eight mules, six of them being laden with the silver. They struck back at once into the hills, and after travelling for two days, ascended a wild gorge. "It is not once a year that anyone would come up here, señor. There is no way out of it. We can bury the silver here with a certainty that it will be safe from disturbance."

"Yes, it will be safe here; and as you want it you have only to make a journey with a couple of mules to fetch as much as you require, carry it home, and bury it in your garden or under the house; then you could from time to time take a few ingots into the town and dispose of them. But to begin with, I will borrow fifty pounds weight of it, and get you to dispose of it for me at Lima. My money is beginning to run short. I shall have to pay for the freight of the gold and my own passage home, and to buy a boat large enough to carry half the treasure. It is not likely that there will be two vessels sailing at the same time, in which case I shall make two trips. As I should not put it on board until the night before the ship sailed, of course I could go home with the second lot."

"I shall never know what to do with a tenth part of this silver, señor. It would never do for me to make a show of being rich; the authorities would seize me, and perhaps torture me to make me reveal the source of my wealth."

"Well, there are thousands of your countrymen in the deepest poverty, Dias; you could secretly help those in distress; a single ingot, ten pounds in weight, would be a fortune to them. And when you die you might get a respectable lawyer to make out a will, leaving your treasure to some charity for the benefit of Indians, giving, of course, instructions where the treasure is to be found."

"That is good," Dias said. "Thank you, señor! that will make me very happy."

They had brought a pick and shovel with them, and, dividing the bags, buried them at some distance apart, rolling stones to cover up the hiding-places, and obliterating any signs of the ground having been disturbed. A hundred pounds were left out, and with this in their saddle-bags they arrived at Lima two days later.

Harry went on alone into Callao. He had no difficulty in purchasing a ship's boat in fair condition. She carried two lug-sails, and was amply large enough for the purpose for which she was required, being nearly thirty feet long with a beam of six feet. He got her cheaply, for the ship to which she belonged had been wrecked some distance along the coast, and a portion of the crew had launched her and made their way to Callao; the mate, who was the sole surviving officer, was glad to accept the ten pounds Harry offered for her, as this would enable the crew to exist until they could obtain a passage home, or ship on board some British vessel short of hands. The boat was too large to be worked by one man, and seeing that the mate was an honest and intelligent fellow, Harry arranged with him to aid him to sail the boat, and each day they went out for some hours. After spending a week in apparent idleness, and getting to know more of the man, Harry told him that he had really bought the boat for the purpose of getting some ore he had discovered on board a ship homeward-bound.

"You know what these Peruvians are," he said, "and how jealous they are of our getting hold of mines, so I have got to do the thing quietly, and the only way will be to take the ore off by night. It is on a spot some eighty miles along the coast. I am going off tomorrow to get it ready for embarkation, and I shall be away about a week. I find that the *London* will leave in ten days, and I shall get it put on board the night before she sails. While I am away, look after the boat. The *Nancy* will sail five days later. I am going to put half on board each ship, as I am anxious to ensure that some at least of the ore shall reach home, so as to be analysed, and see if it is as rich as I hope. But be sure not to mention a word of this to a soul. I should have immense trouble with the authorities if it got about that I had discovered a mine."

"I understand, sir. You may be quite sure I shall say nothing about it."

"How are your men getting on?"

"Four are shipped on board the *Esmerelda*, which sailed yesterday, the others are hanging on till they can get berths. I hope a few will be able to go in the two ships you name, but they haven't applied at present. Some of the crew may desert before the time for sailing comes, and of course they would get better paid if they went as part of the crew than if they merely worked their passage home."

"I am sorry for them," Harry said. "Here is another five pounds to help them to hold on. As an old naval officer I can feel for men in such a place."

Dias, after selling the silver, had, a week before, returned with the mules to the castle, and on his arrival there had sent José to join Harry and bring news to them of the day on which the boat would arrive. Dias and Bertie were packing half the bags, of which the former took with him an ample supply, to get the gold out on the rocks facing the entrance, so that they could be shipped without delay. Great pains were taken in packing the bags so that the three ingots placed in each should be completely surrounded by stones. Anyone who might take a fancy to feel them, in order to ascertain their contents, would have no reason to suppose that they carried anything beyond the ore they were stated to contain.

Harry had had no difficulty in arranging with the captain of the London to take from a ton and a half to two tons of ore the night before he sailed, and three days before this Harry started with the mate. There was but a light breeze, and it was daylight next morning before they arrived. A pole had been stuck up at the edge of the cliff just above the cavern, and as it became dark a lantern was also placed there, so they had no trouble in finding the entrance of the little cove.

"It is a rum-looking place, sir," the man said. "As far as I can see there is no break in the cliffs."

"It is a curious place, but you will find the bags with the ore on the rocks inside here ready for us, and my brother and one of my men waiting there. They will have made us out an hour ago, so we can load up at once and get out of this tiny creek. I don't want to stay in there any longer than is necessary, for if there is anything of a swell we could not get out again."

As they approached the place Harry gave a shout, which was at once answered. The sails were lowered, and the boat passed round the edge of the rocks.

"It is a rum place," the mate repeated. "Why, one might have rowed past here fifty times without thinking there was water inside the rocks. Of course you must have lowered the sacks down from the top?"

"It was a difficult job," Harry said carelessly; "but we were anxious to get the things away quietly. If we had taken them down to the port we should have had no end of bother, and a hundred men would have set off at once to try and find out where we got the ore."

Bertie and Dias had everything ready, and as the boat drew up alongside the rocks on which they were standing the former said, "Everything all right, Harry?"

"Yes, I hope so. We are to put the ore on board the *London* to-morrow after dark; she will get up her anchor at daylight. You have got all the bags ready, I hope?"

"Everything; the others will be ready for you when you come back for them."

"The next ship sails in about a week. Now, let us get them on board at once, I don't want to stop in here a minute longer than is necessary. There is scarcely a breath of wind now; if it doesn't blow up a bit in the morning, we shall have a long row before us to get there in time. This is my brother, Owen; the other is a mule-driver, who has been my guide and companion for the past year, and whom I am proud to call my friend."

"You don't want anything in the way of food, do you?" Bertie asked.

"We have got some here," Harry laughed. "I am too old a sailor to put to sea without having provisions in my craft. Now, let us get the bags on board."

It did not take them long to transfer the sacks into the boat.

"They are pretty heavy," the mate said, "I should say a hundredweight each."

"About that," Harry said carelessly. "This ore stuff is very heavy."

As soon as all was on board Harry said: "Now we can put out at any moment, but I don't want to leave till dark. We may as well begin to get the rest of the bags out here at once. We might finish that job before we start. Then you could come down with us, Bertie, and Dias could pack up the remaining stores to-morrow and start for Lima with the mules, and his wife and José.

"Very well, Harry. I think we can leave the sacks here safely."

"Just as safely as if they were ashore. So far as we know no one has been in here for the past two hundred years, and no one is likely to come in the next week."

By evening all the work was done. The mate had been greatly surprised at the manner in which the bags had been brought on board, but had helped in the work and asked no questions. As soon as it was dark they rowed out from the cove. There was not a breath of wind. Bertie volunteered to take the first watch, the mate was to take the next.

Harry was not sorry to turn in. He had had but little sleep for the past week. Everything had seemed to be going well, but at any moment there might be some hitch in the arrangements, and he had been anxious and excited. Wrapping himself in his poncho he lay down in the stern of the boat and slept soundly until morning.

"I have had a sleep," he said on waking. "I have slept longer to-night than I have done for the past fortnight. Now I will take the helm. How fast have we been moving?"

"We have not gone many miles, and if what tide there is hadn't been with us we should not have moved at all, for the sails have not been full all night. A breeze only sprang up an hour ago, and we are not moving through the water now at more than a knot and a half; but I think it is freshening."

"I hope it is," Harry said. "It is not often that we have a dead calm; but if it doesn't spring up we shall have to row. With two tons and a half of stuff on board it is as much as we can do to move two knots an hour through the water."

"All right, sir! when you think it is time to begin, stir me up."

In half an hour the breeze had increased so much that the boat was running along three knots an hour. By eight o'clock she was doing a knot better. So she ran along till, at four o'clock in the afternoon, the wind died away again, and they could just see the masts of the ships at Callao in the distance.

"I should think that we are about fifteen miles off," Harry said.

"About that," Bertie replied. "We had better get our oars and help her along, she is not going much more than a knot through the water an hour."

They got out the oars and set to work. Occasionally a puff of wind gave them a little assistance, but it was one o'clock before they arrived alongside the *London*.

A lamp was alight at the gangway as arranged, and two sailors were on watch.

"The captain turned in an hour ago, sir," one of them said. "He left orders that the mate was to call him if you arrived. We will soon have him up."

In five minutes the mate and four other sailors were on deck.

"We have got a whip rigged in readiness," the officer said. "How much do the packages weigh, sir?"

"They are leathern bags, and weigh about a hundredweight each."

"How many are there?"

"Forty-six."

"We have got the fore-hatch open, and can hand them down in no time. If you will pass the boat along to the chains forward we shall be ready for you. Shall I send a couple of hands down into the boat to hook them on?"

"No, you needn't do that."

As soon as the boat reached her station a rope with a couple of small chains attached descended. One of the chains was fastened round a bag, and this was at once run up. By the time the rope came down again the other chain was passed round another bag, and in a quarter of an hour the whole were on board and down in the hold. The captain had now come out.

"So you have got them off all right, Mr. Prendergast?"

"Yes. There are forty-six bags. We will say, roughly, two ton and a half; though I doubt whether there is as much as that. At any rate, I will pay you for the freight agreed upon at once. They have all got labels on them, and on your arrival, after being handed into store, are to remain till called for. I am coming on in the *Nancy*. I do not know whether she is faster than you are or not. At any rate, she is not likely to be long behind you."

"I think that possibly you will be home first, sir; the *Nancy* made the voyage out here a fortnight quicker than we did; but it depends, of course, on what weather we meet with. I was on board her this afternoon, and her captain and I made a bet of five pounds each as to which would be in the port of London first. I shall have the anchor up by daylight. Now, gentlemen, will you come down into the cabin and we will take a glass together."

Harry did so, and after emptying a tumbler and wishing the captain a quick and pleasant voyage, he got into the boat and rowed two or three miles along the shore, as a landing at that time of night might cause questions to be asked; and then they lay down and slept by turns until morning broke. A light breeze then sprang up, and hoisting sail they returned to Callao. The *London* was already far out at sea.

CHAPTER XX — HOME

Two days later, Dias, José, and Maria arrived at Callao, having left the mules at Lima.

"Was it got off all right, señor?" Dias asked.

"Yes. It was a pretty near touch, for we had to row nine hours, and only saved our time by an hour."

"And when will you start again?"

"The *Nancy* sails in four days, so I shall go down tomorrow morning. I don't want to run the risk again of losing the boat."

"Well, we shall be stronger handed," Bertie said. "Of course I shall go down with you; Dias says he will too; so we will be able to man four oars, if necessary."

"What have you done with the goods?" Harry asked.

"I sold them all at Lima, señor, to the man I got them from. He took off a third of the price, and said he could not have taken them if it had not been that he had just got an order down from the Cerro mines, and was short of some of the things they had ordered."

"That is all right, Dias."

Harry secured two rooms at the hotel, and they all sat talking far into the night. "I hope you will get your silver down as comfortably as we have got the gold."

"I have no fear about doing that, señor. The difficulty will be for me to know what to do with it. I can never spend so much."

"Oh, nonsense, Dias!"

"I mean it, señor. Maria and I are quite agreed that we don't want any larger house than we have got; and I know that if we did want a big one, there would be all sorts of questions as to where I had got the money from."

"There would be no difficulty in answering that, Dias. You told me how your friend found five mule-loads of silver in the bats' cave. You have only got to say that you found yours hidden away, which would be the truth. José is nineteen now, and you will want to provide him with some good mules, and to put by some money for him when he wants to marry and settle. I know you spoke very highly of an institution at Lima for the orphans of natives. You can hand them over some, and when you and Maria don't want it any longer you can leave them the rest."

Maria cried bitterly in the morning when they said goodbye. "I shall love you and pray for you always, señors," she sobbed. "I shall never forget all your kindness."

"We owe you more than you owe us," Harry said. "You have always been ready to do everything, and you have kept us alive with your merry talk and good spirits. You may be very sure that we shall never forget you."

José was almost equally affected. "You will never come back, señor," he said, as the tears rolled down his cheeks.

"I may some day, José. I think it likely that I shall some day get up a company to drain that lake in the golden valley. The gold will be more useful as money than lying there. It must depend partly upon whether the country is settled. People will not put money into Peru as long as you are always fighting here."

Maria and José would have accompanied them down to the boat the next morning, but Dias pointed out to them that they were apparently only going out for a day's sail, and that if there were any partings on the shore it would at once attract the suspicions of the customs-house officials there.

Accordingly, after a painful farewell, Dias and the two brothers went down to the boat, where the mate was already awaiting them. The voyage was as successful as the previous one had been. On the return journey the wind held, and they arrived alongside of the *Nancy* by eleven o'clock; the bags were all safely in the hold by midnight. The first mate of the ship had two days before been taken with fever and sent ashore, and the captain had gladly accepted the offer of Harry's assistant to take the berth of second mate, that officer having succeeded to the post of the first. Harry had told him that he could sell the boat, and he had, before starting on the trip, done so, on the understanding that it would be found on the beach in charge of Dias when the *Nancy* had sailed.

Harry had given him another ten pounds to provide himself with an outfit, and had also asked him to distribute twenty among his former shipmates for the same purpose, as these had lost all their clothing except what they stood in. The ship's dinghy, with a couple of hands, towed the boat, with Dias in it, to the shore. The muleteer was greatly affected at parting with Harry and his brother.

"It has been a fortunate journey for us both," Dias said, "and I shall always look back to the time we spent together with the greatest pleasure."

"Here is a piece of paper with my address in London. I know that you will have no difficulty in getting letters written for you. Let me hear from you once every six months or so, telling me how you are getting on, and I will write to you. Good-bye! We shall always remember you, and be thankful that we had so faithful a guide here, and, I may say, so faithful a friend."

The voyage home was an uneventful one, save that they met with a heavy storm while rounding the Horn, and for some days the vessel was in great danger. However, she weathered it safely, and when she arrived in the Thames she found that the *London* had come up on the previous tide.

"If it hadn't been for that storm we should have beaten her easily," the captain said. "But I don't mind losing that fiver, considering that we have gained four days on her."

On landing, Harry went straight to the Bank of England and informed the managers that he had two hundred and eighty-two ingots of gold, weighing about twenty pounds each, which he wished to deposit in their vaults until they could weigh them and place their value to his credit, and he requested them to send down one of their waggons to the docks the next day to receive them. On the following evening he had the satisfaction of knowing that the whole of the treasure was at last in safe-keeping. Then he took a hackney-coach and drove to Jermyn Street, where he had taken rooms, having the night before carried there the trunks which he had stored before he left England. He smiled as he spread out suit after suit.

"I don't know anything about the fashions now," he said, "and for aught I can tell they may have changed altogether. However, I don't suppose there will be such an alteration that I shall look as if I had come out of the ark. Certainly I am not going to wait till I get a new outfit.

"It did not seem to me," he said to himself, "that I left a ridiculously large wardrobe before I went. But after knocking about for two years with a single change, it really does seem absurd that I should ever have thought I absolutely required all these things. Now, I suppose I had better write to the old man and say that I have returned, and shall call upon him to-morrow. The chances are ten to one against my catching him in now, and as this is rather a formal sort of business, I had better give him due notice; but I cannot keep Hilda in suspense. I wonder whether she has the same maid as she had before I went away. I have given the girl more than one half-guinea, and to do her justice I believe that she was so attached to her mistress that she would have done anything for her without them. Still, I can't very well knock at the door and ask for Miss Fortescue's maid; I expect I must trust the note to a footman. If she does not get it, there is no harm done; if he hands it to her father, no doubt it would put him in a towering rage, but he will cool down by the time I see him in the morning."

He sat down and wrote two notes. The first was to Mr. Fortescue; it only said:—

"Dear Sir,—I have returned from abroad, and shall do myself the pleasure of calling upon you at eleven o'clock tomorrow morning to discuss with you a matter of much importance to myself."

The note to Hilda was still shorter:—

"My darling,—I am home and am going to call on your father at eleven o'clock tomorrow morning. I am two months within the two years.—Yours devotedly,

"HARRY PRENDERGAST."

Having sealed both letters, he walked to Bedford Square. When the door opened, he saw that the footman was one of those who had been in Mr. Fortescue's service before he left.

"You have not forgotten me, Edward, have you?"

"Why, it is Mr. Prendergast! Well, sir, it is a long time since we saw you."

"Yes, I have been abroad. Will you hand this letter to Mr. Fortescue. Is he in at present?"

"No, sir; he and Mrs. Fortescue are both out. Miss Fortescue is out too."

"Well now, Edward, will you hand this letter quietly to Miss Fortescue when she comes in?" and he held out the note and a guinea with it.

The man hesitated.

"You need not be afraid of giving it to her," Harry went on. "It is only to tell her what I have told your master in my letter to him, that I am going to call tomorrow."

"Then I shall be glad to do it," the man said—for, as usual, the servants were pretty well acquainted with the state of affairs, and when Harry went away, and their young mistress was evidently in disgrace with her father, they guessed pretty accurately what had happened, and their sympathies were with the lovers. Harry returned to Jermyn Street confident that Hilda would get his note that evening. He had no feeling of animosity against her father, It was natural that, as a large land-owner, and belonging to an old family, and closely connected with more than one peer of the realm, he should offer strong opposition to the marriage of his daughter to a half-pay lieutenant, and he had been quite prepared for the burst of anger with which his request for her hand had been received. He had felt that it was a forlorn hope; but he and Hilda hoped that in time the old man would soften, especially as they had an ally in her mother. Hilda had three brothers, and as the estates and the bulk of Mr. Fortescue's fortune would go to them, she was not a great heiress, though undoubtedly she would be well dowered.

On arriving the next morning Harry was shown into the library. Mr. Fortescue rose from his chair and bowed coldly.

"To what am I indebted for the honour of this visit, Mr. Prendergast? I had hoped that the emphatic way in which I rejected your—you will excuse my saying—presumptuous request for the hand of my daughter, would have settled the matter once and for all; and I trust that your request for an interview to-day does not imply that you intend to renew that proposal, which I may say at once would receive, and will receive as long as I live, the same answer as I before gave you."

"It has that object, sir," Harry said quietly, "but under somewhat changed conditions. I asked you at that time to give me two years, in which time possibly my circumstances might change. You refused to give me a single week; but your daughter was more kind, and promised to wait for the two years, which will not be up for two more months."

"She has behaved like a froward and obstinate girl," her father said angrily. "She has refused several most eligible offers, and I have to thank you for it. Well, sir, I hope at least that you have the grace to feel that it is preposterous that you should any longer stand in the way of this misguided girl."

"I have come to say that if it is her wish and yours that I should stand aside, as you say, I will do so, and in my letters I told her that unless circumstances should be changed before the two years have expired I would disappear altogether from her path."

"That is something at least, sir," Mr. Fortescue said with more courtesy than he had hitherto shown. "I need not say that there is no prospect of your obtaining my consent, and may inform you that my daughter promised not to withstand my commands as far as you are concerned beyond the expiration of the two years. I do not know that there is anything more to say."

"I should not have come here, sir, had there not been more to say, but should simply have addressed a letter to you saying that I withdrew all pretensions to your daughter's hand. But I have a good deal more to say. I have during the time that I have been away succeeded in improving my condition to a certain extent."

"Pooh, pooh, sir!" the other said angrily. "Suppose you made a thousand or two, what possible difference could it make?"

"I am not foolish enough to suppose that it would do so; but at least this receipt from the Bank of England, for gold deposited in their hands, will show you that the sums you mention have been somewhat exceeded."

"Tut, tut, I don't wish to see it! it can make no possible difference in the matter."

"At least, sir, you will do me the courtesy to read it, or if you prefer not to do so I will read it myself."

"Give it me," Mr. Fortescue said, holding out his hand. "Let us get through this farce as soon as possible; it is painful to us both."

He put on his spectacles, glanced at the paper, and gave a sudden start, read it again, carefully this time, and then said slowly:

"Do you mean that the two hundred and eighty-two ingots, containing in all five thousand six hundred and forty pounds weight of gold, are your property? That is to say, that you are the sole owner of them, and not only the representative of some mining company?"

"It is the sole property, Mr. Fortescue, of my brother and myself. I own two-thirds of it. It is lost treasure recovered by us from the sea, where it has been lying ever since the conquest of Peru by Pizarro."

"There is no mistake about this? The word pounds is not a mistake for ounces?—although even that would represent a very large sum."

"The bank would not be likely to make such a mistake as that, sir. The ingots weigh about twenty pounds each. I had a small piece of the gold assayed at Callao, and its value was estimated at four pounds per ounce.

Roughly, then, the value of the sum deposited at the bank is two hundred and seventy thousand pounds."

"Prodigious!" Mr. Fortescue murmured.

"Well, Mr. Prendergast, I own that you have astounded me. It would be absurd to deny that this altogether alters the position. Against you personally I have never had anything to say. You were always a welcome visitor to my house till I saw how matters were tending. Your family, like my own, is an old one, and your position as an officer in the King's Naval Service is an honourable one. However, I must ask you to give me a day to reflect over the matter, to consult with my wife, and to ascertain that my daughter's disposition in the matter is unchanged."

"Thank you, sir! But I trust that you will allow me to have an interview with Miss Fortescue now. It is two years since we parted, and she has suffered great anxiety on my account, and on the matter of my safety at least I would not keep her a moment longer in suspense."

"I think that after the turn the matter has taken your request is a reasonable one. You are sure to find her in the drawing-room with her mother at present. I think it is desirable that you should not see her alone until the matter is formally arranged."

Prendergast bowed.

"I am content to wait," he said with a slight smile.

"I will take you up myself," the other said.

Harry could have done without the guidance, for he knew the house well. However, he only bowed again, and followed the old man upstairs.

The latter opened the door and said to his wife: "My dear, I have brought an old friend up to see you;" and as Harry entered he closed the door and went down to the library again.

"Nearly two hundred thousand pounds!" he said. "A splendid fortune! Nearly twice as much as I put by before I left the bar. How in the world could he have got it? 'Got it up out of the sea,' he said; a curious story. However, with that acknowledgment from the bank there can be no mistake about it. Well, well, it might be worse. I always liked the young fellow till he was fool enough to fall in love with Hilda, and worse still, she with him. The silly girl might have had a coronet. However, there is no accounting for these things, and I am glad that the battle between us is at an end. I was only acting for her good, and I should have been mad to let her throw herself away on a penniless officer on half-pay."

Mrs. Fortescue waved her hand as Harry, on entering, was about to speak to her.

"Go to her first," she said; "she has waited long enough for you."

And he turned to Hilda.

He made a step towards her and held out his arms, and with a little cry of joy she ran into them.

"And is it all right?" she said a minute later. "Can it really be all right?"

"You may be quite sure that it is all right, Hilda," Mrs. Fortescue said. "Do you think your father would have brought him up here if it hadn't been? Now you can come to me, Harry."

"I am glad," she said heartily. "We have had a very bad time. Now, thank God, it is all over. You see she has only had me to stand by her, for her brothers, although they have not taken open part against her, have been disposed to think that it was madness her wasting two years on the chance of your making a fortune. Of course you have done so, or you would not be in this drawing-room at present."

"I have done very well, Mrs. Fortescue. I was able to show Mr. Fortescue a receipt for gold amounting to nearly three hundred thousand pounds, of which two-thirds belong to me, the rest to my brother."

Mrs. Fortescue uttered an exclamation of astonishment.

"What have you been doing, Harry?" she asked—"plundering a Nabob?"

"Nabobs do not dwell in Peru," he laughed. "No, I have discovered a long-lost treasure, which, beyond any doubt, was part of the wealth of Atahualpa, the unfortunate monarch whom Pizarro first plundered and then slew. It had been sent off by sea, and the vessel was lost. It is too long a story to tell now."

"And Papa has quite consented, Harry?"

Harry smiled.

"Virtually so, as you might suppose by his bringing me up here. Actually he has deferred the matter, pending a consultation with you and Mrs. Fortescue, and will give me his formal answer to-morrow."

The two ladies both smiled.

"If he said that, the matter is settled," the elder said; "he has never asked my opinion before on the subject, and I have never volunteered it. But I am sure he has not the slightest doubt as to what I thought of it. So we can consider it as happily settled after all. If I had thought that there was the slightest chance of your making a fortune quickly I should have spoken out; but as I thought it absolutely hopeless, I have done what I could privately to support Hilda, always saying, however, that if at the end of the two years nothing came of it, I could not in any way countenance her throwing away the chances of her life."

"You were quite right, Mrs. Fortescue. I had fully intended to write to Hilda at the end of that time releasing her from all promises that she had made to me, and saying that I felt that I had no right to trouble her further; but from what she wrote to me, I doubt whether her father would have found her altogether amenable to his wishes even at the end of the two years."

A month later there was a wedding in Bedford Square. Among those present no one was more gratified than Mr. Barnett, whose surprise and satisfaction were great when Harry told him in confidence the result of his advice, and especially of his introduction to the Indian guide.

It had been arranged that nothing should be said as to the source from which Harry had obtained his wealth, as it was possible that the Peruvian government might set up some claim to it, and it was in Mr. Fortescue's opinion very doubtful what the result would be, as it had been discovered so close to the shore.

Harry never took any steps with reference to the gold valley, for the constant troubles in Peru were sufficient to deter any wealthy men from investing money there.

The correspondence between him and Dias and his wife was maintained until they died full of years and greatly lamented by numbers of their countrymen to whom they had been benefactors.

Bertie never went to sea again except in his own yacht, but when he came of age, bought an estate near Southampton, and six years later brought home a mistress for it.

The End

Made in the USA
Las Vegas, NV
09 December 2024

c4afc607-29ed-4271-adc9-d6c41d391ae8R01